*The*
# LIFEBOAT
# SISTERS

## BOOKS BY TILLY TENNANT

TILLY TENNANT

# *The*
# LIFEBOAT
# SISTERS

*bookouture*

Published by Bookouture in 2023

An imprint of Storyfire Ltd.
Carmelite House
50 Victoria Embankment
London EC4Y 0DZ

www.bookouture.com

ISBN: 978-1-83790-363-4
eBook ISBN: 978-1-83790-362-7

This book is a work of fiction. Names, characters, businesses, organisations,
places and events other than those clearly in the public domain, are either the
product of the author's imagination or are used fictitiously. Any resemblance
to actual persons, living or dead, events or locales is entirely coincidental.

*To the volunteers of the RNLI.*
*Thank you is not enough.*

# CHAPTER ONE

Ava Morrow, youngest daughter of Jack Morrow, had been dreading this day. Every eye in the village would be on her and her family, and things were already going to be bad enough without all the unwanted attention. But her father's funeral had been an intensely private affair, mostly because Ava and her sisters, Gaby and Clara, had decided that their mum was in no state to deal with anything more public. So they'd kept it small, a brief and heartfelt service in the little stone church at the top of the cliffs that overlooked the village. But as many residents of Port Promise had wanted to attend and hadn't been able to, the family had been left with little choice but to hold a more public memorial for anyone who'd missed out.

They'd given it time – six months – time for their mother to heal enough that she'd be better able to deal with the event. This memorial wasn't what Ava would have chosen – not even what her mum would have chosen – but what they'd all agreed – Ava, her mum Jill, and her sisters – had to be done. Just as Jack Morrow had always insisted that he had a duty to the village, one passed down to him by generations of his ancestors, they all acknowledged that they had a duty to Port Promise too.

Jack was one of their sons, the latest and last in a line of men who had built Port Promise and patrolled its seas for hundreds of years. He'd belonged to everyone, not just to his family, and, thus, so did his goodbye.

At least they'd had six months to pull themselves together – as far as a family who'd endured such a tragedy could pull themselves together. They could try to mend and they had, as best they could, but they'd never be the same family again.

Jill had fallen apart in a most unexpected way. She'd always been stoic, practical, someone to turn to in any crisis, but the instant she'd been given the news that Jack had been lost at sea she'd turned into a shadow of that woman, someone they hardly recognised. It was like her fire had gone out, her lust for life evaporated. Her endless curiosity about the natural world had fizzled to nothing, her regular walks on the beach and scrambles around the clifftops had stopped, and even her beloved garden had suffered. And despite the lack of exercise, as she sat staring into space every day on a faded armchair in her sitting room, the weight that had always made her look robust and healthy dropped away. There were bones where there had once been smooth, tanned skin, and hollow cheeks where there had once been blushing plumpness.

Jill had always worn middle age well, still looking as beautiful to Ava as she'd done in the photos from her youth that lined the walls of Seaspray Cottage, their family home. But these days, though she was still beautiful and full of grace, there was a weariness, a sadness that had etched the lines of her face a little deeper.

Ava had been the only daughter at that point with no partner and no other family commitments, and her job giving watersports lessons allowed her to be more flexible, and so she'd taken on most of the caring for her shattered mum. For a short time she'd moved out of the caravan she'd been living in during the summer and autumn before her dad's death and back into

Seaspray Cottage, and though she and her mum had needed each other's support, it had still been the darkest few months of her life. She'd not long gone back to her home and things had started to return to some sort of normality, though it was a very different normal than they'd ever experienced before.

Gaby, the eldest sister, married to Killian, one of the other crew members who'd been on board that night, had been brisk and practical, as their mother would once have been. Ava suspected that even as she mourned her dad, she felt guilt that she was happy her husband had survived. But Gaby could only do so much; she had her own family to take care of. Clara, the middle sister, had wanted to help but had told Ava she didn't know how. She'd had her boyfriend Logan to lean on too. Ava had no one like that and so felt as if the burden had fallen on her shoulders particularly hard, though she did her best to manage it.

Perhaps if they'd found his body Jill might have coped better with his loss. As it was, Ava wondered if perhaps her mother simply hadn't been able to accept that he'd gone because she'd had no proof.

Jill was dressed elegantly today, in a calf-length charcoal dress and heeled shoes – which was strange to Ava because Jill was rarely seen in anything other than her battered old cords and checked shirt and the requisite wellies that constituted her daily uniform, an ensemble practical enough for toiling in the gardens where she grew exotic plants to be sold in the swankier garden centres of the home counties. She looked better than she had done in many months, and she certainly looked more glamorous than Ava had seen her look in a long time. It was obvious she was making an effort to look her best, and that had to be a good thing, but even with her elegant wardrobe and hair done she still looked desperately sad. Despite this, Ava was hopeful that this memorial might turn out to be the point at which Jill finally realised it was time to move on. Perhaps it would be a sort of closure, an acceptance that six months was an awful long time for someone to be lost at sea, and the idea of them walking back through the door having been waylaid by a tide that had taken them off to Scilly or some French coastal town to wait for a lift home was one that really ought to be abandoned.

Ava herself itched to take off the dress she was wearing and swap it for the familiar comfort of a pair of baggy jeans and a nice soft T-shirt. If she could slip on a pair of Birkenstocks even better still – the temperature was rising outside and in the sun trap of the harbour it would be roasting – not the weather for sensible shoes. She only hoped she wouldn't have to wear all these layers for long. It was not yet June, but there'd been several days of unseasonable heat. Everyone on the news kept saying this was how things were going to be from now on. Ava couldn't remember what it was like before – her abiding memories of Port Promise was that it was hot in the summer and always had been. Her mum grew ornamental banana trees and succulents that belonged in South Africa and all sorts of plants that required a more exotic climate, and had done for many years, so it couldn't have just been in Ava's imagination.

She went to the mirror in the hallway to make one last check on her appearance as her mum fussed looking for her handbag and keys and checking the house one last time before they left to meet the rest of the family. With more care than she'd normally show, she smoothed the stray strands back into the grip that was pinning her hair up. In the sunlight coming from the window it looked redder than it was, more like the rich auburn of her sister Gaby's hair than Ava's own muted shade. She had a tan – a happy accident of her job and her outdoor lifestyle was that she almost always had some colour – and her summer freckles were sprinkled across the bridge of her nose.

Her thoughts turned once more to the service. Gaby would be there with Killian and the kids, and Clara would be there with her adoring Logan, but Ava... well, it would have been nice to have someone there, but it didn't bother her that she remained single. In a way it was better that she didn't have a partner – it meant she could devote as much time to her mum as she needed.

'You look nice...'

Ava turned to see Jill coming down the crooked stairs of their tiny cottage. Growing up, it had felt as if they'd all been living on top of one another. The house had never really been big enough for two adults and three kids, but it was the Morrow ancestral home – at least that's what her dad called it, though the idea of an ancestral home conjured up an image of some fifteen-bedroom mansion on a country estate, which was hardly this at all – and there was no way they were ever going to live anywhere else. It had been handed down from father to son, and Ava had learned from an early age that in this part of the world, to own any kind of property made you a very lucky person indeed, regardless of how it had come to you and how impractical it might be. And Seaspray Cottage was undoubtedly one of the prettiest in Port Promise, perched on a vantage point that gave fantastic views of the bay with a south-facing garden that was bathed in glorious sunshine almost all year round. Ava's dad had built a gazebo and her mum had trained vines to cover it, offering leafy shade on the hottest days. The family had often dined out there over the years, crammed in around the table, and if not for the vista of grey cliffs and the broad Cornish accents, it wouldn't be a stretch to imagine them in Greece or Italy or some other glamorous destination.

'Thanks. I don't feel it.'

'I know what you mean.'

'You look lovely, Mum, even if it's weird not to see you in gardening clothes.'

'I do wear other things,' Jill said with a light laugh.

'I know that. But not often.'

'Well, there hasn't been much call for anything else lately, has there?' she replied, her tone brisker now.

It was either that or burst into tears, Ava supposed, and she knew as much because she felt the same. She just wanted to get through this memorial business with as little fuss as possible and then head to the pub to try and forget about it. It wasn't that she didn't care about the memorial or that she didn't think it was important, but it was the opening of an old wound she could do without, especially as she'd spent the last six months trying to heal.

'Gaby and Clara are both meeting us at the harbour,' Jill said.

'I thought they would. I expected Gaby would want to get there a bit earlier so she and Killian could meet up with the crew and go through their slot. He's still thinking of making a speech?'

'As far as I know. Robin too.'

Ava grimaced and Jill nodded in reply. 'I know. Poor Robin. He still blames himself for what happened, feels awful. I'm not sure he'll ever get over it.'

'Well, we've tried talking to him and there's not much more we can do. He took the boat out and everyone gets why; he needed the money. Nobody can undo that now. It'll take time to come to terms with it, I suppose. All such things do.'

Jill turned to her daughter with a melancholy smile. 'When did you get so wise beyond your years?'

'Do you think that's what it is? Wisdom?'

'Yes. What else?'

'I think I'm just telling it how it is. Nothing wise about that.'

'Hmm.' Jill checked her watch. 'We'd better go if we don't want to be late. Ready?'

'As I'll ever be.'

They stepped out of the house, into the sunshine, Ava's stomach churning, and Jill closed the door behind her.

. . .

Ava couldn't think of a single person she knew who was missing – the entire population of Port Promise appeared to be here. She also recognised people from neighbouring towns and villages, as well as representatives from the lifeboat institution's head office who'd occasionally visited her dad, and members of the local government. There were classes of children – far too many to be from Port Promise's tiny school, and so Ava had to assume that others had travelled in from neighbouring schools for the occasion.

Beyond the harbour the sea glinted, gentle undulations of waves that licked the harbour walls. Its millpond surface couldn't have been further from the towering wall of angry waves that had claimed the man they were gathered here to celebrate.

As they'd arranged, Ava and her mum had met her two sisters at the entrance to the harbour and had walked to the space where seats had been set up for the gathering together, along with Clara's partner, Logan. Elijah and Fern, Gaby's children, were spending the morning with Jill's old friend Marina. Aged seven and nine, the family had decided the service was too much sadness for such young souls, but the kids would come to them later for the celebration in the local pub. Gaby's husband, Killian, had bid them a brief goodbye and rushed off to join his crewmates, while the rest of them made the short walk to where a plaque was due to be unveiled in honour of Jack.

Jill and Ava's oldest sister, Gaby, were currently inundated by well-wishers wanting to express their sympathy. Ava and her other sister, Clara, not so much.

'Anyone would think we weren't important,' Clara said drily in a low voice.

Ava gave a sideways look, her response just as quiet. 'We're not. At least, we've always been way down in the sister pecking order.'

'True,' Clara replied. 'Being related to Gaby is like being related to Mother Teresa.'

'If she was a five-foot-eight impossibly gorgeous yummy mummy who's idolised by everyone she meets. I mean, she's even smart as well – it's just not fair! Not that I'm jealous or anything...'

Ava wasn't worried about expressing thoughts such as these to the middle Morrow sister. There was a three-year gap between Clara, who was twenty-seven, and Ava at twenty-four, but a four-year gap between Gaby and Clara, Gaby being older. It was only an extra year, but it had meant that Clara and Ava had become close allies during many sibling disagreements. She knew Clara didn't really take it seriously though, and neither did she. It was simply the natural order of things when you were one of a family of three girls.

Clara grinned. 'You took the words right out of my mouth.'

Ava scanned the crowds. Already the sun was beating down, and it was barely past 10 a.m.

'I think black might have been a bad idea as a dress code today.'

'I wasn't sure about that to be honest,' Clara said. 'I mean, it's not a funeral, but it's sort of like one. I wasn't sure what the deal was, dress-wise. And Dad wouldn't have cared if we'd worn black or not.'

'Dad wouldn't have cared if we'd all turned up in our swimsuits. In fact he'd have probably found that funny.' Ava pushed up her sleeves. 'God, I just want this to be over already.'

'Me too. But there's fat chance of that – it's going to be like the opening ceremony of the Olympics in about ten minutes.'

'Yeah... Dad would have loved it.'

Clara laughed. 'He bloody would! He'd be telling everyone

there's no need but secretly he would have loved all the adulation.'

'Although he would have refused to wear a tie. And he'd have hurried everything along so he could get to the pub after.'

'Obviously.'

Ava let out a long sigh, her gaze going to the sparkling waves beyond the harbour walls. Overhead, a trio of seagulls circled, their cries cutting through the hum of conversation that filled the salted air of the harbour.

'I miss him,' she said quietly.

'Me too. It still hurts like hell, doesn't it?'

'Every day. Sometimes I get why Mum thinks he'll turn up, because even I feel like he might walk through the door... y'-know, in my stupider moments.'

'There's nothing stupid about it,' Clara said. 'I imagine it too.'

'Like, he'd be "Sorry, I took a wrong turning at Dover. What's for tea? Six months of swimming home doesn't half work up an appetite."'

'Something like that,' Clara said. 'Remember when we used to think he was invincible? Like when we were little we felt he could do anything. He was like a real-life superhero.'

'Still is to me.'

'Still is to most of the people who are here today. But not so invincible, in the end.' She paused for a moment. 'What do you think happened?'

Ava turned with a silent question.

'That night,' Clara continued. 'What do you think really happened?'

'What Killian says: Dad went out on the boat when he wasn't supposed to – stubborn as always. Why would you ask that? Has something been said to—'

'No, no.' Clara shook her head. 'I know that's the official line, but sometimes it... I don't know. I just think sometimes it's too simple. It's not like Dad... he was so good at what he did. So strong and smart... I still can't get my head around it.'

'It's hard to imagine, isn't it, but even our dad made mistakes.'

'I know. And I suppose he'd had that bout of flu and maybe he wasn't quite well. But even though he was retired, he'd not long retired and he wasn't exactly old, and he was always so strong and fit...'

'The flu would have knocked him for six, you know. Mum had it, remember, and she was a mess. He never would have admitted that, though. Maybe he was tired, maybe not quite as strong as usual... we'll never know.'

'I suppose you're right.'

'What are you two plotting?'

They both looked at once in the direction of their sister's voice.

Gaby – Gabriella, though nobody called her that – wore black well. She wore every colour well. Five feet eight of pure gorgeousness and by far the most admired woman in Port Promise. She wasn't taller or slimmer than Ava, but somehow she carried herself in a way that made it seem so. Her auburn hair was longer and silkier – though Ava often thought that was because she herself spent so many hours in the sea and in swimming pools as part of her job; her hair was bound to be frazzled. Her eyes were bigger and bluer than Ava's, her movements more graceful and her voice gentler. At least Ava thought so, and it had been a hard act to follow as the youngest kid looking up to her perfect older sister.

'Us?' Ava forced a carefree grin, but for a reason she couldn't put her finger on she felt guilty. Maybe it was the conversation she'd just had with Clara that they'd excluded Gaby from. 'As if we're capable of plotting anything!'

'Hmm...' Gaby's tone was one of mild sarcastic scepticism. 'You say that but you both have that look my kids have when they're planning something they know will get them into trouble if I find out.'

'Gaby,' Clara began in a withering tone, 'I'm twenty-seven. And also not one of your kids. I think we can say I'm way past that sort of thing.'

Gaby flicked a finger towards Ava. 'She's not.'

'Right.' Clara chuckled now. 'On that I'm forced to agree.'

Ava scowled at her. 'Whose side are you on?'

'Whoever gives me less hassle,' Clara said. She looked at Gaby. 'Shouldn't this thing have started by now?'

'I think the reverend is running late,' Gaby replied.

Clara gave her head a slight shake. 'Nothing new there then. Wasn't he late for your wedding, Gab? And for every Christmas carol concert we've ever had since he arrived. I swear he was the rabbit from *Alice in Wonderland* in a previous life. He'll be late for his own funeral – let's face it, it's only fair as he's late for everyone else's.'

'What does he do that makes him run so behind all the time?' Ava wondered out loud. 'It's not like he's got kids at home. As far as I can tell, all he has to do is turn up for stuff – like, that's literally his job, just to be at things.'

'Well...' Gaby nodded towards a bike being stood against the harbour wall by a man in a black suit. 'You could ask him your-self – looks like he's finally here. We'd better go with Mum to speak to him.'

Even as Gaby said it, Jill was beckoning her daughters to follow as she went to greet the new arrival. Ava knew better than to shirk her social responsibilities, though she could have done without everyone watching as they went to talk to the reverend about the order of the service.

She often wondered what the village made of her. The youngest Morrow daughter, of course, that much was obvious. In fact, the youngest Morrow period, now that Gaby was married to Killian, making the youngest members of the family

Smiths, not Morrows. Clara was engaged to be married and had talked about keeping the name, and she might have boys of her own one day, but nobody knew that. The same was true for Ava herself. It was hardly noteworthy, but for a place like Port Promise, where family and tradition meant so much, it was a strange burden to bear. It meant there might be no more Morrow boys to carry the mantle of saving unfortunate souls from the sea, which, more or less, was what every generation until now had existed to do.

That didn't mean there would be nobody patrolling the shores of their village, of course. There was Killian, closest to family but only by marriage, and all the others who volunteered, but there wouldn't be a Morrow. Logan, Clara's fiancé, had no interest, and Gaby had made it clear that there was no way she was going to let her children volunteer, no matter what they or the rest of the village said about it. She'd never wanted Killian on the boats and she still didn't, though she tolerated it.

And yet Ava might still carry the tradition forward – the first Morrow woman to do it. She'd started to think about volunteering in her dad's place. In fact, she'd started to think about volunteering for the service while her dad was alive, the seed sprouting from a suggestion he'd made one day at dinner that she might be suited to take on water safety education at the station, because they didn't currently have anyone doing it. She'd thought about his proposition, but realised quickly that, although it was an important job, it wasn't enough for her.

She'd considered what might be enough, but at the time she'd been busy renovating the caravan she was going to live in and then at work devising and scheduling new sessions, and those thoughts had been pushed to the back of a queue of things she needed to think about. But lately she'd thought more and more about going for the crew. It was a huge commitment but that never stopped her dad. Why should it stop Ava? In fact, surely Ava was better placed to do it than her dad ever was, because right now she had no children or partner to worry about. And she felt that, even if he worried about it, her dad would have been proud to see her step up to the plate.

She'd wondered if she could, though she felt deep down that she should. What would the community make of that? Port Promise was ridiculously traditional and conservative in so many ways – church on Sunday for most, yearly harvest and sea festivals, Cornish dancing, seasonal processions and firework nights. Christmas wasn't Christmas without a stream of lanterns being carried through the streets; likewise, spring was celebrated with the Green Man. But even here people recognised that times changed, so how they'd feel about a Morrow woman on the boats was anyone's guess.

They had female crew members, of course – Maxine, who ran the newsagents, and Shari, who was also church treasurer and did just about any other random job that needed doing – but they were both shore crew with roles that didn't require them to take to sea on rescues. Ava was sure nobody would question her doing a role like that. Then again, hadn't she always gone out of her way to do the things people didn't expect her to?

Ava and her sisters had always been involved in the service in some capacity, of course. It came with being a Morrow, and there was no escape. Support had been offered in fluctuating and varying degrees, according to how old they were and corresponding enthusiasm. As a young child Ava had gone to watch every training launch she could, had cheerfully collected local donations or taken part in larger, nationwide efforts. She'd been obsessed with the boats, excited beyond reason at any chance to be on board during open days, and was proud enough to burst that her dad did such an important job. But all that enthusiasm waned during her teenage years and was only revived by the arrival of Gaby's handsome boyfriend, Killian, and his subsequently joining the crew, which had lent it a sudden new glamour. Of course, older and wiser now, she no longer saw Killian that way at all. Now he was like an overbearing and unwanted big brother.

Her friend, Harry, was the last to join the crew. He'd been on board the night her dad was lost. He'd been like her once, obsessed with the boats, desperate to join up, but, unlike her, he'd actually done it. Despite his intention to join the family cider business, he'd gone off to university in Falmouth for a few years first, at the behest of his mum, who probably hoped he'd get over the idea while he was away, but it hadn't taken long to sign up for training once he'd got back.

In the end, for Ava, it had taken the death of her father to finally crystallise in her own mind her true calling. Her destiny was to follow in his footsteps, to save lives as he did, no matter what it took, no matter the personal risks or costs. She had a feeling, however, that the saving-lives bit might be the easiest part – first she had to convince her family and the doubters of Port Promise she was up to the challenge, that a Morrow woman could do what generations of Morrow men had always done before.

With these thoughts occupying her, she followed her sisters to take a seat at the front of half a dozen tidy rows. The rest were filled by the more important members of the community, while everyone else sat on walls or stood fanning themselves in the heat. The reverend took his place at a podium facing the congregation and everyone fell silent, watching and waiting for him to start the proceedings.

Across the aisle formed by the seating sat Killian, Vas and Harry, who'd crewed the boat with Jack that terrible night. They were all in their uniform, sombre and quiet. Harry fidgeted, glancing around every so often. Ava noticed his parents standing at the back – perhaps they'd arrived too late to get a seat. She held a hand up to acknowledge them, but they didn't see her. Killian looked across at Gaby and she sent a small smile his way.

Behind the crew sat members of the 'higher-ups' as Jack used to call them, managers and coordinators from the lifeboat institute. Then there were prominent community figures – members of the council and local dignitaries (as far as somewhere as small as Port Promise had dignitaries). Some of those were people who'd never uttered two words to Jack during his lifetime, Ava thought wryly, here only to bask in the reflected glory of his memorial, like they'd actually cared about a single thing he'd done while he'd been alive. She'd bet many hadn't even known his name before the accident, because, while the residents of the village had all been raised on the legend of Iziah Morrow and what his descendants stood for, the people who were tasked with the running of Port Promise were often outsiders, local government from nearby towns that had swallowed up the responsibility for smaller ones during countless cost-cutting exercises and often blamed, conveniently and sometimes even unfairly, for every little thing that went wrong in the village. But even they couldn't be blamed for this, Ava thought. This one was all on her dad.

After a few words that Ava couldn't recall even ten minutes afterwards, the reverend asked everyone to stand for the first hymn.

'Now, let us join our voices...' he began.

*Here it comes*, Ava thought, steeling herself.

'Eternal Father, Strong to Save.'

Ava grimaced as she got to her feet. She'd vowed she wasn't going to cry but already she could see what an uphill battle that was going to be. Today was going to be an emotional one, and she didn't do emotion very well.

Daring to glance either side, she saw that her mum was

already crying, as was Clara, and that Gaby was staring straight ahead, which meant she was fighting back the tears too. It was no wonder, when the hymn the reverend had chosen was one of Jack's favourites and a traditional prayer known only too well by mariners everywhere. Singing it, her mouth forming the words almost mechanically, Ava was swamped by a tempest of emotions bigger than any surging wave. While she appreciated the sentiment of the song, and she understood its seafaring significance, she was angry too. Where had this God been when her dad had asked for help?

Glad when it was finally over, Ava took a deep breath and then sat down again with everyone else. Much more of that and she was going to be a wreck in no time.

Then the new operational manager of the station got up to say some words, followed by Killian, whose speech was as soul-less and unimaginative as Ava would have expected from him. Killian had always been a 'say it as you see it' kind of guy, and apparently that stoicism extended to even the saddest and most desperate of situations. It was no wonder Gaby had to keep such a stiff upper lip all the time married to him; she probably didn't get much sympathy if she showed a crumb of passion about anything, so what was the point?

At least Killian's dull speech had been a breather from the rollercoaster of emotions. But that was quickly undone by the combined local primary school choirs. Their renditions of old sea shanties had everyone, not just the family, in tears. To hear those traditional songs, full of covert sentiment, the prayers and fears of the sea once sung by gruff sailors, now offered in soaring and innocent voices that rang out across the bay was all too much. It was beautiful and joyous, but it was also heartbreaking and melancholy, every child taking every word and every note so seriously, as if each of them understood they were under-taking the most solemn of duties, even the youngest.

But if Ava thought that was going to be bad, it was because

she'd clean forgotten that Robin Trelawney, the man her father had saved, was due to speak. She tensed as he stood and faced the gathering, and the space was so silent, it was as if the waves and the gulls had paused to listen too.

He looked strange in his formal suit. Ava had known Robin all her life, as she had many in Port Promise, and she didn't think she'd ever seen him dressed in anything but canvas trousers and flannel shirt in summer, the shirt replaced by a thick home-knitted jumper in the winter. He'd have his waterproofs on if he was working, and those same clothes without the extra protection if not. His hair was impossibly thick and now white, where it had once been a nondescript brown. Today his jacket hung from him in a way that suggested he'd borrowed it from a bigger man, and his trousers were in a not quite matching fabric, as far as Ava could tell, even though they were black just the same.

His hands shook as he unfolded a sheet of paper. Ava had the sudden urge to leap up and throw her arms around him and tell him it would be OK. Sometimes, she felt poor Robin had suffered from her father's loss more than the family had. The guilt had been an impossible weight on him ever since, and he had barely put out to sea, choosing only the calmest days where he once would have braved almost anything.

Everyone knew he'd endured his share of tragedy over the past few years, and her gaze travelled to where his teenage sons sat, looking just as uncomfortable in suits that didn't seem to fit them either. She wondered how they were feeling right now. Would today bring back painful memories of their own loss? Two years had passed since their mum had died. What would it feel like when two years had passed for her dad? Would it still hurt this much?

Robin's voice cracked as he began to speak, and his first words were barely audible. But then he seemed to realise, cleared his throat, and tried again in trembling but louder tones.

'Jack and me go back forever. I can't recall a single day of my life where I didn't say one word to him, even in passing... aside from when the selfish bugger decided to go on holiday somewhere outside Port Promise, and I could never understand why anyone would want to go anywhere outside Port Promise – still can't.'

There was no laughter, though everyone recognised Robin's attempts to lighten the mood. They were, amongst other things, here to celebrate and give thanks for the life of Jack Morrow, as well as remembering that he was no longer with them. Ava gave a tight smile, the best sign of encouragement she could muster, and as Robin looked up from his sheet, he caught her eye and returned it.

'But what I suppose I mean to say,' he continued, 'is that life is strange without him. He didn't just save lives, as he saved mine, but he made this village a better place. He spoke his mind but he always spoke fairly, and he stuck up for those who couldn't stick up for themselves. He hated injustice and he was always kind. He was everyone's friend at school, and I don't mind saying he got me out of many a spot of bother, even when the bother was of my own stupid making.

'I remember once we were out climbing on Old Finn rocks, four of us. And Jack slipped. He was hanging there – no rope, none of your fancy climbing gear, just a daft fourteen-year-old wearing his gym shoes. And I don't know how, but we got hold of him and we pulled him to a ledge, and we all sat there shocked because we knew it was fifty-fifty that he'd have fallen to his death that day. But not Jack. Jack just looked at me and smiled and said, 'One day, when I'm on the lifeboats, I'll return the favour.' He never doubted it and neither did I. But if I'd have known then what that meant, maybe...'

Robin paused and took a long breath.

'The point is,' he said after a moment, 'he did. There are so many people – some sitting here today – who are alive because he didn't die that day on Old Finn rocks. It stretches way beyond this daft little village. There are people alive in America and Australia and France and Norway and all sorts of places, kids born who wouldn't have been if Jack hadn't saved their parents, kids born to their kids even. Jack touched many lives just as he saved them. He was a one of a kind, a Morrow boy, as he always used to say, born to do good, and he did it. He did more good than he would ever know. I would not be standing here talking to you right now if he hadn't come out that night to get me...'

Robin's voice cracked again and he paused, dragging in a steadying breath before he continued, 'And I'll always be grateful for that, but my biggest sadness is that saving my life meant Jack would never save another. But I know it's not about me – it's about Jack today. My friend, my saviour, the best man who ever walked this earth. When you look out to sea from now on, spare a thought for him – I know I will until the day I have no more thoughts.'

Robin sat down, and there was a beat of silence, as if people weren't quite sure how to react to his speech. Many eyes went to the sea beyond the harbour, as if they were doing just as he'd asked, and thinking of Jack. There was a muted applause, and a few people said a quiet 'Hear hear' or 'Well done, Robin', and then the reverend stood up.

'Thank you, Robin. Heartfelt words which I'm sure many would echo. The Port Promise choral society will now sing one of Jack's favourite songs, "Bridge over Troubled Water".'

As if Robin hadn't done enough damage with his speech, this might just finish Ava. Her dad had always said in passing that he wanted this to be played at his funeral, and it had always held significance for her, for that fact alone. Now, it held more meaning than ever. The funny thing was, when he'd made the remark, Ava was certain he hadn't really thought about it. It was merely a song that he loved and it was his way of making that known. She was sure that he could never have envisaged it on such a day as today.

Perhaps they weren't the best collection of singers the world had ever heard – Port Promise was a tiny place, after all, and it had to be a miracle that it contained enough singers to even form a choral society – but their enthusiasm and sincerity more than made up for the odd less than perfect note. And the song had been beautifully arranged, with soaring harmonies that made the hairs along Ava's arms stand up. By the time the last note had faded, there was barely a dry eye amongst the onlookers and Ava was no different. She would have to pull herself together, though, because at this point in the service it fell to the family to say something.

Jill had decided to do it. Ava would have gladly done it, no matter how much she hated public speaking, if only to save her mum the stress, but Jill had been adamant that it had to be her. It was the least she owed Jack, she said, and more importantly, the very least she owed to the community who had rallied around her and her family since his death.

Ava glanced across and reached for her mum's hand, giving it a brief squeeze before Jill got up and headed for the podium. With a desperate but noble presence, she took her place at the microphone.

'Jack, as you all know, is my husband, the only man I ever loved. The first time I laid eyes on him, I think I probably knew we'd get married, which is quite a feat when you consider we were both three. But I suppose that means I always knew there was something special about him.

'There was a time, when we were in our teens, when I felt he was a bit cocky and maybe he needed bringing down a peg or two, but I always felt I was the girl who would do that.

'It took the idiot until he was twenty-one to ask me out, but I didn't mind, because I always sort of knew he'd get round to it eventually. It was like we were fated to end up together. I knew we'd have a good life, and we did. We had an incredible life. He was the most perfect husband, once I'd trained him up, but then I always knew he'd be that too.

'He had a good soul and the ability to see the best in everyone and everything. I never heard him say a bad word about anyone, never heard him speak ill of someone because of their race or religion or the mistakes they might have made in life that had led them to darker paths. He was tolerant and kind to the last, and he believed that everyone had a place and a purpose on the earth, otherwise, why would they be here? He believed that it was his duty to keep everyone safe, no matter who they were. He believed that not just because he was a Morrow and that was what Morrows did, but because that was how he felt independently of his ancestry. It didn't matter who you were or what you did, Jack believed that you had the right to the best life you could have and that you deserved help if you needed it.

'That was the conviction that made him go out on the boats, year after year, in any kind of weather, no matter how tired he was or what was interrupted by the shout. If someone needed help, that was more important than anything else he was doing. He even went out when I was in labour with Clara. I didn't mind, it was just the sort of man Jack was, so why would I complain when he was the most perfect husband in every other respect? I didn't mind that sometimes the sea and the lifeboat came before me, and I know the girls didn't mind that either. We all understood.

'Our lives, and I think the world at large, are a lot poorer for his absence. I can't say it any better than Robin – without Jack, the world would also be missing people who are alive today because of him, so it would be emptier too. And I think knowing that would make him happy, though he'd never want thanks; that wasn't why he did what he did. He did it because he was a hero in the truest sense of the word. He did it because it was the right thing to do, and he believed that if he didn't do it, he could never expect anyone else to. He led by example in every aspect of his life.

'I'm so proud of him and so grateful for the years we've had together. If I could have seen this day coming, I wouldn't have done anything differently. If someone had told me I'd only have a year with him, I'd have taken it gladly. The girls and I loved him dearly and we miss him every second of every day, but there's no resentment. He died doing what he loved, and I know that even if he'd been told he wasn't going to come back from that rescue, he'd have gone anyway.

'I want to finish by thanking you all for showing him such love. He wouldn't have asked for thanks, but I think he would have been chuffed to see you all here today. I think it would have made him feel that his years of service were a job well done, and I think he would have liked that he was appreciated for it.'

Jill stepped back slightly from the mic, and the crowd erupted into applause this time.

This was finally too much for Ava. She was proud of her dad, but she'd never been prouder of her mum than she was right now. Nobody would ever know what it had taken for Jill to write and speak those words, but Ava could guess that it had been some kind of superhuman strength, probably strength even Jill didn't know she had. Ava's eyes filled with tears as the sound of applause filled her ears. And when she finally managed to clear her vision, she caught sight of Harry, his own eyes red and watering. As they connected, his head went down and he wiped his face with a sleeve.

Jill took her seat as the applause subsided, and the reverend asked for a minute of silence while they remembered Jack and all the lifeboat crew who had lost their lives over the generations helping to save others. He asked Jill to unveil a plaque on the harbour wall dedicated to Jack's memory, which she did solemnly. And then the atmosphere suddenly broke, like a wave over a rock, as the reverend declared the service over and everyone began to disperse, talk turning to the Spratt, their local pub, where drinks and food were being provided for anyone who wanted to linger.

Ava, Clara, Gaby and Jill had spent hours the previous day preparing sandwiches, salads and various other finger foods ready for the occasion, and had made dozens of journeys to the pub, leaving it all there for the landlord to lay out for them ready for today. Anyone who wanted to attend would be welcome, even if they weren't a Port Promise resident. This was not a day for exclusion, Jill had decided, because Jack wouldn't have excluded anyone, though Ava wasn't sure how some of the others would feel if a random nosy tourist wandered in and helped themselves to the food.

As they began to trek up the cobbled hill, away from the harbour and up to the ledge where the old pub overlooked the bay – the very same pub that was partly built into the rock, and that had been there so long they would have served beer to Iziah Morrow himself – Jill fell into conversation with the reverend. There was a sense of relief that it was over. Ava felt it, and she knew her mum felt it too. Now, finally, they could move on with their lives. They'd never forget, of course, but today's ceremony felt like a closure of sorts. Now they had to look forward, not back, because that was the best way to honour Jack and was certainly what he would have told them to do if he could.

Gaby was a little way in front with her two children, Elijah and Fern, chatting to Clara, who had her hand clasped in Logan's. At five foot seven, Clara wasn't short, but Logan was so much taller it made her seem so. His dark hair was curly, long enough to cover his ears, and even in a suit there was no hiding his bohemian tendencies. Everything about him screamed artist – or so Ava had often thought.

Ava watched them, his concerned gaze going to Clara often,

feeling oddly adrift. She walked alone, but at least this way, the only person she needed to concentrate on – aside from her mum – was herself. Still, as she looked to see that everyone seemed to have some kind of support but her, she couldn't help but reflect it might have been nice to have someone special to lean on right now.

'Hey...'

Ava turned to see Harry jogging to catch up.

'Hey, Harry. How are you holding up?'

'I was going to ask you the same thing,' he said.

'Oh, I'm fine.'

'Really?'

'Really. I've had six months to get ready for today, after all. Six months to get used to the new normal.'

'I suppose that's true.'

'I think it might be harder for you in a lot of ways.'

'How's that?'

'Well, getting back out onto the water for one thing. I mean, on rescues.'

Harry gave a vague shrug, his gaze going to the ground. 'Truth be told, I haven't been out on any since.'

'I know – Killian mentioned it. You've been given light duties or something?'

'I was told to go and talk to someone. I feel like a tit, though. Everyone else is getting on with things and I'm...'

'Stop that. Nobody thinks that.'

'Killian does.'

'Honestly, he doesn't. He looks at everyone like they've just dribbled on his shoes.'

Harry looked up at her. 'Would you tell me if he'd said anything different? If Killian had said he thought I was being a wet blanket?'

'Of course I would! Any opportunity to drop my holier-than-thou brother-in-law in it.'

Harry gave a low chuckle now, and Ava was glad to see the tension lift from his expression.

'And you're definitely not a wet blanket,' Ava continued. 'You're still volunteering. They ought to be grateful for that much.'

'I'm on the shore crew at the moment.'

'Just as important as seagoing. And you'll get back on the boat in your own time, right?'

'I want to, but...'

'Every time you look at the boat, or your uniform hanging in your locker, or some other small thing it reminds you of that night... I get it,' Ava said. 'It's not just you. Gaby says Killian feels the same way.'

'He's never said.'

'And I bet you haven't either – not to him at least. Honestly, you blokes need to communicate better. How are you supposed to look out for one another if you don't even talk?'

'The service would probably run a whole lot better if the women of the village were in charge.'

'We'd talk a lot more and that would sort things pretty instantly,' Ava agreed. 'You're coming to the pub for a drink?'

'I thought I'd stay for a couple. I owe your dad that much, right?'

'Everyone keeps going on about what they owe Dad. How about you just come because you want to? Dad would have said he wasn't doing favours that needed to be repaid. He was a Morrow boy, he was doing what Morrow boys have always done. You and Killian and the other guys – you all joined because you wanted to, not because of some mad family tradition.'

'But your dad didn't really do it because of that. He wanted to help people. He was a hero.'

'Yes, but he would have said that you were the real heroes.

There was no reason for you to volunteer, no expectations. You just wanted to.'

Harry was silent for a moment. 'Do you really think it's a mad family tradition?'

'I suppose not. I think maybe I get angry sometimes because we'd still have Dad if it hadn't been a thing, or if Dad hadn't been born a Morrow. But it meant a lot to him, so I suppose when I'm angry I have to try and remember that. And because in a strange way the lifeboat service is in every Morrow's blood, even the women, like some kind of inherited family health condition. I'm even thinking I might—'

Ava didn't get to finish. Killian appeared at Harry's side, clapping a hand to his shoulder as he fell into step with them both.

'OK, chief?'

'Glad it's over...' Harry blushed suddenly as he glanced at Ava. 'No offence. I meant to say—'

'None taken,' Ava cut in. 'I'm glad it's over too.'

'It was good, though,' Killian said. 'About time Jack had a decent send-off, something the whole village could get involved in.'

'It was.' Ava nodded as the incline steepened and her step lengthened to keep up with the taller men. 'I think Dad would have approved.'

'He was always a sort of legend to me,' Harry said. 'Obviously he's been around my whole life; he's the reason I wanted to volunteer for the boats as soon as I could swim. He's certainly the person my mum blames for me being on the boats.'

Ava smiled. 'I bet.'

'I seem to recall it was Jack who taught you to swim too,' Killian said to Harry.

'It was,' Harry said. 'One afternoon when I was about five or six he took a load of us to the saltwater lido. Said it was the most important lesson we'd ever have, apart from reading and writing, and reading wouldn't save us if we fell into the harbour.'

'Oh, God, that lido,' Ava said, her smile broadening. 'I still recall the taste of all that water I swallowed when I was learning to swim there as if it was this morning. I think he took practically everyone in Port Promise under the age of twenty-five there at some point to teach them how to swim.'

Harry turned to Killian. 'I guess that means you'll have to do it, now he's not here.'

'Not me,' he replied. 'I haven't got the patience. Didn't even teach my pair. Ava... that one's yours.'

'Maybe I will,' Ava said. 'I suppose it's not a million miles away from my job anyway. Maybe I'll do some of the other things Dad used to do too.'

'Like what?'

'I'll let you know when I've decided,' she said. Though she'd already had firm ideas, she knew this wasn't the time to share them.

'Sounds mysterious,' Harry said.

'Not really.'

Ava was saved from the need to elaborate by the arrival of Vas, falling into step with them, and then a couple of members of the lifeboat shore crew, and by the time they'd reached the pub there was a lively gaggle walking with Ava. The conversation had become less introspective and had turned to anecdotes, mainly about Jack, that had everyone laughing. Ava had heard most of them before, but that didn't mean she didn't enjoy hearing them again. Each time the stories were told they grew and changed, each telling unique, and there was always something new to be learned. Stories from those outside the family made her appreciate her dad in whole new ways, to see him not just as her dad but as a man with a life of his own, a life that she was only ever offered tantalising glimpses into.

'I'll never forget that day when he'd taken a break from exercises when I first joined,' Maxine said. 'It was boiling. He'd stripped off and gone swimming because it was hot and run into a cloud of jellyfish. It was like something out of *Jaws*!' she continued, laughing. 'We all ran out thinking the daft bugger was drowning because he was screaming. I ran into the water with my clothes on – I was about your age then, Ava. Then I realised he was only trying to fight them off. He got out... I know he'd been stung but I had to laugh. Here was this big tough guy that we all looked up to and he'd been floored by some jellyfish, begging Vas to come and pee on his legs to sort out his stings!'

'I suppose he didn't seem so tough after that,' Ava said.

'He definitely seemed more human,' Maxine agreed.

'And we didn't half take the rip,' Vas added. 'It was too good not to.'

'Remember that time someone saw a helium balloon on the water and thought it was a stranded surfer?' Maxine asked.

'Oh, and Jack's face when we took the boat out and he realised... Priceless.'

'And that dolphin who decided he was Jack's best friend. You remember?' Vas said. 'He only showed up and followed the boat when Jack was on board. For about six months he did that. I was convinced he was throwing tuna overboard or something to lure it over and wind us up.'

'I remember that,' Ava said. 'I was little. He used to come in and say, "I've seen Flipper today." I was desperate to see that dolphin, went to the beach almost every day after school, but I never did.'

'It only turned up for him. I think it had a crush on him.'

Ava laughed. 'God, imagine that!'

'Pub looks busy already,' Vas said. 'Anyone would think there was free food.'

Ava smiled. 'It's a shame nobody warned them that I'd made some of it.'

'Serves 'em right if they get poisoned then,' Harry said. He opened the door for Ava to walk in.

Ava laughed. 'Cheeky bugger! I'm allowed to say that but you're not.'

'Don't forget, I was in home ec with you at school; I've witnessed your cooking first-hand. If it can be called cooking at all.'

'Well then, you don't have to eat it.'

'Don't worry,' Harry said. 'Point me in the direction of the stuff your mum made and I won't.'

# CHAPTER TWO

The interior of the pub was already humid. The low ceilings and stone floors, and small draughty windows that were usually cold to sit next to in winter did nothing to keep the space cool today, not with so many bodies packed inside. Harry fought his way to the bar to get a round of drinks, while Killian searched the room for Gaby, who'd gone ahead while the lifeboat crew had all been talking shop, as she called it, with Ava.

'I expect she'll have taken the kids out to the beer garden for the swings,' Ava said.

'Probably.' He frowned slightly. 'You're all right?'

'Of course. I mean, I could have done without this morning, but it's over now and we can get on with celebrating Dad in the way he would have liked. At the pub.'

'I still can't help but feel responsible,' Killian said. 'I know I don't say it, but I think about it all the time.'

Ava looked up at him. 'Responsible for what? For Dad? Nobody blames you. Nobody blames you or Vas or Harry – you know that, right?'

'I do, but it doesn't change the way I feel about it. If only I'd been tougher about him coming out with us—'

'Dad would have pulled rank – you know he would. It was Robin out there, one of Dad's oldest and best friends – there was nothing on earth that would have stopped him getting on that boat to go and rescue Robin and you know it.'

Killian was saved from a response by the return of Harry with their drinks.

'Cheers.' Killian took his pint of bitter. 'Don't mind me, just going to see if Gaby's here and that she's OK with the kids.'

Harry nodded and handed Ava a cider. She turned the bottle to look at the label.

'One of your dad's – don't think I've tried this one before.'

'It's a new one. I know you always like to try them out so I thought I'd get you one.'

Ava took a sip and smiled. 'And as usual, it's pretty good. I don't think I've tried one yet I didn't like.'

'But you'd have to say that with me standing right here.'

'True. The proof will be in how many of these I neck today, even with you not here looking at me.'

Harry grinned. 'So I can tell Dad that's another seal of approval?'

'Absolutely!'

Vas shuffled over and clapped Harry on the back. 'How are you doing there? Could I…?' He glanced at Ava. 'Do you mind if I steal Harry for a quick chat with the higher-ups?'

'Of course I don't.' She raised her bottle at Harry. 'I'll catch you later.'

He looked uncertain as she watched him go and she wondered what he might look so concerned about. But there wasn't much time to dwell on it. Jill came over.

'Sweetheart, could you check in the kitchen for more sausage rolls? I'm sure there must be some because I can't remember putting them all out.'

'They've all been eaten already?'

'Well, there are a lot of burly sailing types here. You know what they're like.'

'Want me to run to Betty's and buy some more?'

Jill shook her head. 'God no! I wouldn't have you climbing that hill again and you can't drive now you've had a drink. When they're gone they're gone, and I think I cleaned out Betty's yesterday anyway. But if there are some in the kitchen then they might as well go out.'

'Of course.'

'I'd go myself but...'

'I know. People want to see you. That's OK – I can sort it. Anything else while I'm there?'

'I don't think so, unless there's anything you see that you know is running out.'

'I've only just got here – I don't have a clue what's running out. And honestly, I don't know how anything's running out because most of us have only just got here.'

Jill shrugged. 'Not a clue. People are hungry I suppose. Thank you.'

Ava went to the kitchen. On the worktop were extra plates covered in cling film, containing sausage rolls, various pies, and sandwiches. Next to them were large unopened bags of crisps and snacks. Ava grabbed all the sausage rolls and took them to the table where the food was laid out.

'Need a hand?' Clara's voice was at her ear.

'It's fine.' Ava turned to her. 'Mum asked me to top up.'

'Greedy lot, aren't they? I've just seen Bob with a plate about ready to topple. I swear he's hoping to take it all home.'

'Probably,' Ava said. 'I expect there'll be some left to take home if people want to – there usually is at these things.'

'Yes, after it's finished and the guests have had their fill – not before. Anyway, have you seen Logan?'

'Not since we got here. Why?'

'Oh, nothing in particular... We had words this morning, that's all.'

'Really? You both seemed OK at the service. '

'Well, I suppose I can thank him for being a grown-up about it for my sake. But I'm worried I might have upset him and we haven't been able to talk properly all day – for obvious reasons. I could do with seeing if things are OK.'

'Hmm. Whatever it was, looks to me like he's over it.'

Clara nodded. 'I hope so, but I think I ought to find him anyway. He's probably talking to some council person or other about doing an art installation somewhere, knowing Logan.'

'Well, that's true. All he talks about is art.'

'No he doesn't.'

'Well what else is he into?'

'Me,' Clara said with a grin.

'Fair enough – can't argue with that.'

'So you're OK?' Clara asked.

'Yes! I'm fine. I'm perfectly capable of whacking a plate of cold pastry out without assistance!'

'Cool, brilliant. I'll catch you later...'

Ava watched Clara push her way through the crowded pub. She saw her stop a few times to say hello to someone or other and then lost track of where she was.

'I bet you're finding this hard work,' Harry said.

Ava spun to see him reaching for a sandwich.

'Oh, hey, Harry. A bit, yeah. My social battery will only run for so long.'

'I know what you mean, but at least I can blend into the background. Everyone wants you.'

'They want my mum or Gaby – they don't want me. And I'm quite happy to have it that way.'

'Well, I want you – how's that?'

'Don't tell your current girlfriend that... What's her name again?'

He shrugged. 'She's gone – we split a couple of days ago.'

'Ah. How are you taking it?'

'It wasn't all that serious so I'm OK.'

Ava picked up a carrot baton and nibbled at it. 'They never are.'

'Harsh.'

'But true. I've totally lost track of how many girlfriends you've had since we were at school.'

'I could say the same to you.'

'I've never had a girlfriend.'

Harry grinned. 'Boyfriends!'

'I've had hardly any, cheeky bugger!'

'Me thinks the lady doth protest... And why are you keeping score?'

'I don't and I'm not, it's just noted.'

'I haven't had that many.'

'Yes you have. Plus, you were at uni in Falmouth for three years, so you probably had a load there I don't even know about.'

'OK, can't argue with that.'

'So shut up.'

'Got it.' He reached for another sandwich.

'You could just get a plate and take what you want all at once, like normal people,' Ava said.

'I could, but then I'd deprive you of my company,' he said, shoving a triangle of bread and cheese into his mouth.

Ava looked beyond him. 'Hold that thought,' she said. 'I'm afraid Mum wants me; I'll catch up with you later.'

Ava fought her way across the bar to where her mum was beckoning her over.

'What's up?'

'It's Robin,' Jill said in a low voice.

'What's wrong with him?'

Jill nodded to a chair in a corner, on which the fisherman

sat, staring into space. He had no drink in his hand like everyone else and no food. He was stock-still.

'I don't think I even saw him look like that after his wife died,' Jill said.

'No, I see what you mean. What can we do about it? We've tried talking to him, more than once.'

'I know, but try again.'

Ava blinked. 'Me?'

'You're good at things like that.'

'I think you're confusing me with Gaby.'

'Yes, but Gaby's busy with the kids.'

'Oh, thanks... so I am second choice... or have you already asked Clara too?'

Jill frowned at her.

'OK,' Ava said, holding up a hand in a gesture of surrender. 'I'll try.'

Ava made her way over. 'Hey,' she said gently.

Robin looked up at her. 'Ah... Ava.'

'Just wondering... you want a sandwich or anything? I haven't seen you eat, and these gannets will have it all if you don't get some.'

'No,' he said. 'Though I appreciate you thinking of me.'

'Well...' Ava paused. She needed to start this conversation without making it obvious she was starting a conversation that was more than simply a conversation. 'Can I get you a drink?' she asked.

'I'm all right as I am.'

'Your boys have gone home?'

He nodded.

'So would you like to come and sit with me and Mum?'

'No,' he said. 'I'm good here.'

'Robin...' Ava dragged over a nearby seat and sat next to him. 'Are you OK? We're worried about you.'

He looked at her with some surprise. 'Worried about me?'

'Of course. You're sitting here on your own not eating or drinking like everyone else.'

He shrugged. 'Doesn't seem right to be enjoying myself when I'm the reason everyone is here.'

'It's not really enjoying ourselves, though,' Ava said. 'Not like that. We're remembering Dad... just in a bit of a rowdy way. In the way Dad would have wanted us to. You know how much he loved a drink in here. And don't you dare keep on saying it's your fault because it's not.'

'But it is!' Robin ran a hand through his unruly hair. 'I don't know how you can even look at me. And you and your mum and your sisters are so kind, even knowing what I've done—'

'You're like family,' Ava said. 'I've known you my whole life – why would we be anything else to you?'

'Because I killed your dad!'

Ava reached for his hand and took it in both of hers. 'Look at me.'

His head went down and he tried to take his hand from her grip but she held on tighter.

'Robin...'

He looked up and flinched, like it hurt to see her face.

'I know you feel guilty and you feel like this is all your fault,' she continued. 'But that's not what Dad would want, and it's not what we want either. Dad knew what he was doing. You said it yourself: he'd have gone out for anyone but especially for his best friend...' She pointed at him. 'You. He knew every time he went on any shout there was a chance he might not come back. That's how it is for all the crew. And if not you, he'd have been out saving someone else – probably people he wouldn't have even liked if he'd known them, people who'd got into trouble being stupid—'

'Like me.'

'No, not like you. You were making a living for you and your boys. You were doing what a good dad should do. If you really want to make it up to us, if you really want to help, please stop blaming yourself. It breaks Mum's heart to see you looking so down.'

'I'll go,' he began, but Ava stopped him.

'That's not what I mean. I'm not expecting you to dance on the tables here today, and I respect that you want to remember Dad the way you feel is best, but don't keep beating yourself up about what happened. It won't bring him back, and he'd hate the idea of you doing it.'

He sniffed, his head going down again. 'I'll try.'

'OK,' she said. 'Are you sure you don't want a plate of food or a drink now?'

He looked up and shook his head. 'I'm not hungry. I'll go and see your mum and take my leave, if it's all the same to you.'

Ava let go of his hand. She'd done as much as she could, and the rest, whether it was here or at home in his own time, was up to him. 'I'm sure she'd like a quick chat with you.'

He got up from his chair and shuffled off. Ava watched him. From an early age she'd watched him take to the sea in his trawler almost as often as she'd watched her dad on his lifeboat launches. Just as she'd told him, he was like family. She wished there was something more she could do to help, because words clearly weren't enough, but she had no clue what else would work. Perhaps, in the end, all they could do was hope that time would make things easier. She couldn't imagine how it felt to carry such a burden, and she hoped she'd never have to find out.


The afternoon turned into early evening. Ava hadn't been lying when she'd told Harry that her social battery was running low. She didn't do small talk at the best of times but was finding it particularly difficult today, especially because a lot of it was with people she hardly knew. She'd been to the kitchen more times than she'd needed to, just to get a breather, but every time someone had come looking for her.

'Honestly,' Jill said, coming in to find Ava sitting on the kitchen stool by herself, staring into space. 'Your sister...'

Ava looked up. 'Which one?'

'Gabriella.'

'Now I know you're annoyed if you're using every syllable of her name. What's she done?'

'Drunk.'

'Is that all? I think just about everyone's drunk now.'

'You're not.'

'I'm not sober either.'

'I know, but it's not like her.' Jill looked worried now. 'Do you think she's all right? She hasn't said much about today – keeps it all in, doesn't she? I'm not sure that's always healthy.'

'I'm sure she's fine,' Ava said. 'Want me to go and talk to her?'

'Not about that. I'm sure we'll have a chance to catch up when she's more sober.'

'OK, in that case I'm going to see if she's as drunk as you think. I might take a photo and save it for next time she gets on my nerves.'

'Ava...' Jill's voice had a warning note to it.

Ava hopped off the stool and put her phone away. 'Chill, Mum, joking. I'll go and find her.'


Ava had seen Gaby neck at least two shots of rum early on. It wasn't like her, but someone had got her involved in some kind of sailing drinking tradition and Ava guessed that by the time her sister had drunk the first one, not blessed with a high tolerance for alcohol, her guard had probably gone down. Things in the pub were getting rowdy – just as Jack would have liked it – and Gaby was suddenly in the thick of it. Ava found her by the bar talking to Bob, husband of Marina, Jill's oldest friend. Bob greeted Ava briefly and was then distracted by someone asking him if he wanted to go outside to smoke.

'Ava!' Gaby curled her arms around her youngest sister's neck. 'Where have you been?'

'Nowhere,' Ava said with a wry smile. 'I've been right here in the pub. I could ask you the same thing, because I think you might have gone off with the fairies.'

'What does that mean?'

'You're a bit drunk.'

'I'm not!'

'How many have you had?'

'Three,' Gaby said. 'No, wait... four... Hang on... there was Sandy's... six. Or seven.'

Just to prove how not drunk she was, Gaby then hiccoughed and started to giggle. This was the point at which Killian arrived. Gaby threw her arms around him and kissed him hard on the lips. Ava had thought her sister tipsy but realised now that she was more than tipsy. PDAs were not Gaby's thing, and so to kiss Killian so passionately in full view of the pub, she had to be fairly drunk.

Ava raised her eyebrows at Killian. 'You've got an interesting night ahead of you.'

'So I noticed,' Killian said. 'And it's usually you we're carrying home – what universe have I fallen into?'

Ava feigned outrage but then laughed. Clearly, if Killian was cracking jokes he'd had more than a few tots of rum too. 'I've no idea,' she said. 'But something's definitely wrong somewhere.'

Killian looked more thoughtful now. 'Maybe I ought to get you home...' he said to Gaby, who waved a hand and spluttered a reply that nobody could understand.

'No way! This is my dad's send-off – the non-miserable one. I'm not leaving this; it would be an insult to his memory.'

'I can't argue with that,' Killian said. 'Nobody liked a noisy night in this pub better than your dad. I hope he's raising a glass in heaven. Still, it's getting on and the kids ought to be settling down.'

'Most days,' Ava said. 'But this isn't most days, surely? Would anyone really be that stressed if your kids had a later than usual bedtime? Why not let them be a part of the occasion like everyone else?'

'Anyone would think it was a party,' Killian replied, his tone full of sarcasm.

Ava shrugged, unfazed by his comment. 'You just said yourself Dad would have loved it. He would have said stop being such a Victorian dad and leave the kids be for a while. They missed the miserable bit this morning... let them have this so at least they feel a part of something.'

'That's true,' Gaby said, sucking on the straw of a cocktail that Ava hadn't even seen her pick up. Had she swiped it from a nearby table? 'You are a Victorian dad.'

'Because I want my kids to grow up with a strong moral compass?' Killian turned to her. 'Is that what makes me Victorian?'

'Nah.' Ava smirked. 'It's all the times you tried to get them up your chimney with that big brush.'

Gaby giggled, and Killian frowned but then seemed to decide there was no point having this discussion with his tipsy wife and flippant sister-in-law.

'Where are they anyway?' he asked.

'In the beer garden,' Ava replied. 'Playing footie with Harry last time I saw. I think Fern might be a bit in love.'

'Definitely!' Gaby agreed. 'Thank God she's not ten years older; I'd have to keep an eye on her.'

'He spares a lot of time for people,' Ava said. 'Kids warm to that.'

'He is a good lad,' Killian agreed. He looked pointedly at Ava. '*You* could do a lot worse than someone like him.'

'Killian...' Ava frowned as she cut him short. 'Don't even go there. Harry... well it's never going to happen.'

'Why not?'

'What, are you working for Tinder or something now? What do you care if I get it on with Harry? And, just so you know, I won't. Gaby knows why.'

'Do I?' Gaby asked. 'Not sure I do.'

'I don't either, so spill,' Killian said, and Ava's frown deepened.

'Fine!' Killian put his hands up in a gesture of surrender, though his expression suggested he was far from finished and he had many more opinions to impart if Ava would let him.

'Right...' Gaby swung around to search the pub. 'Where's Clara?'

'I think she nipped out with Logan...' Ava said. 'Something about the alarm going off at the studio and they needed to check it.'

'Both of them?' Gaby asked.

Ava shrugged. She'd guessed that maybe Clara had spotted an opportunity to have the chat with Logan that she'd wanted all day, but wasn't about to say so, in case it bothered Clara that Ava had told Gaby. 'Maybe they just needed a breather. I expect they'll be back shortly. So until then I'm stuck with Drunk and Drunker.'

'Who?' Gaby asked.

'You and Killian.'

'I'm not drunk!' Killian huffed.

'But you've had more than usual.'

'Usually I'd be waiting for a shout, but the higher-ups have told me to take the day off.'

'So they've told you all that?' Ava asked. Knowing that the

crew were on call every single hour of every day, no matter what, it seemed unlikely.

'Well, they said we could work it out amongst ourselves. Vas didn't want to take time off, so he's got his pager on him. Maxine and Yvan are staying off the sauce too.'

'And Harry's outside,' Gaby said. 'He hasn't had much either.'

'I know.'

'Playing football with the kids.'

'I know that too,' Ava said patiently.

'Why don't you go out and talk to him?'

Ava held in a sigh but then decided that going outside to chat to Harry wasn't such a terrible idea after all. She was getting no sense out of Gaby right now, and amusing as it was to wind Killian up when he was tipsy too, it might still lead to friction, and maybe that wasn't what anyone needed today.

'Actually,' she said, 'now that I think about it, maybe I will have a kick around, show them all how football is really played.'

'You do that!' Gaby returned with a drunken grin.

Ava left them, fighting her way through the bodies now crowding the pub, stopping to speak briefly to one or two, before emerging into the cooler air of the beer garden. Though the sun was still quite high, the garden was almost always in the shade cast by the shadow of the pub itself. It was narrow, mostly rocky with only a razor-thin strip of grass and some hardy plants that allowed it to be called a garden at all. The piss had been taken royally by the locals when the landlord of the time had told them he'd turn the ledge that sat alongside his rock-face pub into a beer garden, but people still used it – though how anyone played on it at all was another thing entirely. Still, Ava had spent many hours of her formative years in this space, sipping on straws bobbing inside bottles of cola, making the best of it while her dad caught up with old friends over a pint in the snug.

Far from the squealing and laughter she expected, the

garden was relatively quiet. It was then that Ava noticed Elijah and Harry kneeling beside a softly sobbing Fern.

'It doesn't look too bad.' Harry's tone was soothing. 'It might sting for a bit, but it won't last long. You can be a brave girl, right?'

'What's happened?'

All three looked up at Ava's question.

'Fern fell over,' Elijah announced.

'Oh.' Ava bent to inspect Fern's wound. Her niece's grazed knee was scraped raw and oozing a little blood in places, but mostly what Ava could see was mud.

'We were just trying to persuade her to let us wash it,' Harry said.

'But she thinks it will hurt too much,' Elijah added.

'I don't!' Fern looked more defiant now, her tears drying.

In many ways, Ava saw a lot of herself in Fern – and a reluctance to show weakness was very definitely one of those traits. Fern wouldn't be down for long and she wouldn't want to look like a baby – especially not to Ava. For some reason, Fern idolised her youngest aunt. Gaby had mentioned it first, but that didn't mean Ava had never noticed, though she'd never figured out why, or what made their relationship different from the one Fern had with Clara, who probably spent more time with them because she often babysat.

'You said!' Elijah fired back.

'It might hurt,' Ava cut in. 'Things often do, but the bravest people don't mind admitting it, even if they need to tough it out.' She turned to Fern. 'Shall I take you inside to clean it? Better that I do it now and it hurts only a little than it gets infected and ends up hurting a lot more.'

Fern glanced between Ava and Harry, seemingly torn.

'Will Harry pick me up?' she asked finally.

'I can carry you in,' he said. 'But I'll leave all the medic stuff to Ava. She's way better at it than me.'

'I'm not going to lie,' Ava said, frowning at Fern's knee as if deep in thought. 'It's not going to be an easy mission. I might have to sew it with thread ripped from my combat gear.'

Harry raised his eyebrows. 'Under enemy fire?'

Ava gave a grim nod. 'I'll cover you. You get the casualty off the battlefield. Ready?'

Harry gave a daft salute as he leaped up to attention, and then he swept a now giggling Fern into his arms, while Ava ran alongside pretending to shoot snipers and Elijah, quickly catching on, made machine-gun and explosive noises. By the time Ava had taken Fern into the ladies toilets, the little girl was as bright as if nothing had happened. Ava cleaned her knee by holding her over the sink and running the tap over it, but Fern didn't complain once, even if she did wince on occasion.

'See,' Ava said. 'I knew you were a tough cookie. Your mum is a Morrow, after all, and us Morrows are tough.'

'Grandpa Jack was tough.' Fern looked up, not sad at the statement but inquisitive, like she wanted and expected Ava to tell her a story about her grandfather's toughness. It was no wonder; Ava had told many of them to Elijah and Fern since his death – so many, in fact, that Gaby had taken her aside for a quiet but stern word that she wasn't to tell any more because it was putting ideas into their heads about the lifeboat service.

'He was,' Ava said. 'He was kind too. That's another Morrow thing.' She gave a jaunty wink. 'Apart from your mum, of course. I have no idea how she got to be so mean.'

Fern giggled. 'Sometimes she's kind.'

'Well, I've never seen it – she must hide it well. But I suppose she's going to be kind to you and Elijah. How could anyone have you two and not be kind to you? After all, you're so darned cool you make everyone want to be kind to you.'

'You're cooler,' Fern said.

Ava grinned. 'Oh yeah, I know that.'

'Harry too.'

'I'm sure.'

'Are you coming to our house later?'

'Do you want me to?'

'Yes! I've got a new game!'

'Oh yeah? What is it?'

'Sports.'

'Just sports? That doesn't tell me much.'

'You know, like tennis and bowling and stuff. On the Wii. Like Wii Sports.'

'You mean exactly Wii Sports?'

'Yes.'

'Well...' Ava folded her arms and pretended to ponder the offer. 'That does sound like fun. Maybe I could fit you in the diary.'

'Yes!' Fern punched the air. 'I'll tell Eli!'

'I'm sure he'll figure it out for himself when I rock up later.'

'Will you take us home?'

Ava raised her eyebrows slightly. 'Now? I thought you were in the middle of a football match with Harry.'

'I think I'm bored of that now.'

'And I suppose you are injured.'

'Yes. Maybe I should do something else.' Then Fern seemed to be struck by a light-bulb moment. 'Harry can play sports with us!'

'I'm not sure he has time.'

'I'll ask him!'

Fern lunged for the bathroom doors and raced out into the pub, nearly taking a punter and his tray full of beers with her.

Ava could have given chase, but instead she shook her head with a wry smile, apologised to the customer (someone she didn't recognise) and then strolled out to the beer garden. She had no issue with Harry joining them and doubted that Gaby or Killian would have either, but she was fairly convinced that Harry would have better things to do. He'd find it hard to refuse, however, unless Ava helped him out. Quite how she was going to do that with any subtlety was another matter.

When she got back out to the beer garden, Fern was already deep in negotiations. She was batting her eyelashes at Harry like some heroine from a thirties cartoon.

'Mum and Dad don't mind at all; they like it when you come to our house!'

'I know,' Harry said. 'And normally I like visiting but I'm not sure today will be a good day for them.'

'I'll ask!'

With that, Fern raced back inside to find one or both of her parents.

Harry watched her go, and then noticed Ava's approach.

'She's not going to take no for an answer,' she said.

'I kind of got that. Normally I'd be happy to entertain them both for an hour, but today... well, it's a weird day, isn't it?'

'If that's your only worry, it might be wasted. Killian and Gaby are both too pissed to be giving sombre reflection to anything right now, even the life of my dad. And before you look shocked' – she gave a wry smile – 'I think that might be a good thing. They're both far too serious all the time. I don't think for a minute Dad would have begrudged them letting their hair down today. The funeral has been and gone and life has moved on whether we like it or not. Dad would say today is a day for celebrating a life lived, not mourning one that's been lost for long enough for everyone to have got used to it by now.'

'You think that's true?'

'Well, he wouldn't have put it quite as eloquently as his obviously smartest daughter' – Ava hooked a thumb at herself and laughed – 'and nobody would have caught a word of half of it anyway because of his ludicrously thick accent, but I'm sure it would have been something along those lines.'

Harry grinned. 'His accent *was* broad.'

'Ridiculous,' Ava countered. 'I mean, who even talks like that, even round here, in the twenty-first century. I don't know how any of his crew had a clue what he wanted them to do half the time.'

Harry was thoughtful for a moment, the smile fading from his lips as he regarded her. 'You're dealing with this so well. I only wish I could be half as strong. I feel like such a—'

'No!' Ava put a finger up to stop him. 'No! Whatever you're going to say, I'm going to stop you right there because I think I know what it is. Everyone's processes are different. Besides that, you were on the bloody boat when it happened and I wasn't. It's bound to affect us differently.'

'You're his daughter.'

'True. But I couldn't have done anything to change what happened that night.'

'You think I could?' Harry asked, looking suddenly crestfallen.

'God, no, Harry! That's not what I meant! I meant there's no reason for me to beat myself up, but you seem to be finding plenty to do that to yourself. It wasn't your fault just like it wasn't mine! I know what Dad was like, and I can't say I'm entirely clear on the details, but I do know he shouldn't have been on that boat in the first place. It was just like Dad to go ahead anyway. He knew the risks, and if he was here now he'd tell you that himself. Harry, you've got to stop blaming yourself for something you couldn't have stopped. Nobody else is blaming you.'

'Sometimes I think—' Harry stopped and shrugged. 'Never mind. Maybe you're right. Thanks.'

'For what?'

'For being so nice.'

'Jesus, Harry!' Ava cried. 'I'm not being nice; I'm telling you how it is! You think I'm being nice? You know me better than that – I'm a raging bitch if you do something I don't like!'

'That's true,' Harry said with a small smile. 'I'm still getting over the 2008 Oyster Festival.'

'Well, you did ask for that.'

'I asked for something, but not for my head to be dunked in a bucket of oysters.'

'At least they were fresh – could have been worse.'

Harry's small smile turned into a more genuine one. 'Seriously, thanks. I needed to hear that.'

'Even if you don't quite believe it?'

'Even then.'

'So I just have to keep telling you and eventually you'll start to believe it.'

'I don't know about that. But I feel better that at least you don't hate me.'

'I could never hate you. Nobody could.'

'You say that, but you didn't feel that way in 2008.'

Ava laughed. 'I can barely remember 2008 – not sure how you can be so upset about it.'

He grinned. 'These scars run deep.'

'Harry!'

They both turned to see Fern running across the garden.

'I'm sure that girl doesn't know how to walk anywhere,' Ava said.

'Mum says yes!' Fern panted. 'And she says can Ava stay with us until bedtime?'

'Did she?' Ava asked. Fern gave an enthusiastic nod. 'She wants me to take you home?'

'I don't know,' Fern said, more uncertainly this time. 'Should I ask her?'

'Don't worry about it,' Ava said. She didn't mind helping her sister out and she didn't mind enabling a well-deserved night off. What she'd said to Harry was true – even the two most strait-laced people she knew needed to let their hair down now and again. As for Ava herself, if she was being honest, she'd had about enough here for one day and the idea of spending a quieter hour with her niece and nephew – relatively quiet anyway – was tempting. They'd expect to be entertained, but she didn't mind that – she'd probably find it as much fun as them.

'So are you coming?' Fern turned to Harry with an adorably beseeching look.

Elijah, who'd been prodding at a clump of grass with great interest up until this point, looked up at Harry now. 'Are you coming to our house?'

Harry looked between the two of them and then at Ava. 'How can I say no to such cool company? As long as you don't mind me crashing your party?'

'God no!' Ava smiled. 'I'll take all the help I can get!'

# CHAPTER THREE

Ava found her mum in the pub talking to Clara. She'd returned without Logan, who'd stayed at the gallery to get it ready for an exhibition the following day, so Ava explained the plan and bid them both a brief goodbye.

'I could take them home if you like,' Clara offered.

Ava shook her head. 'It's fine – you're always sitting for them and to be honest, I could do with an excuse to leave here... sorry, Mum.'

Jill waved away the apology, and Clara nodded. 'I don't blame you. I didn't need to go with Logan to check the alarm but I was glad of the breather.'

Ava kissed them both lightly. Then she went to find Gaby and Killian to let them know she was taking the kids home and ask if she could have a house key. Killian had definitely had a couple more drinks and was far more relaxed than he'd been earlier, while Gaby was due a hangover she wasn't going to forget in a hurry. Ava couldn't help but smile to herself as she, Harry, Elijah and Fern left the pub and set off for her sister's cottage.

.  .  .

Harry had always been easy company. People in the village had always teased them both that they ought to be a couple, but Ava had never seen him like that, though he'd once asked her out, back in high school. Shamefully, when she looked back on it, she'd said yes and then left him standing at the school gates on the day of the date. She'd never understood what had made her do it, apart from some ribbing from her sisters and even then it wasn't like her. Jill had found out, of course, because there were no secrets in Port Promise, and had been furious that she could have been so cruel.

It had taken some time, but Harry had forgiven her. In fact, by the time he'd been away from the village for his three years at university, Ava wondered if he even remembered the incident at all. And Ava didn't feel she'd missed out – it was just the way life played out and she valued him as a friend far more these days.

He'd been his pleasant, humorous self on the walk back, but Ava could tell it wasn't quite his honest mood. Something was there in the background, troubling him. Something had changed. She could only guess that it was somehow connected with his sabbatical from the boat crew since her dad's death, but without asking him outright she couldn't be sure, and with Elijah and Fern in tow it wasn't the right time for a discussion that might take him to a very dark place. If she was being totally honest, a discussion like that might take them both to a dark place.

So Ava joked about this and that as the sun sank into the bay, setting the sea on fire. The night was mild, though this early in the season there might be a frost come the small hours of the morning.

Thistledown Cottage came into view. This was where Gaby and Killian called home. Clara envied Gaby her home, but Ava had often thought it too ordered. The garden was pretty enough, with rose bushes planted in neat rows, sunflowers in lined-up pots along the gable wall and a pristine lawn. The front door was lacquered navy blue, the original wood having been replaced by a smart modern composite, which still looked good but had a manufactured look that bugged Ava. It all suited its owners perfectly, there was no doubt, but Ava preferred her surroundings wilder, like the grounds that surrounded the caravan she'd lived in for the past few months.

She opened the door to let everyone in. Elijah and Fern knew the drill well – they headed straight to a rack in the hallway to take off their shoes before they went into the living room. Harry followed their lead, and while Ava was tempted to keep hers on, just to annoy her sister, she kicked them off and left them on the welcome mat. Then she went through to the kitchen and made coffee and chocolate milk (coffee for her, chocolate milk for Harry and the kids) while Harry helped the children set up the games console.

Things were as lively and carefree as they could be on such a day. And really, in Ava's opinion, the kids were too young to be burdened – and maybe didn't even fully understand it all – and so why make them suffer? They'd face tragedy enough in their adult lives – why not shield them from it for as long as possible? And if she was being completely honest, it felt good for her to think about something other than her dad's loss too.

'At the risk of sounding like your mum,' Ava said as she brought the drinks through, 'I have to insist that you kids store yours on the kitchen table where we can't knock them over and only go to get them to take a sip, and then put them back again. If you spill a drop, my life won't be worth living, and you wouldn't want to be responsible for me being barred from the house, would you?'

'OK,' Elijah said breezily, staring intently at the screen where he was making himself a new player name. Ava was fairly sure he hadn't listened to a word she'd said as she put the glasses out of harm's way.

'What about me?' Harry asked. 'Have I got to put my glass up there too?'

'Well, if everyone else has to stick to the rules then I don't see why you're any different.'

'Yes, Mum.'

'Oi!' Ava warned.

Harry laughed.

'Bowling first?' Elijah called out.

'You said tennis!' Fern tried to grab the controller from him, but he swung it out of her way so violently that Ava felt her decision to move the drinks out of range had been instantly vindicated.

'We can do tennis after!'

'Tennis first!'

Ava sipped at her coffee. 'Can't we compromise?'

Both children looked up with expectant faces, like she'd suggested a new scientific formula worthy of the Nobel Prize.

'I don't know what to compromise with, though,' Ava added. 'What games are on there?'

'There's tennis,' Fern said.

'And bowling,' Elijah put in.

'Hmm, well I already knew about those two, didn't I? Seeing as you're arguing about them. What else?'

'Golf,' Elijah said, 'but that's boring.'

'OK. So no to golf.'

'I like golf,' Harry said.

Ava gave him a withering look. 'You would. I'm trying to negotiate here – stop messing things up!'

Harry chuckled as she turned back to the kids.

'Baseball,' Fern said. 'But I want to play tennis first.'

'We will play tennis, but Elijah wants to bowl first, and one of you either has to give in, or we do something else, otherwise we'll argue about it for so long it will be bedtime and we won't have played anything. So how about we do baseball?'

'We could do rock paper scissors,' Harry offered.

'Yes!' Elijah said. 'We could do that! The winner gets their game first.'

'Well...' Ava pretended to frown as if in deep concentration. 'I suppose that could work...'

Harry stepped in and positioned the children opposite each other, then lowered his arm to separate them.

'Get ready...' He lifted his arm. 'Go!'

Both children went through the gestures of the game.

'Rock!' Elijah exclaimed. 'Rock blunts scissors! Yes! Bowling!'

Fern pouted but then glanced at Harry and clearly didn't want to show herself in a bad light in front of him. So she simply folded her arms and huffed.

'Fine. You win. But we do tennis straight after.'

'Yup,' Elijah said, but he'd already stopped listening. He grabbed the control to continue setting up the game. Ava exchanged a wry smile with Harry.

'So this is what it's like to have kids,' Harry said.

'Are you taking notes?'

'I might be.'

'Good luck then.'

He grinned, and she grinned back at him. Elijah started to flap a hand at them.

'It's starting! Get your controls!'

'Yes, sir!' Ava shouted, putting her coffee down and joining them in front of the television. 'Prepare to have your ass whipped!'


Things had been lively, and it was lucky there were no neighbours for miles, because there would most definitely have been noise complaints. Elijah had won almost all of the bowling games, and Ava suspected he'd played them a lot, knew he was good and that was why he'd been so adamant that they do that one first. He and Ava had paired up for tennis doubles and had won most of their games on that too. But then she noticed Fern looking a bit dejected and, to Elijah's confusion, deliberately played terribly for the last couple to throw the game in Fern and Harry's favour – a fact that wasn't lost on Harry, who gave her a knowing look.

'Right...' Ava put her controller down. 'I think that might be it for sports.'

'But you said we could do baseball!' Fern pleaded.

'I said we could if nobody could settle between tennis and bowling – and we've done both of those now.'

'Please!' Elijah joined in. 'Just one game!'

'Oh!' Ava pointed at Fern. 'I saw that! It was a yawn!'

'No...' Fern looked sheepish, but there was no way she was going to admit it. 'I'm not tired.'

'No?' Ava winked at Harry. 'What do you think, Harry? Did you see a yawn?'

He held his hands up. 'Don't get me involved!'

'I'm not tired!' Fern insisted.

'I'm not tired either!' Elijah chimed in. 'Not one bit!'

'Hmm...' Pretending to look thoughtful, Ava glanced at the clock. 'Well, if memory serves me correctly, your bedtime is ten. And it's past ten now. So that means you must be tired.'

'But Mum didn't say—' Elijah began, but Ava stopped him with a look that he knew better than to argue with.

'I might be a soft touch, but I know a yawn when I see one, and I know that we're already way past your usual bedtime. I think you've got away with it for long enough. And to be honest, I might be asleep myself in about ten minutes, because it's been a long day and even if you're not tired, I am.'

'Me too,' Harry said. 'And I should probably start making my way home.'

'Not yet!' Fern pleaded. 'Just one more game! Like five more minutes!'

'Then five more becomes five more and five more, with you two distracting us in the hopes we don't notice that it's become an hour,' Ava said. 'I've done enough of these bedtimes to know how you two operate.'

'Well...' Elijah exchanged a look with his sister that said they knew they were beaten, but they were still going to have the last word. 'Could Harry stay until we're in bed?'

'What's he going to do while you get ready?' Ava asked.

'He could watch telly,' Elijah said.

'I should go,' Harry said.

'Actually...' Ava gave him a sideways look as an idea formed in her mind, then she glanced warily at the children before continuing. This might be a bad idea or it might be a very good one, but she didn't want them to know anything about it either way. 'I thought we might have a quick chat before you go. I mean... a private one...'

Harry held back an obvious frown. 'Sure,' he said slowly. 'I guess I could... Is it something I ought to be prepared for?'

'No, nothing to worry about.' Ava gave her most reassuring smile. 'I'd just really appreciate your take on something.'

In less than a second, Ava had decided that Harry might well be the perfect person to talk to about her plans to volunteer for the lifeboat crew, and in the process, she might be able to make some headway in coaxing a few healing truths from him too.

'If that's all right,' she added. 'I mean, if you really want to get home then it could wait.'

'No, no that's fine. I can hang on.'

'Great! Why don't you go and get a drink or whatever and I'll tuck these guys in and be right down.'

'Can Harry tuck us in?' Fern asked.

'Um... I think your aunt should do it,' Harry said.

'But he can listen in on the bedtime story if he wants to,' Ava said, glancing at Harry for an answer.

'God, I might end up asleep before the kids,' he replied.

Ava cocked an eyebrow. 'You're saying my story will be boring?'

Harry laughed. 'No. I'm saying I'm knackered! What's the story tonight?'

'Hmm...' Ava looked at Elijah and Fern. 'What are we going for?'

'*James and the Giant Peach!*' Fern said.

'A bit long.' Ava said. 'Unless I go with just one or two chapters.'

'That's no good,' Harry put in. 'How will I get to know how it ends?'

Ava's hand flew to her breast in mock horror. 'You've never read *James and the Giant Peach*?'

'Nope.'

'What kind of upbringing did you have? I've never heard anything so sad! I shall have to have a word with your parents.'

Harry chuckled. 'Well, you know my parents. It was all apples in our house – anything to do with peaches would have been a betrayal of the family business.'

'Oh!' Elijah squeaked. 'I know... can we hear about Iziah?'

'Yes!' Fern agreed. 'Tell us the Iziah story!'

Ava looked vaguely troubled now. 'I don't... Your mum doesn't exactly love... Well, she wasn't...'

Ava stalled. The truth was Gaby hated the fact her children had ever heard that story in the first place. She felt it was to blame for Killian joining the lifeboats and for her father's death. She'd decided it ought to be consigned to history, and that the Morrows had paid their debts to Port Promise a hundred times over, and from now on none of them ought to be risking their necks at sea for the sake of a stupid old tale she wasn't convinced had ever happened anyway.

Elijah and Fern had been rapt the first time Ava had told it, way before her dad's retirement from the crew, when nobody – not even Gaby – had seen any harm in it. The kids had loved it all the other times Ava had obliged too, and she'd be happy to tell it again tonight, especially considering the significance of the day. Gaby, on the other hand, would not see it the same way, and if she found out that Ava had told them the story she'd be pissed off.

Then again, why did Ava have to follow her sister's rules? Ava loved the story. She was proud of the family history and – true or not – she loved the point of the story. Why shouldn't the Morrows keep the shores of Port Promise safe? Someone had to. Why shouldn't it be them? Why should others risk their lives if they weren't prepared to?

'Please...' Elijah clasped his hands together. It was such a comical gesture that Ava had to laugh.

'You two will get me shot!'

'Why?' Fern asked with such sincere confusion that Ava laughed even more.

'Because... I'll tell you the story, but you don't say a word about it to your mum?'

'Why?' Fern asked again.

'Hmm...' Ava paused. 'Because I think she feels like you've heard it too many times.'

'But we like it!' Elijah said.

'I know...' Ava gave a fond smile. 'I know you do.'

'So can we?' Elijah asked.

'With the voices?' Fern added.

Harry raised his eyebrows at Ava now. 'Voices? This I have got to hear!'

Ava grinned as she turned back to their charges. 'Right –

wash, teeth, pyjamas! Record time and no messing, otherwise no story!'

Elijah and Fern raced to the stairs.

'And that,' Harry said wryly, 'is how it's done!'


Ava decided that it was probably better and more appropriate to do the storytelling downstairs if Harry was going to be joining them, rather than in the bedroom that Fern and Elijah shared, and so she snuggled under a blanket with her niece and nephew on the sofa while Harry sat on the opposite armchair with a blanket of his own.

'Everyone ready?' she asked.

Fern rested her head on Ava's arm and got comfortable, while Elijah sat bolt upright, giving his obvious full attention, and Harry grinned and pretended to be a little boy, crossing his legs and resting his chin on his fists.

'I'm ready!' he said.

'OK.' Ava composed herself. She'd heard this story a million times and told it a million more, but she liked to make it sound different every time if she could. The first line, as any good story-teller knew, was the crucial one. 'Before telly and the internet and phones, and even before people took photos or had engines on boats, there lived a man called Iziah Morrow. He had a wife and a house by the sea in a beautiful place called Cornwall – though it wasn't called that back then. In fact, Iziah probably didn't even know where he lived was called Cornwall; he probably just called it home.'

'How big was his cottage?' Fern asked. 'Was it about as big as ours?'

'Nobody knows for sure,' Ava said. 'But I would guess so.'

'Maybe *it is* ours!' Elijah said.

'I don't think so. It's more likely to be Seaspray Cottage where grandma lives than this one, but I don't think it's that one

either. I'm not sure when the Morrow family went to live in that
one, but I don't think it's that far back. Anyway,' Ava added
patiently, 'we're getting away from the story. I'm not sure the
cottage is the important bit. I think that Iziah's cottage was right
by the sea, and that's all we need to know.'

'OK,' Fern said.

'So,' Ava continued, 'Iziah was happy. He loved his little
cottage by the sea and his wife and his boat and his job catching
fish. He'd catch enough fish for them to eat, and a little bit extra
to sell to the people in the other houses nearby so he could get
bread and milk and furniture, and he didn't take a single extra
one, because he respected the sea and he didn't want it to run
out of fish so that he'd starve. But one day a new man arrived
with his wife and built a cottage nearby, and his name was
William.

'Iziah wasn't happy about William, because he was a fisherman too and Iziah was worried that there wouldn't be enough
fish for them both in his bit of sea. Iziah didn't want his peaceful
life with his wife interrupted and he didn't want to share the
firewood and all the other things he needed to live. But William
kept calling to say hello, and once their cottage was built his
wife brought flowers and cakes every day, and eventually they
won Iziah over and everyone became friends. In fact, they
became best friends.

'Iziah and William began fishing together instead of on their
own little boats, and while they didn't catch more than they
needed, they caught enough to sell a few further afield so they
could buy a few more nice things for their wives, and soon they
also had enough money for a bigger boat. And when Iziah's wife
had a baby, William's wife helped bring him into the world, and
when William's wife had one, Iziah's wife did the same for her,
and the children grew up best friends too.'

'Who was William's baby?' Fern asked, a well-rehearsed
question that she'd asked every time she'd heard the story.

'Nobody's sure,' Ava said. 'But we think maybe it's Robin Trelawney's great, great, great, great... lots of times grandfather.'

'And Robin is Amelia's uncle,' Fern said. 'And Amelia is my best friend.'

'Yes,' Ava said. 'It's cool, isn't it?'

'And Robin still goes fishing,' Elijah said.

Ava nodded. 'He does.'

'But the Morrows don't. They save people instead,' Elijah replied.

'I suppose that means they sort of fish,' Harry put in. 'They fish folks out of the sea.'

Ava smiled. 'I suppose they do.'

'Like Dad,' Fern said.

'Yes,' Ava said. 'Like your dad.'

'Do you have to be a boy?' Fern asked.

Ava looked down at her. 'To join the lifeboat crew? Of course not.'

'But only Morrow boys do it,' she replied, looking slightly confused.

'Well, yes, so far. But it doesn't have to be that way.'

'So...' Fern paused. 'I could do it?'

Ava glanced at Harry, who grimaced. She knew exactly what he was thinking, because she was thinking it too.

'I think your mum might have something to say about that.'

'She wants dad to quit,' Elijah said. 'I heard her say it to him.'

'Your dad would definitely have something to say about that,' Ava said, glancing at Harry again.

Elijah nodded. 'He said no way.'

'I bet,' Ava replied. 'But maybe now's not the time to go into that, eh?'

'The storm is next,' Fern prompted. 'That's the next bit of the story, right?'

Ava cocked an eyebrow at her. 'Who's telling this story, you or me?'

Fern giggled 'You! But the storm comes next, doesn't it? Iziah can't make Port Promise until the storm happens.'

'Yes, I know, I'm getting to that.'

Ava tugged the blanket around Fern's shoulders and pulled her close again. 'So one night Iziah and William are out fishing, because, you know, it's best to fish at night when the fish don't see you coming, and they were after this huge shoal that someone had seen, where there'd be enough fish to sell all over Cornwall, even if they left loads of them there, and they'd make enough money to buy their wives lovely new dresses and their children a toy or two.'

'But then the storm came,' Fern said.

'Out of nowhere,' Ava continued. 'Like a wizard had conjured it.'

'Or a witch,' Fern put in.

'Or the god of the sea,' Elijah added.

Ava nodded. 'Or Poseidon himself. Iziah and William were tough old fishermen and they weren't scared at all, but they did think it was time to go home and maybe their wives would have to live without fancy Sunday dresses for a little longer.'

'But they didn't make it,' Elijah said.

Ava looked down at him. 'Hey, who's telling this story? You're giving Harry spoilers!'

'I'll put my fingers in my ears every time he says something,' Harry said. 'Nobody wants spoilers.'

Fern grinned. 'Yeah, shut up, Eli!'

'Settle down, spoiler boy,' Ava said with a wink at her nephew. 'We're getting there. So, Iziah and William were tough old sailors and though they did everything to keep the boat steady and on course, they were taking on water too fast. Iziah knew things were looking dicey and he hoped their wives on the shore would be looking out for them, because if they'd seen the storm begin, they'd know what to do. And sure enough, a minute after he'd thought this, he could see lights through the darkness and he knew that the wives had lit the big storm lanterns so that the men could find their way home. He turned the boat to head for them, but the wind got fiercer and the waves got bigger still and the rain came down so hard it was enough to make a man's head bleed. Sometimes he could see the lanterns and sometimes he couldn't, because sometimes the rain and the waves got in the way, or the boat got spun around, or maybe the lanterns blew out.

'Back on shore, the children prayed for their daddies and the wives kept those lanterns going while the wind roared and the waves crashed against the harbour wall, and out at sea, the tiny boat they wanted desperately to see coming in was tossed this way and that. Iziah and William clung on for dear life, exhausted and beaten, half dead and dreaming of home where it was warm and dry and safe. And then Iziah cheered, because he could see the shore – they were almost there!'

'And then: crash!' Elijah cried.

'Crash!' Ava repeated. 'The biggest wave, the size of the tallest mountain they'd ever seen, came rushing towards them and crashed right over the boat. It was so strong it turned the boat upside down and threw them both into the sea.'

'But another wave turned the boat the right way again,' Elijah said.

'Eli!' Fern hissed. 'Spoiler boy!'

'It did,' Ava said. 'And somehow, though to this day nobody knows how, Iziah managed to get back on board. He looked for William but he couldn't see him anywhere. He could have turned the boat around and headed for home, but he kept on looking, even though the storm was still raging and he had no lights on the boat now. He stayed out until the sky started to calm and the sun came up, trying to find his friend. And then the dawn was clear and bright and the sea was as blue as if there'd never been a storm at all, but there was still no sign of William.

'Finally, Iziah realised he had no choice but to go home without his friend. He hoped that William had somehow got to shore after the storm, on a piece of driftwood, or else washed up and been taken home to get warm by his family. He hoped that he'd find William eating breakfast when he got back, but it was a tiny, tiny hope. And if there was no William when he got back – what then? What would he say to William's family? Iziah felt as if everything was his fault.

'As the boat got closer to the harbour, it passed by some rocks... and there was poor William, lying on them.'

'He was drowned,' Fern said quietly.

'He was,' Ava said. 'Iziah could see it straight away. He went to get him, even though it meant going too close to the rocks, and then he laid him out on the deck and did his best to tidy him up so he'd look as nice as possible for his wife to bury, and then he took him home. Afterwards he made a solemn vow that not another soul would ever be lost at sea while he could prevent it. He called it his promise, and as other people came to fish and build houses and a village grew, he did just that and rescued every single fisherman who ever needed it.'

'And that's how Port Promise began,' Elijah said.

Ava nodded. 'That's how Port Promise was named. Some years later, a proper lifeboat service began and Iziah's son joined up, and ever since then every Morrow boy has volunteered to keep people safe in the sea, just like Iziah.'

'And other people,' Fern said. 'Like Harry.'

Ava smiled at their guest. 'Like Harry.'

But Harry didn't smile back. He looked troubled, though he was obviously trying not to show it.

'Right.' Ava clapped both of her charges on the lap. 'Bedtime!'

Neither exactly rushed – not that Ava had expected

anything else, but at least they complied in their own feet-dragging fashion.

'I'll tuck them in,' Ava said to Harry as they stood at the bottom of the stairs. 'Then I'll be right down for that chat. If you're still OK to stay, that is.'

'Sure, I can—'

They were interrupted by the sound of the front door opening and closing.

Ava looked at Elijah and Fern. 'Looks like we've been rumbled!'

A moment later, Killian and Gaby strolled into the living room.

Killian gave a wry smile as he took in the scene. 'Thought you could get away with a sneaky late one, eh?' he said to his children.

'We were going to bed,' Fern said. 'Honest!'

'Like, literally now,' Elijah added. 'We were just saying goodnight to Harry.'

'So...' Gaby looked up at the clock. 'It's taken a whole hour to say goodnight to Harry? Did you do it in the form of a play? Were there drinks at the interval?'

Ava grinned. 'Something like that.' She gave her niece and nephew meaningful looks, silently trying to warn them that even though their parents were obviously a little tipsy and in a good mood, she still didn't want them to find out about their choice of bedtime story that night.

'I should go,' Harry said, clearly deciding that whatever plans Ava had to talk to him were probably out the window now that her sister and brother-in-law were home.

'You don't have to go on our account,' Gaby said.

'Yes he does.' Killian gave his wife a drunken, leering grin that Ava wished she hadn't seen. It wasn't like she didn't know her sister had a sex life, but she certainly didn't want details. 'No offence, mate.'

'None taken,' Harry said. 'It's late – I wasn't going to be much longer anyway.'

'Hang on,' Ava told Harry. 'I'll tuck these two in and be right down – I'll walk to yours with you.'

'You're not planning on walking back to the caravan tonight?' Gaby asked her.

'I was, yeah...' Ava began, but Gaby shook her head vehemently.

'No way. It's miles out and there are no lights on that road. Stay here – Killian can get the sofa bed made up for you; it's far too late to be walking back to the caravan park on your own.'

'It's fine – I've done it a million times before,' Ava replied.

The park that housed her caravan was a good fifteen minutes' walk outside Port Promise, nestled in a beautiful section of woodland, and although Gaby was right, and the street lights on the road were sparse once she left the village, Ava had never once felt unsafe walking it.

'No, it's not,' Gaby said. 'Besides, it'll be nice to have you stay. You can spend a few hours here in the morning before you go – seems like we never get a chance to spend time together these days.'

They'd spent a lot of time together during the six months since their father's death, but perhaps Gaby had a point. It hadn't exactly been quality time, and mostly it had been spent grieving together, or making plans for a world without their dad, or figuring out how they were going to get their mum through it. They hadn't been just sisters, hanging out and goofing around, for what felt like years. In all honesty it *had* been years, because Killian's arrival changed things long before their dad died.

But staying over meant her chat with Harry would have to wait. Looking at him now, perhaps that wasn't a bad thing. She'd be short on time – the walk back to his place wouldn't take long – and would she have enough time to get any meaningful discussion going? Even if she did, there wouldn't be enough time to arrive at any sort of resolution. Maybe it would be better if she tried to catch him in a few days. In hindsight, maybe she ought to tell her own family about her decision before she told others, and whatever Harry was going through, perhaps that was best discussed when they were both fully sober and less tired.

As if he'd guessed what was in her head, Harry turned to her. 'Ava, you didn't want to... well, did you want to ask me that thing before I go?'

She shook her head. 'It can wait. Maybe I'll catch you during the week?'

'Sure, you know where to find me.'

'Cool, thanks.'

Harry got up from the chair and stretched. 'So I'll be off then.'

'I'll catch up with you in the week too,' Killian said to him, gesturing that he would see him to the door.

As they left the room, Gaby raised her eyebrows at Ava. 'Had a good time here with Harry?'

'Don't start,' Ava replied wearily.

'I haven't started anything—'

'Come on, kids,' Ava cut in. 'Your mum's a bit worse for wear so I'll take you up to bed.'

'Why?' Fern asked.

Ava didn't reply but simply ushered her along.

'But, Ava...' Fern protested as they went up the stairs.

'She's drunk,' Elijah said, sounding like someone who was party to a very important secret.

'Is she?' Fern asked.

'Maybe a little,' Ava said. 'But I wouldn't worry about it now.'

'So you'll be here in the morning?' Fern asked her.

'Looks like it.'

'Yes!' Elijah punched the air. 'So you'll play with us tomorrow?'

Ava smiled. 'I'm sure I can manage an hour. And it's probably a good thing, because I don't think your mum or dad are going to be much good come the morning.'

# CHAPTER FOUR

As Ava had predicted, Gaby was next to useless the next morning. Ava had spent the night on the sofa bed and had slept well enough, apart from being woken at around seven by the sound of her sister vomiting in the bathroom upstairs. She rolled onto her back and grinned up at the ceiling.

'Serves you right.'

A few minutes later Gaby came downstairs.

'Oh...' she said to Ava, her face grey. 'You're up, are you?'

'I wasn't,' Ava said. 'But someone was making one hell of a din in the bathroom.'

'Hmmm...' Gaby padded past and into the kitchen. 'Paracetamol...'

'Blood transfusion is more like it from what I can see,' Ava called after her, the grin back on her face. Gaby had always been the strait-laced sister – Ava couldn't deny that this unexpected and seldom-seen version of her was entertaining.

Ava swung herself out of the bed and followed her into the kitchen. 'Want me to make some coffee?'

'Knock yourself out if you want some,' Gaby said. 'I'm going back to bed while I still can. If the kids get up, can you watch them for an hour or do you have to get back?'

'I suppose I can stay for a bit if you need me to. Is Killian as hungover as you?'

'No idea – he's still snoring.'

Killian walked in as Gaby was saying this. 'No he's not.' He scratched at his belly and gave an exaggerated yawn. 'And he's not as hungover as his wife either – though that's not much of an achievement judging by the state of her.'

Gaby scowled. 'Thanks.'

'Just saying it how I see it.'

'So you want coffee?' Ava asked him.

'If there's one going.'

'I'll leave you both to it,' Gaby put in, sloping past her husband and out of the kitchen.

'There's a sight I haven't seen for a good few years,' Ava said.

'Me neither,' Killian agreed. 'God help us all today.'

'God help *you*,' Ava corrected. 'I'm not sticking around to be snapped at by my suffering sister.'

Killian sniffed as he took a seat at the breakfast bar. The cottage was old and the rooms oddly shaped, and the kitchen was no exception, meaning there was no room for a table and chairs, only a bar and a series of stools parked against one wall. He twisted to watch as Ava put the kettle on to boil. 'Don't fancy staying for lunch then?'

Ava got two mugs from a cupboard. 'Tempting as your lunch sounds, I want to check on Mum.'

Killian shrugged as he examined his bare feet. 'Fair enough.'

Ava turned to him. She took a breath and then continued. 'Kill...' she began slowly. 'Remember after Dad's funeral we had a conversation about' – she glanced through the open kitchen door and towards the stairs before lowering her voice – 'you know... me volunteering.'

'Yes,' he said, the merest hint of impatience in his voice now. 'And I told you to volunteer if you must, in any way you liked except for the way you told me you wanted to.'

'I know. And I've looked at everything. I've been over the vacancies a thousand times and there's nothing else that screams *me*. I've done all that other stuff over the years – fundraising with Dad and getting my lifesaving qualifications and all that sort of thing, but it's just not enough.'

He looked sharply at her now, but she didn't return his gaze. Instead, she poured the hot water into the cafetière to make their drinks. 'What are you saying?'

'I'm saying, you told me to think about it and I have thought about it.'

'I told you to think about it because I thought you'd come to your senses once you had.'

'You don't think I'm good enough?'

'It's not that! Gaby would kill me and you know she would!'

'It's not yours or Gaby's decision and you can hardly stop me – she knows that.'

'Doesn't mean she'd be any happier. She'd never allow it and she'd make me do something about it, no matter what you or I said.'

Ava slammed her hands on her hips and stared at him. 'And what would she be expecting you to do? It's a free country and I'm my own person with my own free will. Realistically, what can she do?'

'Make everyone's life a misery.'

'It's a price I'm willing to pay.'

'It's not one I'm willing to pay. You don't have to live with her.'

'Be honest with me... Would we be having this conversation if I was Gaby's brother and not her sister?'

'Don't be ridiculous.'

'What's the difference then?'

'Gaby doesn't want anyone she loves doing it – she doesn't even want me to do it!'

Ava poured two coffees into the waiting mugs, then went to the fridge for the milk. She was keeping it together but could feel her impatience growing.

'Why are we having this conversation again?' Killian asked into the brief silence. 'I thought we'd sorted it.'

'Because I want to make my own decisions.'

'Think about what you're saying!'

'I am thinking about it!' Ava slammed a coffee down in front of him, the contents sloshing over the side of the mug and onto the countertop. Killian slid off his stool and fetched a cloth from the sink to wipe it up while Ava took her own mug into her hands and simply watched him. 'I've done nothing but think about it – ever since we had that first talk.'

He let out a sigh. 'I can't stop you from doing anything. All I'm asking is have you thought – I mean, *really* thought – about what you're signing up for? What you're asking me to ignore? Don't you think it's unfair on me, for one thing? How am I supposed to square it with your sister? Something like this will put pressure on our marriage.'

'Of course it won't.'

'Your dad would never have allowed it.'

'Dad encouraged me; he encouraged all of us – he loved that we got involved in the service. He wanted me to join!'

'Yes, doing things other than boat crew. Listen, I'm not saying you can't serve, but please do something else. You already have swimming qualifications coming out of your ears – go on the water safety ed team. Train newbies in lifesaving... there must be something else. Learn how to fix engines, drive the launch tractor... There are a million things just as important that need people doing them, and you can do any of them. All I'm asking is not the boat crew.'

Ava put her coffee down for a moment and leaned on the

counter, holding Killian in a steady gaze. 'You thought a lot of my dad, didn't you?'

'You know I did. Everyone in Port Promise had the greatest respect for him—'

'Not just respect. I'm talking about affection.'

'I had that too. He was like a dad to me – to all the crew. You know that, Ava, and I don't know what it has to do with what you're asking me to approve.'

'I'm not asking for your approval; I'm telling you my plans.'

'I know... and I get it. But Ava—'

'I'm doing this *for* my dad. He'd never have said it, but it bothered him that he'd never had a boy – not because he didn't love us, but because he felt like he was somehow letting his ancestors down. And now Elijah isn't going to join the crew—'

'Elijah will make his own decisions when it's time.'

Ava folded her arms. 'You and I both know Gaby will never allow that. She'd have him in prison before she let him go out on rescues.'

'She'd feel the same way about you. Imagine for a minute that you did this and we got into trouble on a mission and you—'

Killian picked up his coffee.

'Gaby would never forgive me,' he finished after a considered pause. 'She'd see it as my fault if something happened to you at sea.'

'All sorts of things could happen to me, at sea or otherwise. She can't stop harm coming to everyone, no matter how much she wishes it. I could walk across to Salty's Chips right now and get hit by a car – if we all thought like that, we'd never do anything.'

'Yes, but we can lessen the risks. And don't throw that line at me – I use it on the daily with your sister and even I know how hollow it sounds.'

Ava's gaze went to the window. Beyond it lay the tiny court-yard garden that was at the back of the cottage, high old walls of red brick and trellises of honeysuckle surrounding a gravelled area filled with fragrant pots and a patio with a table and chairs. There wasn't a lot of space for much else, but they'd never complain. It was an outdoor space attached to a beautiful old house and they knew better than to complain because it was more than many had in those parts. And besides, Gaby would say, they were surrounded by as much outdoor space as they needed in the form of the harbour and beaches and the rolling hills that connected Port Promise to the rest of the county. They didn't have far to go to enjoy the outdoors.

Tucking an auburn lock behind her ear, she turned back to Killian. When Gaby had first introduced him to the family as her boyfriend, Ava had been an impressionable but impetuous fourteen-year-old, the youngest of three girls and very much the pampered baby. Killian was impossibly handsome, and young Ava had developed an instant crush. Whenever he had come to visit, her reaction had swung between barely being able to string a sentence together to showing off in the most horribly embarrassing way, and all the while she'd felt envy and guilt that this was her sister's boyfriend.

But as time went on and Gaby married him, Ava got over her childish infatuation. It was never going to end any other way, of course, but very occasionally she'd see a flash of the man who had made her feel that way, all those years before. For a second, she saw it now: his firm jaw, eyes of winter blue, a resoluteness and strength of character that gave his features dignity. He was a little greyer around the temples these days, and his eyes crinkled a little more when he smiled. But as Ava thought about all this now, she also reminded herself that the qualities she'd once admired in him were the same qualities that meant he'd make her life as difficult as possible as she pushed to join the lifeboat crew. They'd butt heads and the clash would be seismic, because she could be strong and resolute too, as stubborn and single-minded as she needed to be. In many ways, the fight with Killian would be harder than the one to convince Gaby, because he was doing it *for* Gaby, and he was the sort of man who would do right by his family until his final breath, no matter what it took. If Gaby wanted to keep Ava away from the seagoing crew, Killian would do his utmost to make sure that happened.

Knowing all this changed nothing, however. Ava had made her decision. It had been brewing for some time, but the epiphany had come during the memorial service the day before. She'd wanted to sound Harry out first, but that hadn't happened. Perhaps she could have got him on side and it might have made this conversation easier, but she'd never know.

'Where does this leave us?' she asked.

'You haven't listened to a word I've said, have you?' he asked wearily, the question not really a question at all. He couldn't have been surprised that his words had made little impact.

'I've listened.'

'But it's made no difference.'

'Did you think it would? You know me better than that.'

'Don't I just.'

'And you're not going to back down either, I suppose.'

'You know I can't.'

'That's what I thought.'

Ava picked up her coffee and took a sip. There was a noise from the stairs, and a moment later Fern appeared, looking bleary-eyed but smiling.

'Ava!' she squeaked, running to hug her.

Ava exchanged a look with Killian as Fern held on to her. Things were about to get interesting, but for now, all that would have to wait.

Ava sent a brief text to make sure her mum would be home before she went to visit, and a second later her mum phoned to say she'd been planning to text Ava at the same time to see if she'd be home for a visit.

'Great minds think alike,' she'd said. 'Do you want to come to the cottage or shall we go to yours?'

'Which is easier for you?'

'Either, but I would quite enjoy a walk today.'

'OK. So if you want I'll meet you halfway and we can walk to the caravan park together. How's that sound?'

'Perfect,' Jill said. 'Where will you wait?'

'Um... I'll be at the harbour. Where we had the service yesterday. I think I'd like to get a proper look at Dad's plaque, now that all the fuss has died down.'

'All right, sweetheart, I'll meet you there in a short while.'


The half hour Ava had waited for her mum had been spent mostly watching a cloud of gulls following Robin's trawler as it ploughed the waves. They screeched at each other, flocking this way and that with every tiny turn of the boat, never losing sight of it. And then her attention had been grabbed by Harry striding over the sand towards the lifeboat station. She wondered what he was going to do there as she watched him walk in. There hadn't been a shout, as far as she knew.

Seeing Harry head inside the station brought to mind another day, years before, where the weather was exactly as it was today and she'd stood at this very place, watching her dad enter the station.

She'd have been ten, eleven maybe. She couldn't be sure, but she hadn't yet hit her teenage years because she was still obsessed with every lifeboat launch, no matter what it was for. It was a Sunday morning like this. She'd sneaked out of their family home and followed her dad down to the beach, even though he'd told her she needed to stay home and help her mum with the dinner. But he must have known she'd been following him, desperate to see the boat go out, because he'd turned with a wry smile just before he'd gone inside, his gaze trained on the harbour wall where Ava was, and she'd ducked out of sight, afraid that she might get in trouble. But when she looked again, he'd gone.

She waited patiently, and was rewarded with the sight of the doors opening and the boat flying out onto the waves. It never failed to thrill her back then – the drama, the flash of orange and blue as the brightly painted boat crashed onto the sea, the sound of the waves thumping against it, and she never failed to be overwhelmed with pride that her dad was on board. She'd watched it go out, the sun burning her neck as she shielded her eyes from the glare and followed the boat as it went out on a rescue. She watched it go all the way out to another boat, a yacht with a delicate mast, and pull up alongside. They must have been in trouble, she'd thought, but it was all very calm. Some moments later, the boat was coming back in, towing the yacht. Another successful rescue mission.

When her dad came out of the station, she'd hidden again, though she felt certain he'd seen her, before running for home. Halfway back to the cottage, Clara had met her on the road, having been sent out to find her. Jill was furious when she got home. She told Ava that her dad would be too, but Jack had never told Ava off – or if he had, it had been so half-hearted she couldn't even recall it now.

A few minutes later, Harry came out of the station again. She'd have waved and called for his attention, but his head was down and he was moving quickly, and she didn't think he'd hear her so didn't bother after all. She did wave at Betty, however, the owner of the seafront cafe who came out to water hanging baskets full of geraniums outside the front door. It was still quite early in the day, and though there were holidaymakers around – families on the beach playing with buckets and spades and leaping over the foam-topped waves as they rolled in to shore, or strolling the new promenade to admire the views – it didn't seem that Betty was too busy yet. She couldn't have been if she had time to water her flowers, but it wasn't often Ava saw the cafe so quiet.

She'd no sooner decided to go over for a chat than she heard her mum's voice.

'Have you been here long?' Jill asked, making her way over with a huge potted plant in her arms.

Ava stepped forward. 'No… let me take that from you – it looks massive!'

'Oh, thank you, sweetheart.' Jill let Ava take the pot and wiped her hands down her old corduroy trousers. There had been something strangely jarring about seeing her mum in a charcoal dress and pearls the day before – despite the elegance of it – and it was comforting to see her back in her usual gardening clothes.

'Who's it for?' she asked.

'Oh, Marina. I thought, as we were passing her house, we could drop it in. You don't mind, do you? It's just that she's been such a rock these last few months and she and Bob were so lovely yesterday… Anyway, I wanted to thank her and I know she's recently had a patio built so I thought this would sit on it perfectly.'

Ava craned to get a look. 'What is it?'

'It's a cabbage palm… I'd have thought you'd know that.'

'Mum…' Ava laughed lightly. 'Not everyone is as obsessed with plants as you are.'

'Apparently not. I've only been growing them for the past thirty years,' she added wryly, 'why on earth would I expect my daughter to have picked up anything about it?'

'OK, maybe you have a point. I mean, I do know some of them – it's just that this one was a bit close to my face so it was harder to tell.'

'Right…' Jill said, throwing Ava a sceptical sideways look.

Then her attention turned to the harbour wall. 'Did you look at your dad's plaque?'

'Yes, but I thought you might want to as well before we leave?'

'I would like to,' Jill said.

Ava started to follow where her mum led. A minute later they were at the site of the previous day's memorial service. Ava put Marina's plant down for a moment and grabbed for her mum's hand as they read the plaque again together.

*In memory of Jack Morrow, who gave his life to save another. A braver son of Port Promise was never known. His service and selfless dedication to the people of this village will always be remembered.*

'It's lovely, isn't it?' Ava said.

'I suppose so.' Jill paused. 'But I'd rather have him back than all the gratitude in the world. I'd rather he'd been selfish and never gone out that day so I'd still have him.'

Ava looked sharply at her. 'You don't mean that?'

'I mean every word of it. That damned lifeboat... if I'd known before what I know now, I'd have made him leave the service.'

'You couldn't have known. *He* couldn't have known – nobody could!'

'Well, we should have done. Any risk, no matter how small, was too big. I should have seen that; I should have made him give it up the day we got married.'

'You'd never have done that; you know the service meant everything to him!'

'More than his family did – that much is certain.'

'Mum, you know it wasn't like that. Dad—'

'Has left behind a wife and three daughters, left them with more pain than any family has a right to. How could I think anything else? Every time he went out he knew he might not come back, but he still went.'

'Because that was who he was. You never said anything about it all the years he served.'

'Because I believed him when he said he'd stay safe. I was an idiot. If Gaby's got anything about her she'll get Killian away from that boat, otherwise we might one day have two plaques to come and polish.'

Ava said nothing as she turned her gaze back to the bronze memorial plaque. She couldn't imagine Killian giving in to any amount of pressure to quit the boats. And the strength of feeling her mum showed now had completely thrown her. She'd thought perhaps Jill would be upset, worried, a little scared even at the prospect of Ava volunteering but was beginning to see now that things were going to be far more difficult than that. She'd considered breaking the news to her today as they walked to her caravan, so that they'd have time to discuss it and for Ava to make her case. But now she wondered whether there was any case she could make that would win her mum over. But still, she had to try.

Perhaps now, standing here, however, wasn't the time. Jill was clearly upset, feelings dredged up by the memorial still raw. Right now she needed comfort, not conflict. So instead, Ava reached an arm around her mum's shoulder and pulled her close.

'I miss him too. Every day I wake up and wish I could talk to him.'

'Me too. It's daft, but most days I half expect to see him walking up the path to the house or in the garden early doors with his cup of tea, talking to my plants like they're going to answer back.'

'He used to say he was helping you grow them,' Ava said with a smile.

'He did. Silly sod.'

'I think it was his way of working through problems,' Ava replied. 'I didn't always understand, of course, but I think he talked to the plants so—'

'He wouldn't have to burden anyone else,' Jill finished for her. 'I know. He thought it was weak to share his worries and fears, and he didn't want anyone else to have to deal with them. I know that. It was just typical of him – he wanted to be Jack Morrow all the time, the great saviour of Port Promise.' Jill gave a heavy sigh. 'He had so much to live up to with that stupid family legacy. I told him many a time, there was no need, nobody would have thought any less of him if sometimes he wished it would go away...'

'I know, Mum. The thing is, I don't think he ever wanted it to go away. I think he liked being Jack Morrow.'

'It made him feel like someone, that's for sure.'

'And he wanted to help people – he always said that. If he hadn't been on the boats he'd have probably joined the fire service or something. It was just who he was.'

Jill turned to her. 'You always did see him just as he was – sometimes even better than I did.'

'I spent a long time watching,' Ava said with a small smile. 'My whole life. It ought to give me a bit of a clue, right?'

'I think you understand him because you're the most like him too.'

'Maybe,' Ava said slowly, wondering whether this might be a lead into the conversation she was desperate to have. 'I suppose it's Dad's love of the sea that I've caught more than anyone else in the family.'

Jill nodded, her gaze going back to the plaque. 'At least you've chosen to love the sea in a far safer way than your dad did – I ought to be thankful for that, at least.'

'Hmm...' Ava retrieved the mini palm tree and hoisted it into her arms. 'We ought to get going if we're to catch Marina. Doesn't she go out with the ramblers on a Sunday?'

'Oh, she does!' Jill said. 'You're right – we probably ought to go or we'll miss her.'

The day had started out bright but now clouds were blowing quickly across the sky, swallowing the sun every so often before setting it free again as they moved on. Ava had to stop a couple of times to rest the plant pot on a wall.

'This is heavier than it looks,' she panted.

'Let me carry it,' Jill began, but Ava wafted her hand away.

'I've got it.'

They walked away from the harbour, down narrow streets flanked by tiny cottages decked with flowerboxes and hanging baskets, and out onto a wider road that contained a row of stone-fronted shops. Salty's fish-and-chip shop was there, but it wasn't open yet. Ava could see the antique cream tiles of the walls dimly lit inside and the huge steel fryers, still cold. Later, there would be queues out the door. For most holidaymakers – apart from Betty's or the fish shack – this was the place where they'd get their lunches to take onto the beach. Salty's was reassuringly old-fashioned, and the owner, Nigel, in his eighties, didn't see any reason to modernise it now.

Then there was Mona's surf shop. Mona was an out-of-towner who'd settled in Port Promise during the nineties. Ava often sent her students there to buy equipment of their own once their lessons had ended, because what Mona didn't know about her stock wasn't worth knowing.

There was a greengrocer and a florist who regularly bought plants from Jill to sell on, and then there was Horton Hardware, Marina and Bob's store.

The wide store window was single-glazed wood and painted sage green. Ava's dad had always said it was hardly suitable for the winters of Port Promise and he didn't understand why they didn't get a decent plastic one to keep the weather out, but they'd never changed it in all the years Ava had been alive. Hardware stores like this didn't really exist anymore – at least, as far as Ava knew. Renovating her caravan, she'd driven out to DIY stores with her dad plenty of times to get materials and equipment that she couldn't get in the village, and not once had she seen another shop like Marina's.

Hanging from hooks and stands outside the door were sundry items that nobody really used anymore either, like old tin baths and the sets of pokers and shovels that people used for open fires. And all that sat strangely incongruous next to bright buckets and spades, decorative candles and beach windbreakers. In fact, just about anything that could be conceived of seemed to be stocked in Marina and Bob's shop. If you needed fly paper or moth balls or coal tar soap, or a plaster ceiling rose or a thermonuclear warhead, Marina would find it in the storeroom at the back and bring it through with a wink and a price she'd decided just by looking at it. Ava often wondered how the shop stayed open, and Jill had often agreed. But it was loved and used by the people of Port Promise, and so, perhaps, that was the only explanation they needed.

It was Sunday, and so the shop was closed. Jill rang the bell at the front door.

'She's expecting us,' she said to Ava.

A moment later Marina opened up. Her long white hair was fastened into a milkmaid braid and she wore her walking trousers and fleece.

Ava held out the palm tree.

'We brought you this,' Jill said.

Marina broke into a bemused smile. 'For me? What on earth have I done to deserve such a beautiful gift?'

'You've been a beautiful friend,' Jill said, leaning in to kiss her.

'Come in!' Marina stepped back to admit them to the shop.

'We won't stay long,' Jill said as Ava put the plant down on the waxed wooden counter. 'I know your rambling group are meeting today. Just thought I'd drop this in.'

Marina waved a vague hand. 'They'll wait. Bob can go up and stall them for a bit. Or...' She paused. 'You could come with us.'

'Oh, not today,' Jill said.

'You keep saying that,' Marina admonished. 'But I still say it would do you good to get out into the fresh air and meet some new folks.'

'And I will,' Jill replied. 'But I need a little more time before I'm there.'

Ava nudged her. 'You should go, Mum. I think it would do you good as well.'

'I can't go now – we've arranged—'

'You can come to the caravan any time,' Ava said.

'I don't have my walking gear on,' Jill said. 'Not sure I even own any.'

Ava smiled. 'Mum... What do you think you wear every day? Sturdy boots, comfortable trousers and a flannel shirt – I think that's perfect for walking. Right, Marina?'

'Some of those daft sods turn up in flip-flops,' Marina said, laughing. 'You'll be doing better than them. Come on... Bob and I would love it.'

'This is not what I was planning today,' Jill said.

'Sometimes the days that aren't what you planned are the best ones,' Ava said.

'What about you?' Jill asked her.

'I've got tons to do to be honest.'

Jill looked sceptical. 'Like what?'

'Are you saying that because I'm young and live on my own I don't have things I need to do?'

'No, but you do seem very keen to get me rambling with Marina.'

'Because we can both see that it would do you good,' Marina

put in. 'Out of the village and into the hills will do wonders for your mood. And by God, you'll sleep well later!'

Jill paused, then let out a sigh. 'I suppose I could come along, just this once to see what it's like, and only because you've been so amazing this past week with the memorial and everything.'

'That's wonderful!' Marina beamed. 'We can call at your place on the way to the meeting point if you need to pick anything up.'

'I should probably get a water bottle and maybe some more suitable clothes.'

'No problem.'

Ava leaned on the counter. She had to be pleased that her mum had agreed to this – socialising had been low on her list the past six months. It had to mean things were finally getting better. 'My work here is done, I see.'

'Oh, sweetheart... you don't mind that our plans have changed?'

'Honestly, Mum. I'd have been annoyed if you'd said no – poor Marina's been bugging you long enough to join this group.'

'I never said I was joining – I said I'd try it.'

'And you'll love it!' Marina said. 'I guarantee you'll want to go every week once you get out there.'

'I think so too.' Ava kissed her mum on the cheek. 'Right, so I'll see you later in the week maybe?'

'Of course. Let me know when you're free and I'll make us some supper.'

'I will.'

After hugging Marina, Ava left them to it. She'd wanted to see her mum, more than anything to make certain she was OK after the memorial day, but it seemed that this time, Marina would be able to do far more towards improving her mood than Ava herself could. And Ava did have plenty to do. She'd just come to a momentous decision. None of them could stand still, and her mum had to realise that. In time she would, Ava was certain, but for now, there were plans to put in place. She was going to apply as a volunteer for the lifeboat. There were so many tests and assessments she'd have to do before she even got a foot in the door that it might yet come to nothing, but she was going to try.

Ava threw her keys onto the kitchen worktop and filled the kettle, her gaze going to the window as she did. She had the rest of the day to herself and there'd be some decent waves in the bay, and on any other day like this she'd be itching to get her surfboard out. But today, her thoughts were occupied with something quieter. The task she'd decided to set herself ran through her mind as she waited for the kettle to boil, watching a bee visit the scarlet geraniums in her window box.

Everyone referred to Ava's home as 'the old caravan on the park', which implied that it was a beige seventies nightmare deemed too old for paying customers to holiday in, and when Ava had snapped it up at a bargain price and negotiated pitch fees with the site owner (family discounts because Clara worked there), that was true. The outside hadn't changed a lot from the day Ava had taken ownership, apart from new decking, but the inside was barely recognisable. She loved to see the shock on people's faces when they visited for the first time, passing from the drab exterior into her updated interior. What she'd done definitely wasn't what people expected when they saw the outside.

The sofa had been reupholstered and was now a cute candy pink, the windows were dressed with pastel paisley curtains, the grubby carpet replaced by smart wooden flooring and the old plastic dining furniture had been replaced with a gorgeous white-and-chrome table paired with upholstered chairs that matched the curtains. Every available surface contained a plant or a solar lantern that Ava left on the decking by day to charge so she could use them at night to save money. The kitchen units had been painted a willow green, and white blinds gave privacy at night, and the two bedrooms had been painted a primrose yellow and finished with pretty gingham curtains made from fabric Ava had found in a thrift store on a day trip to Falmouth. Until then, Ava had been no seamstress, but Marina had taught her the basics, and from that point, Ava had felt confident enough to make anything else her caravan needed.

Her makeover wasn't perfect – if anyone cared to look closely enough they'd see where the floor didn't quite lock together in one corner, or where she'd snagged the stitches on her curtain hems, or where the paint had streaked on the kitchen cupboards – but to Ava it was home and she loved it. And that was lucky, she'd told Clara, because it would have to be home – it was going to be a long time before she'd have the money to buy an actual house, especially in the area close to Port Promise, where most houses that came on the market were snapped up by out-of-towners for second homes or by investors to rent out at huge profits. People in the village got angry about this, but Ava was more philosophical. What good was getting angry going to do her? This was the way of the world she lived in, and there was little she could do to change it. At least her current home meant she had her own space and didn't have to leave her beautiful village to get it.

She'd never forget the look on her dad's face when she'd first shown him where she planned to live.

'Tell me you're joking,' he'd groaned.

Ava had taken him by the hand, bursting with excitement, to show him the inside. The door had almost come off its hinges as she'd thrown it open, and an overpowering odour of damp had come rolling out.

'It doesn't look like anything now,' Ava said. 'But use your imagination for a minute.'

'I am... I'm imagining that I'm going to be doing a lot of DIY in the next few months.'

'I can do it,' Ava said.

'I know, but it's better with two, right?'

'I mean...' Ava gave her most beseeching smile. 'I would really love your help.'

He sighed. 'I never could say no to you.'

'Oh, Dad! You're the best, you know that?'

And they'd spent the next few months working on it every weekend, her dad's old radio blasting out Beach Boys classics as they worked. They'd ripped out furniture and floors and replaced the bathroom suite and sanded down fitted cupboards, and Jill had brought shrubs and plants from her own nursery for the outside, and when her dad had been called away on a rescue the day they'd been laying the wooden flooring, Ava had simply finished it by herself and beamed with pride when he'd returned and pretended she'd done a good job, even though she could see it was wonky as hell. To get his approval was all she ever craved, and to have this place of her own meant everything. She'd been so happy for those few months she'd never wanted them to finish the project, because once they did she wouldn't have all this time with him. But at the same time, she'd been excited for her new life there.

The day it was done she'd invited her entire family round for a barbecue, and her dad had cremated the sausages with a flame that was too high, but they all ate them anyway and got drunk on cider Killian had picked up from Trevithick's farm.

It had been one of the best days of her life.

The sound of the kettle clicking off brought her back to the room and it was then she realised she was crying.

# CHAPTER FIVE

Ava had a gap in her Monday teaching schedule so she'd decided to get coffee and see who might be about for a chat. She walked into the village, a pair of board shorts and a vest hastily thrown over her swimming costume, the sun warming her shoulders and barely a breeze to stir the air.

Betty, who owned and ran Betty's Cafe, was actually third-generation Betty. Her mum had been called Betty as had her mum before, and all three of them had run the cafe at some point, a family connection which seemed to be a theme in Port Promise. The current Betty was only a few years older than Ava herself, but what she didn't know about making a tasty fry-up or a plate of fluffy French toast sprinkled with sugar and cinnamon and topped with fruit and cream wasn't worth knowing.

Ava's sister Clara had worked there for a while after she'd left catering college, though it wasn't what she'd trained for; although she and Betty were best friends, they'd both agreed that she was massively overqualified. Despite that, Clara still helped out during busy weeks, though her job at the caravan park took up most of her working hours now, and so had to take priority. It wasn't what Clara had trained to do either, but it was better paid and, like most in Port Promise, she and Logan needed the money. He kept the village's art studio, of course, but the income from that was never predictable and very reliant on seasonal custom.

And Betty's was one more place that reminded Ava of her dad. Everywhere in Port Promise, of course, held some memory or other, but he'd taken her and her sisters to the cafe most weekends for an ice cream or a milkshake. Betty senior had run it then, aided by Betty mark II – the current Betty's mum, who now lived in Truro with a second husband – much to the shock of most of the community here, who couldn't understand why anyone would leave Port Promise, not even for love.

Ava recalled those days now as she walked the cobbled pavements, passing the bright coloured doors of tiny cottages, some inhabited by families they knew well, who'd lived in Port Promise for generations, but a good many also owned by strangers as second homes or holiday lets. As the years went by, actual residents of the village seemed to be in decline, although they weren't faring as badly on that score as some of the neighbouring towns and villages. Port Promise, though popular for holidays for those in the know, wasn't as famous or glamorous as the likes of St Ives or St Agnes, and that was the way most in the village liked it. There was trade enough to keep those who relied on tourism going, but not too many visitors that the village was swamped every summer, though its population definitely swelled by three or four times its usual size.

One day in particular came to mind. She'd been sitting on the terrace with her dad and her sisters while her mum was out somewhere with Marina – Ava didn't recall where – and they'd been laughing at a seagull who was stalking someone with a cone of chips from Salty's. They'd been betting on whether the seagull would get the prize or not. Ava's money was on the bird for sure – she'd seen this scenario play out often enough and the gull usually won. She'd just turned back to her towering glass full of chocolate and vanilla ice cream when her dad's pager went off. Every Morrow girl looked expectantly at him. There was no complaint and no disappointment that their time with him would be snatched away. This was their life – this was simply how things had to be. The call would come and their dad would go to sea. They were all proud of what he did, and even from a young age Ava understood its importance, so none of them would ever dream of making a fuss.

Ava had been perhaps five or six. She'd stood on her chair to watch him run down the beach to the station. It was one of the first times she recalled being genuinely thrilled by the sight. He was like an action hero. Gaby had tried to pretend she'd been left in charge because she was the oldest, and old Betty had come to sit with them, pretending that was absolutely right but really keeping an eye on them as Jack had asked her to do should he ever be called away while they were in the cafe. To ensure they'd be content, she'd brought them extra glasses of cola while they watched and waited. The boat had shot out from the station and raced over the waves, and Ava remembered that by this point lots of people had stopped to watch it.

Everyone was watching her dad and everyone could see what she already knew – that he was just about the coolest dad who ever lived. She didn't have a clue what the rescue that day was for or how it had turned out, but it was the rescuing that had stuck in her mind. She had to wonder if that was when she'd fallen in love with the service.

As she turned from a side street, the harbour opened out in front of her. Robin's new trawler was in and he was working on the deck. He waved at Ava, but he didn't make any sign that he was going to get off and come ashore to talk to her. Ava wasn't offended – he probably had a lot to do and only himself to do it. Times were hard for Robin, even harder since his old boat was lost and he'd had to find the money for a new one. There was insurance, of course, but that only covered so much, and he hadn't exactly been swimming in cash before. At least he'd looked relatively relaxed as he'd waved – certainly better than he had at the memorial. Perhaps their chat had helped.

On a low wall, a few feet along from Robin's boat, looking out to sea, sat Harry. He had a takeout coffee in one hand, his phone in the other. Ava couldn't help but feel he looked a bit lost. Killian's comments came back to her, how Harry was struggling silently, still coming to terms with what had happened to her dad, still blaming himself, even though it couldn't possibly have been his fault. Everyone seemed to be blaming themselves. Her dad would not have been impressed by that at all.

'Hey...'

He looked round and gave a smile that was so obviously full of effort Ava wanted to throw her arms around him. He'd been cheerful enough in the Spratt the day of the memorial, but she'd known then that it was taking a huge amount of strength to maintain. Now he was barely hiding his real state of being.

'Morning,' he said. 'How are you doing? Sleep OK on Gaby's sofa?'

'Oh, yeah, fine...' Ava shrugged slightly. 'Not like it's the first time I've slept on there and I've definitely slept in worse places. Killian made us all breakfast too, so that was a bonus worth having.'

'Bacon sandwiches by any chance?'

Ava nodded.

'He does make a good bacon butty,' Harry said. 'No lessons today?'

'I've got a break. I'm going to get a drink at Betty's. Join me if you like.'

'I've just had something.' Harry held up his cup. 'Thought I'd finish off out here, catch a bit of the sun, you know...'

'Right...' Ava hesitated, but even if she wanted to make sure Harry was OK, he looked as if he wanted to be alone. 'Well, you'll send your mum and dad my love, won't you?'

'Of course.'

Ava gave him one last look before going on her way.

Betty looked up from a table she was cleaning and smiled brightly as Ava walked in.

'Hello, stranger!' she called, dropping her cloth down and coming to hug her. She smelled like sugar and lavender, which was a strange thing to think, but Ava had always thought it. Like sugar and lavender were somehow Betty's natural scents, like she was made of those two substances. Her arms were smooth and tanned, and her curled hair glossy and currently a shade that looked like ginger biscuits, and she always gave the best hugs Ava had ever received.

'You saw me at the memorial,' Ava said with a light laugh.

'True, but you haven't been into the cafe for a while.'

'Well, I've been a bit busy, you know. Sorry about that.'

'Oh, I don't mind. Just saying. I know people get side-tracked, but the main thing is you're here now. So what can I get for you today?'

'Just a coffee.'

'Latte, shot of hazelnut syrup?'

'You know me so well!'

'Take a seat, my love. Wherever you like and I'll bring it to you.'

'Sounds good. I'll be outside on the terrace, if that's OK.'

'Of course. I'll be out in a tick.'

Ava went to settle at a vacant table. It was early but already the terrace was almost full. Most were families she didn't know so she assumed they were on holiday. She recognised one or two were familiar faces and so they either came to Port Promise very regularly or were second-home owners.

As she got comfortable, she took a moment to unlock her phone to check her emails and run over the day's schedule once more. She had three sessions booked in and all were full – mostly beginners and intermediates. She always preferred those – people with a bit of experience could be cocky. She had to wonder why those people bothered booking on to her sessions if they thought they knew so much already.

Then she put her phone away and closed her eyes for a moment, letting the sounds of the surf and children squealing with joy on the beach wash over her. The sun was high and strong already and it was going to be a corker of a day. Later she'd take her surfboard out, or maybe swim as the sun went down. Splashing around as the sun set over the sea on a hot day – that had to be in the top ten of life's pleasures.

'Here you go...'

Ava opened her eyes to see Betty putting a cup down.

'Thanks, Betty. How's it going? Busy?'

'Getting there.' Betty wiped a hand on her apron. 'Manageable now. I can't wait for August.' She rolled her eyes. 'Come back and ask me then if I'm managing.'

'I suppose it's all money,' Ava said.

'It is. I suppose I shouldn't complain.' She glanced back at the entrance to the cafe. 'Customers... no rest for the wicked, eh?'

'No worries. I'll catch you later.'

Ava sipped at her drink, her gaze trained on the sand and the ocean beyond, when, from the corner of her eye, she saw Harry leap from his seat on the harbour wall and race down the beach.

A shout? It had to be.

Her suspicions were confirmed when she saw him run in

the direction of the station. He wasn't seagoing, but there would be plenty for him to do on shore. If Harry was heading there, chances were Killian wouldn't be far behind. Vas would probably already be at the station – he literally lived a few yards away and was always first on scene.

She watched the sea. She wouldn't have to wait long. Seven, eight minutes – that was about what it took to launch. And right on cue, seven minutes later, the inshore lifeboat – the compact, more manoeuvrable one that was used for smaller rescues or on calmer seas – went speeding across the bay.

Ava wondered what they were going out for. Someone caught in a riptide maybe? It was pretty common, and she'd even had a few close calls herself out on her board over the years. They'd be scared, and if someone didn't pick them up they'd find themselves way out at sea before they could do anything about it. How relieved would they be to see that boat? She'd never been rescued herself, and she'd never been out on one, but her dad had described plenty to her, and she'd always imagined the looks on people's faces when they'd thought their end had arrived, only to see those rescuers arrive in their orange-and-blue boats with their soothing, calm voices and strong, capable hands.

Ava had thought a lot about how others would react when she announced her plans, and she'd spent weeks second-guessing herself before making her decision. But as she sat here today, watching the boat skim the waves, answering the call from some poor terrified soul, there was no more doubt. Surely, when she explained it, others would understand why she felt she needed to do this? Her family would hate the idea at first, but they'd come round eventually, even if they never loved it. The wider community of Port Promise... well, that remained to be seen. Ava imagined there would be some scepticism – perhaps amongst the older people – but she hoped that there would also be some pride in the fact that she wanted to keep the

Morrow tradition alive. Whatever she was to face, it was easier to ask forgiveness than permission – wasn't that how the old saying went? Ava was inclined to agree. Get the gig first, then worry about convincing everyone it's not the worst idea they've ever heard.

# CHAPTER SIX

Mostly Ava loved her job. There were days where the sea was pond-still, the sun warm and friendly, seabirds swooping around the bay and students wide-eyed and eager to learn. Today, she had those eager students lined up, borrowed paddleboards in hand, waiting at the water's edge where the calm sea called them in. The sun was high and hot, but, even though all the things she most loved about her job were in abundance, today her mind wasn't on it. She'd made her decision and now she wanted to get things started – but that would have to wait for a while.

She stood before them in her wetsuit and gave her brightest, most welcoming smile, and did her best to give them as good as she could manage. After all, they'd each paid a lot of money to be here and it wasn't their fault she was itching to get an application sent off.

'Hi everyone,' she called out to the row of new students. 'My name is Ava. We'll have a quick safety briefing – sorry, I know it's boring but we have to do it – and then we'll get started familiarising ourselves with the boards. Everyone OK with that?'

There were murmurs and nods, and so Ava continued. 'So, first of all, let me explain a few of the features on your life vests.'

A hand shot up.

'Yes?' Ava said.

'Do we have to wear them?' a young man asked. 'Cos, like, I can swim.'

'I'm sure everyone here can swim,' Ava said patiently. 'But it's protocol.'

'But can I take it off? It's getting in the way.'

'I'm afraid not. If you took it off, neither you nor I would be insured if anything were to happen to you.'

'But nothing will happen to me.'

'We don't know that.'

'But I can swim.'

Ava glanced along the line. Some of the other students threw the young man a look of annoyance. She needed to shut this down or they'd spend the next hour discussing his aversion to buoyancy aids.

'I appreciate that you're probably an amazing swimmer – I would imagine everyone here is – but I'm afraid it's the rules. Please understand that if you removed your life vest I would have to ask you to leave the class and there would be no refund.'

The young man started to grumble and tug at his vest, but he didn't argue, and so Ava took that as a sign that the issue was resolved.

'So,' she started again. 'A few signs I might make to you if you're too far away to hear me. There aren't many, but I'd appreciate your attention – you never know, one of these might just save your life.'

'Oooh... I know these!' a girl in a tiny bikini said to her friend. 'I've seen them on that video.'

Ava paused and waited for their attention. But as the girl noticed her and stopped talking, another young man was gesturing to what was obviously his girlfriend sitting on the beach. She grinned and held up her phone to take a photo while he posed, making a hand gesture that was a favourite of surfers, despite the fact that he was in this lesson, so probably didn't surf at all.

Ava sighed. It was going to be a long day.

Ava was waving the last of her students off when she noticed her sister Clara sitting on the harbour wall.

'Thought you'd still be working,' she said as she made her way over, pulling a soft towelling hoodie over the swimming costume she'd had on under her wetsuit. 'Don't you have holidaymakers to book into caravans or something?'

'I'm done for the day and Logan's busy *creating*. So I thought I'd take a walk down here and see what you're up to.'

Ava knew the rule that a parent never had a favourite child, and although she wouldn't have dared say Clara was her favourite sister, she wouldn't hesitate to admit that she found her easier to get along with than Gaby. There was no treading on eggshells here, no rigid sense of morals or propriety. Gaby could be fun, and she was lovely, of course, kind and sensitive, but she could be horribly judgemental and once she made up her mind or took a certain position, it was nigh impossible to change it. Clara was easier going, believed in the adage of live and let live, and was open to discussions on a topic, even if her opinions differed wildly to start with.

'Not a lot,' Ava said. 'I was thinking I might head out on my board.'

'Oooh, I might come with you. It's ages since I surfed.'

'The waves won't be massive—'

Clara laughed. 'Exactly how I like them!'

'That'd be cool then. You can borrow some stuff from the kit room here to save you going all the way home to get changed.'

'Perfect. Can we go for food afterwards?'

'Sounds good to me.'

Clara lifted herself off the wall and dropped gracefully to the ground. 'So what's occurring?'

'What, with me?' Ava gave her a sideways glance as they began to walk in step. 'Not a lot more than when you saw me on Saturday. How about you?'

'Oh, apart from another row with Logan? Not much.'

'Another row. I don't recall you mentioning before that life was one long round of arguments. What's wrong? Is there trouble? Everything's OK, isn't it?'

'Yes... sort of. I don't think it's us, necessarily – it's the stuff going on around us. Things get to you, don't they? No matter how strong a couple is, things are bound to get to us.'

'What sort of things?'

'The wedding plans. And money. Money, mostly. Don't they say that's at the root of all evil?'

'Bloody right there,' Ava said. 'All the things I could do with a bit more money...'

'Yup. I'd sing the song but your ears might bleed.'

Ava grinned. 'But you're OK?'

'I'm sure it's just a blip. I refuse to plan another wedding with someone else – this one's been enough of a nightmare to put me off for life.'

'I told you to run off and do it somewhere in private.'

'I might yet do that. Mum would never forgive me, though, especially now...'

'Yeah, I know. Especially since we lost Dad. I suppose she needs something positive to look forward to. And I suppose that's not helping with the money stress.'

'Yes, weddings aren't cheap, even when you try to do them on the cheap.'

'With that in mind, where do you want to eat? You could come to mine and I'll fix us something.'

'I've tasted your cooking,' Clara said. 'If you can even call it that. How about the fish shack? They do lobster salads now.'

Ava turned and arched an eyebrow at her sister. 'Lobster salad? Haven't we just been talking about how skint you are?'

'I never said *totally* skint, only that we were *discussing* money quite a lot. But where my stomach's concerned, I say it's never worth skimping.'

Ava laughed. 'Well, I love a good fish shack dinner, but I'll leave the lobster to you. I'm sure they'll have something a bit cheaper for me.'

'I'll treat you if you want to try the lobster with me.'

'I don't need you to treat me.'

'But you love lobster!'

'I do, on a very special occasion. God, don't encourage me to eat it all the time – I need some financial perspective. I live in a caravan as it is!'

'Which is why I can totally treat you to dinner.'

Ava made to argue but Clara stopped her. 'Please... let me. It'll be a reward because I actually feel like I need to vent, and you might wish you hadn't come to dinner with me unless I make it worth your while.'

'Hmm, I thought as much,' Ava said. 'Not that I don't love that you wanted to meet up, but I thought there had to be more to it. And while we're venting, there's actually something I could do with getting off my chest, so let's eat your lobster, take it in turns to complain and call it quits.'

'OK but first... surf's up!'

Ava shook her head. 'Seriously, don't! I've had a day of people thinking they're in Baywatch – don't you start!'


Not quite the sun drenched swim she'd been anticipating, but Ava loved the alternative. They'd all got so busy as they'd grown older that Ava and her sisters had precious little time for messing about on the beach like this. As teenagers she and Clara had spent as much time as they could on their boards during the summer months. For Ava, it had become more than that, and while Clara had still dabbled, she'd eventually found more interesting things to do.

They walked into the rolling waves together, Ava's trusty old board under her arm and Clara with a loaned one from the kit room of the watersports academy.

'The sea hasn't warmed much yet,' Clara said, gasping as the first wave broke over her feet.

Ava laughed. 'You're such a wuss! It's early in the season yet, but you've got a bloody wetsuit on! What do you think they're for?'

'My feet don't have a wetsuit on!'

Ava rolled her eyes comically before splashing further out. 'Race you!'

'Race me to where?' Clara called back rushing after her anyway. 'France?'

Ava grinned and threw herself onto the board. She began to paddle into deeper water, chasing the first decent-sized waves, and Clara followed. She looked back and caught her sister's eye. The swells began to grow, the board rising and falling in a gentle rhythm. And then she looked ahead and saw the water grow, and turned her board around to catch the start of the wave that would carry her back towards the shore. Smiling, she felt it underneath her, and as it began to propel her forward, she leaped to her feet to ride it. There was no fairground ride, no spin on a racetrack, no adrenaline-fuelled activity that filled her with this kind of excitement, no matter how many times she came out here.

In the shallows as the wave dropped her, she hopped off her board and turned it to go again, just in time to see Clara following on a wave of her own, only to lose her balance and disappear.

'Wipeout!' Ava cried, laughing. 'You need more practice!' she added as Clara emerged from the sea with her board, wiping water from her face.

Clara frowned as she pulled a strand of seaweed from her hair and held it up. 'I think you might be right!' she spluttered.

'Ready to go again?'

In reply, Clara turned her board and mounted it, and Ava did the same. Side by side this time, they paddled out to find the next wave.

'I don't know why we don't do this more often,' Clara said.

'Because we're too busy being boring adults.'

'Screw that!'

'Agreed!'

The sun warmed her face as she squinted out across the sparkling swells. Ahead of them, further away from Port Promise, she could see another group of surfers. It looked as if they'd come from a neighbouring beach. Apart from them and a few families with children messing around on the shoreline, they had the sea to themselves. Even though this stretch of beach was a fair distance from the village and therefore often quieter, it was a rare thing for it to be this deserted in the summer and something Ava was determined to enjoy.

The next wall of water began to build. Clara pointed to it and Ava nodded.

'Seen it!'

They paddled towards it, turning their boards and waiting for it to lift them. Clara let out a squeal of delight. Ava leaped to her feet; from the corner of her eye, she saw Clara do the same. This time they both stayed on the board until the wave dumped them on the beach again.

Clara grinned. 'I'd forgotten how much fun that is! I need to get Logan into this so we can go together.'

'I'll teach him if he wants to try,' Ava said.

'I'll definitely mention it to him. He's been in Port Promise long enough – can't be married to a Morrow and not surf – right?'

They spent another hour on the waves before agreeing that they were both ravenous and it was time to eat. They both got changed and walked back along the seafront together, laughing like they hadn't laughed in ages. It had done them good individually, and Ava felt it had done their relationship good too. Clara had plaited her wet hair so that it hung down her back. Her features were more delicate than Ava's and less obviously beautiful than Gaby's, but Ava thought she was perhaps, in her own modest way, the prettiest sister. She certainly looked gentler and more approachable than she or Gaby did, and Ava knew that for a fact because everyone loved Clara. Ava could rub people up the wrong way, she knew that, and Gaby was sometimes too opinionated, but Clara was just Clara – kind, helpful, inoffensive, everyone's friend.


Two of the students from Ava's last class were at the shack eating their meals in the covered seating area next to the little timber shed when she and Clara got there. It was the girl in the tiny bikini and her friend. They waved cheerily and pointed to the seafood platter they were both devouring. Ava waved back awkwardly. It wasn't that she minded them being there or even having to make small talk, it was the fact that whatever discussion Clara wanted to have, and anything of a more personal nature that Ava wanted to tell Clara, would have to wait until they'd gone. As the seating area consisted of half a dozen tables, all close together under an old tarpaulin decorated with lanterns and old fishing pots, unless the place was full with rowdy customers so that nobody could hear anyone but their own parties, or completely deserted, there was little privacy to be had.

'Hey, Cormac.' Clara smiled brightly at the man standing at the little takeout window of the shack. 'Busy today?'

'Busy every day,' Cormac replied, offering a warm smile in return.

Cormac had arrived in Port Promise the winter before to take over the business from his uncle, who'd had enough of the long hours in sometimes horrible weather and had decided to retire early. Before that, Cormac had been living in Ireland where the paternal side of his family hailed from, and so he had the most delicious accent. It had been noted by many of the female inhabitants of Port Promise, as had his gorgeous blue eyes and handsome face.

'Not that I'm complaining. Got to make a living, right? If people are coming to give me money, I'm hardly going to turn them away.'

'Well, I for one am glad,' Clara said. 'If things are going well then it means you won't be leaving Port Promise any time soon. We've got quite used to seeing you around and I think everyone would miss you.'

'That's nice to hear!' Cormac's smile spread wider still. 'Sometimes it's hard to be the outsider, so it's good to know I'm being accepted. What can I get you girls today?'

'We're going to try your lobster salad,' Clara said.

'Grand!' Cormac went to a tiny sink to wash his hands. 'I'm glad to hear it. I was thinking about tweaking the ingredients so I could do with some honest feedback about how it tastes.'

'Does that mean we get it for free?' Ava asked with a wink. Clara nudged her but Ava grinned.

'I wish I could say yes,' Cormac replied. 'But I can throw a drink in for you – how's that?'

'A couple of Cokes would be amazing,' Clara said.

'Get yourselves comfortable round the side there,' Cormac said, going to the fridge. 'I'll bring everything out to you.'

Ava followed Clara round to the shaded eating area and

they took a seat. Then she leaned across the table and lowered her voice. 'I hope you don't bring Logan here – you'd have more than money to argue about.'

'What does that mean?' Clara asked carelessly.

'You and Cormac!'

Clara's forehead creased. 'I'm only being friendly.'

'Yes, but it's obvious you fancy him.'

'I don't.'

Ava raised her eyebrows. 'Not even one bit?'

'He's good-looking – nobody could deny that. You said so yourself when he first moved here.'

'I did, but I'm not the one flirting like mad with him.'

'No,' Clara shot back. 'You save that for Harry Trevithick.'

'I don't! You know we're good mates and that's all we are.'

'Oh yeah, of course. Still, I bet there are times now when you look at him and wish you'd never stood him up that time. He was definitely one of those boys who blossomed when puberty hit proper. Who'd have thought he'd end up being so fit?'

'Don't be stupid. We were in high school; he hasn't mentioned that for years. We all do horrible things in high school; it had nothing to do with his looks.'

'Do we?' Clara raised an eyebrow. 'I'm sure I never did anything that horrible. And I seem to recall you being annoyed by his zits or something.'

'I'm sure you did horrible things. Anyway, it was nothing to do with zits. Harry was a spoiled brat back then and he needed taking down a peg or two.'

'Or maybe you were the spoiled brat? Thought you were too good for him.'

'I'd never!' Ava's mouth fell open, but then she frowned as Clara laughed. 'Are you winding me up?'

'I might be.'

'So you're after a clobbering?'

'God no, you'd wipe the floor with me – you always won fights.'

Ava grinned. 'True.'

Clara looked up with a smile as Cormac came over to the table with two plated salads and two drinks. His muscular frame was dressed in black jeans and black T-shirt, with a short white apron tied around his waist. Ava had to admit, if Clara was flirting, she could see why. Logan was good-looking in his own way, but Cormac was an undeniable hottie.

'Two lobster salads and two Cokes. Bon appetite.'

'Looks amazing!' Clara said.

'It does,' Ava agreed, eyeing up a plate piled high with chunks of pink lobster, crisp lettuce, lemony mayonnaise, avocado and topped with ribbons of cucumber and carrot. There might have been paprika or chilli or something sprinkled over the top, but Ava wasn't sure. 'Thanks, Cormac.'

'Don't forget – feedback,' he said as he left them to it.

'You want a point-by-point review?' Clara called with a laugh.

'Absolutely!'

With that he went back into the shack through a side door and shut himself in. At that moment, the students who had been at Ava's class finished their food and left, with a friendly wave at her as they did.

'Right...' Ava dug a fork into her meal and pushed a mound of smothered lettuce into her mouth. 'Let's have it.'

'Have what?'

'The reason you wanted to buy me this outrageously expensive meal.'

'I just wanted to spend some time with my sister. I can do that, right? Anyway, I thought it was you who needed to get something off your chest.'

Ava put her fork down for a moment. She took a breath. And then she said it.

'I'm going to join the lifeboat crew. At least I will if they'll have me.'

There was a beat of silence. Clara didn't look as shocked as Ava might have expected. In fact, she gave a small smile as she put down her fork and held Ava's gaze.

'I had wondered,' she said.

'Really?'

Clara nodded.

'What makes you say that?'

'Well, if anyone in the family other than Dad was going to do it, I'd have put my money on you. In fact I'm surprised you haven't announced this sooner, even before Dad died. I mean, you're the one who loves the water as much as he did and you're practically always in the sea doing one thing or another, like you've always been a regular water baby.'

'And you don't think it's madness?'

'Why would I think that?'

'Because Gaby and Mum will flip. Or so Killian thinks.'

'I'm sorry to break it to you, but he's not wrong there. Have you told anyone else yet?'

'No,' Ava replied. 'I'm picking my moment for Mum.'

'I'd say you might have to pick your moment for Gaby too. How about some time in the next decade? Or even better, once she's in a nursing home and too old to show how annoyed she is?'

'I know she's going to hate the idea, and I get why, but she can't seriously think she can tell me what to do. She has as much right as Killian, which is zero right.'

'She won't see it like that. She'll see it as her duty to save you.'

'From myself, you mean?'

'That, and from certain death. She hasn't been able to deter Killian from the boats and that pisses her off enough, so she'll have a bloody good go at stopping you from joining.'

'I know.'

Ava took a sip of Coke and placed the glass thoughtfully on the table.

'That's not to say that if you want to do it, you shouldn't,' Clara continued.

Ava looked up to see that small smile again. 'It means a lot to me that you're behind me on this. I don't imagine there'll be many.'

'Everyone at the station will be made up.'

'Except Killian.'

'Well, perhaps except Killian, but that's only because he knows he'll get it in the neck from Gaby. I actually think a lot of people will be more understanding than you imagine. You're a Morrow, after all, and it's only a quirk of physiology or whatever that made you a girl. But a Morrow is still a Morrow and why shouldn't you carry on the family tradition, just because you're the wrong sex?'

'Maybe I'm the *right* sex and all the others were wrong,' Ava said with a smile of her own now.

Clara laughed. 'That's the spirit! Or maybe there was never a wrong sex, only wrong social attitudes. Until now that is.'

'The mad thing is, we have female volunteers already, just not seagoing. It's not such a leap from shore crew to sea crew, when you think about it.'

'I don't know about that. I think it's pretty ballsy to go out to sea on a rescue. I take my hat off to you, Ava, I don't think I could do it. Since Dad died, I've thought about it a million times, probably like you have, thought about how I could be doing more to help, how valued my contribution would be, and I've thought about roles I could take at the station, but never once have I even considered going to sea. That's the difference between you and me – you're braver.'

'Maybe just brave in a different way.'

Clara set her cutlery down and reached for her drink. 'I'm

behind you, for what it's worth. If it's what you want to do then I think you should go for it.'

'I already have,' Ava said. 'I sent the application at lunchtime.'

Clara smiled. 'Of course you did. My brave baby sister.'

'Stop saying that. We'll decide if I'm brave if I even get through the training and survive my first shout. We've all seen what it's done to Harry.'

'That's different.'

'Is it?'

'I've always thought Harry was a bit too sensitive for a job like that.'

'He cares; I don't think that's a bad thing.'

'No, true, but I think he probably ought to be a bit thicker skinned. Like Killian. He doesn't let stuff get to him. I bet if Harry makes a mistake he beats himself up over it, but Killian would just move on.'

'Bury it and not talk or think about it, you mean?' Ava said. 'I'm not sure that's healthier. At least Harry externalises what he's feeling and deals with it. Killian just bottles it up. If he's not careful he's going to end up like a hand grenade full of rage. One tease of the pin and he'll go off.'

'Wow!' Clara sat back and regarded Ava with a faint spark of humour in her eyes. 'You've really thought about that, haven't you?'

'Only now, to be honest. It sort of came to me in a flash of inspiration.'

'And do you think you'll be a Harry or a Killian?'

'I think I'll be somewhere in between. I hope so. I hope I can deal with whatever comes without it crushing me.'

'You think Harry's that bad? I know people are saying he's struggled but he's still volunteering at the station, and he hasn't... Has he said something to you? I know you guys used to be close.'

'Not in so many words, but I feel like he's struggling more than he lets on. I would imagine he's putting on a brave face for the rest of the crew, especially Killian. As for volunteering, that's true, but it's a shore role. That's not Harry, is it? He was obsessed with the idea of being on the boat when he was growing up. Ever since I can remember that was all he talked about, and the only reason he didn't join at eighteen was that his parents insisted he went to university first.'

Clara was silent for a moment, picking over her salad. 'I suppose you've tried talking to him? You spent a lot of time with him at the memorial service – did it come up?'

'I get the impression he would have liked to talk about it, but the opportunity never arose. I chatted to him plenty but it was busy, you know that. Not really the sort of place to air stuff like that. And I suppose he might have felt, in the circumstances, that it wasn't the time to bring it up.'

'Circumstances?'

'Well, you know, that we were there to remember Dad. I'd have probably felt the same. I'd have felt that any issues I might have paled into insignificance when you consider that Dad hadn't been lucky enough to survive like Harry did. If you see what I mean.'

'I see what you mean. Harry ought to know nobody would think that.'

'I'm sure he does, but still, I'm sure I wouldn't choose that day to bring my problems up.'

'Maybe we could go see him?'

'You and me?' Ava held back a frown. 'And ask him straight out?'

'Why not? It's not like we don't know him well enough.'

Ava shook her head slowly. 'I think it's something he's going to have to bring up when he's ready, with the right person. I know we're mates, but that doesn't automatically make the right person you or me. If he thinks so, then I'm sure he'll come and talk to one of us when he's ready.'

Clara picked up her cola. 'I'm sorry, but I think you're wrong. I think someone needs to get to the bottom of this and I don't think he'll ask for help. He'll see it as a weakness.'

'He's not Killian.'

'No, but he works alongside Killian, and that guy has an influence on almost everyone around him. All the blokes turn into macho berks when Killian's around.'

Ava grinned. 'What was Gaby thinking?'

'Macho berks are obviously her thing.'

'Harry's not like that. I can't see him being sucked into that mindset; he's too smart.'

'He's still a man who's grown up in a small village where most people's attitude is a stiff upper lip. The generations who've come before have had hard lives and they've had to be tough – changing that isn't going to happen overnight.'

'Sandy's not like that.'

Clara raised her eyebrows. 'Harry's dad is awesome and a breed apart from almost everyone, but I bet even he gets influenced more than you think.'

Ava paused, and then gave a shrug. 'All right, if I can find a good moment maybe I'll drop some hints and see if Harry takes them.'

'I still say just go and see him. If you don't want to, then I don't mind.'

'Maybe...' Ava said slowly. 'Maybe you could. After all, you weren't in our year at school and so you have that older kid thing going on.'

Clara laughed. 'We're in our twenties! I don't think that's an issue anymore.'

'No, but you know what I mean. You weren't as close growing up because you were older so you weren't interested in hanging out. It gives you the right amount of distance, maybe.

You know, distance I don't have in the same way. I just mean he might actually feel more comfortable talking to you about it than to me.'

'OK. I'll see what I can do.' Clara put down her knife and fork. There was still a good half portion of food on the plate.

Ava nodded at it. 'You're not going to eat that?'

'Stuffed.'

'Cormac will be gutted; he'll think you don't like it.'

'Oh, don't worry about that – I'm going to get it boxed and take it home. No fear of me wasting food that good.'

Cormac chose that exact moment to come, whistling softly, to their table. 'How's your lobster?' he asked.

'Incredible!' Clara smiled up at him. 'There's a lot of it, though. Not that I'm complaining, of course.'

'You're finished?' He glanced at the plate and then back at her.

'For now, but I wouldn't mind taking the rest with me if you could do me a takeaway box.'

'No worries.' He looked at Ava, who was still eating. She stuck a thumb in the air as she chewed and he grinned. 'It's going down OK then? Any recommendations?' he asked, turning back to Clara. 'Seeing as you're a chef yourself?'

'Not anymore. I hardly get a chance to heat a tin of beans lately, let alone cook.'

'I bet you miss it,' he said.

Clara nodded. 'I do, but that's how things go sometimes.'

'Aye, I hear ya...' Cormac picked up her plate. 'I suppose life gets in the way for all of us, doesn't it?'

Clara nodded. 'I suppose it does. And your lobster... I wouldn't change a thing – it's completely delicious.'

Cormac grinned. 'That's brilliant. Thanks. I'll just be away with your leftovers and get them boxed up for you.'

# CHAPTER SEVEN

Ava had slept more soundly that night than she had in a long while. It had felt good to share her plans with Clara and to hear Clara's support. So after her lessons the following day, she decided it was time to come clean with her mum and hope she'd get the same kind of understanding. She didn't expect it to be that easy, of course, but sooner or later Jill was going to find out, and maybe leaving it longer would only make it worse, especially if someone at the station let the cat out of the bag.

So that evening Ava trudged the steep hill that led to her childhood home, hair still wet from when she'd pretended to fall off her board and into the sea with a huge splash during the last session to entertain two children (and they'd found it hilarious, so totally worth it), ready to face the music.

But as she let herself into the cottage with her spare key and called out, there was no reply.

'Mum?'

Ava went through the tiny entrance hallway – hardly bigger than a broom cupboard – into the sitting room. Through the vast window she could see the harbour down below, a measureless cauldron of blue encircled by cliffs with ramshackle houses clinging to their faces, and down below the greys of the cobbled streets and the pastel squares of the cottages lining them. From this window she'd witnessed storms and sunshine, spectacular sunsets and magical moonrises, watched for planets and counted shooting stars during meteor showers. She'd watched fishing boats and pleasure cruisers come and go, and seen many launches of the boat that her father went out on to save those in need. It was just a window in a house, but to Ava it was so much more – it was a window on her life, on the many significant and not so significant events that had shaped it.

Behind a pair of matching modern sofas stood an old dresser that had belonged to Jill's grandmother and had been transported to Port Promise from Truro on the horse-drawn cart of a rag and bone man on the occasion of her wedding. Jill's grandmother – Adelaide – was the reason Jill's family had come to settle in Port Promise. She'd married a butcher from the area, which was how her family and Jack Morrow's had ended up so fortuitously in the same village – and how Jack and his future wife were able meet at all.

On the polished surface of the wood stood row upon row of framed photos – of Jack, of long-gone versions of the lifeboat crew, of the children and grandchildren, of Jack and Jill on their wedding day and a small carving of a bucket that Robin Trelawney had bought them as a joke because of their names. There were medals in display boxes that had been presented to Jack and to his ancestors, alongside certificates of commendation.

On the wall next to the dresser was a vast watercolour of the harbour, all inky blues and serene smoke greys, painted by Logan for their last wedding anniversary. On the mantel over the tiled fireplace there were more family photos and a dried-flower arrangement that Clara had made for her mother when she'd taken it up, briefly, as a hobby.

But aside from all these memories, there was no sign anyone

lived here at all. The room was otherwise uncluttered and immaculate and clean as a science lab, and there was no sign of Ava's mother.

'Mum!' Ava called up as she made her way to the bottom of the stairs. 'Are you up there?'

Still no reply, and Ava decided not to go up to investigate but to check the kitchen first.

The kitchen was dominated by a scrubbed wooden table and pastel painted chairs. The units along the wall were free-standing, collected from various craft fairs and antique shops, some renovated by Jill herself and some done by the people she'd bought them from. Ava had always thought it cosier and kinder than some of the clinical fitted kitchens she'd seen in other people's houses, though as she'd grown older she'd realised that it could be a lot less practical. It took a lot of cleaning and maintenance, for all its aesthetic joy. On the table was an empty, tea-stained mug and a well-thumbed horticulture maga-zine, so Jill had recently been in here, even though she wasn't here now. There wasn't much sign of any cooking going on, which was odd, considering they'd arranged to have tea together and Ava would have expected something to be on the stove by now. Had she misunderstood their plans? With that thought, Ava took herself into the garden.

Jill was in her gardening cords and wellies and a soft checked shirt, her grey-threaded hair pulled into a crocodile clip, carefully pruning a rose bush on the patio. She had more exotic species in her greenhouse, and the ones she grew to sell on she mostly kept on a separate plot of land that she rented outside the village where it was sheltered from the harsher winds and colder temperatures that sometimes swept across the harbour.

'I wondered where you'd got to,' Ava said.

Jill straightened up and smiled vaguely. 'Hello. Thought

you'd call on the off-chance? Lucky you caught me. I've been down to the work garden most of the day – just got home.'

'Mum... we made arrangements to have tea. But I can totally go home if you're busy—'

'Oh!' Jill slapped her forehead comically. 'Of course! I'm such an idiot, totally mixed my days up this week! I'm so sorry, I haven't done a thing towards it!'

'That doesn't matter.'

'But I bet you're starving!' Jill put down her cutters and started to yank off her gloves. 'I'll get something going...'

'Honestly, it's fine,' Ava said. 'I'm not that hungry. I can make some sandwiches and you can make a brew and that will be just fine.'

'But it won't take a minute to—'

'Honestly, Mum. Unless you're desperate to eat a whole cooked meal, don't do it on my account.'

Jill started to walk to the house, muttering, and Ava followed her inside. 'I'm such an idiot. I can't believe myself sometimes.'

'You're not. Stop beating yourself up. You're allowed to forget stuff from time to time – you've got a lot to think about.'

'Well, it's annoying.'

Ava closed the door behind her and took off her jacket, hanging it over the back of one of the kitchen chairs. 'What do you fancy?' she asked, going to the fridge and sticking her head in to see what was there. 'Oooh, I see you've got some of that nice cheese. We could have that with some... oh yes, you've got coleslaw.'

'Cheese and coleslaw sandwiches? I'm sure we can do better than that. I got some of that deli ham you like the other day – should be some left.'

'Honestly, cheese is fine. I'm in the mood for something simple – I had lobster with Clara last night at Cormac's place, so I've had my luxury for this week.'

Jill looked round from the sink where she was filling the kettle. 'Lobster? Wow! What's the occasion?'

'Clara wanted to treat me,' Ava said, laughing. 'Who am I to say no to lobster when someone else is paying?'

'Was it nice?'

'Bloody amazing actually. You should definitely try it if you get a chance.'

'Hmmm... maybe I'll see if Marina wants to go with me next week for lunch, if the weather's decent enough to sit outside.'

'It's covered – he's got a tarpaulin set up now and heaters; I'm sure you'd be fine whatever weather it is.'

'Yes, but nobody wants to sit there and stare out at the pouring rain, do they?'

'No, but I think the forecast is good for the next week or so.'

Ava smoothed away a frown. Her mum listened to the weather forecasts on the radio regularly and paid them great attention. She needed to for her work as a gardener, because she needed to know if there was something on the way that might affect her plants. She'd also spent years listening to them with Ava's dad, trying to second-guess whether any forecast might signal a possible call-out for the boats. It had become a baked-in habit, something she did without fail, so she'd know there was no rain in the near future. And yet, she didn't know what the next few days had in store? Did that mean she'd stopped listening to them? Was that because it had become too much of a painful reminder of Jack? Or had she simply forgotten, like she had about their tea arrangements?

'So what do you want on your sandwiches?' she asked, deciding not to express her thoughts out loud for the moment. 'Did you want the ham?'

'Oh yes, I might as well finish it.'

'You want coleslaw?'

'Just salad for me. Thanks, Ava. If you're OK here I'll go and get washed up before we eat.'

'Sure...' Ava pulled a loaf of sourdough bread from an antique crock, the glaze crazed and cracked from years of use, but somehow the wear and tear making it more beautiful. 'I can manage. I'll shout up when it's ready.'

As Jill went out to the stairs, the kitchen fell into silence. Ava could hear her mum's footsteps on the floor above, going back and forth, followed by the sound of the tap running in the bathroom. Despite this, the house felt empty and strangely huge for such a small cottage. Growing up, the fact that it was a compact home and a family of five lived there had often frustrated and annoyed Ava, but these days, stepping in to find only her mum there saddened her. If she felt like that just visiting, she had to wonder how her mum felt, rattling round in there on her own all the time. Looking at things that way, it stood to reason that her mum might seem a little more melancholy these days, and that she might sometimes struggle to find the small joys in her life that it used to be so full of.

Buttering the bread, Ava was deep in thought. She wondered if she ought to offer to move back in. Then again, was that really the answer? She couldn't live there forever – not realistically – no matter how she might worry about her mum. To do that probably wouldn't help either of them in the long term.

As she was looking for the ham in the fridge, her mum returned to the kitchen. She was still wearing her gardening clothes but had brushed her hair and smelled of lavender soap.

'I've got a bit of pruning to finish,' she said in answer to Ava's questioning glance over her shirt. 'I'll do it after we've eaten, so no point in getting changed yet. It doesn't matter anyway – my trousers aren't that dirty.'

'I never said they were. If you're going to be in the garden, I don't mind helping. It's a nice evening – I'd rather be outside making the most of it.'

'You don't want to be gardening after you've had a day at work—'

'I do, Mum. I'd like to. I went surfing with Clara yesterday, and it made me realise we don't do the things we used to do together anymore. I haven't helped you in the garden for ages, so it'd be nice.'

Ava gave the brightest smile she could manage. Perhaps the garden, her mum's favourite place, where she felt relaxed and calm, would be the best place to break her news. She'd wait, choose her moment, and then she'd tell her.

An hour later they'd washed up what few dishes had been made by their quick tea and were back in the garden. The evening was bright, but as the sun began to set, there was a nip in the air and a fresh breeze sweeping in from the sea. Jill went inside to fetch two fleece jumpers and handed one to Ava to put on, along with a spare pair of gardening gloves and some cutters. The scents of the garden were somehow more intense than they were during the day, especially the white star jasmine that clung to the faded boards of the summer house, and clouds of gnats hung in the air.

Ava and her mum made light conversation as they worked, as they had done during tea. Nothing of importance was said, and yet Ava was desperate for the right moment to present itself so she could tell her mum this thing, this momentous decision, the secret that she hated she was keeping. But instead, Jill told Ava about Brogan Scott's new puppy, and Ava told Jill about Harry's dad's new ciders. Jill told Ava about Molly Johnson's first-class degree, and Ava told Jill about the new flavour of cupcakes at Betty's cafe. It went back and forth like this as they worked – more news, more opinions, nothing of consequence – and yet Ava still couldn't see her moment. Maybe there would never be a right moment. Maybe she just had to launch it, like the lifeboat into the sea with all the spray and mess, and hope that when that settled their relationship would still be afloat.

Ava looked up from the rose bush she'd been deadheading and took a breath to begin.

At that moment there was a voice from the garden gate, and they both looked up to see Marina, peering over.

'Thought I'd find you out here,' she said to Jill before nodding at Ava. 'Hello, love.'

'Hi, Marina,' Ava said, relieved and frustrated in equal measure by the interruption. 'Been on the beach? Got a good colour there.'

Marina smiled. 'Oh, it's amazing what a bit of sun will do. I need a tan otherwise people think I'm on the way out. Got some yourself. I see your mum is working you hard.'

Jill unfastened the gate to let Marina in. 'Well, I did say I could manage...'

'I don't mind a bit of mindful pruning every now and again.' Ava looked at Marina, who was holding up a paper bag. 'That looks interesting.'

'Sorry, I didn't bring one for you,' Marina said. 'Didn't know you'd be here. This is for your mum. Just got them in at the shop and thought of her straight away.'

'Oh...' Jill took off her gloves and went to take the bag from Marina. 'You don't have to be giving me your stock all the time!' She opened it up and peered inside, looking up again with a broad smile. 'It's lovely, thank you!'

'What is it then?' Ava asked, going over to look. 'Don't leave me in suspense.'

Jill took out a silver candle and gave it a sniff. 'Eucalyptus and mint, if I'm not mistaken. And what else...?'

'Sandalwood,' Marina said. 'Smells even more gorgeous when it's lit.'

'I'll bet. I'll have that burning later on. Are you staying a while? You fancy a glass of wine?'

'You're busy, and Ava's here, I only called on the off-chance—'

'Don't mind me!' Ava put in. 'I'd be up for a glass of wine if there's one going and I think we're nearly done here, aren't we, Mum?'

'I think we could call it a day,' Jill said, surveying a pile of cuttings. 'We've done quite a lot and the light will be fading soon anyway.'

'Right then,' Ava said, taking off her own gloves. 'You clear up those cuttings. Marina, you can sit down and make yourself comfortable. I'll get the glasses and the plonk.'

Marina was almost like family to Ava, she'd known her so long – certainly she couldn't remember a time when her mum's friend wasn't a regular visitor to Seaspray Cottage. For that reason, Ava had never felt ill at ease in her company, and despite the age difference (Marina was even a few years older than Ava's mum, and so much older than her) she'd always found her funny and entertaining and interesting to be around. This evening was no different – at least, it had started that way.

'That new delivery guy...' Marina gave a theatrical shiver. 'He does something to me that I'm far too old for.'

Jill laughed. 'Honestly! I can't leave you alone for a minute! What would Bob say?'

'I've told Bob he's got competition!' Marina blew a stray hair from her face. She had it wound into a snow-white bun today that accentuated her high cheekbones. She often joked that she didn't know where they'd come from, only that she had to have some Viking in her somewhere. 'He knows anyway – caught me the other day, checking out the delivery man's bum when he dropped some boxes of nails and had to bend over to pick them up. I told Bob if I'd known I was going to get such a gorgeous view, I'd have kicked a whole crate of nails all over the floor and got him to collect them up for me.'

'What did Bob say to that?' Ava asked.

'He said if the guy would have me, he was welcome to try being married to me; it would save him a job.'

Ava giggled and reached for the wine bottle to fill her glass. 'Poor Bob.'

'It's a shame,' Marina agreed. 'I do wear the poor man out. But he knew what he was getting when he asked me to marry him so he can hardly blame anyone else now.'

'So do I need to come to the store and see this delivery man for myself?' Ava asked. 'If he's that good-looking maybe I ought to. I'm not sure what's happening, but we seem to be blessed with good-looking guys in Port Promise right now.'

'Oh yes, that Cormac is quite easy on the eye,' Marina said, smacking her lips.

Ava snorted and Jill burst out laughing.

'Marina! Don't let Bob hear you say that!'

Marina rolled her eyes. 'Like he hasn't seen me looking! Who wouldn't be looking at that man-cake? I bet even Bob looks!'

Ava laughed again, but then, through her laughter, she glanced at her mum and saw that she suddenly had that same melancholic expression she wore often these days, and knew that she must have been thinking about her own husband and about how she was now alone.

'I think we should light that candle,' she said in a bid to change the subject. 'Be nice now it's going a bit dark, and it will keep the bugs from the patio.'

'That's citronella,' Jill said vaguely.

'Oh. Won't eucalyptus do the same?'

Jill's gaze was on the garden and she didn't reply.

'Mum?'

Marina snapped her fingers in front of Jill's face, bringing her back to them rather more abruptly than Ava thought was necessary. But it seemed to do the trick. Jill forced a smile.

'Of course, let's light the candle. I bet it smells lovely.'

Ava went into the house to get it from the kitchen table where her mum had left it. When she returned, Marina was telling Jill about business and how they were thinking of branching out, turning the hardware store that had been in Port Promise for the past forty years into more of a gift shop for the tourists, which was the reason they'd been getting deliveries of more tourist-friendly goods like the candle she'd brought round. Then she turned to Ava as she placed it on the patio table and lit it, and dropped the bombshell.

'So what's this about you volunteering for the crew?'

Ava's head snapped up. 'What?'

'Isn't that right? It's what I heard.'

'The boat crew?' Jill asked sharply.

Ava's stomach dropped. She'd known she'd have to tell her mum, of course, but she would never have wanted to tell her like this. 'I've only thought about it,' she lied, because now wasn't the time to discuss it, and if she told the truth, her mum would never let it go, no matter whose company they were in.

'Not what I heard,' Marina said. 'I heard you'd already signed up.'

Jill almost knocked her glass over as she spun to face Ava. 'What?'

'You've sent in your application, haven't you?' Marina said. 'I think it's marvellous. I think your dad would be very proud.'

'Well he's not here to think anything!' Jill snapped. 'We'll never know if he's proud or not because he'd dead, lost somewhere out there in the ocean because of that stupid boat!'

'He died doing what he loved,' Marina said serenely, seeming not to have noticed Jill's newly agitated state. Or maybe she'd simply chosen not to react to it.

'He died doing the thing this ridiculous village had drummed into him he was supposed to do because he'd been born a Morrow! You think he loved it? You didn't see the times he came back from a shout, eyes glazed over, exhausted, trauma-tised because he nearly didn't save someone, devastated when he'd absolutely failed, angry at the stupidity of some and despairing of others' bad luck. And there were the nights where he knew he'd have to get up after two hours in bed where he couldn't sleep and go to his proper job with all that hanging over him. He didn't love it then!'

'But, Mum,' Ava began, 'he wouldn't have done it for all those years if he didn't—'

'Don't you dare talk to me!' Jill told her. 'Don't tell me you think differently! It's selfish, that's what it is! It was selfish of him to leave me alone doing that stupid job, and now it's selfish of you to even think about following him into it! Didn't you think for one second how I'd feel if I lost you too?'

'Mum, it wasn't like that. I haven't even—'

'Don't lie to me, Ava. I'm not that stupid. I know it's true because I know *you*. I was afraid you might decide to do something like this, but I'd hoped to be wrong because I didn't want to believe you could be this cruel to me. Now I know my faith was misplaced. I was right – you *are* cruel.'

Ava looked hopelessly at Marina. *Thanks a lot.* But Marina still seemed oblivious to the trouble she'd caused. 'Who told you this?' she asked, deciding she didn't have an answer right now that would remotely placate her mum. In fact, she couldn't think of anything else to say but to discover who the architect of her fate had been. 'Killian? Clara?'

It had to be Clara. Only Clara and Killian knew, and Killian would have let things sit, hoping she'd change her mind and there would never be a need to concern himself with it. But surely not? Clara knew how important it was to Ava, and hadn't they discussed how upset their mum would be? Clara would surely know Ava needed to break this news to their mum. Killian could have told Gaby, Ava supposed, but if Gaby had found out her first port of call would have been a dressing-down for Ava herself, not gossiping to Marina about it.

'Maxine,' Marina said. 'She told me you were going to join the crew.'

Ava stared at her. She'd only told Clara and Killian outright, and, if she was being perfectly honest, she'd expected Clara to be the one who'd let it slip. But of course, the shore crew at the station would have had something from head office, some kind of heads-up about her application. She hadn't expected it to go through so soon, but there it was. The damage was done now, and Ava would just have to deal with the fallout.

'I'm sorry, Ava,' Marina said. 'I hadn't realised it was a secret – she didn't tell me not to mention it to anyone, so I thought she was telling me old news.'

Jill took her wine glass and tipped the contents down her throat before slamming it onto the table.

'I'm sorry, Marina, but I'm afraid we're going to have to cut this short. I need to talk to Ava. Maybe we can catch up next week?'

'Oh, right...' Finally, Marina seemed to realise something big was brewing. She finished her own wine and stood up. 'Of course. Call me when you've got some free time.' She mouthed an apology to Ava, not that it was worth much now.

'See you, Marina.'

'Yes, I'm sure you will,' Marina said, and if that wasn't a loaded statement Ava didn't know what was. Perhaps Marina expected Ava to go to the shop and wipe the floor with her at the first opportunity, but Ava had stopped blaming Marina already. What was the point? Her secret was out and it was hardly Marina's fault anyway. The fault lay with Ava herself. Perhaps if she'd sat her mum down and explained what she wanted to do in the first place there'd be none of this. But it was too late for that now; all she could do was try to salvage what she could from the wreckage and hope her relationship with her mum wasn't already permanently damaged.

They both stood up and Marina kissed each of them briefly

on the cheek. Then Jill opened the garden gate to let her out, and they stood in silence for a moment to give her enough time to get down the hill and out of earshot.

Jill rounded on Ava, landing the first blow. 'I can't believe you'd do this to me! After all we've been through this year!'

'I didn't mean to do anything to you; it wasn't like that.'

'Then what did you mean to do? Did you honestly think I'd be happy about this?'

'I thought you might have reservations, but—'

'*Reservations*? I don't recall dropping you on your head as a baby, Ava, but now I see I must have done. Reservations? You're damn right I have reservations and then some!'

'Let me explain—'

'I don't want explanations. I want to hear you say you'll withdraw your application.'

Ava paused. She held her mother in a searching gaze before she spoke again. 'Is that what you want?'

'Didn't I just say so?'

'Even if it's not what I want?'

'I want you safe. Is that too much to ask? Am I wrong for wanting my daughter to be safe?'

'No, but you can't keep me safe from everything, Mum.'

'I can bloody well try.'

'At the expense of any freedom to live my own life? To make my own choices? To be treated with respect as an adult? Is that what you want for me? Do you want to dictate everything I do? Because that's what you're trying to do right now.'

'Oh don't be so ridiculous! This is one thing! I ask so little of you, Ava, you can surely grant me this one thing when you know how much it means to me!'

'But you're asking me to give up something that means a lot to me too – as much as your thing means to you.'

'You couldn't possibly know how much this matters to me.'

'Believe me, I do. You don't think losing Dad hurt me as

much as it did you? You think I haven't considered the implications of joining the crew? That it hasn't crossed my mind at least once that I might end up dying like he did? Of course I have, but doing this means so much to me that it isn't enough to put me off.'

Jill's eyes misted and her reply cracked. 'And knowing what it would do to me isn't enough to put you off either? Do I mean so little to you?'

'Of course you don't!' Ava's own throat tightened. The tears would fall no matter how she might fight them, but she was going to do her best not to let emotions cloud her judgement or weaken her argument. 'You are the most important person in my life! You know that!'

'Then why would you put me through this?'

'I could ask you the same question. Isn't this about more than love? It's about faith and belief. Don't you have faith in me? Don't you believe I'm capable of this? I want more than just teaching people how to mess around on boards. I want more than... I want to matter. I want what I do to matter. I want to make a difference. Even if Dad hadn't drowned, even if he hadn't been born a Morrow, even if I hadn't I'd still want that. I feel like I don't know where my life is going right now or even what it means half the time, but I know that helping to save people, making a difference, could give me that meaning. I've always felt it, but it took a big event, horrible and sad as it is that we lost Dad, to show me what I couldn't figure out for myself. I've been coasting, Mum. I've been coasting along not feeling like the whole version of myself and not understanding why until now. I need this; I have to do it.'

Jill shook her head vehemently. 'I can't... I won't give you my blessing for something that would put you in danger – how could I? What kind of mother would I be?'

'The best kind. The kind who understands that sooner or

later your child needs to be her own person. I'm twenty-four, Mum. Don't you think that moment is long overdue?'

'I treat you like an adult. In every other respect you are your own woman. I'm not stupid – I understand that, and I've never tried to tell you how to live your life.'

'I didn't say you did.'

'No!'

Jill got up and went inside. Ava scrambled to follow.

'What does that mean?'

'You know full well what it means. It means no. I don't care how you try to sell this to me, I will never give you my blessing.'

'I don't need your blessing, Mum. I can still do it if I want to.'

'Then we're in trouble. I won't stand by and lose someone else I care about.'

'I don't know what that means either. It's my decision, Mum.'

'And it's my decision not to watch if I don't want to. Do what you must, but don't expect me to be your mother if you do.' Jill started to fold a teacloth that hadn't needed folding.

Ava stared at her. *'You're disowning me?'*

'If you choose to follow this path I don't see what else I can do.'

The pitch of Ava's voice rose. 'You can support me! You can choose to wish me well and be there for me!'

Jill swung to face her. 'I will never, ever support this, and nothing you say or do will change my mind. You do this and our relationship is forever broken. If you're going to break my heart, might as well get it over and done with at the start, because I refuse to mourn anyone else.'

'It's not set in stone that anyone who joins the boats will die. Hardly anyone ever does.'

'Your dad did! Hardly anyone and yet he did! The odds are

too great, Ava! While there is any possibility at all then the odds are too great for me! I can't do it!'

'And I can't not do it,' Ava replied quietly. 'Sorry, but there it is. I'm not trying to make you sad or scared, and I'm sorry you don't respect me enough to trust me to make my own decisions. But I'm an adult and you don't get to tell me what to do.'

Jill turned away and gripped the work surface. 'Then be an adult. Go and live your life, but leave me out of it.'

'Mum, I—'

'Go!'

Ava hesitated. She wasn't done here, not by a long shot, but realised that the best tactic right now might be to give her mum space to cool down. When they'd both slept on things and had time to think it through, maybe they'd communicate better.

'Right then.'

Grabbing her jacket from the back of the chair, Ava made her way out of the kitchen and left the house, shutting the door gently behind her.

As she walked down the hill and away from the childhood home that had held so many happy memories for her, feeling so wretched that she could hardly imagine the little girl who had once lived there at all, she burst into tears.

# CHAPTER EIGHT

Having a bust-up with her mum was one thing, but having it made public was quite another. Sooner or later, if things dragged on and they didn't resolve their issues, Ava supposed people in the village would find out. It was hard enough to keep a secret of any kind there, but the smallest signs of frostiness between her and her mum would quickly be noticed.

Still, as she walked the cobbled streets back to her caravan, Ava did her best to suck up the tears that had engulfed her as she'd left Seaspray Cottage. She'd tell anyone who needed to know in her own time, but right now was not the time. Besides, there might yet be nothing to tell. She'd give her mum some time and then she'd go again to talk to her, and maybe they could sort this out. After everything that had happened, the last thing she wanted was to be at odds with her mum – she'd already lost her dad, and both parents within six months was really too much, especially when it was entirely preventable.

Darkness had fallen over the village. There were many people still out, but mainly tourists out for an evening stroll. They milled around at the harbour wall where the tide crashed against the grey rock and the first stars winked above them, taking photos and admiring the strings of lanterns that hugged the line of the coast, stretching out in either direction.

Ava walked towards the sea. She didn't need to – in fact, the seafront was out of her way home – but hearing the waves and seeing the moonlight glint on their crests had always calmed her. She hoped they would do that now. She needed a calm, clear head to figure out what to do next.

It had crossed her mind to give up on the lifeboats – or at least on the seagoing crew. Despite what she'd told her mum, nothing was worth them being at odds in this way, and knowing her mum, she knew there would be no backing down on this.

Her steps took her past the harbour, where Robin's new boat was moored, currently in darkness, past the tiny office she worked from when she wasn't giving lessons on the sea, and out towards the cove where she often swam for fun and where Cormac's fish shack stood.

She was surprised, given the time of night, to find it still lit and Cormac serving food. The previous owner had never opened beyond six and he even made a fuss about doing that, closing early when he couldn't be bothered. Smoky flavours hung on the air, so Cormac was still cooking too. At the tables under the tarpaulin was a full house, and standing at the serving hatch of the shack was Harry, tucking into a paper cone filled with juicy pink shrimp, chatting with Cormac as he worked. Their laughter rang out into the night as they shared a joke. While it was good to see Harry looking relaxed and cheerful, she had no desire to stop and began to hurry away. But then they both looked up, and there was no way they'd failed to notice her, and despite her delicate emotional state, Ava knew she was going to have to acknowledge them.

'Hi, Cormac... Harry.' Ava looked at the former. 'You're open late.'

'New hours,' he said. 'Thought I ought to make the most of the trade in the summer months. It was actually your Clara who persuaded me the business was there, and she was right – full house practically all night so far.'

'It's one of the most complained-about things on Tripadvisor,' Ava replied.

'What? My lack of opening hours?' Cormac grinned and Ava tried her best to respond in the way he'd have been expecting, though it took superhuman effort.

'No, just the lack of late-opening restaurants. In fact, I can't think of anyone who opens past six; if you want a restaurant you have to go to the caravan park or outside Port Promise. Fine for most who want a quiet, self-catering type holiday, but people don't always read the reviews and I think they often arrive expecting something like St Ives rather than what we actually have here.'

'I must admit, how quiet it is was a surprise to me,' Cormac agreed. 'Not that I mind it. I think the vibe is just the right balance.'

Ava gave a tight smile. Throughout the exchange with Cormac, she'd felt Harry's eyes on her, and now he spoke.

'Hey... how's it going?'

'Good,' she said.

He looked thoughtful at her reply. In the glow from the interior of Cormac's shack she could see that as he munched on his supper, the cogs were going in his brain.

'You walking back to the caravan park?' he asked after a brief moment.

'Yes. But I'll be—'

'I'll walk with you,' he said. 'If you don't mind.'

Ava paused then gave a weak nod. If he'd chosen this moment to open up to her, despite it being her intention to persuade him, he'd chosen badly. But what else could she say? She didn't want to put him off – she'd have felt awful about that once she'd had time to think it over. And maybe listening to him would make her forget her own woes for a while.

'I'll catch you later,' he said to Cormac. 'Thanks for the food.'

'You're welcome,' Cormac said. 'Remember to leave a review – I need as many good ones as I can get. Need to get rid of all the shitty ones people left for my bloody lazy uncle!'

Harry chuckled. 'Will do, bud. See you around.'

'Yep. Goodnight, Ava.'

'Night, Cormac,' Ava smiled before turning to follow the line of the beach, Harry falling quickly into step with her. He was still holding his package of shrimp, popping them into his mouth as he went.

'You got Cormac to shell those,' she said vaguely, angling her head at them. 'His uncle would have told you to sod off.'

'I nipped round the back and did it before he cooked them. Can't be bothered with all that ripping bits off when they're burning your fingers. It also means I can walk along with you and finish my supper.'

'They smell good.'

Harry held out the package. 'Want one?'

'No, I'm good. I've eaten. But thanks.'

'More for me. So... don't think I'm poking where I'm not wanted, but is everything OK with you?'

'Of course. Why would you ask that?'

'Are you serious? I've known you long enough to see straight away something's not right. One look at your face and I knew it. It's fine; you don't have to tell me if it's personal, but if you need a sympathetic ear then mine is right here. Feel free to use it is all I'm saying. Might help you feel better to talk.'

'I could say the same to you,' Ava replied carefully, and in the light from the lamps that ran the length of the beach, she could see his expression darken a little.

'Maybe. But I think mine feels too big to talk about. And I'm not sure – no offence – you're the person to talk to.'

'I'd never judge – you know that.'

'I know. But still, it'd be weird, and I worry—' His sentence stopped and his gaze went to the horizon.

'Worry about what?' Ava pressed.

He shook his head. 'It doesn't matter.'

'Doesn't sound that way to me. I mean, same goes for you as you just told me. You don't have to share, but maybe it would help, and if you need a sympathetic ear, feel free to use mine.'

'Using my words against me, eh?'

'No, just reminding you that what's good for the goose is good for the gander.'

'What does that even mean?' He turned to her with a faint smile.

'I don't know. Mum says it. Stop trying to get me onto a different subject.'

'I'm not, I swear.'

'Hmm...'

They walked for a short while in silence. Ava was waiting for him to begin, but he didn't. Instead, he munched on his supper until the paper was empty, then he screwed it up and dropped it into the nearest rubbish bin. It was an entirely comfortable silence, the sort only two people who have known each other their whole lives could share, and even though Ava's mind was a swirl of questions – for herself and for him – she was content to let the air between them stay empty for the time being. Perhaps he was deciding how to frame his next sentence, as she was, or whether to share at all, as she was doing too.

Before either spoke again, the entrance gates of the caravan park were in sight.

'It's such a weird journey here,' Ava said finally.

'What do you mean?'

'Some nights it seems to take forever and sometimes I blink and I'm here. Funny that.'

'What was tonight?'

'I blinked and there are the gates. Must be the company.'

'Must be,' he agreed.

'Have you got anywhere to be?'

'Not especially. Why?'

Ava paused. When she'd left her mum's cottage she'd wanted nothing more than to be alone to cry. But now, in Harry's company, she felt ready to talk. Not necessarily about the conversation with her mum, but about anything that might take her mind off it. Harry's problems, if she could tease them out of him, would be a welcome distraction, but just about anything else would be too.

'I've got some nice cider in the fridge. Local company... what's their name again?'

Harry smiled. 'Oh yeah, I think I know that place. The owner's son's a bit of a dick but their cider's good.'

'No, I don't think he is.' Ava returned his smile with one of her own. It was hard not to. The one thing she'd always liked about him was his self-deprecating humour. Despite appearances, there was no toxic masculinity here, no arrogant alpha-male attitudes. He was humble and kind and mindful of how he spoke – that was what made him such a good friend and so popular in the village. She'd once told Clara that he'd been a spoiled teenager, but that wasn't true. She'd only said that to make herself feel better about the way she'd treated him back then. She'd never admit it, but she had many regrets about that. 'So, you've got time for one?'

'I could be persuaded.'

'Good. Come on then.'

Ava led the way through the gates and into the park. They passed the pristine holiday lodges, followed an overgrown path to the maintenance area where the units containing gardening, building and cleaning equipment were kept, and round to where some members of staff had their lodgings. These were older caravans that had been retired from holiday use but were still good as temporary homes. The plot was still pretty, but in a wilder way than the rest of the park. Here, brambles had been allowed to weave their thorny branches into a chain-link fence and scarlet poppies lined the paths, starred by the odd dandelion or clumps of oxeye daisies. Their petals were closed now that the sun had gone down, and a hush lay over the park despite the sporadic sounds of conversation or television noise from someone's home. Ava's own van was in darkness, apart from the solar lanterns that lit her decking.

'It's looking good now,' Harry said as they approached. 'Like the new decking. Are you finished renovating yet?'

'Not far off,' Ava replied, getting out her keys. 'A few bits to do here and there, but it's habitable now, and actually pretty comfy. When Clara first suggested it I thought it was going to be like living in a leaky tin can, but now I'm all set up I love it. Even if a house I could afford came on the market I'm not sure I'd move.'

'Wow, then you must really like it.'

'I do. What I especially love is that it's not in the centre of the village so I can hide when I want to avoid any drama.'

'When you put it that way, is there another one for sale that I can buy?'

'I'm sure you'd hate it.'

Harry followed her up the steps to the door. 'What makes you say that? You think I couldn't rough it?'

'Exactly! I think you'd want your creature comforts.'

'Well, I don't know whether I ought to be offended by that statement,' he replied with a low chuckle.

'Make yourself comfy,' Ava said, directing him to the chairs while she took off her jacket and trainers and went to the fridge.

'Want me to take my shoes off?'

'If you don't mind,' she said. 'Thanks.'

'Well, your flooring looks new, and I wouldn't want to be the one to ruin it with my mucky old boots.' He kicked them off and put them out onto the decking before coming back inside.

'Let's hope it doesn't rain,' Ava said. 'Because I'm pretty sure none of my shoes will fit you if yours fill up with water before you leave.'

'I'm more worried about getting a slug in there,' Harry said, sitting down. 'That's happened before and I wouldn't recommend treading on one.'

'Ugh...' Ava took two bottles from the fridge and popped the caps off them. 'God, I can imagine. Bring them back in if you like – they'll be fine by the door.'

'They'll be all right where they are for now,' Harry said. He accepted a bottle from Ava, who went to turn off the main light and brought a couple of solar lanterns in from outside before joining him.

Ava paused. Harry was staring at his bottle again. He seemed as if he'd momentarily lost himself in there.

'Harry, I'm sorry but I can't not say anything about this. I've tried to mind my own business and I've tried waiting for you to say something, but I can't. Everyone is saying you're really not OK. And I think they're right. You know you can talk to me, don't you?'

He looked up. 'This is about me coming off the boat crew and doing shore duties for a while? Of course I do, but there's nothing to tell. I just need a break until I get over... well, I just need time, but I'm OK.'

'And that's really all there is to say?'

'Yes.'

'I don't believe you.'

'Well I can't do anything about that.'

'Harry... talk to me, please. I know you, and I know you're not right.'

'How can I be right?'

His head flicked up and there was a new animation in his features, like he'd suddenly decided to throw caution to the wind.

'How can I be right?' he repeated. 'But how can I tell you of all people about it? How can I sit here with a straight face and tell you what's wrong?'

'So this is about my dad?'

'Of course it's about your dad! Every time I walk into that station I'm right back there, on that night, when everything's about to turn to shit and there's nothing I can do to stop it! I think about it all the time, every minute of every day. I wonder, what should I have done? Could I have saved him if I'd had the balls to speak up, to argue, to tell Jack he was making terrible calls? I should have said something but I didn't; I just stood there like a melon, nodding, a feeling in my gut that trouble was coming.'

Ava stared at him as he swung the bottle to his lips and drank. He didn't stop until he'd emptied it.

'I don't suppose you have another ten or so of these?'

'There's another in the fridge – help yourself.'

As he went to get himself a second drink, Ava's thoughts were everywhere, like leaves on the wind. She'd known her dad wasn't supposed to be on the boat that night – everyone knew he was meant to stay on dry land since he'd given up boat crew and taken over the management of the station. But what Harry was telling her now meant there was more, much more to the story than anyone in the family knew. But the people who'd been there – they knew. Killian knew, in fact, and he *was* family. Why had nobody said before?

'It wasn't your fault,' she said as he sat down again.

'That's what everyone says, so why does it feel as if it was? I can't sleep for thinking of what I should have done and said. Every time I close my eyes, I see your dad...' He took another swig of his cider. 'Your dad in the water. I wanted to go in after him. I wanted—'

'If you had, you might not have been here now.'

'But *he* might. I might have been able to save him.'

'You were following the rules – everyone knows that. Nobody is blaming you for this.'

'They should! I could have saved him. What good am I on the crew if I can't even save my crewmate? What's the use in me being there now? I've got to face it – I'm never going out to sea again. How can I when I can't...?'

'What?'

'My heart's thumping as soon as I step on board. I can barely see straight and my brain fogs up. I'm a mess, Ava. I don't know if I'll ever be able to go out there again.'

'Have you told anyone at the station about this?'

'Sort of. I told them I needed a few weeks.'

'But it's been months. Aren't they asking? Is nobody checking on you?'

'Of course they are, and I tell them I'll be all right – I just need time.'

'But you won't be! Ask for proper help – ask for a professional!'

'They've offered that but how can I take it? How will that make me look? I'm stuck. I don't want to be thrown off the crew, but at the same time I can't be a part of it.'

'Nobody would throw you off!'

'I can't risk it. If I say something like that, I'll be retired, sent to the bloody gift shop to work the tills on Saturdays or something. But even though I've been allowed to do shore duties, they're asking me about going back to the crew all the time – not pushing, of course, but they want to know. And soon they're going to be pushing for an answer even if they're not pushing me to go out, and what am I supposed to say? It's hopeless.'

'I'm sure nobody would push you for anything. Would it help to tell me exactly what happened that night?'

Harry shook his head. 'No, I can't. You'd wish you didn't know if I did tell you.'

'What happened, Harry? You can't give me that and no more!'

The tables had suddenly turned without Ava even noticing. This was no longer about helping Harry, even though she'd told him so, but about getting to some truth, something he was hinting at but keeping from her. This was about knowing what had happened to her dad that night. There were warnings, ringing in her brain, telling her that maybe knowing these things wouldn't be good, but she couldn't focus on them. There was one overriding drive now, one impulse too strong to ignore. She had to hear the truth, and Harry could give that to her if only he'd open up.

'Please, don't...' Harry said miserably. 'Please don't make me go back there. I can't...'

'Tell me what happened!'

He paused, the pain so obvious in his face that at any other time Ava would have crumbled. But she was too far in now and the obsession, the burning need to know had taken hold, and she didn't care that this was hurting her friend. She held his gaze with her own, demanding the truth that she so desperately needed.

'I'm sorry,' he said, putting down his drink and heading for the door. 'I'm sorry, Ava, I can't do this right now.'

Ava leaped up, but he'd already swept his boots into his arms and was running in his socks down the decking, down the steps and onto the path. In her own socks, Ava gave chase, but Harry was far taller and his long stride soon took him out of her reach.

'Harry!' she called. 'Harry, please... Harry, stop! I'm sorry! Come back!'

She pushed to run faster. She was fit, but she mostly swam and she hadn't run like this in a long time. It wasn't like moving through water; it was jarring, harder on the limbs, and she was soon out of breath. The previous year Harry had run the

London Marathon, and it showed. Soon he'd gone from her sight. Ava stopped on the path.

'Shit!' she panted.

It seemed she was making a habit of upsetting people she cared about today. What was meant to help her feel better about the argument with her mum had made her feel worse than ever. The lifeboats had featured prominently in every aspect of her life since her birth, but today it felt as if the lifeboats were responsible for everything that was wrong with it too.

# CHAPTER NINE

Ava checked her phone again. There were no replies from Harry, her mum or Clara, but there was a new message from Gaby. Ava had opened it but she hadn't answered it because her head was too full of other stuff to get into that particular argument right now. Plus, she had a class full of customers wanting specialist sea-swimming lessons in an hour, and she needed to have her wits about her to teach it, though, with such broken sleep, swimming was the last thing she wanted to do.

She dug her spoon into the bowl of porridge she'd made and slopped some into her mouth, forcing herself to eat what she didn't really want, knowing that she had to fuel up to face the physically active day ahead. But it was like glue as she swallowed it, and she gave up, letting the spoon fall into the bowl with a sigh. Perhaps she'd grab something on the way to the lesson from Betty's if she felt hungrier by then.

As she gulped down the rest of her tea, the phone sitting on the table next to her pinged the arrival of a new message. Gaby again. By now she was probably pissed off that Ava hadn't replied to the first one, and she'd never been famous for her patience at the best of times.

Ava opened it.

*Call me! I need to know what's going on!*

It was obvious without Gaby spelling anything out that their mum had either phoned or been to see her and had told her about the argument. Gaby would undoubtedly take their mum's side too, and she'd probably be more vehement about it than Jill. Killian was right about one thing – she'd never stand for another member of her family going out to sea on rescues, and she'd do anything in her power to stop it. Ava could argue her case and perhaps she'd even win – Gaby wasn't her boss after all – but could she take on the combined might of Gaby *and* her mum? Killian had that advantage at least: Jill would never try to tell him what to do because she wouldn't feel it was her place, so he only had Gaby to contend with. His argument for it had always stuck better too, that there were no more Morrow boys to take over from Jack, and so he was the closest thing, and in a strange way Ava felt there was an odd sort of pride for Gaby in that, despite her fundamental objections.

Wearily, Ava picked up her phone and typed a reply.

*Running late for work. Will speak to you later.*

Gaby wouldn't like being put off, but Ava needed time to think. She also needed time to think what she was going to say to Harry if he ever agreed to talk to her again after she'd upset him, and there was so much trying to get worked out in her brain that she felt like an overheating computer, like the kind you saw in old films where reams and reams of paper spewed from a clunky printer and smoke poured out of a wall-sized console before it finally blew up.

She waited to see if Gaby said anything else, but there was nothing, not even a lazy thumbs up, which probably meant she was mad. Ava came to this conclusion because she could see that Gaby had read the message.

But if Gaby was mad she'd just have to get in the queue.

With that thought, Ava went to grab her equipment for the morning session from the wardrobe.

The morning was overcast and there was a stiff breeze, which suited Ava's mood as she walked down to the cove. The waves would probably be a decent size, but in a way that was good. There would be nervous students, of course, but she could teach them more when the sea was a bit more challenging. When it was flat and calm, they might as well be in a swimming pool – at least that was Ava's view.

In the village, she passed the hardware store, not yet open for business, but then the front door opened and Marina rushed out to her.

'Ava!' she called.

'Oh, hi,' Ava replied in a dull voice. It wasn't Marina's fault, but she was the last person Ava wanted to see this morning.

'Hang on...' Marina hopped to get a slipper on, then yanked at the gate. She was still wearing her nightdress, hurriedly tying a dressing gown over it. 'I wanted to say sorry for last night. I hope I didn't make things too awkward.'

'You didn't do anything wrong,' Ava said. 'Don't worry about it.'

'But I did feel awful about it,' Marina said. 'I didn't realise Jill didn't know about your plans.'

'Honestly, it's not a problem and I don't hold any of it against you. Relax, Marina, there's nothing to apologise for. Mum would have found out sooner or later and she'd have reacted the same way.'

'Would she? I can't help thinking that the way she found out made things worse.'

'Even if it did, still wasn't your fault. You were only repeating what Maxine had told you, and, like you said, nobody had told you not to talk about it. How were you to know?'

'Well... thank you for being so understanding. So we're OK?'

'Of course we are.'

'And your mum is OK?'

'That I'm not so sure about. We're not really talking this morning but I imagine we'll work it out eventually.' Ava hoped her words weren't as empty as they felt right now.

Marina pulled her robe tighter around her. The wind teased strands of hair from her plait. 'Would you like me to talk to her? Might help if someone outside the family lent an ear... impartial party and all that.'

'I'm not sure it would, to be honest, but it's kind of you to offer. Thanks, Marina, but I think we need to sort it out ourselves.'

'Well, if I can help, you must let me know.'

'I will. Thanks.' Ava glanced down the road, then looked back at Marina. It seemed she'd said what she wanted to say, because she simply gave an awkward smile.

'I suppose you're on your way to work?'

'I am,' Ava said. 'I should probably get going.'

'Of course. I'm glad I caught you. Thank you for being so nice about what happened.'

Ava gave a tight smile of her own. She didn't see how she could have been anything else, at least not to Marina. 'I'll catch you later,' Ava said.

'I'm sure.'

Marina turned to go inside, holding on to her gown so the wind didn't blow it open. Ava didn't wait for the door to shut before heading on her way. She had plenty of time, but the sooner she could start work and have an excuse not to think about any of this, the better.

# CHAPTER TEN

With her morning lessons done, Ava decided to pop back to her caravan. She didn't much feel like getting lunch out and wanted just an hour to herself. And so she pulled a hoodie over her swimming costume and stamped her feet into a pair of trainers and set off. The sea was choppier now than it had been that morning, and many of her swimmers had found it quite challenging. She wondered vaguely whether it would even be safe to take people out for body-board sessions that afternoon, but it was a bit late in the day to be cancelling them. She'd figure some way around it, even if it meant keeping things low-key and not taking anyone out too far.

With such practicalities running through her mind, Ava stopped on the road home with an inward groan. Talking to Cormac at the open serving hatch of his shack was Harry. She was about to turn and sneak away when he looked up and noticed her.

'Hey, give me a minute,' he said to Cormac before jogging to meet her. 'I'm glad I've seen you,' he said to Ava. 'I wanted to talk to you about last night.'

'I'm glad too – I wanted to apologise.'

'I wanted to apologise as well. I was weird, and you were asking questions that you had every right to ask.'

'No, I had no right to ask them, and I was the one being weird. I should have realised it would be difficult for you to talk about that night – hell, you were telling me as much – and I shouldn't have pushed you. I'm really sorry.'

'So... we're good?'

From nowhere, she had the sudden impulse to throw her arms around him and she acted on it, pulling him into a fierce hug, fighting back tears. 'Of course we're good!' She buried her face in his shoulder for a moment, trying to compose herself, and it was a surprisingly good place to be.

When she pulled away, Harry looked surprised and confused, and perhaps a little wistful. He gave her a warm smile. 'Maybe we should fall out more often if that's how we make friends again.'

'God no!' Ava laughed, trying not to cry again. 'I hated it! I never want to fall out with you!'

'But, Ava...' Harry began, and he looked troubled once more. Not like he had the night before, but some traces of that same pain was there in his eyes. 'I think we do need to talk. I think I do owe you that. I can understand why you wanted to know more, and maybe it's not fair to keep that from you. Especially if you...'

'What?'

'You know, if you're thinking of going for the boat crew.'

'Oh God... who told you? Let me guess... Marina?'

'Betty actually.'

Ava nodded. She hadn't been wrong – the whole village probably knew by now. It wasn't helpful, but it was just another thing she was going to have to deal with.

'I'm guessing by your expression that it wasn't supposed to be common knowledge.'

'You know this place,' Ava said with a wry smile. 'Everything's common knowledge eventually.'

'I was about to order... want to grab some lunch with me? I'll buy.'

Ava hadn't planned to eat out again, but perhaps this was a good idea. Harry clearly needed to get something off his chest, and it might help her to feel better too – after all, there were few who understood her predicament and how the lifeboat service worked as well as he did. He might even be able to give her some pointers for her entrance tests.

'Go on,' Harry cajoled. 'I'd really like it.'

'Well, how about we go Dutch, then I'll say yes?'

'Sounds fair,' Harry said, smiling as he gestured for her to lead the way back to Cormac's shack.

After a brief chat with Cormac, they ordered. Harry had his favourite shrimp and a side of fries, while Ava had a smoked salmon sandwich with the trimmings. Then they sat to wait for their food at one of the tables under the awning at the side of the shack. Cormac had added some decorative touches since Ava's last visit: seashell displays and reclaimed bits of boat. It seemed as if he was putting his all into this business, and Ava was glad to see it. Cormac was already becoming a popular figure in the community so it was good to see he seemed set on staying.

Ava studied Harry for a moment. He'd always worn his hair close and short, but it seemed to be growing out a little and it softened his features. His skin was tanned – as hers always was during the summer months – from spending so much of his time outside. She wondered if he'd lost weight – he was still well built and it was obvious he was keeping up with the workout routine he needed to stay fit for the boats, but she couldn't help but feel there seemed less of him somehow. She thought about his self-deprecating comment and wasn't sure if that was true – at least not right now. Despite what had gone on between them and what still needed to be discussed, she felt comfortable in his company. They'd spoken about it, got their apologies out, and they understood that it was unfinished business but that was fine, because they both seemed to see it the same way.

They both looked up as Cormac came over with their lunches. 'Makes a change for you to be hanging around,' he said to Harry. 'Usually it's: "Stick it in some paper and I'll be off." I suppose it's all those jobs you have.'

'That would be my fault,' Ava said. 'I've got some time to kill so I persuaded Harry to slow down for five seconds to sit with me.'

'Actually...' Cormac put their meals down and then sat at the table with them. Ava exchanged a faintly confused look with Harry. 'While I've got the both of you here, I wanted to ask something.'

'OK,' Harry said uncertainly.

'There's no point in beating about the bush,' Cormac said. 'I was thinking I might volunteer.'

'For the lifeboats?' Ava asked.

'Sure,' Cormac said. 'Here I am, an able-bodied man, fairly fit, fairly young, and I know they're one or two short down there...'

Harry winced but said nothing to correct him.

'... and I think it would be a good way to ingratiate myself with the local community, you know?' Cormac continued. 'So what do you reckon? Think I might be what they're looking for? And do you think I could fit it in? I have this place to run and that has to be my priority, but I'm not always here.'

'You're here a lot, though,' Ava said. 'You'd have to take time off for initial training. And a shout could come in at any time of the day or night – could you do that?'

'Well, I was talking to your sister about that,' he said.

'My sister?' Ava repeated.

'Aye, Clara. She said she'd be able to help me there – trained in catering, isn't she?'

'But she has a job at the caravan park.'

'Yes, but she said if she knew when I might be training she'd get time off to work here for me. As for the rest... well, I'm not on the crew yet. I'll cross that bridge when I come to it.'

'You could stipulate when you're free,' Harry said. 'I mean, we all tend to run to any shout no matter what, but that's only because we can. If you're not able to – like it would mean leaving the shack unattended – then I'm sure Vas will be fine with that. He wouldn't expect you to answer the page if you can't.'

'I think,' Ava said slowly, 'that if you can find a way to make it work it's a brilliant idea. You're right, Port Promise does need men like you, and we'd be happy to have you on the boats.'

'It needs *people*, not just men,' Harry corrected.

Ava gave him a grateful look.

'I mean, I know it must be painful for you to think about,' Cormac continued to Ava, 'what with your da being lost at sea. I didn't know him, but I heard he was a hell of a fella.'

'He was,' Harry said, and Ava could have sworn there was a lump in his throat as he did. 'One in a million.'

'And I'm sure I could never live up to that, but I'd like to do my bit,' Cormac continued. 'So, you think I should give it a go?'

'I think you'd be amazing,' Ava said.

Cormac looked at Harry. 'You reckon you could put a word in for me?'

'I wouldn't need to,' Harry said. 'If you go down to the station and talk to them, I'm sure they'd be snapping your hand off.'

Cormac smiled. He stood up. 'Well, thanks for the chat. I'll give it some more thought, maybe do some research.'

'That sounds sensible,' Harry said. 'Not like me, who

decided at the age of eight that I was going on the boats with no
clue what it might be like. I didn't bother to find out either.'

Cormac looked grave now. Maybe he knew Harry's story,
but he didn't say so if he did. He surely knew, however, that
Harry had been aboard the boat the night Ava's dad had
drowned. 'Aye, I suppose there are some lessons that are cruel to
learn.'

Ava looked across at the hatch of the fish shack, and
Cormac followed her gaze to see that he had a customer
waiting.

'Enjoy your food,' he said, before leaving them to go and
take their order.

'I really like him,' Ava said as they watched him go. 'Such a
nice guy.'

'He's pretty cool,' Harry agreed. 'Also the kind of guy who
could give a boy like me an inferiority complex.'

'Don't be daft,' Ava said. 'You're pretty cool too.'

Harry turned to her with a bemused smile. 'You know, I
think that might be the first time in twenty-four years you've
ever given me a compliment.'

'I'm sure you're exaggerating.'

'I'm sure I'm not.'

'Well, then I suppose you must have been a loser before.'

Harry's smile faded and his gaze dropped to his plate.

'I don't really think that,' Ava said gently.

Harry looked up again. 'Thanks. How come I feel like it? I
hear Cormac volunteering to go on the boats, you're volunteering... I can't even look at the bloody thing without having a
panic attack.'

'Cut yourself some slack, Harry. What you went through
that night... it would affect anyone.'

'Not Killian.'

'We went through this. Killian is better at bottling stuff up,
but that doesn't make it a healthy way to deal with it. You need

to get professional help. Even if you never go back on the boats you need to get this sorted or it will eat you from the inside out.'

Harry nodded. 'I know. It's just hard to admit I need help.'

'You're admitting it to me – that's the first step right there and you never even noticed you'd taken it. If you look at it that way, it has to be easier from here. If you can talk to me about it then you can talk to someone who's trained to help. If you don't want Killian to know, then talk to Vas; he's a good guy and he'll keep your secret for you. Ask him to arrange someone through the lifeboat service; I know they have people. Dad went once, you know.'

Harry's head shot up from where he'd been picking at his fries. 'Jack did?'

Ava nodded. 'It's normal. It's nothing to be ashamed of to be affected by something that happened on a rescue. For all his: "I'm Jack Morrow, I was born to do this", Dad knew that as well as anyone. You'd have to be a robot to be untouched.'

'Or Killian.'

Ava smiled. 'Or Killian.'

'I will,' Harry said. 'I'll sort something out, I promise.'

'You don't need to promise me anything. That promise is one you owe yourself. You don't deserve to suffer and you don't need to, especially when there's help out there.'

'I know, you're right. So...' He picked up a shrimp and frowned at it. 'Looks like I'll have to peel these ones at the table.'

'Well, I don't suppose Cormac had any warning that you wanted it cooked without the shell today. And at least you can sit down while you're doing it.'

'True. And while we're talking about help, you've done your best for me, so now it's my turn to help you if I can.'

'Oh, I'm fine.'

Harry raised his eyebrows at her.

'OK, I'm not fine but it's nothing anyone can sort but me.'

'Would it help to talk about it?'

'I'm not sure it would. Thanks for asking though.'

'It's what friends do, isn't it? After all, you just did that for me.'

'I suppose I did. I suppose you're right.'

Ava picked up one of her sandwiches. It was full to bursting with wood-smoked salmon, salad and lemon mayonnaise, and half the filling tumbled out and onto her plate. 'I don't know how Cormac makes a profit because I'm sure he gives everyone far too much food.'

'I think it might just be his favourite people,' Harry said with a smile. 'But don't tell the others that.'

'Aww, so I'm one of his favourites?'

'I think so.'

'Or...' Ava gave a mischievous grin, 'he thinks I'm a way to get into Clara's good books.'

Harry bit back a grin of his own. 'Poor Cormac. Gets here and the girl of his dreams is already spoken for. That's rough.'

'It is,' Ava agreed. 'But sometimes that's life.'

'Bad timing. Don't I know it,' Harry said. 'Story of my life too.'

Ava laughed. 'How do you know it? You have no trouble getting girls – you've always got someone on the go. The only thing I don't understand is how you get them in the first place.'

'There you go again, insulting me. I knew the compliment earlier was a blip.'

'Can't have you getting big-headed, can we?'

'No danger of that when you're around.'

Ava took a bite of her sandwich. 'I tell you one thing, whoever marries Cormac is one lucky girl. Imagine eating like this all the time.'

'I bet he doesn't cook at home. I bet he just opens tins of beans.'

'What, like builders don't like working on their own houses?'

'Exactly.'

'Still, I think he's a catch for someone.'

'Hmm...' It was Harry's turn to sit back in his seat and regard her carefully. 'You haven't asked me what I think yet.'

'About what?'

'About you joining the seagoing crew.'

'OK, what do you think?'

'I think if it means that much to you, go for it.'

'You're only saying that because you think it's unlikely to happen.'

'That's not insulting at all. I don't think that; I think it's very likely.'

'You know what I mean. It's easy to say it. Would you want to work alongside me on the crew? And be honest.'

'Yes. I'd work alongside you. I've seen you taking those numpties out on their boards. If you can keep that lot safe in the water, you can do anything.'

Ava smiled. 'Thanks. That actually means a lot to me. It doesn't necessarily help my predicament, but it does make me feel better.'

From her pocket, Ava's phone began to ring. She took it out, frowned at the screen and then put it face down on the table.

'Aren't you going to get that?' Harry asked.

'No, it's Gaby.'

'All the more reason to get it?'

'All the more reason to ignore it. She wants to shout at me. I'm not sure I'm in the mood for any more shouting right now.'

Harry began to laugh softly, but then his face dropped as he stared at a spot past Ava's shoulder.

'Um... you might not be able to ignore Gaby after all.'

He nodded at where he was looking, and Ava swung around in her seat to see a furious Gaby walking towards them, phone at her ear.

'Ignore my call, would you?' she snapped as she got to the table. 'Hey, Harry.'

'Gaby...' Harry said, before putting his face down to look as small as possible while he ate his lunch.

Ava wished she could do the same. She looked up at her sister. 'I was going to phone you back after we'd finished eating.'

'Really?'

'Yes really.'

'Well can you hurry it along? We need to talk.'

'I've already arranged to have lunch with Harry now; can't it wait?'

'Don't mind me,' Harry said, with the faintest look of reproach at Ava's throwing him under the proverbial bus. 'We can catch up any time if you need to talk to Gaby. In fact, I can ask Cormac to put this in a takeout container if—'

'No!' Ava said firmly. 'If Gaby wants me, she can wait.'

It was obvious Gaby was about to give Ava a mouthful when Cormac came over.

'Oh, hey, Gaby. How's your family? Were you wanting to order something?'

'Um...' Gaby was suddenly flustered, which gave Ava a certain satisfaction to see. She could be as rude as she liked to Ava, even a little bit to Harry, but she couldn't bring herself to be rude to someone like Cormac, who was a relative newcomer to the village and so didn't know her like everyone else did. If there was one thing old strait-laced Gaby liked better than a rant of righteous indignation it was to give a good impression. 'I'm actually fine, thanks, Cormac. I just needed to have a word with Ava.'

'Could I perhaps get you a drink then while she eats?' Cormac asked. 'On the house. And actually, while you're here, could I get your opinion on something I've been thinking about?'

Harry looked at Ava and she returned it, not quite knowing

what to think. Cormac was probably going to ask her opinion on his plan to volunteer for the boats, and who knew how she'd react to that, given her current agitation and that the boats were mainly the reason for it. One thing Ava could be sure of – the next few minutes weren't going to be dull.

'Um... sure...' Gaby sat down.

'What'll it be then?' Cormac asked.

'Just a glass of water, thanks.'

'I can do you a cola.'

'Water's perfect, honestly.'

While Cormac was getting Gaby's drink, Harry was wolfing down his lunch at a speed usually the preserve of astrophysics. A few moments later his cutlery clattered onto his plate and he stood up.

'Have to be back at the... you know... got to help my dad. Good to see you both...'

'Bye, Harry,' Ava said with a knowing smile. He didn't want to be there when the fireworks started, and she could hardly blame him for that. 'Thanks for the chat.'

'You too,' Harry said. 'See you later, Gaby.'

'Yep, see you, Harry.'

As Harry left, Cormac returned with Gaby's water.

'Thank you,' she said as he sat at their table again. 'So what is it I can help with?'

Ava shoved the last of her sandwich in her mouth and stood up. 'So, I'll leave you two to chat.'

Gaby glared at her. 'You're going?'

'Yep, got to get back to work, got a class arriving. Sorry, sis. See you, Cormac.'

She was laughing to herself as she walked away, imagining the look on Gaby's face. She'd have to have that conversation sooner or later, and it would almost certainly be one where Gaby wiped the floor with her about upsetting their mum; Ava could almost predict word for word how it would go. But that was a conversation she wasn't ready to have right now. She'd have felt sorry for leaving Cormac with her, only she knew Gaby would never be rude to him.

As she walked back to the cove and to the office to get ready for the next class, she thought about what Harry had said. His insistence that he'd serve alongside her without hesitation, and that he'd trust her, felt like a good sign.

# CHAPTER ELEVEN

*Fancy a night out? From what I've heard sounds like you need one and I definitely do!*

Ava read Clara's message, her forehead wrinkled into a vague frown.

*Does it mean travelling? Only I've got an early start.*

She did have an early start – that was no lie – but she was also exhausted, the kind of emotional exhaustion that only a slump in front of the TV with a stiff drink would fix.

*Not far. Just the beach. There's a barbecue on. Maybe someone will bring a guitar or something. I think Harry's going to be there...*

Ava put her phone on the kitchen counter and went to the fridge to get some water. She'd not long finished work – later than usual because she'd had a pile of admin to do afterwards, and the sea had been as rough as she'd suspected – not so rough to call off the class, but rough enough to make everything harder on her limbs.

She wasn't sure why Clara felt the need to mention that Harry would be going. *She might as well* have ended *the text with* an eggplant *emoji and* be *done with it...*

Her phone pinged again as she kicked the fridge door shut, still trying to decide if she could be bothered with the beach barbecue or not. She went over to the counter to see this one was from Gaby.

> *Don't forget I need to talk to you. I'm coming over as soon as I've fed the kids.*

> *Sorry, won't be in, got plans. Another time?*

She couldn't escape Gaby forever, but that wasn't going to stop her from trying. Maybe an evening on the sand chomping on burgers wasn't such a bad idea after all. Then the phone rang. Ava stared at Gaby's photo on the caller ID – smiling at some family picnic or other. The woman at the other end of this call almost certainly wasn't smiling right now.

Ava let out a sigh. Might as well get it over with. She took the call and put it on speaker.

'Hi, Gaby. What's up?'

'What's going on with Mum?'

'I'm sure you already know that or you wouldn't be ringing to tear a strip off me.'

'She says you're joining the lifeboat crew.'

'I'm applying – there's a difference. Doesn't mean I'll get in.'

'Of course you will! You're exactly what they need. The question is: have you gone completely mad?'

'I don't think so. Nobody's mentioned anything weird I'm doing to me.'

'You think you're so funny. Mum's out of her mind about this!'

'She told me to get out. She said she didn't want to see me again.'

'She's scared! She's already mourned her husband – she doesn't want to go through something like that again. I don't think she could – it would finish her. Surely you know that? Or are you that self-absorbed?'

'I get it. But, self-absorbed or not, I have to do what's right for me. I want to live my life, not the one my mum or you or anyone else wants for me.'

There was a sharp silence on the line. Then Gaby spoke again. 'So you're willing to fall out with Mum on this scale, just so you can live this life you think you want?'

'I don't *think* I want it; I know it's what I'm meant to do.'

'Since when?'

'Since I realised it. At the memorial. I had a moment; I just knew. What does it matter?'

'It matters because it all seems a bit sudden to me. Typical Ava, doing things on impulse.'

'I never do things on impulse – you know that! If anything, I overthink every bloody thing. Maybe a bit of impulse is what I need.'

'*What you need* is to speak to Mum. She's devastated by this.'

'I will.'

'When?'

'When she's calmed down.'

'Ava.' Gaby's tone was growing more and more impatient with every second on the line. 'She's never going to calm down unless you tell her you've changed your mind.'

'I'm not going to change my mind.'

'So... what? I've got to live the rest of my life tiptoeing

around between my sister and my mum because they can't get along? Is that fair to me or Clara?'

'Clara understands.'

'Doesn't mean she wants to see one or the other of you but is never able to see you both in the same room again.'

'Mum will come round – it won't be like that for long.'

'She won't!'

Ava leaned her head on the worktop and closed her eyes. Was she asking for the world? Wasn't she trying to do a good thing? Anyone would think she'd kidnapped a whole bunch of puppies to make a coat, not volunteered to save lives.

'Ava...'

Ava lifted her head. 'Yeah, I'm still here. I just don't know what you want me to say.'

'Say you'll fix this.'

'I'll fix this.'

'And mean it!'

'I do... I do, honest. I just don't know how.'

'It's easy.'

'I know, I tell her I'm not volunteering for the boats after all. I don't want to do that, though.'

'I don't care if you want to or not, you have to. Unless you're going to tear what's left of this family apart, you're going to have to give in just this once.'

'Feels like I'm always giving in.'

'Oh, don't be so spoiled, Ava! You're worse than Eli and Fern!'

'That's not fair.'

'What's not fair is you putting Mum through this. Killian told me you'd talked to him about it too.'

'So I suppose he got it in the neck for not telling you.'

'No, I know why he didn't tell me, because he thought he'd talked some sense into you and there'd be nothing to tell. Sign he doesn't know you like we do if he thought you'd ever listen to reason.'

Ava picked up the bottle of water she'd taken from the fridge and opened it. 'I'll talk to Mum,' she said. 'At least I'll try, but I can't promise anything.'

'What does that mean?'

'It means I can't say how it's going to go. If she's as angry as you say, even my apology won't be enough.'

'But you're not only going to apologise, are you? You're going to put it right.'

'I haven't decided yet,' Ava said stubbornly. The more Gaby pushed, the less she wanted to comply. It wasn't her fault; it was just the way she'd been built. She knew that maybe she'd have to give in eventually, but it wasn't going to be down to this conversation with her sister. She'd decide if that was going to happen, nobody else.

'Please, Ava...'

Ava looked sharply at her phone. Gaby suddenly sounded desperate, and that wasn't what she'd expected at all. Her sister was an all-guns-blazing sort of problem solver, the unelected and unofficial but undisputed boss of the family, and she knew it. She told people to jump and they asked how high. When she spoke, everyone listened. It annoyed the hell out of Ava, but that didn't mean she was immune to Gaby's influence. So to hear her asking, almost begging now...

'Please,' Gaby repeated. 'I just want everything to go back to normal. The last few months have been hard enough without this. Please talk to Mum and fix it – I don't care how you do it, but please do it. She's beside herself, and you know she's as stubborn as you are and she's not going to back down. I know you don't want to, but could you take one for the team, just this once? Killian will put a word in at the station – you can have any other job you want.'

Ava put the bottle down and ran a hand through her hair. It

was still tangled from the sea and would need a good dollop of conditioner, though that thought was vague as it floated through her consciousness.

'I'll try,' she said.

'You'll go and see her tonight?'

'I can't because I don't know what I'm going to say yet. And I'm supposed to be going out with Clara.'

'You can't leave it another day.'

'I'll message her tonight to go round tomorrow. By then I'll have it figured out.'

'Right,' Gaby said, though Ava could tell she wanted to argue with the plan. 'And you'll let me know?'

'I'm sure Mum will do that.'

'But I want to hear from you. I don't want one side of the story – I need both.'

'Fine, I'll speak to you when I've spoken to her.'

'Right.'

There was a pause.

'Where are you going with Clara?' Gaby asked.

'Oh, just a drink. Some random get-together on the beach... not sure who'll be there.'

'Good. Sounds like fun,' she replied vaguely.

'You could come,' Ava said. 'It's not an exclusive thing or anything.'

'Can't,' Gaby said. 'Killian might get called out and I don't want to ask Mum to have the kids tonight, not in the current circumstances.'

Ava chewed on her lip for a moment. Gaby actually sounded sorry that she hadn't been able to come, which made Ava feel guilty that they hadn't asked her in the first place. Although it had been Clara's idea, so Ava really had nothing to feel guilty about. Perhaps it was only a general sort of guilt for... well, more or less everything right now.

'What if I could sort things out with Mum tonight and she'd have the kids for you?'

'It's all a bit short notice, isn't it? You go with Clara; I'll do something with you two another time.'

'OK, if you're sure.'

'Yes. Speak to you tomorrow then?'

'Yes. Bye, Gaby.'

'Bye.'

Ava ended the call and reached for her water, staring thoughtfully at the darkened screen of her phone the whole time. Maybe she ought to see her mum before she went out to meet Clara. If Jill was as distraught as Gaby said, then it was cruel to leave it another day.


Jill wasn't answering her phone or picking up messages, but Ava decided to go to the cottage anyway. Her mum was often in the garden and her phone in the house, so it wasn't unusual for her not to respond, and Ava needed to do this before she met Clara. When she got there she knocked, and, getting no response, let herself in with the spare key to find the house and the garden both empty.

So much for sorting things out quickly.

Closing the door behind her, she stepped back out into an evening that threatened rain. Nothing torrential, but the sky was dull and the air was damp and salty, and there'd be some drizzle before the night was out. It was still warm – warmer, in fact, than it had been when she'd been teaching earlier that day, and the sea had calmed.

Ava took the path that would lead her to the harbour wall and along the line of the bay back to her caravan, dialling Clara as she did.

'Hey, Mum's not in. She's not with you, is she?'

'No,' Clara said. 'I haven't seen her. Have you checked with Gaby?'

'Gaby would have let me know if Mum was there, considering it was her idea for me to see her. I suppose it's just going to have to wait until tomorrow after all. If she turns up there in the meantime will you let me know? I'm going to walk through town to see if I can catch her, but otherwise I'll make my way to yours.'

'OK. See you shortly.'

'Yep.'

Ava ended the call and put the phone in her jeans pocket. She wasn't unduly worried – her mum would probably be at Marina's house, bending her ear, and it didn't take a genius to figure out what – or who – the main topic of conversation would be.

# CHAPTER TWELVE

The thing about Harry's dad, or so Ava had always thought, was that he looked as if someone had made a paper copy of Harry, scrunched it up and then smoothed it out again. He looked exactly like Harry, only very wrinkly. She'd once told Harry that, and he'd laughed and told her it was a good indication for anyone who wanted to marry him of what he'd look like in forty years, and that it would probably put them off.

That exact thought crossed her mind again as she watched him walk across the sand towards them.

'Hello you lot!' he said, beaming. 'Have you been conned by the promise of a barbecue too?'

Ava smiled. She, Clara and Logan had arrived at the allotted space on the beach to find there was no barbecue. Logan had insisted that he'd heard it right from the customer in the gallery that day, but that hadn't stopped Clara and Ava from taking the royal rip out of him. They hadn't let it spoil their evening, though. Clara had grabbed some bottles of wine and cups from the flat and they were busy drinking those now, Ava insisting that she didn't care about food because they could get far drunker far quicker without a silly barbecue. Down the beach there was a group of young people playing chart music from a portable speaker. They'd got a fire going and were toasting marshmallows on it, and despite Ava saying she didn't want food, the smell wafting over was pretty incredible.

'Sandy!' Clara and Ava both leaped up to furnish him with hugs.

'Didn't know you were coming tonight!' Clara said.

'Well, Harry mentioned it. Said he'd meet me here. Don't suppose you've seen him?'

'No, but we haven't been here long. Maybe he came down and went again, thinking there was nobody he knew down here,' Ava put in. 'Who told you two about a barbecue?'

'Well, Harry told me,' Sandy said.

'And I told Harry,' Logan added sheepishly.

Ava sat on the sand again laughing and patted it for Sandy to join them. 'Never mind,' she said. 'We've got booze at least. And we can always run to Salty's for a takeaway if we get hungry.'

'I could get some chips for us now,' Sandy offered.

'I *could* eat...' Clara replied. 'And it might be a good idea to go now before they get too busy...'

'I'll come with you,' Logan said to Sandy. He looked at Ava and Clara. 'So do you both want something?'

'Just chips for me,' Clara said. 'Lots of vinegar... tell Salty they're for me and he'll know how much.'

'I'll have the same,' Ava said. 'Not so much of the vinegar. And maybe I'll have some scampi too... And maybe a pickle on the side...'

Clara laughed. 'Want half a cow with that?'

'Hey!' Ava stuck her tongue out. 'I've had a busy day!'

'Right...' Sandy turned to go. 'If Harry comes, tell him where we are, and if he wants something he'll have to text me.'

'Will do!' Ava called back. She turned her attention to the party further down the beach. They didn't look like locals – at least, she didn't recognise anyone. 'Maybe if we get drunk enough we could go and crash that party,' she said. 'Looks like fun.'

'It does,' Clara said. 'Though things like that have started to make me feel old.'

Ava turned to her. 'Seriously? You're not exactly retired yet!'

'Yeah, I know. But you wait until you're twenty-seven and you'll see what I mean.'

Ava leaned back on her elbows and let the breeze lift her hair as she watched the group going back and forth, some teasing each other, some lounging on the sand as they ate, some toasting mallows over the fire, some kissing while others splashed about in the waves.

A few minutes later, Clara nudged her and pointed to a spot a few feet away, where Harry's dad was making his way over the sand. Arms full of parcels of food, he was being accosted by a trio of girls. Presumably they were asking him where he'd got the chips, as he was pointing back to the promenade and doing his best to direct them. Then he pointed to their group, started to wiggle his hips as if dancing, and they laughed. They beckoned him to join them, and though he shook his head, he pretended to dance again.

Ava giggled to herself as he then handed his parcels to Logan and started to boogie, and the girls laughed even harder.

He really didn't care how daft he looked. It was kind of lovely, and made Ava feel strangely emotional. Sandy always lived his best life, which was perhaps the only kind of life anyone ought to live, but it also made her think of her own mum, who was trying to do that while rebuilding what was left of it now she was a widow. She'd been that happy and carefree once, with Ava's dad at her side. She'd always loved her life while he'd been a part of it.

Ava had understood that losing him had been like losing a part of her soul, and here she was, ready to take another part, just to satisfy some silly itch, to honour some family legacy that her dad had never asked her to honour. If her dad was here now, what would he say? What would he want her to do? Ava thought she knew, even if she didn't want to acknowledge it. He'd probably ask her to take care of her mum, whatever that meant, no matter how hard it got. He'd ask her to do that for him and Ava would say yes, because she'd do anything for him.

Ava laughed and also cried a little, and she didn't know which one she wanted to do most.

Logan was making his way over when her attention was caught by someone striding over the sand to where Sandy was chatting to the girls. By now they'd dragged him across to their campfire and were introducing him to the others. Harry had seen his dad, but apparently not anyone else, and was now going over, either to rescue him or join him, and Ava quickly decided that, even if Sandy didn't know it, he probably needed rescuing. She wondered whether to try to catch Harry's attention but figured Sandy would be back soon enough for his chips and would bring Harry with him, so she settled down to wait. After their recent soul-baring chat, she needed to know that he was OK, so it was good to see him arrive looking well.

After a couple of minutes of Sandy introducing him to the others, Ava watched as a redhead nudged him and offered her beer. He smiled down at her and shook his head. They talked some more, and there seemed to be a lot of laughter. The redhead got out her phone and waved it at him. He took the phone and typed on it.

Ava held back a frown. He was giving her his number.

'Sandy's got a new crew,' Logan said, laughing as he joined them.

'I'm going to see if Harry wants chips,' Ava said tersely, pushing herself up and striding across the sand.

'Hey, Harry!' she shouted as she made her way over. He looked up from his conversation.

'We've got chips – want some?'

'Um, yeah... that would be good.' Harry nodded uncertainly. The girl who'd been talking to him gave Ava a once-over and moved away.

'They've asked us to join their party,' Sandy said, laughing. 'I'm a bit too old for that sort of thing, but—'

'You're never too old!' a black-haired girl said, grinning. She looked at Ava. 'You could all come over if you like.'

'No thank you,' Ava said.

Harry stared at her. 'What's this? Ava Morrow turning down a party?'

'It's just that we... we have our own plans. And Clara said it's making her feel old, so I don't want to make her uncomfortable.'

It wasn't exactly how Clara had put it, and Ava didn't know why she was deflecting her own dislike of the group onto her sister. She didn't even know why she suddenly disliked them so much.

'So did you want to come over and join us or not?' she added.

'I'll come and get my supper,' Sandy said.

'Awwww!' the girls all chorused. 'Don't go, Sandy!'

He laughed again. 'I'm far too old to keep up with you lot. But it was lovely to meet you. Enjoy the rest of your holiday!'

Sandy turned to leave. Harry nodded to the group then followed him, and Ava did the same. She glanced back once and noticed that the girl who'd taken Harry's number was watching them. Her frown deepened as she saw Harry glance back too.

She wondered what he was looking at. And the notion came suddenly, from nowhere.

She really hoped he wasn't looking at the girl he'd just met.

# CHAPTER THIRTEEN

As predicted, Ava had stayed out too late and had drunk far too much alcohol. In the end, Sandy and Harry hadn't stayed long, and the group of youngsters who'd befriended them soon moved on. Ava, Clara and Logan had watched the first stars pepper a velvet sky and made a good fist of naming many of them before Clara and Logan had finally walked Ava back to her caravan and then gone home themselves. This morning she was paying the price, but at least the sun was out and the sea was calm and her early class of students weren't too much trouble – which made a welcome change. She'd had a text message from her mum too, who wanted to meet up to talk. Despite her thumping head, Ava was hopeful this would be a good thing. Perhaps everything was about to work out after all, because she was certain that the news she was going to give her would smooth things over.

With her first class gone, Ava's schedule showed a private session next. She waited on a seat by the office, her face to the sun, soaking it in. Ten minutes after start time, a notification sounded on her phone to tell her she had new emails, and she opened them up to one from the student, unable to attend his lesson due to a family emergency.

Ava put her phone away and went into the office to pull on some tracksuit trousers and a loose T-shirt. The last-minute cancellation left her with a spare hour, so she decided to stroll to Betty's to get a latte. The sun was shining, she had an unexpected break, the paracetamol she'd taken first thing had banished her hangover and everything was good.

Betty looked up from a table she was clearing. The cafe was almost full, the air bright with laughter and chatter and sweet with cinnamon and sugar and coffee. Through the gingham-curtained windows lay the sea, dappled with sunlight.

'Good morning, Ava,' she said. 'What can I get you?'

'A latte, if you can manage it,' Ava said, going to the counter. 'It looks as if you're heaving so there's no rush.'

'You want that to take out?' Betty asked, balancing a pile of plates as she came over.

'Probably should – don't want to leave the office unattended for too long.'

'No worries.' Betty went behind the counter, dumped the plates in a sink and pulled some milk from the fridge. 'How was last night?'

'Oh...' Ava smiled. 'So Clara told you about that?'

'I saw her first thing. It wasn't pretty.'

'I think she drank way more than I did and I was in a bit of a state. God knows how she's feeling. But it was good. Logan was there too.'

'And Harry Trevithick, so Clara says?'

'He came down with Sandy.'

'Ah. Of course, she did say that. Sandy was his usual self too, by all accounts.'

'God yes, everyone's best friend. I bloody love Sandy.'

'Don't we all!'

Betty was silent for a moment as she frothed the milk. The door of the cafe opened and Cormac rushed in.

'Hey, Ava...'

'Hi, Cormac.'

'Betty,' he said, going to the counter. 'I'm sorry to ask, but I don't suppose I could take some change from you? I'm clean out.'

'Sure,' Betty said, without turning around. 'What do you need?'

'A few pound coins, maybe about twenty?'

'I don't think I have that many.' Betty turned around with Ava's cup and put it on the counter before opening her till drawer and looking in. 'I can give you ten, but that's all, I'm afraid.'

'I'll take what you've got,' he said, putting a note on the counter. Betty counted out the coins and tipped them into his waiting palm. 'You're an angel,' he said. 'Thanks.'

Betty laughed. 'I wish everyone thought so.'

Cormac went to leave and then turned back and looked at Ava. 'You never said the other day that you were volunteering for the boat crew.'

Ava didn't even bother to ask who'd told Cormac, because by now it could be anyone living in Port Promise. 'I didn't think... well, you were talking to Harry about it and I didn't want to steal your thunder.'

'I hope it goes well for you,' he continued.

'Me too. Have you made up your mind about it?' she asked.

'Um... maybe. Sorry, got to go, catch you later.' Cormac dashed out again.

Betty pushed Ava's latte across the counter.

'Thanks,' Ava said, deep in thought as she handed the money over.

'I hope you don't think I'm prying...' Betty's voice cut into her thoughts. 'But Clara told me you'd had a bit of a disagreement with your mum about joining the crew.'

'Yes. I was hoping to clear it up with her yesterday but I didn't get the chance.'

'She was in here yesterday afternoon with Marina,' Betty said. 'She seemed...'

'What?'

'I hate to say this, Ava, but she seemed really upset.'

'How upset? You know what, never mind. Thanks, Betty.'

'See you later.'

With a growing feeling of regret, Ava took a detour past the lifeboat station before she headed back to work. She stopped to look up at it. Was joining the seagoing crew really worth losing her mum? It didn't seem Jill was going to back down, and Ava could see why, even if she didn't agree. She could do other things, she supposed, just as she'd planned to before. They always needed people to teach water safety, and that was just as important, right? Maybe more, because then fewer people would need rescuing.

With a sigh, she turned to leave, but then, from the corner of her eye, she saw Vas at the window, calling her over.

As she made her way across the promenade, he opened the station door.

'Need a word!' he said.

'What's up?'

'How are you fixed for next weekend?'

'What for?'

'Your fitness tests, dummy!'

Ava stared at him. 'My application was approved?'

'Not yet, but you get through these and the medical and you're pretty damned close. Did you seriously think they were going to turn you down?'

'Well, I don't know...'

Vas narrowed his eyes. 'I have to say, I thought you'd be more excited.'

'I am.' Ava forced a smile. 'I'm surprised, that's all.'

'I don't know why – you're a perfect candidate. The service would be mad to turn you down.'

'Thanks.'

'So next weekend...? Can you make it? I can't fit you in before then—'

'Vas... this is all amazing, but can I get back to you? I mean, I need to check my schedule first.'

'Sure.' Vas looked puzzled but he nodded. 'Let me know as soon as you can, will you? I want to get you started as quick as possible.'

'I will.'

Ava turned to leave. She had to get out before she started to cry. She'd finally got what she wanted and now she was going to have to turn it down. She had to, because the alternative, she now realised, was losing her mum, and she could never do that.

Ava texted her mum when she got back to her office and this time got a reply.

*Can we talk please?*

*I think it's about time we did.*

*I could come after work. Is that OK?*

*Yes. That would be good.*

Her mum was in the garden when Ava arrived. 'I picked up some cream cakes,' she said.

Jill took off her gloves. On a bench in front of her was a row of small pots with seedlings in them and larger pots that looked as though they were being prepared for potting on.

'They look nice,' she said as Ava opened the bag to show her. 'Want a cup of tea?'

'Please.'

Ava followed her inside. The atmosphere was stilted and a little weird, but considering they'd been at each other's throats the last time they'd been together, it was probably the least they could expect.

'Would you like a sandwich?' Jill asked as she washed her hands in the sink. 'I've got some chicken.'

'Sounds good.'

Ava took a seat at the dining table. Jill dried her hands and went to the fridge.

'I'm sorry,' she began, paused with her fingers wrapped around the door handle.

'Me too,' Ava said. 'I'm the one who really should be saying that. And I've been thinking... I'm going to withdraw my application.'

Jill closed the door, her arms loaded with packs of salad and meat, a look somewhere between surprise and relief on her face. 'You are?'

Ava nodded. 'If it's going to come between us then it's not worth it, right?'

'I only had your best interests at heart, you know that? I was worried about you.'

'Well, I don't want you to worry any more. I'm going to volunteer for something else. Something shore-based.'

Jill took the lettuce to the tap to rinse. 'That's really what you want?'

'Yes,' Ava said. 'That's what I want.'

'Hmm.' Jill looked up at her. 'Ava, I can't tell you how relieved I am to hear that.'

'Good. Then we're all right?'

'Ava, we were always all right. Did you really think I'd lose my youngest daughter over this? I would have hated it and I would have fought tooth and nail to put you off, but I would never have wanted to lose you; I'd have given up before that happened.'

'I was so—' Ava broke off, a lump in her throat.

'I was worried too,' Jill said, going over and taking Ava into her arms.

'I thought I'd lost you. I thought you'd never speak to me again.'

'All bluster – I can't believe you didn't realise that. You should know me well enough by now. After all, it's exactly how you are.'

'I know, Mum. I'm so sorry for putting you through all this.'

'I don't want you to be sorry. I understand what you were trying to do. And your dad would have been proud to see it. Sit down – let's eat.'

Ava nodded and did as her mum asked. Jill returned to the sink to get the lettuce she'd washed.

'So we're friends again?'

'Of course.'

'Thanks, Mum.'

The kettle clicked off and Ava went to fill the teapot, relief flooding through her. She'd given up something that was important to her, yes, and perhaps if she'd stood her ground she might have got it in the end, but this meant more. Being here, with her mum, everything well again, meant the world.


They were clearing up the leftovers when there was a knock at the front door. Ava went to get it and found Gaby on the doorstep.

'Don't have your key?'

Gaby shrugged. 'Don't like to use it these days,' she said in a significant tone. 'I'd rather knock so Mum can...'

Ava lowered her voice. 'I get it. She can pull herself together before she sees anyone. I walked in on her crying once too. Anyway, she's in the kitchen.'

'And I take it,' Gaby said as she let the front door close and followed Ava through, 'that you two have settled your differences? At least you don't look too stressed.'

'I think so.'

'Good. That was another problem I could have done without.'

'While we're on the subject—' Ava stopped mid-sentence as their mum looked up from wiping over the kettle and smiled broadly at her oldest daughter.

'Didn't expect to see you today!'

'I thought I'd drop by on the off-chance. Kids are at after-school club so I have a bit more time.'

'You want a cup of tea?'

'If you're making one.' Gaby sat at the table and put down her handbag. She looked up at Ava. 'Are you staying for one?'

'I've already had about ten,' Ava replied. 'I should probably think about getting back to the caravan – got some scheduling to do.'

'Right. That thing you were about to ask me...? Want to do that before you go, or is it a long discussion kind of thing?'

'I'm not sure. It's not about me – it's about Harry Trevithick.'

'Ah...' Gaby gave a knowing look. 'If you're worrying about him, you shouldn't. The higher-ups have spoken to him and he's said he's all right, just needs a bit of a break from the boats.'

'That's just it – he's not all right.'

'But he says—'

'We all say a lot of things, don't we? Doesn't make them true. We all say the things we think will spare others the stress of trying to make things right for us. But he's not OK, Gab. I'm no expert, but I think he has post-traumatic stress or survivor's guilt or something like that. I think he needs proper intervention. He says he'll get it, but... well, I think it might help if he hears it from Killian; you know, if Killian tells him there's no shame and he ought to see a counsellor or whatever. He looks up to Killian – they all do, even more so now Dad's not there.'

Gaby was thoughtful for a moment. 'I suppose I could speak to Kill. I can't honestly say that it will make things better for Harry.'

'It might make things worse,' Jill cut in, bringing some mugs to the table. 'I'm not sure Harry will appreciate you sticking your nose in.'

Ava turned to her. 'What would Dad have done?'

'There's no way of saying,' Jill replied briskly. 'As he's not here.'

'All right then,' Ava replied. 'What would you do? If it was me or Gaby or Clara going through what Harry's going through, what would you do?'

'That's different. Perhaps if his mum or dad were to be doing this, he might be more... well, he might see why. But you're not his mum or dad.'

'But I am a friend who cares about him.'

Jill shook her head. 'I think you ought to be careful where you stick your oar, that's all.'

Ava huffed. Gaby gave her a sharp look and Ava checked her rising irritation.

'Sorry,' she said. 'It's just hard to see him like this. Surely you'd both want to help too? You've both known Harry his whole life, like I have. You must have noticed the changes in him.'

'Of course we have,' Gaby said. 'I've seen changes in all the crew, everyone who was on board that night – nobody could live through that and not be changed.'

Ava looked at her. 'Even Killian?'

'Yes Killian!' Gaby's tone was exasperated now. 'Of course Killian! Just because he doesn't go around weeping doesn't mean it hasn't got to him.'

'Harry doesn't go around weeping,' Ava said.

'I never said he did!' Gaby shot back.

'Girls...'

They both turned to see Jill frowning.

Ava looked back at Gaby. 'So will you talk to Killian or not?'

'If you think I should, then I will.' Gaby gave a slight shrug. 'But don't blame me if it doesn't go the way you think it will.'

'I wouldn't dream of it,' Ava said. She looked up at the old station clock on the wall. 'I should be going.'

Jill went to hug her. 'Thank you for coming.'

Ava paused with the softness of her mum's cheek on hers and closed her eyes. 'Love you, Mum.'

'I love you too.' Jill let go and wiped her eyes.

'I'll let myself out.' Ava kissed Gaby a brief farewell and then headed for the door. As she emerged onto the road outside and began to march down the hill, she was content that she'd done a lot of very good things that day.

# CHAPTER FOURTEEN

Ava loved Logan's art. There were paintings like his in galleries all over Cornwall, aimed very much at the tourist trade – colour-washed seascapes in blue and gold hues, gentle, inoffensive, easy on the eye. But Logan's were different if you looked hard enough. Here and there an aggressive tick of colour, a darkness that gave them a sense of excitement, an edge that betrayed his city roots and the artistic ambitions Clara had talked about. The gallery itself was also like many others – minimally decorated in shades of white to avoid detracting from the real draw – the paintings. In this small space they had installed a desk of pale wood, but the walls were white and the planks of the old floor were whitewashed, and from the ceiling hung square glass pendulums encasing clear bulbs. As with almost every other building in Port Promise, the windows showed a view of the sea, now a curve of indigo as the twilight began to fall.

Clara and Logan were carefully moving a huge canvas between them when Ava arrived, an impressionist-inspired view of the harbour on a bright day.

'Hey!' Clara said. 'What brings you here?'

'A chat,' Ava said. She nodded at the canvas. 'That's cool. A new one?'

'Yup!' Logan grunted. 'And heavier than it looks!'

Deciding there wasn't an angle she could approach from to help that wouldn't actually hinder progress, she stepped back and waited patiently for them to put the canvas down where they wanted it. Then Logan gave Clara a significant look.

'Taking a break?' he asked, glancing at Ava.

'Yes,' Clara said. 'Give me a few minutes.'

'No problem – I'll nip in the back for a drink. Come and get me when you're ready to start again.'

'So what's this chat?' Clara asked.

'I went to see Mum.'

'I heard; Gaby told me.'

'What do you think?'

'I think I'm glad there's no more drama, but I'm surprised you're backing down.'

'I know, but what else was I meant to do?'

'I didn't say I had an answer, only that I was surprised... so you fancy a glass of wine? We've got some left from a gallery open evening. In fact, I bet Logan's guzzling it in the back right now.'

'He did say he was getting a drink – just not what sort.'

'He did, didn't he? Sneaky little bugger.'

Clara slid herself from the desk and went into the back room, emerging a moment later with half a bottle of red and two glasses.

'So you're happy with your decision?'

'I'm as happy as I can be. It's worth it, I think. Isn't it?'

'Of course.' Clara sipped at her wine. 'If that's your priority.'

'It would be yours, right?'

'I couldn't say. I don't know what I'd do. It's hard, feeling unfulfilled, like you had something important taken away from you. I know that much. Maybe harder for you, of all people.'

'Why me?'

'Because you're you. I know it must have taken a lot to back down on this.'

'It's not that big a deal. I can do something else. Gaby's in charge of fundraising at the station for a start – I'm sure she'd find me loads to do.'

'Yep, I can just see you rattling buckets on the harbour.'

'I'm only saying... it's a for instance. There's always some way to be involved in the service, even if I never set foot in the station. Dad was always trying to get me to take on water safety ed. I suppose I could do that.'

'I can just see that too. I don't imagine for a minute you'll be able to stay away from the launches.'

'I always kept away before.'

'No you didn't! You were forever badgering Dad to take you to drills and stuff. You even used to beg to go out on rescues!'

'I was about eight!' Ava said with a smile. 'I don't think anyone was taking me seriously.'

'All I'm saying is, I'm surprised it took you so long to say you wanted to join.'

'Yeah, I know. I suppose in a way it was because Dad was there.'

'Why would that stop you?'

'I think...' Ava picked up her glass and studied the red depths of the wine. 'I suppose I was afraid of embarrassing him. Like I'd be there and I'd be shit at it and then everyone would be to him like, there's your Ava, hopeless isn't she? And I might somehow make Dad ashamed. Because he was this big deal around here and I was always so mindful of that.' She looked at her sister. 'Didn't you ever feel like it's impossible to live up to our name? Like you were never good enough to be a Morrow?'

'I can't say I've thought about it as much as you seem to.

The difference is I'm not obsessed with the lifeboats, but that brings its own sort of guilt. I always felt guilty that I'm not involved and I can't say I want to be. Logan doesn't serve; I don't do anything – not even that much fundraising anymore. I wanted to go into something completely different.'

'Dad got that – he didn't mind at all. He never expected you to be obsessed with the boats.'

Clara took another sip of her wine and any further discussion was halted by Logan coming in.

'Sorry, just need to get my phone from the desk.'

'Don't mind us,' Ava said. 'I think I've said what I needed to say. It wasn't that much in the end.'

'Right. So this is about Harry Trevithick then?' he said, tapping the side of his nose.

Ava stared at him and then at Clara. Had Clara told Logan about Harry's problems? But if she had, Logan didn't seem very sympathetic. 'No... wait, why would we be talking about that?'

'Well, you're into him, right?'

Clara shot her fiancé a warning look. He returned it with one of confusion.

'Am I not supposed to say that? But I thought everyone said it?'

'God, you're an idiot,' Clara sighed. 'We don't say it to Ava... or Harry for that matter – *do we*?'

Logan shrugged. 'I don't see what good that does anyone. How can they get together if they don't know they like each other?'

'I don't like him,' Ava said. 'Not in that way... We're good mates, that's all.'

Logan laughed. 'Said every couple in denial ever. Honestly, just have sex and get it over with – everyone can see you want to.'

'Logan!' Clara snapped. '*Not helping*!'

'I think it is,' Logan replied carelessly. 'One day they'll thank me.'

'For your information,' Clara added, 'Harry is seeing someone.'

'Who?' Ava asked, more sharply than she meant to.

'That girl he met on the beach.'

'The redhead who gave him her number even though she'd said all of one sentence to him?' Ava asked. 'Oh, that will end well. She's not right for him at all.'

'They never are, are they?' Clara said with a knowing look.

Ava put her glass down. 'It's not my fault he's got terrible taste.'

'If he's got such terrible taste, why don't you do something about it?' Logan asked.

'Like what?'

'Like point him in the direction of the girl who's right for him.'

'I would if I ever met her.'

Logan chuckled. Shaking his head, he left them again. Ava frowned as she watched him go.

'He might have a point,' Clara said.

Ava turned to her. 'Don't you start!'

'I'm not, I'm only saying you never like any of Harry's girl-friends. Why do you suppose that is?'

'I've told you why.'

Clara raised her eyebrows.

'Me and Harry... that's not where we're at. He's like a cousin or something.'

'Well, in your average Jane Austen, cousins get married—'

'Can we change the subject?' Ava huffed. 'You've just said Harry's dating someone, so what's the point of discussing it?'

'The point, dear sister, is that if you told him you wanted to give things a go I'm sure he'd drop her like a hot potato. Even you can't be stupid enough to have missed how he looks at you.'

Ava picked up her wine and knocked back the last of it. She and Harry had always been good friends, but it had always seemed they were on the same page when it came to anything else – the timing had so often been out, but even if it hadn't, she'd always believed that their friendship was too good to complicate with messy variables like romance. As things were now, she knew where she stood with him and she knew she could rely on him. They didn't have to see each other often to know that they'd get along and have a laugh the minute they bumped into each other. But had there been something else for him that whole time? Had he wanted more? Was it her fault he'd never said? And maybe she did have feelings for him now, though she couldn't actually remember when that started. This month? Last month? A year ago? Ten years ago? How was it only now that she was beginning to acknowledge them at all? What had changed?

# CHAPTER FIFTEEN

The one event that drew all the town together in one place was approaching – the annual Port Promise oyster festival. She'd be there, as she was every year – as would all her family – and Harry would be working at his dad's cider stall, as he did every year. It was a brave resident who didn't turn up, and the rest of the village would spend the following twelve months talking about it so much that they'd never miss another.

This year was no different. Preparations had begun weeks before, but behind the scenes and barely noticed apart from by the people who were undertaking them. Bookings for stands were being taken by the staff at the tiny council offices, the caravan site had undergone an extensive programme of garden maintenance and cleaning to welcome out-of-towners in to join the festivities, fishing boats had been washed and lacquered so that the hulls gleamed, every lamppost on every street had a hanging basket of summer blooms, and every box in every window of every cottage had the same. Stonework and pavements were jet-washed, while Betty and Cormac were taking on extra supplies, renovating furniture and adding flourishes to their welcoming decor.

The day before work got fully underway things were hectic. Hardly a road wasn't blocked at some point or other by a delivery van or lorry, and though tempers flared, everyone understood it was necessary – apart from the odd annoyed tourist, of course, but the villagers were used to that. Then the bunting went up and the party feeling really kicked in. The ramshackle, meandering streets of Port Promise were no strangers to bunting. There were many events over the summer months that called for the walkways to be zig-zagged by colourful, fluttering triangles of cloth, but none was a bigger or more important feature of the village calendar than the annual oyster festival.

Fishing, like most livelihoods connected to the sea, was an important part of the heritage and identity of Port Promise, as intertwined with its history and lore as the Morrow family themselves. The fishing industry around these waters – such as it was in the twenty-first century – was still precious to the village, even if it struggled to keep up with the industrial harvesting that took place on further shores. The oyster festival was a celebration of this, a celebration of keeping traditions alive, a way to bring the community together and, more cynically for those who stood to gain, a way to bring tourists in.

'Couldn't have got a better day for it.'

On the morning of the festival, Ava glanced across and smiled at her mother's remark as they walked the cobbles to the harbour. This felt new, being friends again, almost as if they'd gone back to the beginning and started afresh. She was glad. Nothing was worth losing her mother, and so she also tried to keep the voices of dissent from her mind. So she'd given up her dream? So what? People sacrificed far bigger things for the people they loved. It was worth it to get her mum back.

The iris-blue sky and the sun spilling over slate rooftops, warming cottages of dove-grey stone with tiny front doors all the colours of the rainbow, window boxes bursting with flowers or herbs and picket fences leading to little garden paths certainly helped to buoy her mood too. Such welcoming prettiness could hardly fail, even though Ava had walked these streets hundreds, if not thousands of times during her life. The street fell gently away to the harbour, and from this vantage point they could see the glittering swells of a sea stirred by a brisk breeze.

'The only thing that stops this from being perfect is that your dad isn't here,' Jill added.

It was a very big thing, even if it was the only thing. Probably worth a million other gripes that might ruin the day. Life had been hard, and harder for Jill, possibly, than anyone else, but her statement said a lot more than she'd intended. Perhaps she was finally coming to some sort of acceptance, emerging from that dark tunnel of grief that had almost paralysed her since they'd lost Ava's dad. Perhaps now, with that and Ava's agreement that she wouldn't join the lifeboat crew after all, they could move past this difficult period and become mother and daughter in the way they ought to be, in the way they always had before all this trauma had almost ripped them apart.

'He loved the festival, didn't he?' Ava said.

'Never missed it. We always came here together, right back from the first year we were courting. And even before that, when I used to come as a girl with my parents, Jack would be here with his mum and dad, hanging around, and I'd always see him somewhere or other doing something daft. I think I always loved him, long before I even knew it. Always there, my entire life, until now. Sometimes it feels as if Port Promise was built with him already installed, like he'd grown from the ground with the trees and grass.'

'I suppose, in a way, that's true, when you consider the Morrow legend,' Ava replied.

'I suppose so,' Jill agreed. 'The Morrows and Port Promise. Like...'

'Like chickens and eggs?'

Jill laughed lightly. 'Like chickens and eggs – exactly. Nobody knows who came first, but you can't have one without the other.'

Ava pointed to a row of stalls and owners setting up on the harbour approach. Most of them were people from out of town who Ava didn't know that well – the villagers didn't mind businesses from neighbouring areas getting involved in the festival, because the business owners of Port Promise would be invited to their events in return and there was plenty of trade once the tourists and visitors arrived. They were set up to sell treats like sweet waffles, plump Mediterranean olives and sun-dried tomatoes by the tub, toffees and artisan chocolate and flavoured gins. One of them, however, was being manned by Cormac, who'd obviously decided that his shack was too far from the main action and had brought a mobile version to the centre of the village to trade. 'Shall we go and have a quick word?'

'We probably ought to,' Jill said.

'Morning!' Cormac looked up just as they were deciding to go over and hailed them. 'How are you this fine morning?'

'Someone's happy,' Ava said as they walked across the street to his stall.

'Well, the weather's perfect, my salmon smoked perfectly and all the stars seem to be aligned for my first oyster festival.' He rubbed his broad hands together. 'Hoping for a good day's trade.'

'You'll probably get it,' Jill said. 'It's always busy.'

'Yes,' Ava agreed, 'and hardly anyone actually eats the oysters, so I'm sure your perfect smoked salmon will fly off the shelves.'

'Everyone eats the oysters,' Jill chided.

Ava laughed. 'No they don't! Only the folks who pretend to like them because it makes them look sophisticated.'

'I like them,' Jill said.

'Ah,' Cormac put in, 'but that's because you *are* sophisticated, Mrs Morrow.'

Jill flushed quite adorably and Ava smiled. It was lovely to see.

'So your whole family will be here today?' he asked.

'Yes.' Ava shot her mum a knowing glance. 'Gaby and Killian and the kids and Logan and Clara...'

'It'll be good to see them.'

'Clara's going to be late,' Jill said to Ava. 'She sent me a message to say something had come up – I think Logan's probably holding them up trying to finish one of his canvases.'

Ava glanced at Cormac, who'd now turned to chalking prices on a board, probably deciding that he ought to at least look as if he wasn't listening.

'I suppose they must need the money for the wedding,' Jill added, her blue eyes on the sea, the coarse greys that had escaped her clip now whipping around her face. 'He certainly seems to spend night and day in that studio painting. Shame that. He must feel as if all that passion has gone from a pleasure to a necessity – can't be good for the creative soul.'

'Well,' Ava said brightly, 'that's the thing, isn't it? However you can earn a crust round here, you have to take it gladly – right, Cormac?'

He looked up from his sign, where he'd created quite an accomplished drawing of a fish. 'You do that.'

'I don't think Logan really wants to come,' Ava added.

'He should be here,' Jill insisted. 'It's the oyster festival.'

Ava shrugged. 'I don't suppose it's a big deal to him, being from London and everything. And I don't know if he even likes oysters.'

'Liking oysters isn't the point; being here is the point. It's about the village coming together.'

Ava couldn't quite decide whether her mum was annoyed with Logan or not. She'd gone from defending him to now reprimanding him in his absence.

'Again,' she said patiently, 'I don't suppose he sees it that way. He didn't grow up here, so it doesn't mean anything to him.'

'But Clara's a Morrow. That should mean something to him if he's going to marry into the family. She's the reason Port Promise exists!'

'While I'm sure Clara would love to claim that, I'm pretty sure the existence of this place isn't just down to her.'

'You know what I mean.'

'Not sure I do and not sure how that changes anything. The existence of any of us is down to Iziah and his wife doing the dance of lurvvveeee...'

Jill rolled her eyes and Ava grinned, then she turned to see Cormac grinning to himself too.

'You never take anything seriously,' Jill said.

'I don't take *those* things seriously,' Ava replied, choosing not to add that all she'd done was be serious for the past six months and she was sick of it. 'Our family has contributed to the village over the years, sure, but all this reverence is silly. You said it yourself when—'

Ava stopped. Jill had more or less said that as part of her argument about why Ava shouldn't join the lifeboat crew, and to remind her now might be to dredge that argument up again when it ought to be over.

'Your dad didn't think it was silly,' Jill cut in.

'Yes he did. He was all about what we could do for the village, not the other way around. That promise Iziah made – Dad took that seriously, of course, but not all the other daft stuff. And I reckon a hero like Dad would have volunteered for the lifeboats no matter whether he'd been born here or not, even if there'd never been a pledge made by a guilty-feeling ancestor one stormy night. Dad would have done it because it was the right thing to do and because he wanted to keep people safe, and because nobody knew the seas around here like he did, and so why shouldn't he use that knowledge to do some good?'

It was all Ava could do not to follow this up with a renewal of her case to follow in his footsteps, but she held her tongue.

'I've said it before, but he sounds like he was one hell of a fella,' Cormac said into the gap, and both Ava and Jill turned to him as if surprised he was there. 'I'm only sorry I didn't get to meet him.'

'He was,' Jill said with obvious pride.

They were distracted by a voice hailing them. Marina was making her way down the cobbles in a pair of linen flares and a sleeveless blouse, her long white plait tied with a band and draped over one shoulder.

'I wasn't sure you'd come this year,' she said to Jill as she approached, pulling her into a hug.

'Of course I was going to come,' Jill said. 'As if I'd miss it!'

'Well, I'm glad to see you down here and I'm sure everyone else will be.' Marina smiled at Ava. 'And how are you, my darlin'?'

Ava smiled warmly. 'I'm good.'

'You still doing work on that caravan? Only we're selling off some shelves – thought you might want first dibs,' Marina said.

'That would be brilliant,' Ava said. 'I'll come and have a look when I get a minute.'

'So you're still enjoying the gypsy life?'

'I love it!'

'Now you do.' Marina swept a hand down her plait absently. 'But you wait until the wind is howling around it and there's snow on the ground.'

'That's what I've been saying,' Jill put in. 'I've told her to move back into the cottage when it gets too cold over there at the park.'

It was strange to Ava how, in all the years she'd been on the earth, youngest sibling of three, she'd never recognised that being the baby of the family often meant being treated that way. It was also strange that, although her father had been as guilty of it as everyone else, he'd done it in a way that was all affection, as a dad who simply wanted to cling to the last of his children for as long as possible. The others did it too, but not in the same way.

When her mum and her sisters babied her, it was more like they didn't trust that she was capable of doing anything for herself, like they felt they needed to take responsibility for her where they could, that they thought she wasn't mature enough to deal with anything. She had barely been involved in the practicalities of her dad's death, for instance, had been given no task around the administration of his estate or the arrangement of his funeral. She'd wanted to be involved in those decisions, to be given things to do, and yet Gaby – to a greater degree – and Clara – doing what Gaby told her – had taken every aspect out of Ava's way, insisting that she didn't want to deal with such matters and insinuating that she didn't know enough of the world to try. And if that were true, surely it was because nobody would ever let her make mistakes for herself.

She'd grown up in a sleepy Cornish village that only came alive for about ten weeks a year every summer when the tourists arrived, cosseted and cuddled and not allowed to take any kind of responsibility. But she wasn't that little girl anymore. Wasn't it about time she was allowed to take control of her own life? Wasn't it time to take risks, to fail or succeed but to make those decisions herself, no matter the outcome? She was sick of people telling her what she was and wasn't capable of, what she ought and ought not to do, of everyone telling her they knew better. Perhaps they did, but even then she didn't want to hear it. She wanted to throw herself at life and see what happened.

She was shaken from her musings by Marina's voice. 'Lots of new stalls this year...' She glanced at Cormac, who gave a little salute.

'Don't mind me.'

'Oh, I don't,' Marina replied with a look of pure lust. 'You can have as many stalls here as you like.'

'Who else?' Jill asked.

'Benson's farm,' Marina said, tearing her gaze from Cormac's broad chest. 'Bringing their fresh milkshakes down. And' – she lowered her voice to a gossipy whisper and leaned in – 'some new cider maker.'

Ava frowned. 'Not the Trevithicks then?'

'Nope.' Marina straightened up again. 'What do you make of that, eh? Personally, I don't think it's right. Organisers should have known better. We've got one cider maker around here and they ought to be the only stall at the festival.'

'I suppose they must have thought there was room for two. There's always a massive queue at Trevithick's stand.'

'With good reason,' Marina said. 'Locals will only buy from them.'

Ava thought it was more likely because they were usually the only cider stall but decided it might be churlish to say so.

'I suppose there's going to be enough business for the both of them,' Cormac put in cheerfully.

Marina rounded on him, her lust seeming to have evaporated instantly. 'And would you be happy if there was another fish shack here?'

'Well...' Ava cut in, hoping to rescue him. 'There will be. There's going to be lots of seafood here because... Well, it's a seafood festival.'

'*Oyster* festival,' Marina corrected.

'Yes, but as we've established, there's a lot more being served up than oysters. I'm sure Trevithick's will be fine.'

Jill nodded. 'That's what Sandy says. He's not worried – he knows all the locals will buy from him.'

'I might try the new place,' Ava said glibly but then laughed at the looks of horror on both her mum and Marina's faces. 'Joking! Of course I won't – I wouldn't dare! I'll be getting my cider from Trevithick's!'

'I wonder how young Harry is,' Marina said. Ava looked sharply at her. 'All that business with... well, you know. Can't imagine what that poor boy must be going through, but by all accounts he's not faring well. And yet, he's perfectly cheerful when he comes into the store. Funny that.'

He was hardly going to walk around Port Promise sobbing, Ava thought, but it was yet another thing she didn't say to Marina.

'I expect he's talked it through with Killian or Vas,' Jill said, and Ava kept her mouth shut there too.

'I'm surprised you don't know anything about it,' Marina said, looking very deliberately at Ava.

*If I did, I wouldn't tell you.*

'I know about as much as anyone else,' Ava said, keeping her tone neutral.

'Because you two used to be quite an item,' Marina continued.

'No we weren't. We've never been together, Marina. You must be confusing us with someone else.'

'Then you definitely liked him.'

'Oh, yes,' Jill agreed. 'I think you did once. But he had a girl-friend by the time you'd made up your mind about it.'

'God, Mum, I was about thirteen! Harry's a mate now, that's all. And not even that close, apart from the lifeboat connection. I mean, we have a laugh if we see each other out, but we don't go drinking together or anything.'

'You see him all the time!' Jill said.

'It's hard not to whenever I go in the Spratt,' Ava replied. 'When you go in there, you're drinking with the whole village whether you want to or not.'

'That's true enough,' Marina said in a tone that suggested Ava had discovered the meaning of life rather than simply observing that the village's one small pub was about the only place anyone could get a decent pint.

'Grandma! Ava!'

All three women turned to see Elijah and Fern racing down the road towards them. Jill put a panicked hand out.

'Slow down! It's steep – you'll fall!'

Neither took a bit of notice, instead speeding up and crashing into Jill and Ava, throwing arms around them and laughing.

'You'll be the death of me!' Jill chided, but she was smiling anyway. They looked up at Marina with a courteous hello.

In their wake, strolling down the hill hand in hand, were Gaby and Killian. Gaby looked gorgeous, as she always did, in a white cotton dress that flattered her sun-kissed curves.

That old familiar pang of envy settled in Ava's gut, unwanted but unavoidable, like it was a built-in feature of their relationship, something in her DNA that meant she'd always feel this way. She knew Clara felt exactly the same. They both loved Gaby, but that kind of perfection was hard to live up to, even harder not to sometimes feel bitter about. She was the gorgeous sister who'd caught the gorgeous husband and had the gorgeous kids. She was serene – outwardly, at least – measured and confident and assertive without being aggressive in a way that Ava could never hope to live up to. Ava often admired her and sometimes resented her for the very same reasons.

And here she was, looking the part as always, with her wide blue eyes, lashes long enough to look false though they were all natural, glossy auburn hair sitting on her shoulders. She looked like she hadn't even tried, and she probably hadn't because she didn't have time and didn't need to. Ava had been happy with her own appearance before she'd left the caravan that morning, wearing a cute denim dress that was one of her favourites, her own hair slightly sandier than Gaby's and piled into a bun, but now she felt dowdy.

'Morning!' Gaby greeted everyone with a broad smile. 'Good day for the festival, right?'

'Isn't it?' Jill said. 'Let's hope it holds.'

'Forecast looks good,' Marina said.

Ava chanced a glance at Killian as the others exchanged pleasantries. He was his usual unreadable, unflappable self. She was desperate to talk to him about Harry, but it would have to wait, because this definitely wasn't the time. Then she felt someone tugging on her hand and looked down to see Elijah looking up at her.

'Can you take us swimming today?'

Ava's forehead wrinkled slightly. 'Today? It's a bit... well, there's a lot going on. Don't you want to be at the festival?'

'Eli says it's boring,' Fern said. 'And he hates oysters.'

'I never said that!' Elijah exclaimed. 'You're such a—' He looked at his dad and instantly clammed up.

'Want me to let you in on a secret?' Ava asked. Both children turned expectantly to her. 'Oysters are like sprouts at Christmas – at least they are around here. Nobody really wants to eat them, but there's one day a year where it's sort of the rule and we all have to.'

'Speak for yourself.' Marina sniggered, aiming a molten glance at poor Cormac, who was still trying to get his stall set up in peace. 'I'm partial to a good shuck.'

Jill giggled. Gaby smiled and even Killian managed a grin. Elijah and Fern looked as if they wanted to laugh – recognising something funny had been said even if they didn't quite understand what it was.

'Aren't we all?' said Ava. 'But why do I get the feeling we're not talking about oysters now?'

'Oh Marina,' Jill said, still laughing. 'How does Bob cope?'

Marina winked. 'He likes a good shuck too, so we shuck together. Speaking of Bob, I probably ought to find him. I think he was supposed to be helping the reverend with the raffle and, to be honest, I believe I'm supposed to be helping too.'

'That's about right,' Jill said with a smile. 'You'd better go and find him then, before you get in trouble.'

'Trouble?' Marina said breezily as she began to walk away. 'Trouble gets into me!'

Gaby turned to her mum, shaking her head. 'That one, they broke the mould when they made her, right?'

'Oh, that they did.'

'Clara not here yet?'

Jill shook her head. 'They're in discussions about whether to keep the studio open today or not. I expect she'll be down at some point, even if Logan isn't.'

Gaby turned to her husband. 'Thank goodness you've got a normal job, eh? Your computer goes off and then I have your undivided attention... oh, no, hang on, then you get called out to sea to rescue someone.'

Killian looked unfazed by the barbed comment. 'Let's not start that today. Can't we have five minutes where we don't talk about it?'

'Yes, if I can have five minutes where you're not on that boat.'

'I'm not on it now.'

'Miracles never cease, do they?' Gaby turned to Ava. 'At least you've got that nonsense out of your system.'

Ava gritted her teeth and decided that silence was the best response here.

'Come on, be fair,' Killian said, and Ava had to do a double-take. Was this Killian, about to defend her? 'I wouldn't call it nonsense.'

'I would when it involves my sister.'

'But it's not nonsense,' Killian insisted. 'It's just not the right job for Ava. There are plenty of other roles and I'm sure she's looking at those – right, Ava?'

'Yes,' Ava said levelly, though she didn't feel that calm. Here they were again, her entire family telling her what she needed, what she should and shouldn't do, how to live her life. Everyone else knows what's best for baby Ava. She was looking at other roles, and she'd probably end up doing one of them, but that wasn't the point. She'd wanted to go out on the boats and everyone had done their best to stop her, and it still needled that she'd had to give in, even though the decision had been taken gladly to save her relationship with her mum. That mattered more than anything – of course it did – but Killian's patronising defence was hardly helping her come to terms with it.

Ava's glance went to Elijah and Fern, who were doing their best to follow the exchange.

'Are you going to rescue people?' Fern asked, her expression full of admiration. 'Like Grandpa Jack?'

'Sort of,' Ava said carefully.

'There are lots of ways to help people,' Gaby put in, gathering them around her as if she needed to shield them from some horrible truth that might be coming. 'And not all of them mean going out to sea in storms.'

'That's true,' Ava said. She glanced at her mum to gauge her reaction to the current topic of discussion. She looked back at Ava, clearly doing the same.

'I don't know about anyone else,' Killian said into the gap, 'but I'm about ready to go and see what we can eat.'

Gaby threw him a withering look. 'Seriously? You've not long had breakfast.'

Ava grinned, relieved that the moment of danger had passed. Whether Killian had diverted it deliberately or not, she silently thanked him. She turned to Gaby. 'And your point is? If nothing else, today is about stuffing your face and drinking until you pass out. I, for one, intend to honour that particular Port Promise tradition.'

'That's what your dad used to say,' Jill put in. 'Of course, he

didn't say it in quite such a direct way, but he definitely prac-
tised what you're preaching.'

'Good,' Ava said. 'So if nothing else, today is about doing
what Dad would have wanted us to.'

Gaby nodded. 'He'd have said it was good for the community spirit or some such nonsense. In other words, he wanted a
drink and was trying to make it look like a charitable act.'

Jill smiled. 'That's also true. Community spirit comes in
many forms, I suppose.'

'What,' Ava chipped in, 'like in rum bottles?'

Jill's smile grew. 'Oh, your dad did like a drop of the old
navy juice. I think, if he hadn't grown up in Port Promise as a
Morrow with his future on the lifeboats already mapped out for
him, he'd probably have joined the navy. One way or another,
that man was destined for a life on the sea. I found a bottle of
rum the other day, you know, cleaning out the shed. Your dad
must have stashed it there. Goodness only knows why – probably thought I'd shout at him if I found too many in the house or
some such nonsense.'

'You would have done,' Ava said.

'Probably,' Jill agreed. 'But it only came from a place of
love.'

'See...' Gaby turned to Killian. 'It's not nagging, it's love.'

'Not when you do it,' Killian shot back. 'When you do it, it's
terrifying.'

'Marriage must be lovely,' Ava said with a wry smile at her
sister and brother-in-law. 'Living in perfect harmony... it's so
inspiring.'

'You'll be laughing on the other side of your face when it's
your turn,' Gaby replied.

'That's assuming I bother to get married,' Ava said. 'Looking
at you two and seeing the stress it's caused for Clara and Logan
just getting engaged and planning the wedding, maybe I won't
bother.'

'Mum, can we get ice cream?' Fern asked.

Gaby looked down at her. 'It's a bit early.'

Ava laughed. 'You're so uptight! Thank God you're not my mum! Let them have some ice cream.'

'But it's so early – they've not long had breakfast.'

'Yes, but it's festival day. If we're all about to start cider sampling, then I'm sure the kids can have some ice cream.'

'*You're* about to start on the cider,' Gaby reminded her. 'The rest of us aren't planning to pass out before noon.'

'I won't be passing out at all – I'm no lightweight like you are.'

'Well, you say that...' Killian cut in.

'I could drink you under the table, mate,' Ava replied.

At this he started to laugh. 'That sounds like a challenge.'

'Take it how you want.'

'Ah, well, you see, I'd take you up on it too, but I've got to stay sober, right? In case there's a shout.'

'I bet that's it,' Ava said. 'Not that you think you'd lose.'

Killian laughed 'Oliver Reed would lose. But I'll walk up there with you to say hello and maybe one wouldn't hurt.'

He really was trying very hard with Ava. Guilty conscience, perhaps? She had to wonder. Still, she liked this Killian better than the one who turned up to lecture and generally made life as difficult as possible for her.

'Sounds good to me.'


Harry was connecting pipes to barrels when Ava, Killian, Gaby, Jill and the kids arrived at the cider stall. He looked up with a goofy grin as Killian hailed him. 'Morning!' Killian said. 'Working hard I see.'

'And I see you're not,' Harry shot back. 'Come for your first of many?'

'Ava has. I've got to keep my wits about me,' Killian said.

'Oh... of course.' Harry straightened up and wiped his hands on a cloth.

Ava swept her hand at the candy-striped awning he stood beneath. Rows of barrels were on the floor behind him, practical steel ones that held the cider, while on a shelf above were decorative oak ones that – so he'd told her one year – actually held nothing at all and were designed to make everything look rustic. Not that it wasn't rustic – their family business took cider very seriously and they did almost everything in the traditions of the family who'd gone before – but there were aspects of production where it simply didn't make sense not to take advantage of new technology. Along the temporary bar were a row of taps displaying the names of each brew alongside stacks of disposable cups. In a bid to be sustainable, the year before they'd trialled returnable glasses, but hardly anybody had returned them, so it looked to Ava as if they'd given up on the idea. 'Stall looks good. I see you've got even more new ones on.'

Harry looked down at his taps. 'Yep, Dad thought they were about ready to go. He's on fire at the moment – keeps coming up with new flavours. The trick right now is keeping up with him.'

Ava pointed at one. 'Drink Lady?'

'It's a pun, see? On Pink Lady, like pink lady apples.'

'Oh, does it have pink lady apples in it?'

'Well... the thing is, they're not actually good cider apples so... we sort of made it taste like that but... actually, why don't you try it and you'll see what I mean.'

'Can't argue with that,' Ava said.

Harry looked at Killian. 'Do you want to try it?'

'I wouldn't say no. You're having one yourself?'

'Oh, no,' Harry said cheerfully as he got two glasses from a stack. 'I'm on standby today like you. Can't imagine there'll be many out on the sea with this going on, but you never know. Best to stay sober, just in case.'

'Good man, absolutely,' Killian said.

'So you're setting all this up and you can't have any?' Ava asked. 'Seems a bit harsh.'

'That's what it's like on the crew,' Killian said pointedly, and there was no mistaking his veiled warning that the decision she'd made to stay off the boats ought not to be reviewed.

'Harry's not on the seagoing crew,' Ava pointed out stubbornly but then immediately wished she hadn't when she glanced at Harry. He looked suddenly crestfallen and she knew why – she'd reminded him of a fact that caused him great pain and guilt. God, she was stupid. 'I mean...'

'It's a commitment,' Killian continued, seeming to address them both now. 'Not a passing fancy.'

'I'm sure everyone knows that,' Ava said tartly, trying to indicate without words that Killian ought to shut up because Harry looked more miserable with every passing second.

Killian suddenly seemed to understand, and he threw Harry a look of silent apology. Then they all ignored the moment, which was the only thing they could do other than to dive in and head for a conversation that couldn't be had here and now.

Harry turned on a tap and drained a little cider, holding it up to the light before throwing it down a tiny sink behind the bar. Then he drained some more and did the same, before finally deciding he could serve it.

'What do you reckon?' he asked as they both took a sip.

'A bit sweet for me,' Killian said.

'I think it's really good,' Ava said. 'Tell your dad I approve. Where is he, by the way?'

'Still bringing bits down from storage,' Harry said. 'He'll be here shortly if you want to say hello.'

'Definitely,' Ava said. 'I haven't seen him since the beach.'

'Doesn't get down the hill very often these days,' Harry said. 'Too busy inventing new ciders like a mad scientist.'

'He can invent as many as he likes if they're all this good.'

Ava took another sip of her drink. It was sweet and crisp and really did taste like a pink lady apple, even if there were none in it. 'Is he going to do another autumn special this year?'

'I think he's planning some sort of Halloween-themed one,' Harry said. 'He bloody loves Halloween!'

'Sounds interesting...' Killian handed his empty glass back to Harry. 'How about a half of your Killer Crunch this time, just to be sociable?'

'Oh, that stuff's like paint stripper,' Ava said. 'No offence, Harry.'

'None taken. There's a cider for everyone, right?'

'And just because it tastes strong doesn't mean it's a higher proof, right?' Ava added, a challenging look at Killian.

They were interrupted by the sound of Gaby hailing them. She made her way over with Elijah and Fern, who both had ice creams as big as their heads. Ava couldn't help but smile. She might talk the talk of a strict mum, but in reality Gaby adored her kids so much she couldn't help but spoil them.

'Come and see the rabbits, Ava!' Fern cried.

'Rabbits?' Ava glanced at Gaby.

'There's a petting zoo,' she said. 'Must be a new thing.' She turned to Killian. 'Get ready, I have a feeling we're about to get pressganged into a pet.'

'Come and see!' Fern insisted. 'They're so cute! Come and see, Dad!'

'Bloody hell, I'm trying to have a quiet drink here...'

'Killian!' Gaby warned. 'It's ten minutes out of your day to look at some bunnies; indulge them. And you shouldn't be drinking – it's practically breakfast time. A wife might be inclined to think you were developing a drink problem—'

'But there's hardly anything...'

With a weary sigh, Killian drank his half and handed the empty glass to Harry. Then he held out a hand to Fern, while Gaby took Elijah's.

'Rabbits then,' Killian said. 'Come on – let's go look at them.'

Once they were out of earshot, Harry turned to her. 'So you changed your mind about the seagoing crew?'

'Yep.' Ava took a mouthful of cider.

'What changed? You were set on it.'

'I thought, was it worth losing my mum for it? She went mental when she found out, said she'd never forgive me.'

'I suppose, when you put it that way, I'd have done the same. What will you do instead?'

She shrugged. 'I'll come and talk to Vas, see if we can figure something out between us.'

'Whatever you decide to do will be valued, you know?'

She looked up to see Harry give her an encouraging smile. This morning he wore a soft navy T-shirt showing his toned arms and an apron tied around his trim waist, and he looked...

And there it was again, the feeling she'd never even realised was there. But this was Harry... surely not? After all these years of friendship, why should she start feeling this way now?

A sudden crash snapped her out of it. They both spun round to see Harry's dad struggling towards the stand with his arms full of equipment and a good deal of it on the pavement behind him.

'Dad!' Harry raced over. 'You're supposed to use the barrow!'

'Couldn't find it,' Sandy puffed.

'You can't carry all this – you're meant to be taking it easy.'

Ava went over. 'Let me help...' She grabbed some tubing from the road. 'What's this about taking it easy?'

'Oh, Harry making a fuss about nothing,' Sandy said. 'I had a funny dizzy spell. Probably some kind of virus – you know how this stuff gets around.'

'You went white as a sheet,' Harry said.

'When was this?' Ava grabbed another piece from further down the road.

'This morning.' Sandy dumped the equipment on the bar. 'I was fine ten minutes afterwards.'

'Stay at the bar,' Harry said. 'I'll go to the van for the rest. I should have done that in the first place instead of listening to you – might have known you'd ignore everyone's advice and do it your way.'

Sandy pulled a face and mimicked his son in a way that made him look like a strangely wrinkled child. Ava laughed.

'Come on, Sandy... I'll stay with you, and you can tell me about all these new ciders you've been dreaming up.'


There weren't many takers for glasses of cider at that time of the day. In an hour or so the stall would be inundated – it always was – but for now, Ava was enjoying chatting to Sandy as he finished setting up.

'How's your mum doing these days?' Sandy asked.

'I think she's getting there.' Ava handed him a towel to mop up a drip from a connector pipe.

'You know, I still expect to see your dad's Land Rover pull up at the farmhouse from time to time, him getting out with that daft grin of his to chew the fat for an hour.'

'I know,' Ava said. 'I think we're still processing that he's never coming back, even after all these months. Sometimes I see someone on the street, by the station, or walking past the window of my caravan, and for a second I think it's him. Then I remember that it can't be him and it feels like the first shock all over again. But I suppose that will go eventually.'

'It gets less often,' Sandy said. 'But my dad's been dead for thirty years and still, on the odd occasion, I see someone on the street and for a second I think it might be him.'

'Harry never knew your dad, did he?'

Sandy shook his head. 'More's the pity.'

'I think that's the saddest thing for me – if I have children, they'll never meet my dad.'

'But I expect you'll bring him to life in stories for them.' He gave her a good-natured wink. 'I've heard all about your stories. Apparently you spin quite the yarn.'

'Do I?' Ava asked with a bemused smile. 'Who told you that?'

'Harry.'

'Oh! He was round at Gaby's when I was babysitting the kids.'

'That'll be it. Said he'd have listened all day.'

'I'm sure he wouldn't,' Ava said with a grin. It faded quickly as another thought occurred to her. 'Please don't tell Harry I was asking, but... how is he?'

Sandy gave a knowing look. 'You're not asking about his general health, are you? It's hard to tell with Harry – he's very closed like that.'

Ava nodded slowly. 'He said he wanted to go on the boat crew again.'

'Yes. His mum wasn't overly pleased with that idea.'

'Sounds familiar,' Ava said wryly.

'I would imagine most mothers would want to keep their sons from danger.'

Ava smiled. 'But not dads?'

'Of course. But being a man comes with certain expectations, doesn't it? We might be scared to death, but we can't say so.'

'Why not? I don't see why it's so different for men than women. If we can talk about stuff then why can't you?'

'If only the world were that simple,' Sandy said with a chuckle as he twisted a tap.

'I think things ought to change then.'

'Isn't that what youth is about? Hoping for change?' He

twisted another tap with a grimace. 'When you get to my age you learn not to expect too much.'

'Sandy...' Ava said with a smile. 'You're not *that* old.'

'Not in my head. Sadly my body has other ideas.'

'I don't believe that. I saw you throwing shapes at the beach the other night.'

Sandy burst out laughing. 'Is that what I was doing? I'm glad to have a name for it at last! Let me tell you, I knew about it the next day!' His laughter faded. 'I do think that's my only regret though – that we didn't have Harry while we were younger. I'd have liked to have been able to keep up with him a bit better now than I do.'

'I think you do fine. And I'm sure Harry does too.'

'And I worry that we won't live long enough to see him settle down...'

'Oh my God, Sandy! You're definitely not *that* old!'

'I'm almost seventy. And he does seem to be taking his sweet time about it. Girls come and go but he never seems... well, they never last long.'

'That's because he doesn't know how to pick the right ones,' Ava said.

'You're right.' Sandy gave her a strangely shrewd look. 'He doesn't.'

'So he's seeing someone at the moment?'

'Not that I know of. If you've heard different, then you've heard more than me. Not that he rushes home to announce every time he gets a new one.' Sandy chuckled. 'Often the first we know of it is when he's sneaking her out of the house in the morning. Drives his mum crackers, I can tell you.'

'Is she mad about him bringing them to the farmhouse?'

Sandy winked. 'Only mad that she doesn't get to sit the wench down and give her some breakfast before he packs her off.'

Sandy bent down to fiddle with a tap, chuckling.

Ava laughed. So Harry was single after all? Or was it just that Sandy was clueless at this point about any potential relationship? But even if he was, did that change anything for her?

It was as these thoughts were running through her head that she realised Sandy was suddenly very still and very quiet. When she looked properly, he was hunched over the bar, and his breathing seemed all wrong.

'Sandy...?'

There was no reply, and then he stumbled backwards and crumpled to the ground.

'Sandy!'

Ava dropped to her knees and turned him onto his back. His breathing was shallow and his skin had suddenly turned grey.

'Sandy?'

There was still no reply. He seemed conscious – his eyes were open – but he didn't seem to be registering anything that was going on around him. It had all happened so quickly and silently that she couldn't quite believe what she was seeing. A moment ago they'd been joking about Harry, and now this.

She checked his pulse and her stomach dropped. She'd learned about this in her first aid training, though she'd never seen it and she couldn't be sure, but... it looked like a heart attack. Not like the ones you saw on films that were all dramatic and obvious, but the ones that happened in real life, that killed people because they were sneaky and pretended to be something else.

Ava fumbled for her phone. She had to keep a cool head, and usually there was no one cooler than her in these situations. She was trained to deal with them, after all, as a lifeguard and in her job, but it was different when it was someone close to you, the stakes somehow higher, the emotions more real and more terrifying.

'What's happened?'

Ava spun round to see Harry with his arms full of boxes. He let them drop to the counter and got to his knees.

'Dad...?' He turned to Ava. 'What's wrong with him?'

'I don't know... I think maybe he's having a heart attack.'

'Shit... have you called the ambulance?'

'I was just about to.'

Harry got his phone out. While he spoke to the emergency services, Sandy began to whisper, but it was hard to tell what he was saying – if it even meant anything at all. Ava tried to sit him up.

'We need aspirin,' she said. 'Harry, can you get some?'

'Aspirin?' Harry ran a hand through his hair. 'Aspirin... where the hell do I get that from?'

'My mum will have some – go and find her.'

'Where is she?'

'I don't know... try the petting zoo – that's where the kids were going, last I saw them. She might be there with them.'

Harry raced off. Ava turned back to Sandy.

'Hang in there,' she said gently. 'A bit of aspirin and a hospital stay – we'll have you raving again in no time.'

She rested her finger on his wrist and tried to swallow her panic as she noted that his pulse was slower. She felt so help-less, simply sitting on the floor with him as he fought for his life, but until the ambulance came or until Harry returned with the aspirin that might give Sandy a fighting chance, there was nothing she could do. She could only stay with him, try to make him comfortable and reassure him that he wasn't alone – though she had no clue how lucid he was at this point and whether he even knew she was there or not. He seemed to drift in and out of consciousness, and it was hard to tell what was going on, even for her, who'd had more hours of training for this scenario than she could count.

Sick of waiting, she reached for her phone and dialled Gaby's number – the first one on her recent call list.

'Where are you?' she asked as Gaby answered. 'Actually, never mind, is Mum with you?'

'No, why?'

'Where is she? Do you have aspirin in your bag?'

'No, only paracetamol – you know Elijah's allergic...'

'Shit, of course. You need to find Mum now; I need some aspirin and she always has some. Is Killian there?'

'Yes, but—'

'I need him at the cider stand – now! I think Sandy's having a heart attack.'

'Right,' Gaby said briskly, 'we're on our way. Have you called the ambulance?'

'Yes, but... don't bring the kids.'

'I'm not stupid, Ava!'

'I didn't say you were! It's just...' Ava looked down at Sandy. He looked like she imagined someone recently dead would look. She wouldn't have wanted to witness this as a child and she didn't think Elijah and Fern ought to. 'Just send Killian!'

Ava ended the call and looked up to see Harry return.

'Got them...' He held out his hand to show her a pack of tiny pills.

'How long for the ambulance?' she asked.

'They couldn't say. This is the trouble with being in the middle of nowhere. It's fine until there's an emergency.' He kneeled down. 'I just give him this?'

'He needs to chew it, if we can somehow get him to.'

Harry took a pill and prised his dad's mouth open, though it wouldn't go far. He shoved the aspirin in. 'I don't think chewing is an option.'

'Then we'll have to hope it dissolves in there and still does the trick.'

Harry stared at him. 'It's hopeless.' He looked up at Ava. 'We're going to lose him, aren't we?'

'Not if I've got anything to do with it.'

'Let me sit with him,' Harry said, holding out his arms.

Ava moved as gently as she could from her position cradling Sandy's head and shoulders and allowed Harry to slip into her place. They both looked down at him.

But then he was suddenly very still, and his breathing almost disappeared until Ava couldn't tell if it had stopped or not. She checked his pulse again.

'Lay him on the floor,' she said tersely. She looked up at Harry. 'CPR – yes?'

Harry put his head close to his dad's face for a moment. 'I think so.'

'You want to do it?' she asked.

'Yes... I think I can...'

'You can!' Ava said. 'Just do it!'

She watched as Harry got to work. He'd been trained in this, just as she had. She could have done it, but she understood that Harry needed to. If they could save Sandy, then maybe they could save Harry at the same time. She was conflicted – was she making things worse? Should she have done the CPR herself? But she had to believe that it was Harry's destiny to save his dad and in doing so regain some of the confidence he'd lost when he hadn't been able to save hers. The universe owed them this – she could only pray that it agreed.

After minutes that seemed like years, she detected movement. Harry saw it at the same time and paused.

'He's back!' Ava cried. 'You did it!'

Harry heaved a sigh, tears filling his eyes. He looked at Ava through them. 'Thanks,' he said.

'It was all you.'

'No it wasn't.'

They both looked down at Sandy. He wasn't out of the woods yet, but they'd brought him back from the brink and surely now the path was clearer, even if it was still long.

There was movement in the corner of Ava's eye, and she

saw Killian running towards the stand with a bag strapped to him.

'Went to get the defib from the station,' he panted.

'Not sure we need it at the moment,' Ava said. 'But keep close by until the ambulance comes in case we do.'

Killian let the bag slide to the ground and joined them on the floor. He put his fingers to Sandy's neck, then glanced at Harry and gave a grim nod. 'He'll be all right.'

Harry nodded too but didn't reply. Perhaps he didn't trust his voice not to crack – Ava knew she'd be the same.

It was then that others started to arrive. Vas was first, having followed Killian from the station.

'What can I do?' he asked.

'Not much right now,' Killian said. 'Maybe keep the crowds away – you know what folks are like at the sniff of drama.'

'Right...'

Vas took up position at the front of the stand. Ava hastily scribbled a notice on the chalkboard that they were closed and put it out at the front. At least she could stop customers coming over, even if they couldn't stop curious onlookers.

By now, Sandy seemed to be coming round a little. He didn't say much but he seemed to be taking things in. Maybe it hadn't been a heart attack after all, Ava thought, though she couldn't imagine what else it might have been. There she was again – overthinking things.

As her mum arrived, so did the ambulance. Gaby showed up a few moments later, having left Elijah and Fern with Marina. She was followed a moment or two later by Clara, who had somehow learned of the drama. News really did travel quickly in Port Promise. Sandy was hauled onto a stretcher and taken into the ambulance.

'I should go with him,' Harry said. 'I've phoned Mum, but she shouldn't be on her own at the hospital.'

'I agree,' Ava said.

'But I think Dad wants me to man the stall.'

Ava gave a weary smile. 'Of course he does.'

'So I'm torn. I don't want to give him the stress of losing a good day's takings but I don't want Mum to be dealing with all this—'

'I'll man the stall until you can get back.'

'It might be all day.'

'Then it's all day.'

'Do you even know what you're doing?'

'You manage it – how hard can it be? I bet Clara will help me. And if we're stuck, we can phone you, right?'

Harry gave a small smile. 'I don't know what I would have done without you today. You were bloody amazing.'

'You saved him.'

'But you spotted what was going on straight away. I didn't. He was ill this morning and we never saw it.'

'Because he would have played it down – you know your dad. Like you said, he'd have been thinking about the day's takings more than his health.'

'Still... I don't know how I'll ever be able to thank you.'

'It's nothing. It's what friends do, isn't it?'

'But I couldn't... your dad...'

'Stop it!' Ava said firmly. 'Stop that right now! It's different and you know it is!'

'Mr Trevithick...'

Harry turned to see the ambulance driver beckon him.

'Got to go,' Harry said to Ava. 'You're sure you can manage?'

'I mean, don't blame me if the stall is a mess when you get back to it, but we'll muddle through.'

'Call me,' he said as he walked away. 'Anything you need to ask, call me.'

'I will – stop stressing! Go to your dad!'

# CHAPTER SIXTEEN

The day that had started like so many other oyster festivals had certainly taken a most unexpected turn. Ava could never have imagined when she woke that morning she'd be selling cider alongside her mum and Clara, while Killian fetched and carried. In a strange way, it was fun. It was like playing pretend for a while, getting to sample a different life, one that belonged to someone else. They were busy, and they often didn't know what they were doing, but as she'd promised Harry, they muddled through, even had a laugh, but all the while thoughts of Sandy and his family were in their heads.

Harry called often to check in. His dad was stable and the prognosis was good, and he said on every occasion it was entirely down to Ava's quick thinking, though she didn't see it that way at all. She told him all was well at the stall (it looked as if someone had lobbed a grenade in at some point, but they were managing the constant queues) and to stop worrying. They all took turns to have a break, though Ava didn't feel as if she needed one. But Killian had insisted she take her mum for a cup of tea and a sit-down while he and Clara kept things ticking along, and she could hardly argue with that.

'It's been a weird day,' Ava said as they walked slowly towards Betty's. Betty didn't have a stand at the festival – she didn't need to; she was so close to the event people went to her if they wanted to, though she'd always have customers spilling out onto the pavements with cups of tea and coffee, too large in number to fit inside. They'd be sitting on her tables and chairs, and on nearby benches or perched on kerbs or balanced on the harbour wall. Today was no different – in fact, because of the good weather, Ava thought today was perhaps the busiest she'd ever seen it.

'It has,' Jill agreed, wiping a hand down the apron she'd forgotten to take off. 'I feel as if I've had a bath in Trevithick's cider. I'm sure I'll be washing it out of my clothes for the next year.'

Ava laughed. 'Me too. I wonder what Dad would have made of all this.'

'Goodness knows. I'm sad he didn't get to see it. I'm sad he didn't get to see you today – he'd have been so proud.'

'I didn't do anything much.'

'That's where you're wrong.' Jill stopped and looked at the queue spilling out of Betty's door. 'Do we really want to stand in that for a cup of tea? Perhaps Gaby will make a flask at the house and bring it to us.'

'Want me to phone her?'

Jill nodded and, while Ava did the necessary, leaned on the wall and stared out to sea.

'It looks so peaceful, doesn't it?' Jill nodded at a stretch of blue that was calm as a village pond. 'You couldn't even imagine it being dangerous looking at it now.'

'No,' Ava agreed, turning her own gaze out to the bay. 'You really couldn't. It's a funny sort of love-hate relationship we have, isn't it? Us and the sea, I mean.'

'Most days I hate it since your dad went.'

'Only most days?'

Jill turned to her. 'Less and less as the weeks pass. I suppose that means I'm moving on. Makes me feel guilty, though.'

'I know, but it's how grief works, isn't it? At least, how it should work. Dad wouldn't want you to mourn like the first day forever.'

Jill let out a sigh but didn't respond. Ava rested a hand on her mum's and studied her features. Grief was a strange thing. While it had steeled Ava and made her want to fight for the memory and legacy of her father, it had sent Jill into a spiral of misery that had taken some getting out of. For a while, the Morrow girls had feared they'd lose her in the depths of a despair that was as deep and cruel as the unpredictable ocean that had claimed their dad. It looked as if things were finally changing for the better. If that were true, Ava would lend as much support as her mum needed to get her life back on track – a life that was now a different one, but one that still mattered. She and Clara and Gaby – they needed her. They needed her as much as they'd done as children – maybe even more so. They needed her in different and more subtle ways, but her presence in their lives was perhaps more important now than ever.

But she also needed them, and Ava had never seen that in the way she had since her father's death. It had always been one-sided before – her mum had given and she'd taken. For the first time in her life, she'd begun to recognise that it had to work both ways. That was why she'd finally found peace with her decision to abandon her ambitions for the lifeboat crew.

'Want to go and see Dad's plaque?' Ava turned to her mum. 'It'll be a bit quieter down that end of the harbour. I can text Gaby to tell her we'll be there.'

'That'd be nice,' Jill said.

Ava led the way. It was still so new and so shiny, and strangely small and unimposing, screwed to the harbour wall almost discreetly in a way that apologised for existing at all. Even then, Ava wondered what her dad would make of it. He'd say it was a fuss over nothing, but secretly she thought he'd be quite pleased that someone had taken the time to do it for him.

Jill bundled a corner of her apron around her hand and lovingly wiped it over. 'Silly thing's all mucked up.'

'It looks fine,' Ava said, putting an arm around her. 'He'd have liked it a bit mucked up. Remember how he always used to complain if you went mad cleaning for visitors?'

'"I never asked to live in a show home",' Jill mimicked. '"Can't find a bloody thing." Oh, and his boots – bane of my life, those boots. They were always lying somewhere for me to trip over.'

Ava smiled. 'They were. He didn't care. "Spick and span at the station", everything like clockwork but, at home…'

'I suppose it felt like a busman's holiday to have everything at home as organised as it was at the station.' Jill turned to Ava with a watery smile. 'I feel too young to be a widow. I think sometimes, knowing what I am, saying the word to myself – that's almost harder than everything else. I thought we had years left. I thought we'd go together when we were old and couldn't feed ourselves any longer. I mean, I'm not young, I know, but I'm not old either. I've got all these years ahead of me without him. What do I do with them?'

'I don't know,' Ava said. 'I wish I could say something that would magically give you the answer, but I can't. Sometimes… I'm twenty-four but I still feel like a stupid kid. I thought I'd have my dad forever, until I could work out what being an adult was and how to do it properly.' She shrugged. 'It's not fair but we have to live with it now.'

'You have me,' Jill said.

'I know. I'm so glad of that. And I have Gaby and Clara too, so I guess I have a lot more than some. If Harry had lost his dad today… well, it made me realise I'm lucky to have you lot, because he's got no one except his mum and dad, and his mum is nowhere near as tough as you.'

Jill turned to the plaque and gazed at it silently for a moment before she turned back to Ava.

'It's funny, but seeing you take charge like you did today... I'd never seen you like that before. You reminded me so much of your dad.'

'Did I?' Ava gave a bemused smile. 'I suppose that's kind of cool.'

'He'd have been so proud.'

'He'd have been telling me how I was doing it wrong too.'

'Probably.' Jill smiled. 'It's made me think.'

'Oh?'

'About your plans... your future. I can't help but feel you're planning it around me. In fact, I know you are.'

'Not exactly—'

'But I asked you to give up your ambition to join the crew.'

'It doesn't matter about that—'

'It does. I've thought about it a lot, and I've realised it's unfair. I've realised that I'm saving you only to smother you. I couldn't keep your dad safe, and he wouldn't have thanked me for trying – in fact, he'd have hated it and resented me. And yet I'm trying to do that to you.'

'I'll never resent you, Mum – you know that.'

'I know. But what I'm trying to say is that if you still want to do it, I'm giving you my blessing.'

'Mum, I appreciate you saying that, but if it's going to cause you pain or stress then I don't want to do it.'

Jill gave a small smile. You're so much more capable than I ever imagined – I saw that today. To me, you were still my littlest girl, still my baby who I had to protect, but today it hit me – you're a woman, and a smart and brave one who could give so much to the world if her daft old mum wasn't holding her back.'

Ava began to cry. It had come from nowhere. Perhaps it was

the drama of the day, the pent-up adrenaline, but whatever it was, the tears were pouring down her face.

'Oh, Ava... I didn't mean to upset you!' Jill pulled her close and hugged her tight.

'You're not,' Ava sobbed. 'You're giving me the most lovely compliments and it's just that I...'

'It's OK. I think I understand.'

Ava pulled free of her mum's arms and wiped her eyes. 'I don't want to worry you.'

'I know.'

'And I don't ever want to put you through the pain you went through over losing Dad.'

'I know that too.'

'When I was asking for your blessing, I never wanted to make things hard for you.'

'I know you didn't. I know you were doing what you were born to do. You're a Morrow – you were always going to want to do something with your life like that, but I never noticed it coming. I should have realised. I thought because Gaby and Clara hadn't joined the service in such an active way, I'd escaped any of my daughters doing it. I'd thought it was the end of the line for Iziah's promise, and after losing your dad, I thought good riddance.'

'No... I get that.'

'But you can't escape who you are, and I can't be that self-ish. If you want to go on the boats, go on the boats.'

'Mum...?'

'I mean it. Port Promise needs people like you... isn't that what you told Cormac... and Harry?'

'How did you...?'

'Seriously?' Jill gave a wry smile. 'There are no secrets around here no matter how hard you try.'

'You can say that again!'

Jill pulled her into another hug, and they stayed that way for a few moments, until they heard Gaby's voice.

'What's going on here then?'

They pulled apart and both smiled as they wiped away tears.

'Oh,' Ava said, 'just having a chat... as you do.'

'I've been phoning you,' Gaby said.

'Have you?'

She handed them a flask. 'Because I didn't know where you were!'

'Oh!' Ava clapped a hand to her mouth and grinned at her mum from behind it. 'Sorry! I was meant to text you to tell you we'd moved but I forgot!'

Gaby rolled her eyes. 'Thanks so much for making me run around town like an idiot.'

'Yeah,' Ava replied, 'but town is only about a mile wide so...'

'That's not the point – it's bedlam around here today and having to look after the kids by myself isn't exactly helping.'

'I know,' Jill said. 'But I'm sure the Trevithicks appreciate you letting Killian help.'

'Right, I suppose so,' Gaby said. 'I'm going to see if he's OK.'

'Where are the kids?' Ava asked.

'With Marina.'

'Still? She'll be exhausted,' Jill said.

'So you're not entirely on your own with them,' Ava added.

Gaby scowled and Ava thought better of pressing her point.

'I'll be back for the flask in a bit,' she said.

'We'll be at the stand as soon as we've had this,' Jill said. 'We'll bring it back to you there, if you're going to see Killian.'

Gaby waved a hand to acknowledge their plan as she walked away.

'I don't know how she got so bossy,' Jill said as they watched her go.

Ava giggled. 'You're not supposed to say that about your kids.'

Jill smiled 'Doesn't mean I don't love her. I love you all dearly, but I can still see who you are.'

'Warts and all.'

Jill kissed her on the head, then opened the flask. 'My beautiful girls have many faults, but warts are definitely not on the list.'

# CHAPTER SEVENTEEN

The sky was blue, a patchwork of clouds blowing quickly across it casting light and shade as each one crossed the sun. Ava stood on the sand and watched as the lifeboat performed its regular practice manoeuvres. She'd seen it launch from the station and wondered if Harry was on board. One day soon, if luck was on her side, she'd be out there too. Vas had fast-tracked her fitness tests and her medical and now it was all about getting the formalities out of the way. Not that she'd be going to sea on rescues any time soon, even after that. A good eighteen months of training and assessments were waiting, but at least she'd be working towards it and doing her bit at the station in other ways. The journey had begun.

It had been a week since the oyster festival. Sandy was home from the hospital and taking it easy, doing very well by all accounts, though Ava hadn't yet been up to see him. She was waiting for an invite, not wanting to put them out if they weren't yet ready for visitors. She'd sent a text every day to Harry, though, and his replies had been positive. He had a lot to do around the place, he said, but was happy to do it if it meant his dad getting well again.

So she was surprised to hear her name being called and to see Harry striding up the beach towards her. He was in his uniform – a dressed-down version – but it suited him. In fact, Ava was forced to admit, he looked pretty damn good. He looked like the sort of man who'd pass you in the street and make you hold your breath while you looked again.

As he got closer she could see him holding something down by his side. As he greeted her, he held it out.

'Flowers?' Ava frowned. 'For me?'

'Yes. I saw you from the window of the station; I've been meaning to call by the caravan so... well, you saved me a trip.'

'But...' Ava took the posy from him. 'You've never bought me flowers.'

'That's true,' he said. 'But you've never saved my dad's life before. Actually, when I say it out loud like that I realise that flowers are a bit shit. I should have got you a car or something.'

'*You* saved your dad's life,' Ava reminded him. 'You did the CPR.'

'Only because you told me to. Honestly I was all over the place; all my training went straight out of my head. It was your quick thinking that was the make or break of it.'

'Well...' Ava put the flowers to her nose. She could detect a faint scent, but the breeze from the sea snatched it away. 'I love them. Thank you. Although, if the car is still on offer...'

Harry grinned. 'What are you up to?'

'Standing here watching the boat. No lessons this morning. What about you?'

'Doing some maintenance around the station. I helped with the launch and now I'm waiting for them to come back in.'

'So you're not back on the crew yet?'

'I'm not ready.'

'I think it's good you recognise that.'

'That's what Killian said. He said it shows maturity.'

'God! Praise from Killian! What next?'

'I know. If he doesn't watch it, people will start to think he's a functioning human being.'

'They will – imagine that. How's your dad?'

'He's good. Watching a lot of cricket.'

'And listening to some One Direction?'

'That's banned – far too exciting.'

'And cricket isn't?'

'Have you ever watched a cricket match?'

Ava laughed. 'I see your point.' She hugged her flowers to her chest and looked up at him. 'How's your girlfriend?'

His forehead crinkled. 'What girlfriend? Who told you I had one?'

'Nobody. I was just checking the current situation, because there's usually someone lurking about. So you don't have one?'

'Nope. Don't have time right now. You know, a ton of work to do while Dad's out of action and stuff here at the station so...'

'Yeah, of course. I suppose that makes sense.'

Her gaze went out to the water. 'Looks as if the boat's coming back in. Will they need you?'

'Not yet,' he said. 'I bet you're looking forward to joining.'

'I am. I'll be as impatient as hell – just so you know. Eighteen months is a long time.'

'Knowing you, you'll do it in twelve. You'll fly through those competencies.'

'I hope so.'

'I know so. I'm really glad you're coming to join us.'

'Are you?'

'Of course. You're amazing! You're going to be amazing.'

He smiled down at her, and she was gripped by the urge to pull him into a kiss.

'Harry. I—'

She never got to finish. His pager bleeped. He took it from his pocket and frowned.

'Well, at least the boat's warmed up,' he said tersely. He looked up at Ava. 'Sorry... got to...'

'Yeah, yeah of course.'

'This'll be your life soon!' he shouted as he raced towards the station. 'Never a dull moment!'

*Never a moment to say something that needs saying either, apparently*. Perhaps it was for the best she didn't get to tell him about her new feelings. Perhaps it would have ruined their friendship. It would have most certainly complicated working at the station together. And maybe these feelings weren't even real. Maybe they were only a result of all the drama lately and the flowers and his dad's near-death... and maybe when things calmed down she wouldn't feel like that.

Putting the flowers to her nose and sniffing them again, she decided that yes, that must be it. She watched as the inshore boat took off across the waves. There were more important things to think about and, like Harry, she didn't have time for romance.

# CHAPTER EIGHTEEN

Ava's job meant she often slept soundly. A combination of fresh air, sea and physical exertion were the perfect conditions for it, and the quiet little corner of the park where her van was tethered meant there was little to disturb her.

But tonight, sleep was nowhere to be found. Even though she'd had a few glasses of wine with Clara and then walked home the long way round on top of all the other demands of the day, it was gone 2 a.m. and she was still wide awake.

Fed up with tossing and turning in her bed, she got up and padded through to the kitchen, where the solar lights hanging from the decking balustrades outside her windows cast their warm glow through the glass and into the room. She didn't need to switch on any other lights as she filled the kettle and set it on the stove to boil. Then, with a cup of camomile tea in her hand, she went to the sofa and sat, pulling a throw over her legs to stave off the night's chill.

She supposed, as her gaze rested on the moon outside her window, she ought not to be surprised that she couldn't sleep, considering all the new developments in her life. Things were about to change beyond recognition, and things were also about to get very busy. She'd have her job and her family, and any free time she might have had would now be spent at the lifeboat station.

And, on top of everything else, there was Harry. Her emotions on this subject were more jumbled than on anything else. Try as she might to put any romantic notions of him out of her mind, she couldn't. She'd wanted so badly to kiss him on the beach it had taken her completely by surprise.

Her gaze went to the vase on the table where she'd displayed his flowers.

The more she thought about it, the more the fog cleared. Why had Harry been such a constant in her life? Many men came and went but he had always been there. Was it because, on some level, she'd always recognised him as a soul mate? Deep down, had she always known they were meant to be together? Was that why she'd instinctively (and often unfairly – even Ava couldn't deny that) hated every girl he'd ever introduced her to?

Eventually her thoughts tied her in knots. She leaned back on the seat and closed her eyes with an exasperated sigh. Overthinking again – she wished she could stop just long enough to figure out what she wanted.

Then her eyes snapped open and she bolted up. To hell with overthinking!

Throwing off her blanket, she went to get her phone from the bedside table and unlocked it.

*I need to talk to you. Can we meet up tomorrow?*

Her heart pounding, wondering if she was about to do the craziest thing of her entire life, Ava pressed send on the message. She stared at the screen for a moment, until it went dark.

Stupid – it wasn't like he was going to be watching for her text messages in the middle of the night. He wasn't going to be watching for her text messages at any time because he had better things to do.

Ava checked the time. Her schedule was pretty light for the following day but it wouldn't be made easy if she was exhausted. With one last glance at her phone, she got back into bed, pulled the covers over her shoulders and tried to empty her mind so she could sleep.

At some point Ava had dropped off, and she woke with her alarm to find a reply from Harry. He'd sent it early that morning.

*Sure. Meet at Cormac's for lunch?*

Ava typed a reply to confirm and then, jittery all over again without understanding why, she went to take a shower.

Throughout the morning, Ava's emotions had swung between wanting desperately for her early sessions to be over to wishing lunchtime might never arrive. She'd done her best to focus and hoped none of her students had noticed her weird mood – she supposed it helped that many of them were holiday-makers and so didn't know her and didn't have a clue what her normal mood was, and probably assumed she was always this scatty.

As the morning session ended and she found herself with a two-hour gap, she went into the office and paid particular atten-tion to hair that she normally left to dry on its own, using the hairdryer in the changing rooms and applying a little serum to smooth the ends. She patted on a light layer of foundation and added a slick of mascara; she wanted to look nice but didn't want it to be too obvious that she'd made an effort, because that would be weird, given that this was just Harry and lunch at Cormac's shack. Finally, she sprayed some perfume that Clara had given her the previous Christmas, then put on a pair of nice jeans instead of her joggers and headed out.

Her steps were impatient, but she had to slow herself down because the sun was high and it was warm and she didn't want to be sweaty when she got there, and... *Why the hell am I this stressed? It's lunch with Harry – you've done it a million times.*

'Hi, Ava!'

Marina waved from across the street but Ava couldn't stop. Harry wouldn't have cared if she was a minute or two late but she could barely string a coherent sentence together right now as it was, let alone make small talk with her mum's friend, so she simply waved back.

'Can't stop – sorry!'

'Always rushing,' Marina said with a smile. 'See you later.'

Ava breathed a reply that Marina probably didn't hear and marched on. She had to get there, she had to do this now or she'd lose her nerve and she'd never do it.

*Don't overthink it.*

If she thought about it for a minute, she'd turn around and go back to the office and she'd never speak of it again. Harry would marry some redhead he'd met at a beach bonfire and she'd probably have to be godmother to their redheaded children or something just as horrible.


When the shack finally came into view, Harry wasn't at a table as she'd expected. He wasn't even at the hatch chatting to Cormac. He was perched on a nearby wall. Ava stopped in her tracks as he looked up and saw her. He didn't look happy. Without waiting, he slid off his seat and strode over.

'What's wrong?' she asked, because it was obvious something was amiss.

'I've just left the station.'

'Oh. Did something happen there?'

'Killian happened. What did you say to him?'

'I haven't said anything to him,' she replied, feeling flustered. She never got flustered and she couldn't say she cared much for it.

'So you didn't tell him about our conversation?'

'Which one?'

'You know which one!' Harry glanced over his shoulder, then lowered his voice. 'You know which one! I told you stuff I've never told anyone because I thought I could trust you.'

'You can—'

'You know what this place is like. Now Killian thinks I'm falling apart and everyone will know about it. The last thing I need is all those pitying looks.'

'I didn't tell Killian… I told Gaby. I didn't tell her everything, I just said… Well, I wanted to help.'

'It didn't help, Ava. It made everything so much worse.'

'How?' Ava's wits began to recover and she began to feel aggrieved at his tone. 'How have I made it worse? How could it possibly have been worse than it was?'

'Because now Killian thinks I'm a pathetic basket case! You know what he told me?'

Ava shook her head.

'He told me to man up! Don't you think I've tried to do that? Don't you think manning up was the first thing I tried?'

'I didn't say you had to *man up*,' Ava replied tartly.

'No, but you had to go and meddle, didn't you? I told you I would get help, but I wanted to do it in my own time and in my own way. I thought you would have understood that.'

'I do!'

'Then why did you have to go and tell Gaby that I have post-traumatic stress disorder?'

'Because you bloody well do!' Ava yelled. 'And you're being an absolute tit about it! You can't bury your head in the sand and expect it to just go away!'

He stared at her, shaking his head. 'There's no talking to you, is there? There never has been. All these years we've known each other, you'd think I'd have got that by now. You can never be wrong about anything, can you?'

'I'm not wrong about this,' she snapped.

'That's not the point! You can't fix everything. You have to lose this stupid saviour complex you've carried around your whole life! Being Jack Morrow's daughter doesn't mean you can do anything you want – you're just like your bloody dad! He never knew when to back off either! And if it wasn't for him and his stupid superhero—'

Harry stopped dead and suddenly looked mortified. 'Leave me alone,' he said quietly now, almost guiltily. 'Don't try to help me again; it's the sort of help I can do without.'

He started to walk away, head down, shoulders hunched.

'Harry!' Ava called after him, but he kept going. 'Harry, please... I'm...'

What was the point? He wasn't listening. She could fall to her knees and grovel but it wouldn't make a bit of difference.

Cormac's voice in her ear made her spin around. He was standing behind her with his hands in his apron pocket, watching Harry go.

'Trouble between you two?' he asked softly.

'You could say that.'

'It's a shame, but I'm sure things will work out. You always seem like the best of friends to me.'

Ava shook her head. 'I'm not sure it will this time. I think I might have blown it.'

'My ma always says there's nothing that can't be mended, only death.'

'That's just it – I think it's death that might be part of the problem.'

'Ah... your da?' he asked with a shrewd look.

She nodded.

'And Harry blames himself for what happened?'

'I'm not sure who he blames,' Ava said slowly. 'I thought he blamed himself... Maybe I was wrong. But if I am, I don't know what to do about it. I don't even know how I feel about it.'

Cormac patted her on the arm. 'I'm sure you'll work it out. Are you staying for something to eat?'

Ava shook her head. 'Not today, Cormac, thanks. I'm not as hungry as I thought I was.'

# CHAPTER NINETEEN

Ava didn't see Harry for the rest of that week. She'd gone from shock to hurt, to a refusal to accept blame, to resentment, to anger, and then to sadness and a growing fear that she'd made a mistake so big it might just have ruined her entire life. But the one thing she believed, something unflinching and unchanging during that week, was that she ought to stay out of his way and keep her head down. No more trying to fix his problems, no more trying to figure out whether he was The One. If all she managed to do at this point was salvage a lifelong friendship that really mattered to her, then she'd see it as a job well done and happily take it.

She did, however, lock horns with Killian. He couldn't speak to people in the way he'd spoken to Harry and be allowed to get away with it. He had no right to ignore a cry for help or respond to it as he had. Harry had taken it remarkably well under the circumstances, but to someone else, Killian's attitude might do real harm. And for once, Gaby had taken Ava's side over her husband's and had told him much the same thing. It made Ava feel a bit better but didn't change the fact that the damage had already been done.

But those things had to be put to the back of her mind when she was called to do her fitness tests. She'd been doing her own training in her spare time ever since she'd been given the go-ahead, and so she felt confident when the day came. It was good to think about something else too, things that she had control over. It was up to her whether she passed or failed; there were things she could do to influence the outcome here. And so she'd thrown herself into it – running fast, swimming hard, hauling lead weights from a swimming pool – proving herself worthy. She'd been elated to pass with flying colours, but, given the effort, hardly surprised. And the medical was as straightforward as it got. Then she had the call.

'Congratulations,' Vas had said in warm tones. 'We'll see you next week to start your training!'

The first person she called was her mum. She wasn't sure what kind of reaction she was going to get – she imagined Jill would have mixed feelings. But she wanted to share her news with the person who mattered most to her.

If Jill was upset or disappointed, she didn't say so. In fact, she simply suggested that they have a family get-together so they could all celebrate.

They met at Seaspray Cottage that evening. By the time Ava got there, Clara and Logan, Gaby, Killian and the kids had already arrived. As she walked into the kitchen where Jill had laid out nibbles and drinks, everyone started to clap.

Ava stopped and stared.

'Well done!' Clara ran to hug her. Jill followed, and then Gaby, and Ava realised it had taken a lot for her to do that.

She gave them all a grateful smile. 'I haven't actually done anything yet!'

'You got in,' Killian said. 'That's a feat in itself, let me tell you.'

Fern stepped forward and handed her an envelope. Ava opened it up.

'Wow! This is so cool – thank you!'

'I drew you,' Fern said. 'Elijah did the boat.'

The outside of the card was a regular shop-bought congratulatory greeting card, but the children had embellished it with glitter and paint and their own messages such as 'awesome aunty' and 'world's best lifesaver'. And inside were more drawings of a boat on the sea with two figures standing on board, and another drawing of – presumably – Ava, judging by the hair – standing on shore in a superhero pose – and more messages about how brilliant they thought she was. A lump formed in Ava's throat. Was that really how they saw her?

'I love it,' she said. 'I'm going to put it up on my locker so I can see it every time I go to the station.'

Next Clara gave her a gift bag. Ava peered inside. 'You didn't have to get me stuff!'

'It's nothing. They're just things I'd want if I'd been at sea in bad weather. You know, when I got back on dry land and went home.'

Ava took out the items one by one. There was a jar of luxury hot chocolate, some rich moisturising cream, a hair mask, foot soak and a pack of strong throat sweets.

'It's a sort of care package,' Clara explained.

'You never got me one of those,' Killian told her.

Clara grinned. 'That's Christmas sorted for you then.'

Jill had potted a special plant arrangement for her to take back to the caravan, while Gaby had gifted her a bottle of Navy rum, apologising that she hadn't had much time to get anything more original but that it would do much the same job as the hot chocolate Clara had given her, only in a far more potent way.

'I don't know what to say.' Ava beamed at them. 'I didn't expect this much fuss.'

'I don't know why,' Logan said. 'It's impressive from where I'm standing. I couldn't do it – I know that much.'

'I haven't done it yet.'

'I couldn't even get as far as you have!' Logan added, and Clara gave his arm a brief squeeze.

'Your talents lie elsewhere,' she said.

Ava looked at them all standing in front of her. All the people she loved most in the world... well, almost all of them. Her dad was missing, of course, but she hoped, somehow, he might be looking down on her and he might be a little bit proud.

The reminder pinged onto Ava's phone early morning – not that she'd needed one. Her lifeboat training began today and she'd lain awake thinking of little else. Today was the first of many sessions. There were many steps to take, things from first aid to navigation to pyrotechnics to be mastered and tested on. For each she would have to be signed off by her trainer before she could move on to the next. Today was only the start. It was going to be meticulous and sometimes boring, about putting God into the details, and it was going to require patience – something that didn't come naturally to Ava. There was so much to learn before she'd even be allowed near her first sea rescue, and keeping her enthusiasm and impatience in check might test her more than any competency assessment she had to pass.

Her boss had given her time off to go to the station today, and she was conscious of the fact she'd be asking for a lot more over the coming months. It felt strange, as she brushed her teeth and stared at her reflection in the mirror, mulling over what the morning might bring, to be heading somewhere other than her usual Monday morning teaching sessions. She'd offered to work some weekends and more unsociable hours instead, which had actually suited the school well because a lot of learners liked weekends so they could fit sessions in around their own jobs or cram them into mini-breaks. She was on the rota to do the next two; the weekend after that was the Port Promise charity triathlon, which included a sea-swimming leg, and she'd offered to be on lifeguard duty for that, as she had done every year since she'd qualified. Killian and Cormac were competing in the event this year, and even if it hadn't been a tradition of hers to volunteer as lifeguard, she'd have come down to watch – there was no way she'd miss it. All that meant no free weekends, more or less, for the next month. Then again, her social life was so dire these days at least it would be a welcome break from the boredom.

It wasn't that she had to avoid anywhere Harry might be, which, in a place as small as Port Promise, was no mean feat, but things were so cringingly awkward since their falling-out that she didn't know if she could face him. Not that she'd be able to avoid it at the lifeboat station, of course, but at least it would be in a professional capacity and in the company of others, which would help to defuse the situation. And perhaps their schedules wouldn't clash for ages anyway. She wasn't yet serving as a fully-fledged member of the team and so was mostly there training on the weekdays, and he worked during the week and was only there doing his drills at weekends. Thinking of it that way, it could be ages before she was forced to spend time with him, and that suited her just fine.

She didn't need to ask to know he was still angry with her for trying to help him, and though that made her angry in return, it also filled her with shame that she'd gone about it in such a clumsy way. It hurt her to see him trying to bottle up his problems when there were people around him who could help, if only they knew the full extent of his suffering. With neither of them willing to back down, the only option was to go on avoiding each other.

His loss, she thought as she rinsed her mouth. They could have had something good, and they very nearly did. If only he'd swallow his stupid macho pride and accept some help, they might still have a chance. But she wasn't about to apologise for being a good person, and if he was expecting an apology he was going to be disappointed.

She'd detoured via her dad's memorial plaque and had spent a moment buffing it with the sleeve of her jacket, silently seeking his guidance and support and wishing desperately she could get an answer from him. It still hurt. People had told her time would heal the pain, but that wasn't what was happening. The pain was still there and she suspected it would always be there, but it was changing, becoming something new. It was no longer like a knife to the heart whenever she thought of him, but rather a duller pain, like a stitch from running too hard and too fast, and perhaps, in time, it would become a background ache, ever present but not enough to knock her off course. She'd wondered many times what he might make of this decision of hers, and she'd tried to reassure herself that he'd be pleased about it. The nagging doubt that he might not be was something she couldn't allow space to grow, and so she'd shut out any other possibility.

The skies over the sea were grey, but the air was warm and humid as Ava moved on. There was rain in it, but nothing heavy, only the sort of drizzle that found its way beneath umbrellas and hoods. Jill would be on her allotment now, tending her plants, the humidity sending her grey hair into spiralling curls. Ava wondered if her mum was thinking about her this morning, and how she might be feeling about a day she'd never wanted to see. She'd made the most wonderful fuss of her at the family gathering – everyone had – and Ava was grateful for the outward show of support. And there had been a lovely text that morning wishing her luck, and Ava was grateful for that too. She resolved to make time to call at Seaspray Cottage later.

Robin's boat was in the harbour as she passed by, and he was on deck, cleaning his windows.

'Hey, Robin!' Ava called.

He turned and smiled. His smiles looked painful these days. Ava had to wonder if they'd always been like that and she'd simply never noticed, or whether the sight of her and her family was what caused it. No matter how many times they'd told him her dad's death wasn't his fault, it seemed he would take the guilt to his own grave. Despite this – and perhaps because of it – Ava made extra time to acknowledge him whenever she saw him and to be as cheery and warm as possible.

So she went to the harbour wall and called over to him. 'Boat's looking good.'

Robin pulled off his cap, ran a hand through his thick white hair and nodded. 'It'll do,' he said. 'Starting your training today?'

Ava smiled. 'How did you know that?'

He shrugged. 'Everyone's talking about it.'

'Oh God, are they?'

'It's something worth talking about, ain't it?'

'Well, that doesn't mean a lot – most things are worth talking about round here.'

'True... but Jack Morrow's daughter on the boats... That's got folk excited.'

'In a good way?' Ava asked uncertainly.

Robin clamped his hat back on. 'Depends who you ask.'

'I suppose it does,' Ava replied doubtfully. 'Well, I should probably get on... don't want to be late for my first day.'

'Aye...' Robin went back to his bucket and dipped his cloth into it. 'Mind how you go.'

'See you, Robin!'

At the station, Ava noticed the front doors were wide open, so there was no need to punch in the code at the back to get in. Instead, she went round to where the bow of the all-weather lifeboat was exposed to the elements and called out, expecting

Maxine – who she was meant to be meeting for her training today – to pop up from somewhere, hands covered in paint or grease or wax or some other maintenance-type thing, her fluffy blonde hair pulled into its usual perky ponytail. But there was no answer.

So she went in and found the door that led to the offices and locker rooms, and pulled it open to reveal a corridor lined with photographs. She knew exactly where to look to find her grand-father, great-grandfather and great-uncles, standing proudly with their crews in the uniforms of the day next to boats that looked primitive compared to the one that went out today, black-and-white grainy images of her own personal family history. She'd seen them a million times before, but they'd never connected with her in the way they did today. A lump came to her throat as she came face to face with her grandfather, smil-ing, arms folded across his broad chest. She'd been little when he'd died – not at sea like her dad, but of a creeping cancer that nobody had known about until it was too late – and she could barely remember him, but she remembered the stories her dad loved to tell.

She moved along the row, her gaze falling on framed news-paper clippings recounting daring rescues and more photos of different crews – some containing Morrows and some not, though her ancestors were never far away.

And then there was a portrait of her dad, leaning against the boat with a cigarette hanging from his lips and a grin on his face. It had been taken many years before – probably before she'd even been born, because he'd quit smoking shortly before Clara's birth. His hair was dark and thick, sticking up at daft angles, like he'd just pulled off his safety helmet, and he was dressed in dated waterproofs that the service had since replaced with more modern versions, over a thick knitted jumper. She'd seen this photo before, but not with the obituary that now accompanied it. The date of his death was there and the years of his service were documented, as was a brief description of the circumstances of his death and a tribute to his heroism.

It caught Ava unawares, and the emotion she'd been holding back all morning threatened to engulf her. She wanted to stand and linger – she could have stared at the photo for hours – but if she did her sadness might win. She had to put it away – for now at least. There was a time to dwell on her dad and to process this, but now wasn't it.

As she heaved a breath and steadied herself, a noise from the far end of the hallway caught her attention. A door opened, but it wasn't Maxine standing there. It was Harry.

Thoughts of photos and obituaries were forgotten as he gave her a curt nod. 'Morning.'

'Oh…'

Ava scanned the room beyond the doorway frantically, hoping to see someone – anyone – following Harry out. But there was only Harry, his gaze cold and formal. On another day – maybe even another moment on this day – she might have given as good as she got, but it threw her and she blushed.

'I'm meant to be starting my first competency today,' she said.

'I know. I'm meant to be going through it with you.'

'But I thought…'

'Maxine had to go to see Charlie's teacher. Something urgent or something… I don't know. Anyway, I said I could step in.'

'Well, that's… that's kind of you,' Ava said stiffly, finding her feet again. If he could handle this professionally then so could she. It couldn't be that hard, could it?

'I'm only doing my bit for the station,' Harry said as stiffly as her. 'It's no big deal.'

'That's good… I'd hate to think I was a hassle.'

'It's no hassle.'

He turned back to the doorway. She noticed his choice of

words. She'd said she didn't want to be a hassle, but his reply had avoided all reference to her. *It's* no hassle, he'd said, like the *situation* was no hassle, but he hadn't denied that *she* might be. She tried not to let it mean anything.

'Shall we get started?' he asked, his back to her as he walked towards the rooms beyond the corridor. 'The sooner we crack on, the sooner we can both get back to other things.'

This time she bristled at his choice of words. There was no mistaking his meaning. He wanted to get this over and get her out of his sight. It was a struggle, but she fought to contain her rising annoyance.

*You're here to learn and you can be the bigger person – screw Harry and his attitude.*

If he thought he was going to put her off he was sadly mistaken. Maybe, after all that had happened between them he no longer wanted to serve alongside her, but as she wasn't about to give up, he was going to be disappointed in that regard too. Ava was going to do this. She was going to nail it too. She was going to fly through this training and all the other training, and she was going to be brilliant and do her father's memory proud. She was going to repay her mum's faith with success. And so Harry could be as salty as he liked because it would only make her more determined to succeed.

She followed him. 'So what's first?'

'Equipment checks,' he said shortly.

'I know about that. My dad—'

'You know how to put it on, I'm sure, but you don't know how to check it for potential issues. And even if you think you do, you need to be shown.' He turned to face her.

'I'm just saying—'

'Well, for once, don't. Listen to what someone else has to say. I realise you're not very good at that but try very hard.'

Ava scowled at him now, heat rushing to her face. She could

easily have exploded, but though it got harder every minute she spent in his company, she held it in.

'Fine,' she said. 'I get it.'

'Come on.' Harry turned away again. 'We'll start in the kit room.'

Most of what Harry showed her she'd seen her dad do many times over the years, but she needed him to sign off this training session. Considering their fractious start, however, it was taking superhuman strength to listen and nod and not offer a single contradictory opinion on anything he said, but she did it anyway.

Underpinning her prickling annoyance was a sense of sadness. That she and Harry had come to this: sniping, bitching, sarcastic barbed comments… even dislike. On his part, of course, because she could never truly dislike Harry no matter what he did. If anyone had told her a month before that this was in their future she'd have laughed in their face. But here they were, and there went all those years of friendship, lost in one confused instant, like they'd never happened at all.

Saddest of all was the way he looked at her. In all those years, no matter what she'd done – and she'd done some stinky things, the worst of which was standing him up for a date – he'd never looked at her so coldly, in a way she'd never imagined her easy-going friend could look at anyone. It made her realise just how badly things had gone.

Was this really all her fault? she wondered as he showed her how to inspect her waterproofs for unseen holes. And if it was, could she salvage it, or was all hope lost?

'Are you even listening to me?'

Ava blinked up at him.

Harry, it seemed, had been telling her something important, but what it was she had no clue.

He frowned. 'I suppose you think you know all there is to know already? You might, but it makes no difference. I have to show you, and you have to demonstrate that it's gone in.'

'It *has* gone in!' Ava fired back. 'And yes, I did already know... some of it anyway.'

'Some of it?' Harry's tone dripped with sarcasm. 'Well that's OK then. As long as you know some of it, no need to waste my time here. Let's pass you straight away. Let's pass every competency right here and now and get you on that boat.'

'At least one of us would be going out on the boat,' Ava snapped, but as soon as the words had left her mouth, she clapped a hand to it, her face burning with shame. 'Harry, I'm so—'

'I'm trying to help you,' he said quietly. 'And you're right – the sooner we can get you through your training the sooner you'll be on the crew, and God knows they need the extra hands.'

'Harry, I'm sorry. I didn't mean—'

He shook his head and stood up, letting the waterproofs he'd been holding fall to the floor. 'Let's have a break. In fact, Vas will be here soon – he can finish up with you.'

Ava shot to her feet as he walked to the door. 'Harry, wait!'

But he didn't wait. The noise of his exit echoed around the building as he let the door slam shut. Ava rubbed savagely at tears springing from nowhere. It wasn't anger – at least she wasn't angry with Harry – but maybe she was angry with herself. Why couldn't she keep her stupid mouth shut? Why did she have to keep making things worse? She'd already lost his friendship, but now her stupid temper threatened his cooperation as a colleague too, and she needed that more than anything else he had to offer. They'd never be an item – she'd come to terms with that now. Losing him as a friend stung too, but this...? She couldn't jeopardise this opportunity, no matter what else happened, not when she'd fought so hard for it.

She took a deep breath and followed him outside.

He was sitting on the harbour wall a few yards from the station. The wind had picked up and it tugged at his shirt as he looked out on a sea that danced and twitched, petrol-blue shot through with serpentine silver currents.

'I'm sorry,' she said as he looked up at her approach. 'I'm really sorry for being a dick. I'm tense; I just need this to go well. And I'm pumped, I suppose – a bit too pumped. It comes off as cockiness and I know you wouldn't be the first to say it. I'm trying to be better and I'd really appreciate your help.'

He studied her for a moment before he spoke. She wished she could tell what he was thinking but, for once, she couldn't read his expression. She'd always had a pretty good idea what was going on in his head over the years – he'd always been so transparent in that way. But not today. The wind lifted her hair and whipped it around her face and she reached to tuck it behind an ear.

'Knowing you as I do,' he said slowly, 'it took some balls to admit what you just did.'

She nodded. 'So you're back on board? This training means more to me than anything. I can't screw it up, but if you leave me to my own devices, I might just do that. You know how stupid I get.'

'I don't know about stupid... I do know you're going to have to keep that ego bottled up for a bit.'

'I don't have an ego, you cheeky...'

Ava paused as she detected the ghost of a smile on his lips.

'You shit,' she said, relaxing a little. 'You've got to wind me up, haven't you?'

'You're such an easy target, how could I resist?'

'I really am sorry,' she said, and though her apology was for her actions here and now, it was so much deeper than that. He'd reminded her of what she'd lost and for that she was truly sorry.

'Say it with actions, not words,' he said.

'I will. Give me one more chance and I will. I won't let...' she wanted to say what had happened between them but checked herself. The last thing she needed now was to remind him of all the reasons he had to hate her. 'I won't let anything get in the way; I'll be the model student.'

He paused, studying her again for a moment before finally hopping off the wall. 'OK,' he said. 'Let's give it another go.'

# CHAPTER TWENTY

One of the first things new recruits did was to go out on the boat. Not to rescue anyone, but to see if they would be OK with it. A surprising number of people got seasick without ever knowing they were prone to it, and even if they'd been out on boats before, it was often a very different experience on the lifeboat. Ava had completed her first few training sessions, but she still hadn't managed to do this one.

And so it was her turn today. She'd been excited about it ever since Vas had given her the date, and had almost leaped out of bed when her alarm had gone off. She felt like a kid now, swamped in her uniform and layer upon layer of safety gear as she stood waiting to board, but she was also filled with the most enormous pride. It shone from her, and even Killian gave a smile of approval as she bounded over to him.

'Morning!'

'Good morning,' he said with a wry smile. 'You're in a good mood.'

'I am!'

The station had a larger all-weather boat and a smaller inshore boat. Today, Ava was due to go out on the small one. It

was more like a dinghy, a squat, sturdy motorboat that was agile
and compact and could be quickly launched for smaller rescues.
Often this was used for people trapped on the rocks by unexpectedly rising tides or to pick up surfers or people in inflatables
who'd been dragged from shore by unseen currents. It was
pulled into the sea on a raft by a tractor. Ava had watched this
one launch far more times than the big one because it was used
more. She'd even been on it during open days at the station, but
only ever sitting in it on the sand. Today was the first time she'd
ever be at sea in it.

She'd spent years of her childhood begging her dad to take
her out in it, of course, but he'd always impressed upon her that
it wasn't a toy and she couldn't just take day trips in it. And
then he'd laugh at the look of intense disappointment on her
face and would offer to get her an ice cream from Betty's
instead.

She bounced on the balls of her feet, charged by a heady
mix of excitement, trepidation and the looming enormity of her
new life. Today's trip somehow made it all real. It wasn't dry
training; it was real action. She had chosen this. No, she'd
*fought* for this, and she'd won, and now she had to make it all
worthwhile. Today really felt like the proper start of it.

'How you feeling, Ava?' Vas strode down the corridor.
'Ready to go?'

'God yes!'

He smiled at her. 'If only your dad could see you now.'

Ava laughed. 'He'd have a heart attack!'

'He'd probably be stressing,' Vas agreed. 'But he'd be very
proud.'

'I like to think so too,' Ava said, her smile broad but edged
with sadness. 'At least, I hope so. I suppose I still have a long
way to go to earn that pride.'

'You've got this far – further than most,' Killian said.

'Absolutely,' Vas said with a fond smile.

Ava wondered whether he felt more of a duty to take care of her than he did others. Was he as happy with this situation as he appeared to be? After all, he'd been on the boat the night her dad had died, just as Killian and Harry had. But Vas's reaction had never been easy to read. Did that mean he'd coped better than they had? Maybe she'd ask him one day.

'Imagine if I turned out to be seasick after all!' Ava said, laughing. She felt strangely giddy, and even more strangely nervous. 'I mean, I know I'm not because I've been on tons of boats, but can you imagine if it suddenly happened! That would be hilarious!'

'It bloody wouldn't,' Killian said. 'It would have meant all those arguments with your sister were for nothing.'

'You won't be,' Vas said. 'We're just going through the motions with you.' He glanced at Killian. 'Shall we go?'

'I'm ready if Ava is,' he replied, turning to her.

She nodded, butterflies doing circuits of her tummy. 'I'm ready!'

As they made their way to the boat, Ava saw Harry come into the station. He gave her a small smile and she returned it. Maybe that was a good sign?

A few minutes later she was aboard as the boat sped across the bay. She'd been in speedboats before, and on jet skis and yachts, but none of it could compare to this. Somehow this was so much more exciting than any of that. Daunting, when she thought about the missions she might undertake in the future aboard this boat, but that future was so much closer now, and how could she be anything but excited about it?

The sea was calm but the boat still rose and fell as it skimmed the waves, hitting the surface each time with a thud. She shared a manic grin with Killian.

'Who could have imagined I'd be taking my girlfriend's

annoying little sister out on drill one day?' he shouted. 'Not me when I first walked into your mum and dad's cottage!'

'I was annoying?' Ava pretended to be offended.

'God yes!'

She laughed, as he did. If nothing else, it was good not to be at loggerheads with her brother-in-law. There had been friction enough. Ava suspected Gaby was still unhappy about her training, and even more annoyed that their mum had backed down, but Killian at least had seen some middle ground where he was trying his best to reassure his wife while also supporting Ava's decision. And she had to admit, training sessions with him were a lot easier than they were with Harry since she and Harry had fallen out.

Ava looked to the horizon, the wind blasting into her face, and smiled.

'Feeling OK?' Vas called to her.

'Yep!'

As Vas turned back to the helm, Killian pointed to a yellow shape in the water. Ava saw it at the same time.

'They're a bit far out, don't you think?'

Ava squinted to get a better look and saw that it was two boys in an inflatable dinghy. She nodded.

'Vas!'

The helmsman turned and Killian pointed. 'Shall we have a word?'

Vas turned the boat, slowing down as they approached the boys.

'All right, lads?' Killian shouted.

The boys looked up, a mixture of awe and sheepishness on their faces.

'Yes,' one of them said.

'You're a bit far out,' Killian said. He waved a hand at the horizon. 'Riptides out here – you need to be careful. Doesn't take much to get caught in one, then you're off. Ever been to America on a dinghy?'

The boys both shook their heads.

'It's not as much fun as it sounds,' Killian said with a faint smile. 'I wouldn't personally recommend it.' He unwound a safety line and tied it to a handle on their boat. 'If it's all the same to you, we'll tow you back. Better to be safe than sorry, eh? You want to jump aboard with us?'

The boys both nodded, and Ava was pretty sure this was an offer they couldn't refuse. They hadn't been in immediate danger, but she understood why Killian wanted to bring them back in. At their age, she might have even found this exciting.

Once she'd helped Killian to get them aboard, Vas set off for the beach, their inflatable trailing behind.

'It's the little wins,' Killian said to her. 'They mount up and they matter as much as the big ones. This is why we do what we do, right?'

Ava nodded and smiled as she looked at the two boys. In small ways, their lives would be changed by this event forever. Maybe the crew had even averted a tragedy that nobody had seen coming.

Now, more than ever, she was sure this was where she was meant to be.


Ava had got back from her trip buzzing with excitement. They'd called it a day on the training, but Vas had recommended that she get stuck into some of her manuals to speed things along. So, still dreaming of her morning flying over the waves, she was sitting at one of Betty's outside tables, feet up against the wall that separated the terrace from the promenade, tilting the chair back and forth on two legs, exactly the way she'd have done at school and had often been reprimanded for.

You'll fall backwards and hit your head, her teacher would say, but that only made her want to do it all the more.

She'd read the same sentence three times now and it was no clearer. Training manuals were dull – there was no way around that. That was something else she'd learned at school: for her, reading about something was no substitute for doing it. But then, Ava had always been more of a doer than a reader. It didn't help that the sun was shining and the sea was blue and inviting, the breeze that lifted the hair from her neck mild and salty. Above her the gulls swooped and called, and what she most wanted was to climb on her surfboard and spend her precious afternoon messing about on the water. Or, better still, she thought as her gaze drifted back to the ocean, she could go out on patrol again with the boat, making sure nobody was getting into trouble.

The two boys they'd picked up were now on the beach playing Frisbee. Ava watched them for a minute, before reminding herself that she needed to finish reading this book some time this millennium.

Screwing her eyes tight, she shook her head to clear it and then tried again.

This time, Betty's voice broke her concentration.

'Sorry,' she said as Ava looked up. She angled her head at the empty coffee cup on the table. 'Just wanted to know if you were done with that.'

'Oh, yeah...' Ava pushed it across the table towards her before going back to her book.

'Anything else I can get you?' Betty asked, causing Ava to look up again.

'A functioning brain would be good, if you have one to spare.'

'Sorry,' Betty said with a soft smile. 'I'm afraid I need all the brain cells I can get for myself.' She nodded at the book. 'It's tough going? A lot to learn, I suppose.'

'To be honest – and I know I shouldn't say it – it's boring.' Ava rested the open book face down on the table to save her place and stretched. 'I mean, it's obviously important, but it's detail. I've never had a lot of patience for detail – I'm the sort of person who gets instructions for a new telly, throws them straight into the bin and grabs the remote to start fiddling. So this is all quite challenging for me.'

Betty shrugged. 'I don't know... I quite like small stuff. Then again, I'm not like you.'

'I suppose not.'

'I'm happy shuffling round this cafe all day,' Betty continued. 'The nearest I get to the sea is looking at it from this terrace. Some people are born to be daredevils but I'm afraid I'm not one of them – wouldn't get me within a mile of a lifeboat, unless it's to take sandwiches to the station for the open day.'

Ava smiled. 'I wouldn't say it like it's a bad thing. People like me get into a lot more trouble. In fact, if not for people like me then the lifeboats wouldn't need so many... well... people like me.'

Betty laughed lightly. 'So the answer is for everyone to try very hard to be boring like me?'

'No, not boring. Sensible. I'm under no illusions – I'm definitely not the sensible Morrow sister, and the others would agree. I'm sure my mum wonders where she went wrong with me.'

'I'm sure she's proud,' Betty said. 'Clara is. She couldn't be prouder. She thinks it's amazing, what you're doing here.'

Ava gave a bemused smile. 'She said that?'

Betty nodded.

'Blimey... I suppose I'll have to start being a bit nicer to her then.'

Betty's light laugh was almost musical. 'So you're sure you don't want anything else? Another coffee maybe?'

'Actually, I probably should... might help to focus me.'

'No problem.'

Betty's gaze went to the steps that led to her raised terrace. Ava followed it to see Cormac bounding up them, two at a time.

'Hey, Cormac,' Betty greeted him with a warm smile.

'Betty... Ava...' Cormac tipped his forehead with a finger.

'What are you looking so pleased about?' Ava asked.

Cormac came over to the table, grabbed a nearby chair, spun it round and sat astride it, leaning his chin on the back and grinning madly at her.

'I'm in!' he said.

Ava sat up. 'Wait... you mean the lifeboats?'

'Yeah! I mean... eventually. But I've passed all the entrance stuff.'

'That's amazing!' Ava's grin matched his. 'We'll be training buddies!'

'That we will. Should be a blast, eh?'

Betty shook her head, glancing from one to the other with a wry smile. 'Mad, the pair of you. Congratulations, Cormac. Can I get you anything? I don't have champagne but a celebratory coffee on the house?'

'That'd be grand,' Cormac said. 'But in a takeout cup, if you don't mind – I've got a ton of stuff to do at the shack; just wanted to catch Ava here with my news.'

'No problem. I'll be back in a tick.'

'Thanks, Betty.' Cormac turned back to Ava. 'So you're booked for some training at the big college in Dorset?'

'Not yet. I will be as soon as I sort out a date I can go.'

'Can I book on the same sessions? I was thinking we could travel together, save costs. What do you think?'

'That sounds brilliant.'

'Grand. So when you're ready, let me know and we'll book it at the same time.'

Ava gave a vague frown. 'Who's going to look after the

shack for you? Are you going to have to close it while you're away? It's going to be a couple of days.'

'I was hoping your sister would be free to help me out. I asked her a while ago and she agreed in principle, but I guess I'd need to run the dates by her when we know.'

Ava smiled. 'Only Clara would agree to take a holiday from one job to go and do another one.'

'I can't think of anyone I'd trust more, and I'm grateful she'd consider it. I'll have to think of something good to make it up to her.'

'She won't care about that – she'll probably enjoy the change. After all, catering was what she trained to do at college, but there's not much call for it manning the reception desk at a holiday park.'

'Lucky for me, eh?' Cormac said.

'Very,' Ava replied. 'In that case, we ought to run some dates by her before we get our training booked in Poole.'

'Have you been to the big college before? I thought, maybe, with your da...'

'No. Dad went a couple of times but I've never been. I think the surrounding area is pretty cool – a fair few pubs and bars and stuff nearby. It means after-school hours should be fun too.'

Cormac's mad grin spread over his face again. He looked like a kid waking up on Christmas morning. 'I can't wait to get started!'

Ava picked up her book and showed it to him. 'Well, if you want to read this and tell me what's in it so I don't have to, you're more than welcome.'

'I would, but that'd be cheating, wouldn't it?'

'I wouldn't call it cheating... more a shortcut. Or a sharing of knowledge? A friend helping a friend?'

'I don't know... I'd call it an answer for everything.'

'That's me!'

Cormac's grin faded a little. 'Just so I know – how's your man Harry?'

'What do you mean? You see him as much as I do.'

'Yeah, but I don't feel I can ask. He's still shore crew, not back on the boats? I don't want to put my foot in it and say something I shouldn't when I see him.'

'Oh... well, as far as I know – though I'm not exactly socialising with him at the moment and it's a long story so please don't ask – he's looking to join the boat crew again soon, but I don't think he has yet.'

Cormac nodded. 'That's good.'

Betty came back and put Ava's cup and saucer on the table before handing a takeout version to Cormac. He peeled back the lid and sniffed before giving an appreciative nod.

'Your memory must be incredible. You don't even have to ask either of us how we take it – you just know.'

'With regulars it's not that hard – and especially with Ava, who's been coming here for years and ordering the same thing.'

'That doesn't make me sound at all boring and predictable,' Ava said.

'You can't always be mad excitement,' Betty said. 'I think we'll allow you to have the same coffee every day.'

'Well, I ought to be getting on.' Cormac put the lid back on his coffee.

'Me too...' Betty glanced at a table where a stack of plates and cups had been left by a departing family. Cormac watched as she went over and scooped them into her arms. Then he leaped from his chair and rushed to the cafe door to open it for her so she could take them inside.

Betty beamed at him. 'Thanks, Cormac!'

'Any time.'

Ava sipped her coffee, watching the adorable interaction. Cormac really was a great guy, and she couldn't think of anyone she'd rather have with her as she trained for the lifeboats.

# CHAPTER TWENTY-ONE

Her training was picking up pace. Though she still struggled with the written aspect of things, from a practical point of view Ava was flying through the competencies she needed to display to join the seagoing crew. For now, she was helping to maintain the boats alongside her studies, making sure they were ready to launch at a moment's notice, and although it wasn't exactly what she wanted to do, she took great pride in it. But today there would be no lifeboat activity, because she'd promised to be on duty as a lifeguard for the annual Port Promise triathlon, as she did every year.

Most of the competitors did it to raise money for local good causes, and the lifeboats always figured large in the beneficiaries, so Ava had always been active in the event in one way or another. Once or twice she'd competed and she'd loved it, but she was really only good at the swimming bit and had never finished with the top scorers, and so was content to volunteer to keep the other competitors safe, which, according to her dad, was even more important. Besides, there were few people qualified to do it, so every hand on deck was valuable. She didn't see any reason to change things this year, even though her dad would be missing. If anything, it was all the more reason to step up, knowing he'd be proud of her role, keeping people safe in a different way than he'd done, but keeping them safe nonetheless.

Today, the sun of the previous week had given way to a low pressure that had turned the sky heavy and grey and the sea almost the same colour. The temperature had taken a dip too – despite it being summer, it was still cool enough for Ava to need a fleece over her lifeguard uniform.

'It's a good turnout.' Vas handed her a coffee and then gave another to Harry, who was standing silently at her side, looking out to sea. They'd barely spoken since his arrival to assist as second lifeguard, apart from the exchange of cool civilities that hardly meant anything at all. They'd been like this for the past couple of weeks, ever since Ava had started her training. She wanted to ask whether it was because he still hadn't forgiven her for trying to get trauma counselling for him, but she didn't trust herself not to tell him how idiotic he was being and that was hardly going to help matters.

Poor Maxine, who was helping out as a steward with Vas, had been standing with them while Vas went to get their drinks. She'd done her best to lighten the mood, but even she must have been able to feel the chill between Ava and Harry that had nothing to do with the weather front that had turned the sky grey and damp.

'God, do I need this!' Maxine took the third cup from Vas and wrapped her hands around it. 'I don't feel as if I've woken up yet. I bet Killian's been up for hours already, probably done a cross-Channel swim and a Tour de France to warm up for it.'

Ava grinned. 'You know him so well.'

Fitness-mad Killian and Gaby were both competing in the triathlon to raise money for the lifeboat service. Logan had said he'd have a go too, though his swimming was going to be slow. Clara had told him she was proud of him anyway, just for trying, and didn't care how long it took him to finish. Ava suspected, though she didn't say, that he might only be so keen to compete because Cormac was. She suspected quite a lot of men in the village might only be competing to stop their partners ogling the impossibly handsome demigod of an Irishman as he completed the course. Ava expected him to do well, though she had to concede that Killian would probably give him a run for his money.

Jill had Elijah and Fern with her to enable Killian and Gaby to compete, while Cormac had closed his fish shack for a few hours, assuming there wouldn't be a lot of demand for crab sandwiches until early afternoon, by which time the triathlon ought to be over – at least for him if he was fast enough, he'd joked. Ava imagined he'd simply carry on running past the finish line and over to his shack to open up in his race gear, and would have barely broken a sweat doing it.

'I'd better go and find Robin,' Vas said. 'I think things are about to kick off.'

'No need...' Ava pointed to a figure fighting his way through a crowd of laughing and joking competitors and supporters, who were doing a good job of blocking the promenade. 'He's here.'

'Morning!' Robin smiled tensely.

'How are you?' she asked warmly. 'We were just saying what a good turnout it is today, considering the weather's not the best for it.'

'Should raise a fair bit for the good causes,' Vas added.

Robin nodded. 'It should. And I suppose having all those teams from the neighbouring villages soon makes up the numbers. They've really travelled in this year for it.'

'I hear we've got a team from Sennen,' Maxine said.

Robin gave a low whistle. 'All the way down there?'

'The event gets bigger every year,' Ava said.

'Almost too big,' Maxine said. 'We're only a little village, after all; we can barely fit all these crowds in.'

'I think folks have got to hear about…' Vas looked at Ava. 'Well, your dad was in the news, wasn't he? A bit of publicity brings it to people's attention, and I think they want to support the service in whatever way they can.'

'It's nice,' Ava said. 'I'd have competed if I wasn't roped into doing lifeguard duty.'

'You don't have to do lifeguard duty.'

Ava turned to Harry, who was now speaking for the first time since Robin had joined them. She gave a vague frown. 'I know, but who else is there? We hardly have enough volunteers with lifeguard experience as it is.'

'It's a shame though,' Maxine cut in. 'I reckon you'd be right good at this.'

'The swim,' Ava said. 'I did it a couple of times, remember? Last time I was about eighteen, I think.'

'Oh, now I do!' Maxine said.

'I was crap on the cycling leg and even worse at running, and I doubt I've improved any since then. It'd be a laugh and I'd be doing it for a good cause, but I'd definitely humiliate myself.'

'Well, you're doing *this* for a good cause,' Vas said. 'And it's commendable that you are because this is definitely not the fun stuff of the day.' He glanced at his watch and then looked up at Robin and Maxine. 'We'd better get to our stations – things are about to start.'

As they left with an airy wave, around a hundred swimmers began to make their way towards the beach.

'Come on,' Ava said to Harry. 'We'd better get to it too.'

They walked in silence to join the swimmers getting ready for the first leg of what would probably be a gruelling day for many of them. Ava would have tried to make conversation, but she could see how today was going to go and she simply couldn't be bothered. Then she heard a shout from the promenade.

'Ava! Harry!'

She turned to see Elijah and Fern leap from the walkway and onto the sand, tearing across to meet them. Jill and Marina followed at a rather more sedate pace, carrying a pair of bags that Ava quickly assumed were Killian and Gaby's kit for the next couple of legs of the race.

'Hey!' She bent down for a hug from each child, and to his credit, even if he wasn't in the mood, Harry gave them both a high five.

Then Ava straightened up and scanned the crowds of swimmers.

'Seen your mum and dad yet?' she asked Elijah and Fern.

'There!' Fern shouted, flinging an arm out. 'Mum, Dad!' She began to wave madly.

'How are you feeling?' Ava called out.

Killian grinned and flexed his muscles, while Gaby, who was putting on a swim cap, simply rolled her eyes at him.

'What do you think?' she shouted back to Ava.

'I think one of you is more excited about this than the other.'

'Bingo!' Gaby called back.

At that moment, Cormac strolled past. Spotting Ava and Harry and the others, he stopped.

'How are you all this fine morning?' he asked.

'We could ask you the same thing,' Jill said. 'Ready to go?'

'I'd say he looks *very* ready,' Marina put in. 'Fit... he looks very fit. And ready for action.'

Ava tried not to grin at Marina's blindingly obvious reaction to seeing him in his swim gear. She couldn't blame her – even she had to admit there was more than a little of the Adonis about him this morning.

'I am,' he said. 'I haven't done as much training as I'd have liked, but I'm as ready as I'll ever be.'

'We've got the easy bit today, that's for sure,' Ava said. 'I'm sure you'll do amazingly.'

'I don't envy you,' Jill said.

Ava laughed. 'I do!'

'If you like, you can enter next year and I'll take your spot as lifeguard,' Cormac said. 'Of course, I have to become a lifeguard first...'

Ava smiled. 'That would be cool.'

Cormac looked at Harry. 'Or you, of course, if you wanted to do it.'

'I'm good where I am,' Harry replied. 'This is where I'm most useful.'

Cormac nodded. 'Well, I'd better get to the starting line. 'Could I ask a favour? Would some kind soul take care of my bag for me?'

'We'll keep an eye on it for you,' Marina said, almost falling over herself to take it from him. 'We'll be at the finishing line when you need it.'

'That's grand, thanks.'

As they watched him join the other competitors, Ava lowered her voice slightly. 'It's such a shame he doesn't have anyone here to cheer him on.'

'We can do that,' Marina said. 'In fact, the whole village will be cheering him on.'

'Yes, but not a family or partner,' Ava said. 'And he's so lovely it doesn't seem right that he doesn't have anyone like that.'

'It doesn't bother him,' Harry said. 'Not as far as I can tell.'

Ava's gaze was trained on Cormac as she replied. 'You don't know that for sure though.'

'I don't, but he always seems happy enough.'

'I don't suppose he has a choice.'

'Of course he does,' Harry said. 'Nobody forces him to stay in Port Promise if he doesn't like it.'

Ava spun to face him. 'What kind of thing is that to say? Why shouldn't he stay here? His business is here, after all, and he's working hard to build it. And he's working hard to be a good member of the community.'

'We all work hard,' Harry said.

'Says the man who works for his dad!' Ava shot back.

Jill cleared her throat loudly and Ava knew why. The exchange was tense and anyone who didn't know better might think Ava and Harry didn't actually like one another.

Perhaps they didn't, not now; at least, not anymore. The idea filled her with a sudden sadness. And perhaps a lot of that was down to her, but lately, for whatever reason, when she was around Harry she couldn't help but be confrontational. He seemed to bring out the worst in her, and it seemed she did the same to him. The old Harry would never have been so ungenerous towards Cormac. She wished she could have the old Harry back.

'Your mum tells me you and Cormac are off to the big training centre in Dorset soon,' Marina said – as she so often did, completely failing to read the room before she spoke. 'That'll be so much fun.'

'It'll be hard work,' Ava said.

'Hmm...' Marina looked dreamy for a moment. 'I spent a weekend with a sailor in Poole... Way back before I met Bob. It was... well, let's just say we saw quite a lot of the hotel room...'

Jill laughed. 'Marina! Young ears!'

Both Elijah and Fern were looking at them. They might have been young but they knew a conversation they weren't meant to understand when they heard one, and obviously, like any kid, it made them want to know what the grown-ups were being so secretive about.

Ava laughed too. 'I don't know about that – we're likely to see very little of our hotel. I'm quite looking forward to trying a few of the bars on the quay, though.'

From the starting line on the shore, Cormac turned and waved at them. He'd got into his wetsuit and it was tight enough to show the definition of his muscles even beneath the thick fabric.

'I bet you are,' Harry muttered.

'Come on, kids!' Marina said, her gaze trained on Cormac's fine figure too. 'We'd better take these bags to the finish line so everyone can get onto their bikes for the next bit. Don't want to hold anyone up, do we?' She turned to Jill, who seemed torn as she looked at Ava and Harry for a moment. Did she feel the need to referee the sparring match they seemed hell-bent on engaging in?

'Right,' she decided finally. 'So we'll see you a bit later?' she asked Ava.

'You will.' Ava went over to give her a hug, and Jill took her briefly to one side.

'Are you all right?' she asked in a low voice.

'Of course. Why?'

'Well... I know there have been some difficulties between you and Harry but... frankly, I didn't realise how bad it was.'

Ava shook her head sadly. 'We can't seem to get past that whole me trying to get him help thing.'

Jill glanced at Harry, who was talking to Fern, then back at Ava. 'I don't think it's just about that.'

'What's it about then?'

'Cormac,' Jill said simply.

Ava blinked. 'Cormac? What's he done?'

'Nothing, directly. But he's joining the crew, isn't he?'

'So am I – I don't see your point. You think Harry's feeling as if he's being pushed out? But when I first told him I was thinking of joining he was happy about it.'

'Yes, and I'm sure he was – about *you*... But you're not Cormac, are you?'

'I still don't know what you mean.'

'Look at him...'

Ava's gaze followed her mum's down the beach to where Cormac was limbering up ready to enter the water.

'He's all muscles and confidence,' Jill said. 'And with Harry going through... well, not being himself these days, it must feel a bit threatening. He probably worries that Cormac will take his spot on the boats and he won't be able to get it back.'

'That's daft... everyone runs for a shout if they can – there are no spots as such.'

'Yes, we all know that, but it doesn't change things. He might feel Cormac is favoured. And then there's the fact that you and Cormac are getting so close...'

'No, Mum, I'm going to stop you right there. We're not getting close in *that* way. And I joined the boats before Cormac, so if anyone is a threat to Harry's spot, it's me. There's no need for him to take anything out on Cormac.'

'Yes, but you're not a man. And you're... well, you're *you*.'

'Meaning?'

Jill sighed. 'I shouldn't have to spell it out for you. Try to put yourself in Harry's shoes for a moment. He thinks he has it all figured out and then... well, everything falls apart, and next thing he knows, you and the man he feels threatened by are off to Poole together.'

'As colleagues, yes. To train. It's no different than if I'd been going with Harry.'

Jill raised her eyebrows.

'It's not,' Ava said. 'Whatever we might have started, I've since realised it would never have worked. It's better I find that out now than get into a doomed relationship with him. We're better as friends.'

'You're hardly that these days, as far as I can tell.'

'Things are difficult right now,' Ava said bluntly. 'And I don't know if they'll get better, but I hope they will.'

'I know, darling. I hope they will too. I know how fond you've always been of him. In fact, we're all fond of him.'

Ava was about to reply when the starting pistol cracked across the bay and the crowd of swimmers raced into the sea in a mad flurry of splashing limbs. Ava saw that Harry had already taken up position further up the beach and was watching the water.

'I'd better get to my station, Mum.'

Jill kissed her lightly. 'I'll see you later.'

Ava watched for a second as her mum collected the children and Marina and made her way to the finish point with the bags, and then took up her own position to watch the sea.

The swim was a short section compared to the cycling and running, but that didn't mean it was easy. For most, in fact, the sea swim would be the toughest and slowest leg, especially when conditions turned against them, like they had today. The sea was lively – though, of course, had been deemed safe enough to proceed – and would definitely give the challenge of swimming against tides and currents an extra dimension. Everyone was aware they had to be quick because the morning promised to hold the calmest weather – towards the middle of the afternoon the wind was expected to be stronger and the sea more restless still. But that didn't worry Ava too much – she expected all the swimmers to be done within the next hour. As for pulling someone out, in all the years she'd been helping as a lifeguard she'd never once had to rescue a competitor. So, even with all the variables, she felt relaxed as she watched the line of people take to the water and begin to swim the first part of the course. At least, as relaxed as she could be after yet another run-in with Harry.

The spectators on the beach erupted into cheers, egging their nearest and dearest on. As the swimmers began to make headway, the crowd started to move down the beach to follow. Ava kept a close eye on the water, but allowed herself a brief scan of the supporters too. Elijah and Fern were hopping up and down madly, clapping and shouting for their parents, while

Jill and Marina watched the action with more restrained applause. Of course, there was nobody for Cormac, so Ava took a little detour to the water's edge and yelled, 'Come on, Cormac!' before going back to her post.

All this time she'd expected to see Clara supporting Logan, but there was no sign of her. Ava was puzzled, but she'd have to solve the mystery later, because now she was engrossed by the race – watching because that was her job today but also because she was genuinely interested.

The initial glut of competitors had started to spread out, so that the stronger swimmers grew their lead, streaking ahead, while the average ones formed a large clump around the midsection and the stragglers fell valiantly behind. Ava wasn't sure, but Logan looked to be occupying that last group, while Cormac was steaming ahead at the front. *Poor Logan.* He wouldn't like that, but maybe he'd make time up on the next two events.

As these thoughts occupied her, there was a tap on her shoulder and Ava turned to find Clara there.

'Hi!' Ava gave her a brief kiss. 'I wondered where you'd got to.'

'Oh, we were running a bit late – as usual. Logan had to go straight down to the water and jump in – no time for socialising or anything.'

'How's he doing?' Ava asked.

'I can't actually see him,' Clara said.

'Is that...?' Ava pointed to a head with a white swim cap.

'It could be...' Clara craned to get a better look. 'Although it might not be. Knowing his terrible sense of direction, he's probably halfway to Guernsey by now.'

Ava laughed. 'I won't tell him you said that.'

'Please don't – I can't deal with another row.'

Ava's smile faded. Should she ask her sister what that meant?

'Gaby's doing well,' Clara said into the gap. 'Considering...'

'Considering she's done practically no decent training towards it... at least, that's what she says.'

'Yeah, she's like that kid at school who says they did no revision but finishes top of the class and you know they actually spent the last six months cramming like mad and just pretend to have done nothing so they look amazing.'

'The thing is, she does look amazing at everything.'

'And she'll want to beat Killian, so...'

'I know. God, it must be so tiring to be Killian and Gaby – they're so ultra-competitive, even with each other. How did the kids get to be so cute and chill?'

Clara grinned. 'Oh, I can see Cormac! God, he's racing; I didn't realise he was such a good swimmer.'

'Me neither,' Ava said, her gaze fixed on the line of competitors as it grew longer still with the leaders extending their gains and the stragglers getting further behind. 'I mean, of course I knew he could swim, but I'd have had him down as more of a cyclist looking at him.'

'Maybe he is. Imagine if this is his worst discipline and he's this good at it. Nobody else will stand a chance.'

'God, yes. Everyone will hate him!'

'I can't imagine how anyone could hate Cormac, even if he did wipe the floor with everyone else here today.' Clara gave Ava a sideways look.

Ava kept her gaze on the sea, but she felt her sister's questioning study. 'What?'

'I'm just... well, you and Cormac have become good friends recently.'

Ava rolled her eyes. 'Not you as well. Come on, you know me better than that.'

'Do I? I know you're not backwards at coming forwards – I'm surprised you haven't asked him out.'

'That's because I don't fancy him.'

'Seriously?'

'No. He's not my type.'

'Ava, he's everyone's type.'

'That's silly. And anyway, I don't think I'm his type.'

'I think you've got a lot in common.'

'I've got a lot in common with Marina but I'm not going to go out with her.'

'Want to know what I think?'

'No, but I'm sure you're going to tell me anyway.'

'I think you're still holding on for Harry.'

'God no!' Ava turned to her. 'Really, no. That ship has most definitely sailed. And, to be honest, I'm finding him a total arse these days. I can't imagine what possessed me to think we might be a good fit. He was an arse at school, and even if he looks like he's changed, he hasn't.'

'Harry's being an arse?'

'Yes.'

'And that's one-sided, is it? Just him and nobody else?'

'I made one mistake!' Ava said tersely. 'And he wants to keep punishing me for it. What am I meant to do? I've tried apologising and I've tried to be as nice as I can but it's never enough. I don't have the energy for it, and now I have to deal with him at the station too.'

'You could quit.'

'That's never going to happen. If he doesn't like me being there, he can quit.'

'I mean, it's probably best if neither of you quits – Port Promise needs you both.'

'Well, all I can say is I hope, if Harry goes back on the boats – and I *do* want him to because I'm not that heartless – I end up going out on shouts with Cormac more than I do Harry. And not because I fancy him, but because there's no drama with him. Harry's being such a bellend I can't deal with it anymore. I mean, how old are we? Old enough to be past this teenage angst!'

'Um... Ava...'

Ava suddenly realised that she'd been ranting and Clara had been very quiet, then she noticed that Clara was looking at a spot slightly beyond her. She turned and saw the yellow T-shirt before she realised it was Harry. He'd been hidden from view by a spectator, it seemed, because she hadn't seen him before, but he was definitely close enough to have heard her. She braced herself for the onslaught, but he simply stared at her for a moment before mumbling an excuse.

'Moved up the beach... most everyone's past the midpoint now...'

And with that he walked off to stand closer to the finish line.

'Shit!' Ava groaned.

'You can say that again. Sorry, Ava, I only just noticed him before you did or I would have told you to shut up.'

'It's not your fault. Why does he keep making me feel as if I'm kicking a sodding puppy or something?'

Clara looked at her. 'Is it him making you feel that way, or do you feel that way because maybe you're being a bit of a bellend too?'

Ava scowled, but Clara ignored it.

'Oh, I can see Logan now!' she yelped. 'I'd better go down with his towel.'

'Shit...' Ava muttered again as she watched Clara dash down the beach. 'Shit, shit, shit...'

Much as it pained her, she needed to go and talk to Harry to try and clear things up. Again. Or did she? Now that she thought about it, she had no way of knowing he'd actually heard what she'd said. He hadn't said anything about it and the beach was quite noisy and there had been people in between her and him and he might not have caught much – if any – of what she'd said. And she hadn't meant it – not really, even though she'd told Clara she did. She was starting to feel cornered by him and she felt like lashing out, but maybe Clara was right – maybe she only felt that way because she was being the bellend here, not Harry.

Her attention turned back to the swimmers. Even if she did want to go and sound Harry out, she could hardly do it now. With growing restlessness, she tried to concentrate on what was going on in the water.

Some of the faster swimmers were now getting out, ripping off wetsuits and towelling down ready to take to their bikes for the cycling leg. The route for this was the longest section of the course. It ran along the coast as far as the village of Perthalenny and back again. As the crow flew, along a decent A road it wasn't that far, but taking a meandering clifftop road with steep gradients and breathtaking drops, it was far longer and more challenging, especially challenging for those who didn't ride all the time.

As she'd expected, Killian was among the leaders. He strode out from the surf like some sea god, up the beach to where Jill and Marina were now waiting with the children and his and Gaby's bags. He tore off his wetsuit and left it on the sand, not even bothering with the towel Marina offered (rather hopefully, Ava thought), pulled his jersey on over dripping hair and ran to where the bikes waited on the promenade. Cormac followed shortly afterwards.

'Well done!' Ava shouted.

He turned and grinned. 'I'm about ready for a pint!' he said, stripping his wetsuit off as he went. 'Shame I've got a bike ride and a run first! Fancy coming to the Spratt for one afterwards?'

'I think a lot of people are, so I expect I might. But what about the shack?'

'Ah...' His voice was more muffled as he began to jog out of earshot. 'Surely I've earned one before I go to work?'

'You surely have, training buddy!'

'You know what they say?' he shouted as he went over to take the towel Marina was offering. 'The team that plays together stays together.'

'I've never heard that, but I like it!'

She smiled as she watched him run for the bikes, then turned her attention back to the sea. By now, Gaby was out. Ava called as she jogged past.

'Well done, sis! Ready to give up now?'

'And let Kill win?' Gaby panted. 'Not bloody likely!'

Ava grinned. Then Logan appeared, far sooner than she'd anticipated, and she noted with some approval that his time would be faster than she'd imagined if he could keep up this pace for the other two legs. She waved and called out her encouragement, but he was so out of breath he could barely form a reply before he staggered to Clara to get his cycling gear.

Another few minutes and Ava's lifeguard duties were almost done for another year. While she kicked around waiting for the last few stragglers, Maxine came over to join her.

'Well, all that effort and it's over already.'

'Our bit,' Ava agreed. 'Are you staying to watch the rest?'

'I expect so. Look…' She nodded at an approaching figure. 'Here's Harry now. Are you staying?' Maxine asked him.

'Dad's got a tent set up for afterwards. I said I'd help him. Don't want him overdoing things after…'

He glanced at Ava and she nodded. Whatever else was happening between them, they'd always be bound by many things, and the day they'd had to save Sandy's life was one of them.

'Is he well enough to be working?' Ava asked.

'That's what I said, but he's been working since just after it happened. I keep telling him to take it easy and I'll do it all, but then he sneaks in the shed when I'm not there. I can't stop him, but I can make sure he doesn't overdo it.'

'So you won't be coming to the Spratt?' Maxine asked. 'A load of us are going for a drink after the triathlon's over.'

Harry's gaze flicked to Ava again before he replied. 'I don't think so.'

'I'll come to the tent to say hello to Sandy,' Ava said. 'I'd like to see how he is. Maybe I'll hang out there for a while.'

'Isn't Cormac going to the Spratt?' Harry asked.

'Yes, but everyone will be there so...'

'Still, I'm sure you'd rather—'

'Harry!'

They looked to see Sandy waving from the promenade. Harry held a hand up.

'Got to go,' he said, turning to Ava and Maxine.

'Wait...' Ava began to follow him as he went, 'I want to say hello...'

He nodded and they walked the beach in silence. Then, at the promenade, Ava rushed to hug a beaming Sandy.

'It's so good to see you looking well!'

'Aye...' Sandy said. 'And you're a sight for sore eyes too. My guardian angel.'

'Oh...' Ava waved away the compliment. 'You know Harry did all the hard stuff.'

'I know, but I also know you did your part. How's the triathlon been? Had to rescue anyone today?'

'Oh, no, it's been brilliant and no rescues necessary. I think Killian's somewhere in the leading pack. In fact, he looks pretty good; he might even win this year. Imagine that! We'd never hear the end of it!'

'And how's your sister getting on?'

'Gaby? Not sure. She was just behind Cormac and just in front of Logan getting out of the water. I think her bike time might be slow – it's not her best discipline – but she's a quick runner so she'll fly that bit.'

'Aye...' Sandy nodded like a sports pundit on the TV, taking it all in. 'And how's your mum these days?'

'She's good,' Ava said. 'Thanks for asking. She's somewhere around looking after Elijah and Fern. I can find her if you want to say hello.'

'Don't worry yourself,' Sandy said. 'We've got to get set up, but if she wants to come over to the stand later for a word, I'd like that very much.'

'I'll tell her when I see her.'

With the pleasantries over, Sandy suddenly looked shrewd as he cast a glance between her and Harry, clearly holding back a frown.

Had Harry said something to his dad about the state of things between them? Or had someone else? There were no secrets in Port Promise and word often got around, no matter how carefully they were kept. She suddenly felt awkward.

The moment was saved by Maxine's arrival.

'Hey you!' she greeted Sandy. 'Looking well!'

Ava didn't feel like socialising quite as much as she had a few moments before.

'I might go and look for my mum,' she said.

'OK,' Maxine said. 'I'll see you later at the Spratt maybe?'

'Maybe,' Ava said uncertainly.

She was walking away, scanning the beach for her mum, when she heard her name being called and turned to find Harry jogging to catch up with her. Her heart sank. Had he heard her ranting earlier? Was he about to tear a strip off her? She didn't think she could take any more hostility.

'Ava... Look, I just wanted to say I know I'm being... Well, I'm sorry.'

Ava stopped and turned to him. 'There's nothing to say sorry for.'

'There is. I'm dealing with stuff, but that isn't your fault and I shouldn't keep making it about you.' He paused, scuffing the sand with the toe of his shoe before he looked up to speak again. 'What I wanted to say is: Cormac's a good guy. If you like him then you should go out with him.'

Ava clamped her hands on her hips and stared hard. 'Oh, I should, should I? I'm so glad you stopped me to say so. I've been pining, you see, waiting for one man to hand me to another, so now that I have your permission, I'll go offer myself to Cormac, shall I?'

Harry's hands flew into the air. 'What have I done wrong now?'

'What? I have to tell you?'

'Yes! I thought this was what you wanted! I'm telling you if you want to go with Cormac, I won't make a fuss!'

Ava prodded his chest. 'You don't get to tell me anything! How is this anything to do with you? I'm not a toy to be swapped about! And for your information, I don't fancy Cormac, and I'm pretty sure he doesn't fancy me, but even if I did, *I'd* decide what to do about it, not you or anyone else!'

'But I thought... I was trying to be cool about it. I was trying to be a good friend!'

'It's not! It's not cool, Harry! You keep doing this! I don't... I don't know what you want from me and it's driving me crazy!'

He scowled. 'Well I don't know what you want from me either and it's driving me crazy too! So maybe we should both give up trying!'

Ava took a breath. She wasn't going to cry, though she felt the lump driving up her throat. It was angry crying, but Harry would see it as a weakness and she wasn't going to give him the satisfaction. 'I just want... I just want us to be normal again.'

'So do I, but I don't think we can.'

'Why not?'

'Because stuff's happened.'

Ava rolled her eyes. 'This again? I told Gaby you needed help; I didn't know it would be so offensive to you, but I've said sorry a million times. Can't we move past it? How many more times do you need to hear sorry from me before we can?'

'It's not that.'

'Then what?'

He shrugged, the fight gone from his eyes now. 'There was a time when I thought… for a while I thought we'd…'

'Get together?' Ava finished for him. 'Me too, but then you went and got weird about it.'

'I didn't get weird about *that*.'

'I know.' Ava sighed. 'I interfered where I wasn't wanted. I get it; I screwed up. Enough, Harry, please. For the love of God, can't we let this go?'

He studied her for a moment. 'I suppose I should have seen this coming.'

'Seen what coming?'

'I should have learned… I should have learned from the past.'

'What does that even mean?'

'That we're not good for each other – at least, not as anything but friends. It's why we've never been able to get together. We're not meant to be anything other than friends, so maybe we should stop trying to make it happen.'

'I don't recall you trying all that hard. Not with your millions of other girlfriends.'

'Then you weren't looking properly. Ava, I've always liked you, but you always made out that you didn't like me. Why would I have asked you out? In fact, I seem to recall that the one time I did, it didn't end well.'

'We were at school!'

'I know.'

'So we're grown-ups now. You could have said something to me, because that's what grown-ups do.'

'I know that too and I wanted to, but I felt as if… well, we know now it's a good job I didn't say anything.'

'That's really how you feel?'

He shrugged. 'Isn't it how you feel?'

'I don't know, but it's nice to know where I stand. I'm not worth the effort, apparently.'

'That's not what I'm saying; you don't understand—'

'Oh, I understand. When things are difficult, you do what you've always done – you give up.'

'That's not fair,' he said with such reproach that she couldn't look at him.

It wasn't fair and she knew it. So why couldn't she stop? Why did she always say the worst things to him? It was like a compulsion, something she couldn't control.

'I can't have this conversation now,' she said.

'We have to have it sooner or later.'

'Do we? I thought it was the women who liked to talk, while you guys just bottled it all up and went on your merry way. This is only one more thing to keep to yourself, right?'

She didn't wait for his reply. She turned and walked away, sand kicking up beneath her trainers, and he didn't follow. He didn't even call to stop her.

This had gone too far. She had to wonder if it had gone so far they'd never be able to work effectively together on the lifeboats. If they couldn't move past this awful, messed-up episode, Ava was afraid the answer to that question would be no, they'd never be able to do it. Working together, going out to save lives, it needed trust and patience of the sort they simply didn't have in each other right now. Once, they'd had it in buckets; surely it couldn't be so hard to find again if they put in the effort?

Ava couldn't think straight with all the noise and bustle on the beach and promenade, and she certainly didn't want to sit around waiting for the triathlon to end. She checked her watch. There would be time to take a breather; she could head out to a quiet stretch of the beach and take some time away from the crowds and still be back to see the first of the competitors finish their runs. The watersports office she worked from wasn't far and nobody would be there today. She had a key and it would be a perfect place to spend a moment alone collecting her thoughts.

# CHAPTER TWENTY-TWO

The breeze had picked up, even during the last half hour. It whipped Ava's hair around her face as she strode down the beach, the crowds thinning with every step. As she moved away from the village and everyone in it, she felt lighter. The sea was stone-grey and the surface danced, but it was as beautiful as always. Whatever its state: calm or tempestuous, blue or grey, cold or warm, and despite what pain it had inflicted on her family, she couldn't help but love it, and she knew her dad had always felt the same.

Jill had said recently that Ava understood what made him tick better than anyone because she was the most like him, and since she'd had time to digest that, Ava had realised it was true. No matter what the sea gave or took, no matter what it did, she was forced to love it, just as her dad had been. It was in her DNA, it was a part of her she couldn't separate from the whole, it was in her soul, embedded so deeply that nothing could take it out. This was her home, her life... her everything.

At the hut, Ava unlocked the door and slipped inside. The office where she booked appointments and did class rotas was tiny – barely enough room for a desk containing chewed pens and a laptop, and a filing cabinet. A door led to the kit room, which was far larger and took up most of the building. It had to be bigger – it contained all the equipment she and the students used for lessons. As part of her role she was tasked with maintaining it all and so she knew where everything was and that every item was ready to go at a moment's notice.

Her gaze went to the window, to that sea, that piece of her soul. It was frisky, but she'd been out on worse.

Her decision made, she let herself into the kit room and pulled a wetsuit in her size from a rack. Normally she'd have her own but not anticipating a need for it, that was at home in her caravan. She pulled the borrowed one on and then chose a body board. She'd have surfed, but there weren't the right sort of waves today, and as long as she was out she didn't much care.

Taking a lungful of air as she closed the office door behind her, Ava's mouth curled into a smile. She zipped the keys into a waterproof compartment in her wetsuit and clutched the board to her as she set off for the water. Usually, going out alone, she'd zip her phone into that same pocket too, knowing it would be perfectly safe in there, but today she didn't feel like taking it out. It wasn't a situation she'd recommend as a teacher, but she wasn't planning to be out long or to go far, and if she was being perfectly honest, she was glad of the peace. This way, nobody could disturb her with stuff she didn't want to talk about. For the next hour, it would just be her and the waves and the sky. If people's heavens were all different according to what they'd loved in life, then hers was going to look a lot like this.

Padding into the surf, anticipation bubbled in her. It didn't matter how many times she did it, that feeling of stepping in, of the cold on her feet, of the water rising around her, of that final breath of expectation before she took to her board, never got old. Some people lost themselves in meditation or yoga, but Ava had this.

Often, she'd see other surfers, body boarders, paddle-boarders or kayakers out on the water. Today, almost everyone was at the triathlon and so it was only her, a kayak going in the opposite direction, some noisy seabirds and a curious seal watching from the rocks of the headland that jutted out to sea. Ava wondered if it was the same one she'd seen often and whether she could get close enough to see it better, but whenever she'd tried before it would be gone before she'd got near the headland. But without expecting any success, she decided to push that way, because there was a first time for everything and the current seemed happy to take her in that direction anyway.

With each swell, the board lifted and then dropped as it ebbed away again. Ava's limbs were lazy as she pushed through the water, the waves doing much of the work. For anyone less experienced the rate she was travelling at might have been alarming, considering she had so little control over it, but Ava had spent enough years on this sea to know what she was doing. Not that she was ever complacent, of course; nobody knew as well as she did how quickly the sea could turn, but for now she was content that all was well.

The sea stretched out ahead of her, and the clouds, shades of light and dark, were layered onto the grey of the sky. Every so often the sun would break through, but it was rare and weak. Days like this, the ones the tourists didn't care for, had their own beauty.

Close to the headland, Ava thought she saw a head in the water. It disappeared and emerged again. After a moment she could tell it was a seal, floating on its back eating a fish. She looked to the rocks, and there was her seal. So there was more than one? She wondered if they were a family. A moment later she saw another slipping from the rocks into the water.

If she hadn't come out on her board she would never have seen this, and she couldn't help but smile as she watched them: one content to nibble its fish, another relaxing on the rocks and another swimming around in mad circles.

She moved closer. The one on the rocks seemed to sense she was near and disappeared into the sea to join the others, instantly slipping beneath the surface. Ava's smile grew. One of these days she was going to get closer, even if she had to bring a bag of fish to tempt it over.

The wind lifted her hair and sent a little shiver down her neck. The sky seemed darker than it had a moment ago, the sun that had struggled intermittently through now swallowed by a heavy grey mass of cloud. Maybe she ought to head back. The triathlon would be coming to an end and people would be wondering where she was. At least, some would, but others would probably be glad to see the back of her for a while as much as she'd been glad to see the back of them for this short, precious respite.

She turned her board and began to paddle with the current so that she could edge towards the shore on it instead of fighting with the sea. And then she thought she heard something calling. Seabirds? But it didn't sound like seabirds usually sounded.

Craning to look over her shoulder, there was no bird she could see that might make a sound like that. But as she did, it came again. She stopped paddling and strained to listen over the boom of the waves hitting the rocks of the headland. It was hard to tell.

As she scanned the dark finger of rock jutting out to sea, she saw a flash of red, which became two distinct figures of what looked like a man and a young boy. She hadn't seen them before. Where had they come from? Maybe they'd been making their way around the headland behind some of the higher formations. However they'd got there, it looked as though they were in trouble, because the boy was on the man's shoulders while he waved and shouted to her.

Ava's brain worked quickly to assess the situation as she turned her board, fighting the sea now to get to them. Progress was slow, but it gave her time to work things out. As she looked, she could see that a path she knew to be there at low tide was no longer visible and so presumably they'd been cut off by an unexpected surge. She could see that there was no clear route up the rocks that wouldn't be perilous – if not impossible – but to go back the way they'd come was impossible too.

As she drew closer she could see that the boy was about seven or eight – around Fern's age. The man was already waist deep as the tide climbed the rocks.

'Hey!' Ava straddled her board and called over. The man waved his arms in the air, shouting something, but the wind carried away what little sound would have reached her over the surf smashing against the headland. 'I can't hear you!' she shouted. 'I'll come over!'

Ava began to scoop with her hands to move the board, but now she was using every bit of her strength. And the closer she got, the more she was tossed about.

Suddenly, there was a shift in the current, and the sea began to pull her alarmingly towards the rocks. This was worse, and she tried to slow her progress. If she got too close, there was a danger a rogue wave would dash her against them. She should have turned around and gone to get help, but instinct wouldn't let her. The pair needed her and she had to answer the call.

'Have you phoned for help?' she yelled.

'What?'

'Have you phoned for help? Coastguard!'

The man called back but Ava still couldn't hear him. She couldn't even tell if he'd understood her question.

'Coastguard!' she yelled again, miming a phone call with her hand.

He shouted a reply but it was no good; Ava couldn't make it out. Senses heightened, every nerve taut, she let the current take her closer, acutely aware of the danger she was now putting herself in.

'Have you called for help?' she shouted again as she cut the distance between them. She was close enough to see seaweed draping the rocks and creatures clinging on around the water-line. This wasn't good.

'Phone's wet!' the man shouted back.

Ava's heart sank. She'd hoped that would be his first reaction and that a rescue party was already on its way. So only she knew they were stranded, and she didn't have her phone on her. She could have cursed her decision to leave it at the office, but that was hardly a useful thing to do. Now, she had a simple decision to make. She knew this stretch of the coast and she knew that the water would go way higher before it receded again, and way higher than the ledge where the pair were stuck. Before they were done, both man and boy would be submerged. What she couldn't tell was how fast that would happen and whether she had enough time to make it back to shore, retrieve her phone, call for help, and for the lifeboat to launch and save them before their ledge was inundated.

Ava glanced towards the beach. It wasn't that far, but in these conditions far enough to be a risk. Was it a risk she was willing to take? But then, the alternative was just her, trying to get them to safety alone on a board. Maybe she could have put one person on her board and pushed them back to shore – but two of them? And one a grown man? Her board simply wasn't big enough. They could all cling on and use it to aid their swim back, but she couldn't be certain they'd all be able to keep hold that long, and she didn't know what she'd do if one of them happened to let go and got swept away.

There was nothing else for it, as far as she could see – she was going to have to get as close as she dared and take them one at a time. The boy first, and hopefully Ava could trust him once they were back to raise the alarm while she went back for the man.

Using every scrap of her strength to keep the board steady, she let the sea carry her closer.

'I'm Ava!' she called. 'You've got no phone? So you haven't managed to call for help?'

'It got wet,' the man said. 'In my pocket. Big wave. Not working.'

Ava might have asked how they'd come to be in their current predicament and why the man hadn't had a bit more sense, but there wasn't time. Besides, she knew how easy it was to get caught out, even when the situation seemed benign. An unpredictable tide, a sudden change in the wind... it didn't take much. She wondered if they'd been chasing the same seals she'd seen, but the answer to that would have to wait too.

'Can you both swim?' she shouted.

The boy looked alarmed at her question. 'All the way back?' He looked to shore, then back at Ava.

'No,' she said. 'I can't get to you, but if you can come a little way out then I can grab you, pop you onto my board and push you to the beach. Can you manage that?'

The boy shook his head.

'Cal,' the man said. 'It's the best way to get back.'

'One at a time, I'm afraid,' Ava said. 'I'd have to take Cal first... It is, Cal, right?'

The boy nodded.

'Then I'd have to come back for you,' Ava continued to the man.

'You don't have a phone then?' the man asked.

'Sorry, no. Didn't think I'd need it. Maybe Cal can raise the alarm when he gets back and help will come before we have to do the second trip.'

Ava didn't believe that would happen, but she wanted to embolden the boy so he'd make the trip and figured if she made it so he felt like a protagonist rather than a victim, that might do the trick. The truth was, she didn't even know if there was time for her to get back for the man, but she had to try and she had to get Cal to safety first, knowing that the man would want that.

Cal looked at Ava, his eyes wide with fear, then shook his head again. She could see why he was reluctant; even as she'd been talking to them the surf had been crashing against the rocks with more force. And she was being drawn closer even against her will – a couple of times she'd stuck out a foot to try and steady herself and had connected with rocks below the waterline; she was fairly sure that she'd caught one so hard her foot was bleeding. But she didn't show her discomfort and she tried to look as carefree as possible to instil some confidence in Cal.

'It's fine, I promise,' she said. 'All you have to do is get to me and I'll do the rest. I'll be so close it'll be one stroke and you'll be here. And you know what? You're in luck today because I actually teach people how to ride these boards, so you're getting a free lesson. Have you been on one before?'

Cal shook his head.

'OK,' Ava said. 'Well, after this you might like it so much you want to do it again. And if you come and see me at my office, I'll teach you for free, just for being so brave today. How's that sound?'

Cal looked up at the man. 'Dad…?'

'I know you don't want to leave me here,' the man said, 'but Ava's right. This is the best way. You can run and get help.'

'My phone isn't far away when we get back,' Ava said. 'You can phone the coastguard while I come back for your dad, and I bet the lifeboat will get to these rocks quicker than I do.'

'How do you know?' Cal asked.

'Because you know the other reason you're lucky today? I'm training to join the lifeboat crew, so I know them all, and my dad used to do it and so did my granddad and my great granddad, and they're all fast and brave and they save people all the time. But first they need to know we need them, and they won't know that unless you and I head back to shore to call them.'

'But you could go back and call for us,' Cal said. 'I could stay here with Dad.'

Ava exchanged a look with Cal's dad. She'd put a brave face on it, but while there was a chance Cal and his dad would be able to hang on for a while longer, there was an equal chance an unexpectedly violent wave could wash them both into the sea. She didn't want to take that risk, and she didn't think Cal's dad did either. She didn't expect either of them wanted to take the risk of trying to get on her board either, but as far as she could tell, it was the lesser of two very bad choices.

'It'd be quicker and better with your help,' she said to Cal. 'I could really do with it.'

'Go on...' The man grabbed his son's hand and gave it a squeeze. 'You can do this... for me?'

Cal looked down at him, at the sea, and then back at Ava on her board. Her heart lifted as she saw him give the tiniest nod. 'OK.'

His dad lowered Cal from his shoulders and into the water. Cal flinched as the waves soaked his legs. He was visibly shaking and Ava had to wonder whether he was going to be able to do this after all.

As his dad lowered him, he began to squeal. 'I can't do it!'

'I'm not going to lie,' Ava said, 'it might be a little rough until you get to me.' She held out a hand, bracing the other against an outcrop to keep her board steady. 'All you have to do is get in the water, reach out and I'll catch you.'

But Cal froze and he began to cry, clinging to his dad. 'I can't!'

'You can!' Ava urged. 'It's only a few strokes and I swear I'll get you.'

'No, it's too scary!'

Ava hesitated. And then she slid off the board and struck out for their ledge. More than once a hand or a foot connected with something hard and sharp, and more than once she swallowed a mouthful of seawater, but for a strong swimmer like her, even though it was rough, it wasn't far. All the time, however, she was aware that her board was being washed out of reach. She could swim for it, she thought, even with Cal, as long as it didn't move too far away, but that window was small and they had to do it now.

Pulling herself onto the rocks, she reached for him. 'We have to go now!' she said, all pretence that everything was fine and relaxed gone. Even as she did, she was picked up by a swell and then dumped again, her arm cracking against the rock. Biting her lip to keep from crying out, she decided quickly that everything was still functional, even if it hurt like hell. She couldn't let Cal see her in pain, though; nor could she let him see the building fear that she wasn't going to be able to do this.

'Cal, please... you have to trust me. We can do this, but we have to go right now or my board will float away.'

Cal shook his head, crying. 'It's too far – I can't do it!'

Ava whipped around again and this time struck out for the open sea. Her judgement was failing her; she didn't know what to do for the best. This time, as she swam to retrieve her board, every wave wanted to take her back to the rocks and she was already exhausted. For every inch forward, she seemed to get carried two back. But now her priority was her escape vessel, which was currently drifting around the headland.

With every stroke she took it seemed to get further away. But then it snagged on an outcrop and at the same time the current seemed to ease, and she pushed to swim harder until her hand made contact and she hauled herself onto it for a moment, letting her head rest on it while she caught her breath.

This time, as she pushed free of the rocks, the sea wanted to take her around to the far side of the headland, and the current that had brought her here was trying to prevent her getting back to Cal and his dad. But there was no way she was leaving them, even if letting herself get carried out was a good idea – and right now she was so tired it was tempting.

As they came into view she could see that the water was rising rapidly and things were looking ever more desperate. She pushed on, her muscles burning. She owed them this. She'd never met either of them before today, but she owed them. She at least owed it to Cal's dad, who knew the risks of letting her take Cal to shore and leaving him there, where he might not make it, and was willing to do anything to save his son. Ava's dad would have done the same for her; Killian would have done the same for Elijah and Fern. She had to get Cal to safety, no matter what it took.

This time she tried to get the board closer, though with every swell it was being thrown against the headland. Cal was clinging to his dad. Seeing Ava, he transferred his grip to a jutting crag nearby, the water now to his shoulders and hitting his face.

As she watched, Ava's worst fears were realised. A wave bigger than any yet lifted her board and crashed against the rocks. It pushed her into them and washed Cal into the sea.

Ava looked frantically for him, scanning the surface, but there was no sign of the little boy.

'Cal!' she yelled, panic beginning to grip her. 'Cal!'

She looked up at his dad, who was poised, ready to dive in after his son, when Cal emerged, coughing and spluttering, breath rattling as he gasped for air.

Ava slid off the board and grabbed for him, catching his collar and hauling him through the water until she could get a grip on his torso. The moment she had him, she swam for the board that was already moving away again. Fingertips connected only to lose it, and then a second time, while Cal thrashed and cried in the protective circle of her other arm.

Finally she got hold of the board and shouted to him. 'Grab hold of the sides!'

She pushed him onto the board. It almost tipped up, sending him into the water again, but Ava managed to steady it, and a few moments later he was lying on it, face down, sobbing.

'The worst bit's over,' Ava said. 'All you have to do now is hold on with all your might – OK?'

She was lying, of course, because the worst bit was far from over. They still had to get free of the pull of the surf that wanted to throw them back onto the rocks.

Ava began to kick with everything she had, and for what seemed an eternity it felt as if they were held in place. She didn't look back at his dad – she didn't dare – but could imagine the fear on his face as she struggled, wondering if she and Cal were going to make it after all.

Slowly, so slowly it barely registered, the pull lessened and Ava began to make progress. With every stroke towards the beach and the calmer water of the bay, she was more exhausted but her optimism grew.

At last, fifteen minutes later, she pulled the board onto the beach.

'Stay there!' she told Cal, who was sitting on the sand now, looking as if he was in profound shock. She ran for the office, fumbling in her waterproof pocket for the keys and opening up with shaking hands to retrieve her phone. She was dripping as she went inside, leaving a saltwater trail behind her.

Back on the beach, Cal was looking out to sea. He turned at the sound of her voice.

'I need you to be brave one more time,' she said, dialling a number and handing him the phone. 'I don't have time to talk, but I need you to tell the person who answers where your dad is so they can get the lifeboat out, right? Can you do that for me?'

Cal took the phone. 'I don't know what to say.'

'It's the headland off Port Promise beach near where the watersports academy is. It's called Promise Rocks. They'll know it. Can you remember that?'

Cal nodded. As she turned away, a tinny voice answered the call and Cal began to speak into the phone.

Ava didn't linger. She picked up her board and raced down the beach to paddle out again. The lifeboat might get there in time and it might not, but she couldn't take the risk. If she could make it back, there was a chance she could save Cal's dad. She knew what her colleagues at the station would say. She'd been trained better than this – the rules said not to take risks, not to endanger herself as she endeavoured to save someone else. She knew all that, and yet she had to try, even if she became a victim in the process.

The sea was harsher than it had been even moments before. Either that, or Ava was simply so tired now it seemed that way. Whatever the reason, she struggled this time, every kick, every scoop, every muscle involved in keeping the board moving ached and burned. Vaguely, she thought that maybe the triathlon would be in the final throes and she wondered if anyone had realised she was missing. Would they think to look for her? She hoped so with all her heart, because as strong as she always pretended to be, as brave and independent as she wanted people to believe she was, she no longer wanted to do this alone. She wanted her friends on the boat to come and get Cal's dad and then to get her. More than anything, she wanted this to be over so she could stop fighting the sea and get some rest.

But she had to push those thoughts away. She kept going even though every muscle screamed and the sea didn't want her to get back, pushing and pulling with every stroke, and eventually the rocks were close enough to see Cal's dad. He was now chest deep in the surf, clinging to an outcrop. His relief at the sight of her was written all over his face.

Maybe her balance had been off or maybe she'd been too tired to keep her wits about her, but she was about to call to him when a rogue wave crashed over the board and took it from her.

As she went under the roaring surf, the sea flipped her over and over, so that she didn't know which way was up and which way down. By the time she surfaced, it was too late to do anything about the rocks hurtling towards her. All she could do was brace for the impact.

Hands outstretched to take the blow, she landed heavily enough to jolt the breath from her lungs. Immediately, the sea sucked her away and threw her back for a second assault, and this time she felt something crack.

'Ava!'

She gasped as she looked up at Cal's dad, fighting to cling on against the sucking, push-pull of the waves that wanted to dash her on the rocks again, to keep doing it until there was nothing left of her.

'Where's Cal?' he shouted. 'Is he safe? Did you make it? Wait, I'm coming down to you.'

Ava managed to raise a hand. 'No!' she gasped.

Water beating at her face, she looked for the board but couldn't see it. Had it been carried away, around to the far side of the headland again already? She'd try to swim to see but she didn't think she'd make it this time, and there was a pain in her chest that didn't seem good at all. But without it, they were stuck.

She searched again. Could she make it, even against the current, even feeling suddenly sick, even though she knew she was injured? The currents were worse at the tip of the headland; it was some way round before they eased a little.

But then she saw the board and relief flooded through her. It was only a short distance away – surely she could swim that far?

Ava reached out, poised to push off from the rocks to try and reach it when the pain in her torso ripped through her on a whole new level. From the moment she'd hit the rocks that second time she'd known something wasn't right, but the sudden movement had switched the pain up from bearable to excruciating.

She almost lost her grip on the rocks as another wave crashed over her. When it subsided, she was gasping for air. She was used to cold water and had a wetsuit on, but she was beginning to feel a creeping chill, deep in her bones, like the sort of cold that could never be warmed again.

'Ava! Are you OK?'

She looked up to see Cal's dad. She could see the fear in his face, that he knew something was very wrong and was powerless to help, that he knew in rescuing Cal she'd only put herself in danger in his place.

Was this the destiny of all Morrows? she wondered, gritting her teeth against the pain. Was every generation destined to lose someone to the sea? Was it a price they paid for their lives next to it?

She closed her eyes and tipped her face to the sky. She could feel the spray like freezing rain, could taste the salt in it, could smell the seaweed, the roar of the swells as they crashed against the rocks filling her head.

The boat would come, she told herself, fighting the exhaustion and pain. She just had to hold on. If she had nothing else to believe in, she had to believe in her team, in the people who were already a second family to her. They'd come, and she and Cal's dad would be saved, and it would all be in a day's work for them. She might end up feeling stupid about needing to be rescued, considering she was training to join them, but if losing her dad had taught her anything, it was that nobody is bigger than the sea. Anyone could get caught out if the circumstances were against them; she wouldn't be the first and she wouldn't be the last.

'Ava! Out there!'

Her head was beginning to spin as she looked up to see him pointing. A boat was speeding their way, a boat she knew well, a handsome boat of orange and blue. If she'd had the strength she'd have smiled, but all she could manage was overwhelming relief. They'd come through for her, as she'd known they would.

The engines of the smaller inshore boat growled over the booming surf as they pulled alongside. Vas was at the controls, with Killian and someone else on board.

Ava frowned. 'Harry?'

Since when had Harry been back on the boat crew? She looked again – was she mistaken? But even beneath the helmet and safety goggles she'd know that face.

He stepped out of the boat and onto the rocks, immediately chest deep as Cal's dad was.

'You OK?' he asked. 'Any injuries?'

'I'm fine,' he said. 'I think Ava's hurt though.'

'Can you get on the boat?'

'I think so.'

While Harry helped him, Killian called to Ava. 'You're hurt? What's wrong? Can you get on board?'

'I'm fine.' Ava grimaced. 'I can—'

She cried out as she tried to move again.

By now Harry had Cal's dad safe and he turned sharply to her. 'What's wrong?'

'I think... had a bit of an argument with the rocks.'

'Let me guess,' Harry said, going to her. 'The rocks won.'

'I did my best,' Ava said weakly. 'But my ribs are a bit more fragile than the rocks.'

Harry stepped off the boat again and into the water. In his safety equipment he was far more surefooted than she'd been, and it was nothing for him to pull her from the water and sweep her into his arms.

'You're stronger than you look,' she said, feeling woozy and not entirely sure if any of this was happening or not.

Harry grimaced as he passed her to Killian before getting back onto the boat himself.

Vas started the engines.

All that effort, Ava thought as Harry wrapped her in a blanket. All that struggle. It had taken superhuman strength for her to get this far, and yet they'd pulled up alongside and plucked her out of the water like they were pulling a leaf from a swimming pool.

'God, I'm shit,' she said.

Harry sat at her side while Killian gave Cal's dad a blanket. 'Don't be stupid. You're amazing. That lad you picked up... he told us what you'd done. Not many would have done the same.'

'But... should have left it to you guys... look at the state of me now.'

'You made a call. None of us knows if we'd have made the same one, but I'd like to think we would have.'

'You saved my son.'

Ava looked across at Cal's dad, who gave her a grateful smile. In it was contained more than gratitude – it was all the things he'd never be able to put into words for as long as he lived. She understood that. She didn't need to hear them to know that he felt them.

'I suppose I did,' she said with a weary smile.

'You're shivering,' Harry said.

'I'm freezing,' Ava replied. 'I think it's shock... you know, the injury...'

'Probably,' he agreed, reaching to put an arm around her and pulling her close.

'Ow!' she yelped.

'Sorry... I'll try to be gentler. Just trying to keep you warm. I don't want... well, you know. I don't want anything... I don't want to lose...'

Ava closed her eyes. The wind whipped at her face as the boat sped back to land. She'd have to remember to send someone to pick up Cal if they hadn't already – he'd be waiting at the academy wondering what was happening. He probably needed blankets too. And someone to keep him warm. Not like this, of course…

Was her mind wandering? Perhaps. But it was kind of nice. Like being here next to Harry, wrapped in his clumsy arms was nice, even though her ribs hurt every time he tried to warm her up.

'Does this mean we're on again?' she asked.

He let out a soft chuckle. 'Have we ever been on at all?'

'I felt like there was a time… not at school, of course. I was horrible then. I'm sorry.'

'It's all water under the bridge that. I probably deserved it.'

'No, Harry… *I'm sorry*. About everything. Ever. I've been an absolute pain and—'

'Me too,' Harry cut in. 'Let's not go over that again.'

'Let's not,' Ava agreed.

It was getting harder to shout over the boat engines, even though there were so many things she still wanted to say, and so she fell to silence, allowing herself to drift in Harry's arms. They were friends right now. Who knew what would change, but this, here, this was good. She felt safe and protected here at this moment. She'd never been one to play the damsel in distress, but she figured, just this once, she'd earned it.

# CHAPTER TWENTY-THREE

The vast front doors of the station were open. Ava walked in to find Vas, Maxine and Killian there.

'Here she is!' Vas gave her one of his dazzling, toothy smiles. 'And looking a lot better than last time we saw her.'

'I'm sure I couldn't have looked much worse,' Ava said ruefully.

'Oh, I don't know,' Maxine put in, 'I've seen you after a lock-in at the Spratt.'

'True.' Ava took a large box of chocolates from a bag and held them out. 'For you guys. I mean, it's not much in the circumstances, but just to say thanks. I appreciate what you did for me the other day and... well, I hope you all enjoy them.'

'You didn't need to do that,' Vas said.

'Though I'll totally eat them,' Maxine added, taking the box.

Killian was watching with mild amusement as he wiped his hands on a rag. 'All I can say is I hope you're not going to be this much of a liability when you qualify for the boat crew.'

Ava smiled. 'I can't promise that.'

'But then you'll have the proper equipment and a team

behind you,' Maxine said. 'So when you need to be heroic, you won't have to do it on a crappy body board.'

'That's true.'

'And next time, could you try to make it a day where I'm not competing in the triathlon,' Killian said. 'I was in the lead when that shout came in. I mean, *I lost to your sister*! I'm never going to live it down!'

'Technically, you couldn't have lost to her because you didn't actually finish,' Ava said mildly. 'She's no way of knowing she'd have beaten you in the end.'

'Don't you think I've told her that?'

Ava grinned. 'And I bet she was having none of it.'

'What do you think?'

Ava's grin widened. She looked at her friends – *her crew* – and she was full of love and admiration for every one of them. It went deeper even than that – these were her people; this was where she belonged. But someone was missing.

'Where's Harry? You've got a drill, right? I thought he was back on the boats...'

'Well, not officially...' Maxine said. 'I mean, he pelted down here when the shout went up because he thought Killian wouldn't be able to make it and he wanted to... well, he knew it was you out there, so he wanted to make sure we had a full crew.'

'I made it back shortly afterwards,' Killian said. 'But by then he was suited up and insisted he went out with us.'

'Aren't there supposed to be rules about that sort of thing?' Ava asked.

Killian raised his eyebrows. 'It was you. None of us wanted to stay behind.'

She smiled, tears in her eyes, almost overwhelmed by his words.

'But in answer to your question,' Maxine said, tilting her head to the doors, 'he's here now.'

Ava turned to see Harry walk in. He stopped dead at the sight of her. There was a strange look on his face, somewhere between embarrassment and affection. Ava wasn't certain what sort of reaction she'd been expecting, but she felt as if something had changed between them on the boat that day. There hadn't been time to talk – she'd been whisked off to the nearest hospital – and in the days afterwards she'd stayed at Seaspray Cottage being fussed over by her mum. There'd been an exchange of polite texts: Harry's to ask how she was and hers to thank him for his part in the rescue, but that had been about it.

He was already in his uniform, a sports bag slung across his shoulders, golden skin and wheat-blond hair, eyes the colour of a winter sea. Ava couldn't recall him ever looking so good. It was like he'd suddenly got taller, prouder... She couldn't put her finger on what it was, but she liked it.

'Hi!' he said, glancing at everyone before his gaze settled on Ava again.

'I came to bring chocolates,' Ava said, feeling uncharacteristically shy all of a sudden. 'To say thanks, you know.'

'Right...'

'I won't stay,' she added. 'I mean, if you've got a training launch to get on with, I'll clear out of your way. I only came because I knew this was where I'd catch you all—'

'Don't be daft!' Maxine said, throwing an arm around her shoulder. 'You stay if you want to! You're one of us now.'

'You never know, you might learn a thing or two,' Killian said in an impish tone. He went to the hull of the all-weather and patted a hand on it. 'This is called a *boat*... it goes on the water.' He pointed to the doors. 'Out there...'

'Funny!' Ava wrinkled her nose at him and everyone laughed. 'But' – she glanced at Harry again – 'maybe I'll leave you to it. Don't want to get in the way.'

'You won't be,' Harry said. 'Stay if you like.'

Ava was about to reply when she heard familiar voices

coming from the open doors. A moment later, Jill appeared with Gaby, Elijah and Fern.

'Knock knock!' Gaby called.

'Hey.' Killian bent down and his children ran into his arms. 'Come to see Dad be awesome?'

'Yeah!' Elijah said fervently.

Ava aimed a puzzled glance at Gaby. Under normal circumstances, she'd want to keep her kids far away from a situation that might make the lifeboat service seem glamorous or appealing, and yet, here she was, bringing them to a practice launch. What had changed?

'We thought,' Gaby began, as if she'd read Ava's mind, 'well the kids thought... as you'd all brought my little sister back safe and sound... they wanted to come down and watch.' She sent a smile full of love at Killian. 'See our heroes at work, you know. And who am I to argue with that?'

Though she was certain it would prove to be a temporary blip, Ava was glad to see Gaby so supportive for a change. She glanced at her mum, who gave an encouraging smile.

'We'll be coming to watch you soon, Ava.'

Ava laughed. 'Oh, God, don't do that. Me trying to look heroic is a recipe for disaster.'

'I don't know about that,' Jill said fondly. 'I think you look heroic all the time.'

'And looking heroic is not the same as *being* heroic,' Gaby added. 'It's what you do that counts, not what you look like.'

Ava blinked. Could this be the same two women who'd fought hardest to keep her away from the lifeboat crew united in giving their blessing? Even encouraging her with kind words and compliments? The world had gone mad. She'd have to get battered on Promise Rocks more often.

'You'll watch with us, Ava?' Fern asked, looking up at her aunt with awe. She almost always looked at Ava with awe, but today it was on a whole new level.

'Sure.' Ava offered her hand for Fern to take. 'We'll go outside, eh? Maybe get a bit further away – don't want to get splashed when the boat hits the water.'

'Yes!' Elijah punched the air. 'It's amazing when it goes into the sea! I want to get splashed!'

'No you don't,' Gaby said sternly. 'Right then...' She went to kiss Killian, then beckoned everyone to follow her out.

Harry smiled at Ava as she went – she only wished she could work out what it meant. Was it just a smile? Or was it something more?

As they made their way along the beach to a safe vantage point, they were hailed by Clara, walking across the sand towards them.

'Morning!'

'Is there a family outing today?' Ava asked. 'Because nobody told me about it.'

'Betty said there was a drill today,' Clara said. 'I thought I'd come and look – figured someone would be here if I came down.'

By now, not only were her family there, but Ava could see that a few holidaymakers had stopped what they were doing and were watching with curiosity. The station had a news page on the Port Promise website and anyone interested enough would be able to check it out and see that the lifeboat was scheduled for a practice launch this morning. Either that, or they found out the moment it flew out of the doors and into the sea, which was probably a lot more exciting.

'Here we all are then,' Gaby said wryly. 'No matter what, you'll never find a Morrow far from a lifeboat.'

'Seems that way,' Jill agreed. 'Can't keep them away from the bloody things.'

Ava turned to her, half expecting to see disapproval in her features, but she was smiling. There was melancholy in it, but that was to be expected. She was probably thinking about Ava's dad. Ava was thinking about him too right now. She'd stood on this spot year after year as a child, waiting for the launch with the same anticipation, knowing he was on board. She'd always been filled with the most indescribable pride at the thought of it. If nothing else, this was a day to remember those happy moments, and she thought he'd want that more than their sadness at his loss.

An alarm sounded, and a sudden hush fell over the beach. A few moments later the boat came flying out of the station and into the sea with a boom, sending spray high into the air.

'There it is!' Elijah yelled.

Fern bounced on the balls of her feet. 'Yay!'

The gleaming boat cut through the water at speed, until it was a few miles out, and then began to turn circles and figure eights, zooming this way and that as it went through manoeuvres.

Ava was distracted from it by the sight of Harry striding up the beach to them. So he hadn't gone out with the boat?

'How are you?' Jill asked him meaningfully. 'I see you're still shore based.'

'For now,' he said. 'But I'm going to be seagoing soon. Just got to get through my medical.'

'So you're feeling better?' she pressed.

'Yes,' he said. 'I'm ready, at least. I have to face the boat sooner or later.'

'You already did that,' Ava said. 'And thank you again.'

'Yeah...' He rubbed a hand across the back of his neck and gave a lopsided smile. 'It wasn't quite the way I'd planned to go back, but I think it actually did the trick. I just thought... well, I thought about what it meant, what I might lose...'

His sentence stuttered to a halt. Perhaps he felt awkward – her entire family was there, after all, and Ava felt he had some-thing significant to say that was meant for her.

'If you have time,' she said carefully, 'maybe we could meet in the Spratt... I'd like to buy you a drink to say thanks.'

'No need – you've already thanked me enough.'

'No, but I'd really like to. Or if not the Spratt, somewhere else.'

Harry opened his mouth to reply but then closed it again, his gaze now on someone walking across the beach. Ava turned to look.

'Here he is!' Gaby called over. 'Our new triathlon champ!'

Cormac grinned and blushed in the most adorable way. He nodded a greeting to everyone. 'Aww... only because your man was called away.'

'Hey, however you won it, you won,' Gaby said. 'What brings you down here?'

'Same as you,' he said. 'But I see I'm a bit too late,' he added, looking at the boat out at sea.

'Yeah,' Harry said. 'Sorry, man. But there'll be plenty more – and eventually you'll be on board, right?'

'Right!' Cormac grinned at Ava. 'Can't wait. How about you, training buddy? Although you've already been in the thick of the action, or so I hear. Didn't even bother to qualify before you're out rescuing people.'

'God, it wasn't like that,' Ava said. 'In the end it was me who needed saving.'

'Not how I heard it,' Cormac said.

'Well... you'd have done the same,' Ava replied, wishing everyone would stop bringing it up.

Harry clapped Cormac on the back. 'I'm sure you would. Fancy helping to get the boat back in?'

'I'd be able to?' Cormac asked, looking like a kid who'd just been told he could visit the pilot in the cockpit of a plane.

'I don't see why not. You'll have to learn it anyway.'

Cormac looked expectantly at Ava, but she shook her head. 'I'm injured, so it's just you this time.'

'Oh, yeah, of course.'

'Have fun.'

She forced a carefree smile for them both, and then Harry led Cormac back to the station. It was good to see Harry was comfortable with Cormac again, but the fact that he'd seemed so keen to get out of her way troubled her. The hopes she'd held that they'd reached a new understanding and might yet rescue their friendship were fading with every step he took away from her. Things had been polite and courteous, but that wasn't what she wanted from him.

'He's on the right track,' Jill said as she watched them go. 'Harry, I mean.'

'I hope so,' Ava replied.

'He definitely looks better,' Clara said.

'What's wrong with Harry?' Fern asked.

Ava looked at her. 'Nothing.'

'Then why are you all talking about him?'

'Oh...' Ava looked at Gaby for help. How much did she want to share?

'Well,' Gaby said, 'he's been kind of down and not really himself.'

'Oh.' Fern frowned, then she looked brighter again. 'I could make him a card and I bet that would help.'

'Don't be stupid,' Elijah said.

'I made one for Marina when she had flu and she said it made her feel loads better!' Fern replied with a look of pure indignation.

'I think he'd love that,' Gaby said. 'When we get home, you make a card for him and we'll pop up to Trevithick's farmhouse with it.'

'Ooh, I love it there,' Fern said. 'Harry's dad gives us apples.'

'Well, much as I'm enjoying standing here, I've got things to cook,' Jill said. 'Shall I see you all later for our picnic?'

Ava glanced at the station as everyone confirmed their

attendance. Should she go in and try to talk to Harry again? Should she wait for the boat to come back in? But then she looked at her mum, and she couldn't help but feel she'd neglected her over the last few weeks. Not deliberately, but since she'd given her blessing to Ava's lifeboat application things had been so hectic there'd hardly been a moment – not for anything consequential anyway.

'I'll come and help you,' Ava said.

Jill frowned. 'Don't you want to...?' She nodded at the station.

'Nah.' Ava threaded an arm through her mum's. 'I've got all the time in the world to see that place. Besides, what am I going to do in there with two cracked ribs? I'd rather come and help you in the kitchen today.'

Jill beamed at her. 'I'd love that,' she said.

'Then I'm ready when you are.'


It had been such a lovely afternoon that Ava was glad she'd put her mum first for once. They'd baked a broccoli quiche with eggs from Marina's chickens, scones, and chocolate cake covered in hundreds and thousands for the kids. All the while the warm kitchen had been filled with the scents of their cooking and the sounds of their easy laughter. It had been a long time since Ava had spent an afternoon like this; just her and her mum, getting along, no drama, no friction or conflict. In fact, she didn't think they'd been so easy in each other's company since her dad had died. It made her realise how much she'd missed it.

Later, as they'd taken a break to sit outside with drinks, Clara joined them. Then all three of them had put the finishing touches to the food: Clara mixed home-made coleslaw with her 'secret ingredient' that she'd never divulge but always made it the best coleslaw Ava had ever tasted, and made the most incredible feta salad, while Ava buttered bread for the sandwiches and Jill filled them with ham and cheese. Finally, they packed everything into an ancient basket they'd been using for family picnics for as long as Ava could remember.

They trekked down to the beach together, and because everyone wanted to stop Ava to ask how she was and to talk about the rescue on Promise Rocks, it took them almost an hour to get there. By the time they did, the sun was already on its downward journey and Gaby, Killian, Marina and the kids were busy tucking into Gaby's offerings.

'I see you decided not to wait for us to start on the food,' Jill said with a wry smile.

Killian grinned. 'Took you long enough! We thought we'd have to send out a search party!'

'Ava's a local celeb,' Clara said, putting one end of the basket down on the sand while Jill lowered the other. 'It's not our fault everyone wants to talk to her.'

'Must be a slow news day,' Killian shot back, and Ava grimaced at him as he started to chuckle.

Jill spread the blanket for her, Clara and Ava to sit on, while Ava began to unpack plates from the basket.

'Careful!' Clara rushed to take them from her.

Ava laughed. 'I can lift some plates!'

'I'm sure you can, but why do it when I'm here?'

'Because... well, when you put it that way, you might have a point.'

'I'd take advantage of the fuss while it lasts,' Killian said, leaning onto his elbows and regarding her with some humour. 'Once you get the all-clear from the hospital your training will kick in proper and you'll wish someone could do it for you.'

'That's never going to happen,' Ava said.

'Actually, I can see that,' Gaby replied. She turned to her husband. 'You'll have to throw a lot at old stubborn pants before she admits it's too much.'

Ava turned to her, indignant. 'What's that supposed to mean?'

'I'm sure I don't have to spell it out.'

'I'm afraid you *are* quite stubborn,' Jill said.

'Headstrong, I'd say,' Marina offered.

'Opinionated,' Clara said.

'Annoying, actually,' Gaby put in.

'Oh.' Ava grinned as they all started to laugh. 'You all think you're so funny, don't you? If I have all those "qualities"' – she made speech marks in the air with her fingers as she turned to her mum – 'where do you think I got them?'

'You can't blame Mum for all of them,' Clara said.

'Some of them I suppose I can take the blame for,' Jill replied, her features softening as she lifted a stray lock of hair from Ava's face and tucked it behind her ear. 'Your determination and bravery... those you got from your dad, and I'm very glad you did.'

'You're brave too,' Ava said.

'Only because I was forced to be,' Jill sniffed. 'You choose to be.'

There was a moment when, conscious of the entire family looking at her, Ava suddenly felt overwhelmed with love as complete and engulfing as any towering wave.

'Right!' Killian said, clapping his hands together and getting to his feet. He wandered over to their picnic basket. 'I've been waiting for you to get here – Gaby said Clara was making coleslaw...'

Gaby shook her head. 'Never let a moment get too sentimental, right, Kill?'

'What?' Killian looked up from the tub he was opening.

Gaby laughed. 'Never mind.'

. . .

Marina had gifted Elijah and Fern a kite from her new stock. They were currently flying it further along the beach, aided by Killian. Ava lay on her back, looking up at the clouds racing across the sky. She'd eaten her fill, but that didn't mean she wouldn't go back in for seconds as soon as there was space. Gaby and Jill were talking to Marina about her plans for the store, while Logan had joined them and was lying with his head in Clara's lap, telling her about a new commission. All might have been well with the world – about as perfect as it could be, in fact – if not for one small problem that still nagged at Ava.

'Penny for them...'

Gingerly, Ava pushed herself to sit. Harry was standing on the sand. 'Oh... hey.'

'Am I late?' he asked. 'Killian said everyone was going to be here but... where are the others?'

'Who?' Jill turned to him. 'We're all here.'

'Oh... well...' Harry looked embarrassed and confused. 'He said it was a crew thing.'

'No,' Jill said, 'just us.'

Gaby looked shrewdly at him. 'Must have been a mix-up. But if Killian has invited you, maybe stay for a while? I'm sure he'll be back over in a minute and he'd want to say hi.'

'Oh...' Harry's gaze went down the beach. 'I guess I could walk over to have a word?'

'You could,' Gaby said. She glanced at Clara.

'Oh, yes,' Clara said. 'Maybe Ava could go with you. I bet you'd like a walk, right, Ava?'

'Oh, no...' Harry began. 'I wouldn't want to disturb—'

Ava knew a set-up when she saw one, and while she wasn't going to throw this opportunity away, she'd be having words with her family later. 'I could actually do with a walk.' She got to her feet. 'I probably need to move... getting a bit stiff.'

'Right.' Harry dug his hands in his pockets as he waited for her.

'See you two later!' Clara called impishly.

Ava frowned and Harry looked more embarrassed than ever.

'God, I'm so sorry about them,' Ava said in a low voice as they started to walk. 'They mean well, but...'

'It's OK,' he said. 'I'm kind of glad. I wanted to talk to you, but I didn't know... Well, it just seemed too awkward.'

'Look, what I said about a drink at the Spratt... it's too soon, I know now. I'm sorry – I should have kept my stupid mouth shut—'

'No, I liked that you asked. But I thought you were only asking because you felt you ought to.'

'Why would I do that?'

He shrugged. High in the air above the sand, Elijah and Fern's scarlet kite spun this way and that. The low sun glinted from its slick cord where it caught. Ava could hear the kids' laughter from here. She looked to see Killian had the string and was pretending to run away to steal it from them.

'Maybe you felt like you had to thank me for the rescue,' he said into the pause.

'Of course I did, but it wasn't just that. Harry. I hate how we've been the past few weeks.'

'Me too!' he said fervently.

'I want to say sorry,' she got in first. 'I don't want you to say it because you have nothing to be sorry for. You were right – you told me something sensitive and in confidence, and it wasn't for me to tell anyone else, even if I thought I was helping. I do think I can fix everyone and sometimes I don't wait to ask if they want to be fixed and it's a fault; you're right about that too.'

'It's not the worst fault a person could have,' he said with a small smile. 'As faults go, it's not a bad one at all. I know you were acting from a place of kindness. I'm sorry I reacted so badly; I was...' He sighed. 'It caught me by surprise. I'd gone to talk about getting back on the seagoing crew and then Killian started on me – you know how he is.'

'I do,' Ava said ruefully. 'I should never have asked Gaby to get him involved; I don't know what I was thinking.' She nodded to his figure on the beach. 'Seems like he's trying to put things right. Asking you here today, I mean.'

'So there never was a crew thing?'

'Of course not,' Ava said, laughing. 'I'm really glad we're talking again, even if it is Killian's doing. I hated when we weren't friends. I mean, we're friends now, right? This means we're friends again?'

'I think so. I know it was sort of my doing, but I hated it too.'

'It was never your doing. I get it now. I should have understood – listened to what you were going through instead of trying to fix you.'

He stopped and turned to look at the lifeboat station. Ava halted at his side.

'It's funny,' he began slowly. 'I was on the boats before, but going back to them, it feels as if I've never done it. Now, going into it with my eyes open, that makes it feel different. When I was growing up... well, you know, I'd always wanted to do it. I suppose I had this romantic notion of what it was, about being all manly and heroic. But after that night with your dad... I know what the job really is. Deep down, I'm still terrified. This thing, it's terrifying. It's thankless and hard when it doesn't go your way, and sometimes it makes everyone you love hate you for doing it, but I know now that I have to. I feel like I'm trained and I'm fit and able, and I ought to be there, like a duty, but a duty I don't mind having. I think if anyone understands that, it's you, right?

'I don't want you to back off. I want you to be able to say what you think, and if you see that I need help, I want you to feel you can give it. I was wrong to push you away. I ought to have appreciated what I had. I saw your struggle, how you had practically zero support when you wanted to join up, how everyone you loved pushed back against it, and I should have done more for you. It makes me feel ashamed, even more ashamed to see now how I added to that. And then, when you were stuck out there on Promise Rocks and I saw how close we came to...'

Ava reached for his hand. 'Thank you. It means a lot to hear all this. I never expected you to jump into an argument between me and my family – you wouldn't have stood a chance anyway – but I appreciate that you cared.'

'That's just it; I'm not sure I did. Every time I saw you I felt so guilty. When you wanted to join up I knew it would be great and I tried to be supportive, but at the same time I didn't know if I could get past the fact that Jack's daughter was going to be on the crew with me. I didn't think I could handle it, and I took that out on you. As much as I wanted you to succeed, there was a selfish bit of me that wanted to put you off. If you failed, then I wouldn't have to face that day and all the memories it would bring back.'

'I had no idea...' She looked up at him. How had she not seen this? How could she have been so blind? 'I'm sorry, I never even thought about it like that. I must have seemed so clueless and insensitive.'

'I didn't mean that—'

'I know, but I'm saying it. Harry, not once, not even for a second have I ever thought what happened that night was your fault. Nobody does, and nobody thinks there's anything you could have done about it. Dad made his choices, and if he was here, he'd admit that the blame was his alone.'

'You say that, and I know you mean it, but it's not so easy to accept.'

'What can I say to change that?'

'I don't know. I wish I did, because I hate this. I hate that I can't even ask you...'

'Ask me what?'

'Because I want to...'

'Harry... I'm going to come right out and say this, and I'm not going to let you tell me no again. Come for a drink with me. And I don't mean just hanging out. I mean, let's give this thing a go. It's crazy what we're doing. I want to be with you. And you want to be with me, right?'

'More than you could know!'

'Then what are we messing around for?'

He relaxed into a smile. 'I don't know.'

'I don't want to mess around anymore. Kiss me, you big idiot.'

He leaned in, his lips touching hers as the salted breeze whipped around them and the waves rolled onto the beach.

However they'd got here, however they'd cocked it up until now, all that mattered was this. With Harry there'd be no awkward first dates, no second-guessing what every sentence meant, what every exchange might signal, where their lines were drawn or whether they were moving too fast. This was Harry, and she'd known him her whole life, and she already knew everything about him she needed to know to see that this was real and this might just be forever.

As they broke apart, the sound of applause reached her. They turned as one to see Killian clapping and the kids jumping up and down as if they'd been in on the plot.

'Don't you have a kite to watch?' Ava shouted over.

With a grin, Killian turned back to his game with the children.

'You know we'll never hear the end of this?' Harry said.

'Yeah, I know. I guess we'll just have to learn to live with it.'

He was moving in to kiss her once more when an urgent bleep turned his smile into a vague frown. 'You're joking,' he groaned. He pulled away and fished in his pocket, lifting the pager out to look.

Killian raced down the beach, Elijah and Fern following in his wake, the kite trailing behind them and swinging madly. 'Time to go, big fella!' he shouted, clapping Harry on the arm as he passed.

Harry looked at Ava, his features clouding. 'You'll be here? When I get back, you'll still be here? And you'll still feel the same? Only, when you have time to think, you might—'

'Might what? Realise that I like you even more than I thought I did?' She laughed. 'Don't worry, I'll be here. In fact, I'll come to the station with you. I might not be fully trained and I might have dicky ribs, but I'll find a way to help out, and it's as good a place as any to wait for you.'

He reached for her hand, and together they ran for the station.

Inside, Vas was barking out instructions as the crew kitted up. Harry looked her way and smiled. He seemed relaxed, ready to go. Killian was already dressed and striding to the boat; Maxine was in charge of communications while Harry got into his waterproofs and fastened them up. Ava had felt pride many times for this team and for the ones who'd gone before, but never like she did today. No matter what else was happening, they answered the call without a second thought.

This was her life now too, and she wouldn't want it any other way.

# A LETTER FROM TILLY

I want to say a huge thank you for choosing to read *The Lifeboat Sisters*. If you did enjoy it, and want to keep up to date with all my latest releases, just sign up at the following link. Your email address will never be shared and you can unsubscribe at any time.

*www.bookouture.com/tilly-tennant*

I'm so excited to share this book with you. I can't stress enough how writing it gave me new insight into how incredible the RNLI is and how lucky we are to have it.

I hope you enjoyed *The Lifeboat Sisters*, and if you did, I would be very grateful if you could write a review. I'd love to hear what you think, and it makes such a difference helping new readers to discover one of my books for the first time.

I love hearing from my readers – you can get in touch on my Facebook page, through Twitter, Goodreads or my website.

Thank you!

Tilly

# KEEP IN TOUCH WITH TILLY

https://tillytennant.com

facebook.com/TillyTennant
twitter.com/TillyTenWriter

# ACKNOWLEDGEMENTS

I say this every time I come to write acknowledgements for a new book, but it's true: the list of people who have offered help and encouragement on my writing journey so far really is endless and it would take a novel in itself to mention them all. I'd try to list everyone here, regardless, but I know that I'd fail miserably and miss out someone who is really very important. I just want to say that my heartfelt gratitude goes out to each and every one of you, whose involvement, whether small or large, has been invaluable and appreciated more than I can express.

When the idea to write about a family serving on the lifeboats was first discussed with my editor, I admit that I knew very little about the RNLI. I'd seen the stations of course, during holidays up and down the coast, and being from Dorset I knew there was a training centre there which I've driven past many times. I'd donated on occasion too, stuffing a few pounds into a bucket, like many of us, but that was the extent of my involvement.

But then I started to write this series and everything changed. I began to talk to people who volunteered in the service, I watched videos and read accounts of real-life rescues, and through that research I began to understand what truly unique and incredible people those who serve are.

They are selfless, unflinching, dedicated, brave and generous. Most answer 'the shout' whether it's day or night, summer or winter, during Christmas lunches or family weddings, whatever they're doing, in all kinds of weathers and sea conditions. There is no question and no complaint – they just run for the station. Almost all do it without pay or reward, juggling their commitment to the lifeboats with other jobs and their family lives. And yet, they venture out where most of us would turn and run. I can't think of any other organisation quite like it. There is no funding for the service other than charitable donations, and yet, somehow, they keep going.

I'd like to thank the RNLI for their help in writing this book. In particular, the folks at Lytham St Annes, Poole and Aldeburgh. And a very special thanks goes out to Caron Hill at Aldeburgh lifeboat station, who gave so generously of her time and patiently answered all my questions (so many of them!) about life in the service.

If you would like to donate to keep this vital service going, you can go to www.rnli.org and do so there. Not only can you donate, but you can also find out more about what they do and how important it is.

I also want to mention the many good friends I have made and since kept at Staffordshire University. It's been ten years since I graduated with a degree in English and creative writing but hardly a day goes by when I don't think fondly of my time there.

Nowadays, I have to thank the remarkable team at Bookouture for their continued support, patience and amazing publishing flair, particularly Lydia Vassar-Smith – my incredible and long-suffering editor – Kim Nash, Noelle Holten, Sarah Hardy, Peta Nightingale, Alexandra Holmes and Jessie Botterill. I know I'll have forgotten someone else at Bookouture who I ought to be thanking, but I hope they'll forgive me. Their belief, able assistance and encouragement mean the world to me. I truly believe I have the best team an author could ask for.

My friend, Kath Hickton, always gets an honourable

mention for putting up with me since primary school, and Louise Coquio deserves a medal for getting me through university and suffering me ever since, likewise her lovely family. I also have to thank Mel Sherratt, who is as generous with her time and advice as she is talented, someone who is always there to cheer on her fellow authors. She did so much to help me in the early days of my career that I don't think I'll ever be able to thank her as much as she deserves.

My fellow Bookouture authors are all incredible, of course, unfailing and generous in their support of colleagues – life would be a lot duller without the gang! I'd also like to give a special shout-out to Jaimie Admans, who is not only a brilliant author but is a brilliant friend.

I have to thank all the incredible and dedicated book bloggers (there are so many of you, but you know who you are!) and readers, and anyone else who has championed my work, reviewed it, shared it or simply told me that they liked it. Every one of those actions is priceless and you are all very special people. Some of you I am even proud to call friends now – and I'm looking at you in particular, Kerry Ann Parsons and Steph Lawrence!

Last but not least, I'd like to give a special mention to my lovely agent Hannah Todd and the incredible team at the Madeleine Milburn Literary, TV & Film Agency, especially Madeleine herself, Liv Maidment and Rachel Yeoh, who always have my back.

I have to admit I have a love-hate relationship with my writing. It can be frustrating at times, isolating and thankless, but at the same time I feel like the luckiest woman alive to be doing what I do, and I can't imagine earning my living any other way. It also goes without saying that my family and friends understand better than anyone how much I need space to write and they love me enough to enable it, even when it puts them out. I have no words to express fully how grateful and blessed that makes me feel.

And before I go, thank you, dear reader. Without you, I wouldn't be writing this, and you have no idea how happy it makes me that I am.

Printed in Great Britain
by Amazon